THE COLLATERAL DIVIDEND
A Financial Thriller

E.R. WYCHWOOD

This is a work of fiction. Names, characters, places and incidents either are the product of the author's imagination or are used factiously, and any resemblance to actual persons, living or dead, business establishments, events or locales are entirely coincidental.

THE COLLATERAL DIVIDEND / ER Wychwood

Copyright © 2023 ER Wychwood.
All rights reserved.

This book, or parts thereof, may not be reproduced in any form without the express written permission of the author or publisher. The scanning, uploading, and distribution of this book via the Internet or via any other means without the permission of the publisher is illegal and punishable by law.

ISBN: 9798850717384

Printed in the United States of America
10 9 8 7 6 5 4 3 2 1

THE MAN FROM OFCOM

The early morning phone call couldn't have been worse. Gaillard gazed out the window at the rising haze over Paris. The room fell silent, intermittently interrupted by distant construction sounds. He rose from his seat and noticed Piere, his head of security, standing nearby. "Piere, I thought I told you to get rid of that tie," he said casually. Then, inhaling deeply, he erupted in anger, hurling the bookshelf to the ground, causing a cacophony of crashing paper and wood at his feet.

Startled, Gaillard's wife looked up from her book. "Where do you think you are?" she sternly asked him. Gaillard stood there, breathing heavily. "If you're going to lose your temper, do it elsewhere. I won't tolerate it here, nor will he," she said, pointing at Piere, the head of security, who stood sheepishly.

Gaillard stared at her for a while, then took another deep breath. He glanced at Piere, wiped the sweat from his brow, and gestured for someone to clean up the mess. "And for the love of God, I told you to get rid of that god-awful tie," he added, pointing toward the doorway. He noticed a tall glass of water on a side table and walked over to it. From his pocket, he took a metal case, retrieved two capsules, and swallowed them before turning his gaze back to the window. As the door leading to the hallway creaked, Gaillard looked in that direction, took another sip of water, and left the room.

Once they were in another room down the hall, Gaillard inquired, "He said no?" His breathing was now more controlled. The double doors leading to the wood-laden conservatory remained closed. Piere had his phone on the table, tinkering with a recording.

"Look, I'll have to report this," said the man from Ofcom. "I don't want to, but you've left me no choice. Gaillard can go to hell."

"We can't let that happen," Philippe Gaillard pleaded with exasperation. "I don't care what you do, who you contact, but fix this. We need to capture that market by the end of the year, Piere."

At that moment, Gaillard's phone rang. He had specific expectations for the call. The ring awakened the man who had made the original offer to the man from Ofcom. Lazily, he stared at the ceiling before finally answering the call.

Gaillard spoke calmly in English, "Do you know who this is?" "Yes," came the reply.

1

E.R. Wychwood

"Good. I need you to take care of this. He's a crucial client to us. If he doesn't come to dinner, I'm sure any reasonable gesture of goodwill would suffice."

"Somewhere like J Sheekey off Martin's Court?"

"Yes, J Sheekey should be fine," Gaillard confirmed. The man on the other end of the line had unsightly teeth and unkempt hair. He listened without question. When Gaillard finished, he snapped the phone shut, donned a suit, swallowed two pills, and proceeded with his day.

By eleven fifteen, Gaillard had uncorked a bottle of wine. He checked his phone every ten minutes, anxiously awaiting news from London. Finally, ten minutes to one, a hushed stillness fell over the Southbank. The man from Ofcom often strolled along the riverbank, observing ships passing by and tourists navigating the convoluted roads of Southwark.

It was a damp and overcast day, with only a few lingering souls on the street. The man from Ofcom noticed two figures across the street and decided to keep his distance. He pulled up his raincoat collar, tightly gripping his briefcase, and quickened his pace, feeling the dampness seeping into his skin, causing a dull, throbbing ache.

As the man from Ofcom continued south, he spotted a suited figure smoking a cigarette near the Victorian viaduct. He thought nothing of it, assuming it was just an office worker on a break. The figure flicked the cigarette and donned a surgical mask before hastening his steps, following closely behind the man from Ofcom. Suddenly, the figure seized the man from Ofcom's shoulder, forcefully pushing him against a wall, holding a stiletto tightly in his hand.

"Now, let's not make any rash decisions here," the man from Ofcom said, attempting to slide back. He handed the figure a wad of cash from his wallet. "That's all I have on me," he said, trembling.

The figure handed him a folded piece of paper. "Put it in your pocket," the muffled voice beneath the mask instructed. The man from Ofcom complied, shivering, avoiding any sudden movements. He tried to reason, "I can help you. You don't have to make a living like this." His scuffed briefcase lay sideways along the wall. He wondered if it was worth crying out, but the noise from Borough Market suffocated any potential outcry.

The figure lunged forward, stabbing the man from Ofcom in the chest. He felt a warm, piercing pain spreading across his shoulder, causing him to stagger backward and slump toward the ground. The figure repeatedly stabbed him until the sound of the knife cutting through air and flesh was replaced by muffled groans and pleas for help. The man from Ofcom weakly attempted to grasp the figure but was too injured to seek revenge. His hands fell limp, and he collapsed in a heap, his shirt stained red, puncture wounds covering his body. The figure glanced down the narrow alley, turned, and ran until exhaustion overcame him.

*   *   *

There were few things that Paul Irving hadn't covered. He had spent most of his youth immersed in academia, and it showed. If anything, he was a kind man, but there was a cruelty to his eyes. Often, his whimsical looks extracted what he needed with dizzying persuasion.

It took a special mind to be so committed to a topic, so enthralled by its very nature, that one wished to spend long periods of time thinking and writing about it. There was a certain level of obsession required, a touch of insanity, to desire such a thing. And that was Paul.

Paul wasn't crazy, per se, but he certainly couldn't deny being obsessed. It had been a long time since his days as a graduate student, but somehow his thesis had found its way into the hands of some influential people. Ironically, he had once tried to bury it. Someone had told him that any good piece of work would eventually be loathed by its author. That was part of growth, they had said. And Paul had indeed grown. His work had been sponsored by the U.S. Department of Defense, focusing on spy and terrorist networks, financial engineering, and logistical operations. But people were no longer interested in that. Paul had been a bit naive. That kind of salacious work belonged to the Cold War era.

Paul had been in his office since 8:15 in the morning. He looked out the long window across the snow-covered meadow. Virginia was boring, or at least Langley was. He had spent the past three years here, holed up for hours on end at the Central Intelligence Agency campus. His office was dull and overlooked a pristine lawn sloping into the tree-dotted foothills. He hadn't bothered to bring in any photos to adorn the walls; they remained bare, a builder's white. It all felt temporary.

It wasn't that he didn't enjoy his work. He did. But part of the reason he had come here was to put his skills to use. His degrees in mathematics and political science had garnered great interest on Wall Street, where he had been involved in structuring financial instruments. But he had wanted to be involved in something more. Langley had initially provided that opportunity. There was more money than sense in the halls here, and outside-the-box thinking was encouraged. But Paul had been stuck managing digital assets. He had wanted to be part of the innovative projects, but had been held back.

"Paul," Ted Hawthorne stood at the office door, gesturing down the hall. Ted was short, stalky, and much older. "Do you have a minute?"

"Yeah, sure, Ted," Paul replied, slightly timid. He cleared his desk, locked his computer, and joined Ted at the door. "Should I be worried? What's this all about?"

Ted shrugged, unsure himself. Having been at the company for nearly twenty-five years, he had survived many culls, but he suspected the upcoming one would be his last.

The past month at Langley had been tumultuous, with a sense that the world was spiraling into chaos. Ted felt the weight of it all, the anxiety in the mornings sometimes making it difficult to get out of bed. The intelligence services were flooded with information, overwhelmed by the abundance of data and unsure how to manage it all.

Less than a year ago, Langley had ceased using drones, but the event that led to their suspension had only been leaked to the press recently. The CIA was no longer involved in targeting individuals with unmanned combat vehicles or issuing kill orders. Ted had been the oversight assistant-director of the operation that brought it all to an end. He had already received a subpoena to attend a congressional hearing. While people had shown tolerance for collateral damage, political fallout was messier. Non-military operations resulting in deaths were no longer defensible, and everyone at Langley knew it.

Paul wondered if Ted was about to deliver his marching orders, fearing that he might be dragged into the mess. Ted had always been more politically astute than Paul, skilled at navigating the political landscape. However, now it seemed like a burden. Paul questioned whether Ted knew he would never return to the field after what had happened. Who would trust him with a command?

As they entered the elevator, Paul asked, "Are we headed to the Director's office?" when Ted pressed the button for the seventh floor.

"Dunes wants to see both of us. I just found out," Ted replied wearily. It was nearly three, and he had another hearing in an hour. "All this grandstanding for us to be in the same place a year from now. These things are becoming too political."

"What about the DNI? Do you think he'll be sacrificed?" Paul inquired.

"Who knows?" Ted shrugged at the idea. The Director of National Intelligence had initiated the suspension of the drone program, making him politically tolerable. Capitol Hill clamored for heads to roll, and blaming the intelligence community had become popular. Conspiracies were running rampant, with some at Langley's sister agency, the NSA, alleging that Russian bots were fueling the flames.

On the seventh floor, they encountered a small seating area and a desk with a woman sitting behind it. Paul led the way around the corner, followed closely by Ted. The woman stood up and came around the desk, gesturing toward the heavy wood door on the right side. Above the door, a large light well emitted a bland green hue.

"Afternoon, boys," she greeted with a hint of discontent. "Head on in." She pulled the door open, revealing two men sitting around a coffee table. The man closest to the door caught Paul's eye, and he hurriedly placed his coffee cup on the coaster and stood up.

The room exuded warmth, featuring a high ceiling with soft lighting and a large red Persian rug anchoring the seating area. Not far back, a desk displayed a tattered American flag framed on the wall.

"Ah, Ted," the man closest to the door said, lurching forward to shake Ted's hand. Paul recognized him as Brian Redding, the Director of National Intelligence, an experienced spymaster.

"Brian," Ted said, leaning forward to shake the speaker's hand. Paul recognized the face—it was Brian Redding, the Director of National Intelligence, an old spymaster. Redding gestured to a chair on the far side of the room.

"You must be Paul Irving," he said, offering a handshake to the younger man. "I'm sure you know Director Dunes," he pointed to his colleague. Dunes remained seated in a chair on the other side of the coffee table. "Ted," Dunes grumbled. "Do we still have jobs today, or do those quacks on Capitol Hill think we invented the moon?"

"We've had better days, Greg, fighting the war on its toughest front," Ted replied.

Dunes snorted. "Are we losing?" He had the look of an old boy thrown out of an Ivy League school circa 1968, as if he hadn't left the campus since. Thick black-framed glasses adorned his face, and he wore a white dress-shirt with point collars. He could have easily fit in at NASA.

"Frankly, I think it's better if we keep quiet for a while. It's been a tough month," Redding said, breaking the awkward silence. Ted and Paul had been curious about why they were called to this meeting.

E.R. Wychwood

Paul was too anxious to ask. As the youngest and least senior in the room, he felt it wasn't his place.

Ted glanced over at Redding. "Say, what's this all about, Brian? Why have you called both of us here?" Redding ignored Ted and turned to Paul. "Coffee?" He collapsed into a leather chair and poured a cup from the center of the table. "Please. Cream, half sugar."

"I'll let you figure out what you'd like in it," Redding said, handing the cup to Paul. He watched as Paul poured a packet of sugar into the cup. Then Redding looked up at Ted. "I'd like us to have a frank discussion here if you're both fine with that." He stared intensely at each man, making Paul slightly uncomfortable. Was this some sort of power play? "Paul, I had the opportunity to read your Master's dissertation. You then went on to Mayer Kleid on Wall Street in their tax structuring team, right?" Paul felt a wave of heat wash over his forehead, and his fingers became numb.

Redding was methodical, surgical. He rested his hands lethargically on the armrests, his left thumb rotating his wedding band around his ring finger. "Did you join the Agency because you wanted to run black-ops front companies like the ones you cooked up in your thesis?" Redding picked up a binder from the coffee table. Paul wasn't sure what to say.

"There's no shame in that, son—hell, I'm almost certain Greg joined because he watched Goldfinger," Redding continued, leaving a long silence. "I thought it best to discuss this with both of you. I intend to maintain the ban on drone targeted killings indefinitely, and to be clear, the CIA will no longer be conducting operations of that nature." A groan of dissatisfaction filled the room.

"So, what does that mean?" Ted asked.

"Greg and I think Paul might have the solution. There are some lawyers in the building who believe there are legal loopholes to allow for human assets to carry out—uhm, we're calling them selected dispatches now. This would all occur under extremely narrow circumstances."

"What are you suggesting here, Brian?" Ted inquired.

"Well, it's quite brilliant, Paul, it really is. I'm appalled we haven't capitalized on your expertise before this," Redding said, leaning forward. His hand rested on top of the printed paper. "What myself and others envision is to implement this. Paul, you would have the opportunity to manage something I'm sure you've only ever imagined would remain a theory, but I believe in this." Redding cleared his throat. "We have an entire playbook here that would allow us to fabricate an organization with the right balance between oversight and extensive operational capabilities." He pointed at the thick document on the coffee table. "It's all there. It just needs to be built."

"Of course, we think we have one or two suggestions on how things might be improved. We have some relationships with people whom we think—of course, the NSA would be keen to have some input," Dunes said, fiddling with the rim of his coffee cup.

Ted frowned as he looked at Paul. "So how the hell is this going to play out? Are we just going to one day open up a new targeted killing program within the NCS as if the last time never happened?" He wasn't one for melancholy but rather a political realist. Morality had been thrown out of consideration long ago. "Though I do know a few more people who'd be interested," Ted added, sensing that they were going ahead with this idea without consulting him.

"Ted, we all know people," Dunes replied condescendingly, twiddling his thumbs in the chair. "Without going into detail, we acquired some funds—enough for a sizable endowment. We could use your help, Paul, to structure a private front company. We're thinking of a Dutch stitching orphan company at the top, with a corporate stack connecting to a Delaware limited liability company. We'll leave it to you to work out the exact specifics. Brian has kindly offered to set up the firm on a ten-year contract to provide encryption algorithms for the intelligence community. From now on, all encrypted messaging between members of the community will use those algorithms. I'm sure you can figure out why we did that. It was actually another one of Paul's ideas," Dunes explained, while Redding rotated his coffee cup slowly.

"We're giving you pretty free rein here, gentlemen. Obviously, we have the capabilities to keep things in line, but our intention was never to set up a CIA program," Redding stated.

Ted asked about their exact intentions, and Redding raised his hand to cut him off. "I've appointed you as a senior analyst in the Office of the Director of National Intelligence, so you can have official access to information on the hill." Redding cleared his throat. "My intention in all this isn't to give you termination directives. You will be entirely independent. The primary purpose will be to track and independently conclude whether a target should be terminated." Redding had thought this through extensively. He had considered how to covertly communicate that someone was a person of interest, and he decided that including a keyword in the target files to show up on a search engine back at Grip was the best approach. Closing the legal loopholes had proven impossible.

E.R. Wychwood

Director Dunes cleared his throat, sitting forward and looking at Ted and then Paul. "Our entire legal framework is founded on the notion of pre-domestic and pre-emptive self-defense. It is vital to continued national security, and I don't see this changing anytime soon." Dunes outlined that the program's legality, as outlined by Paul's dissertation, operated along the fringes of the intelligence community. It fell under the veil of the government when convenient, but operated beyond it when necessary. It was a dangerous line to walk. The legality came from a combination of complex legislation, allowing them an extremely narrow margin to operate within. The legal framework without drones was challenging to apply, and it had taken Paul months to orchestrate the right wording to both rule out drones and simultaneously allow the act of targeted killing to remain. It was to be extrajudicial but still legal, justified as self-defense or pre-emptive defense of others.

Ted found all of this rather interesting. When he asked how they had found such a loophole, Paul gave a big smile. He had spent a great deal of time thinking about it. He explained that it had come to fruition twofold. "Gerald Ford's famous executive prohibition of assassinations was intended only to prohibit the killing of foreign political leaders," Paul said. He went on to explain an old, long-standing judicial opinion that had authorized the intelligence community to violate criminal laws. Paul presented the information mischievously, fully aware that the Constitution's Due Process Clause meant nothing when applied to foreign aliens abroad. But he knew something more than that. It was the core of why his dissertation would work so well after the CIA's targeted killing program was suspended. The DNI, perhaps intentionally, had been very specific in his wording, providing them with a narrow avenue to exploit. He had banned the use of drones, not humans.

Dunes then informed the group that the bill, which would crystallize the legal loopholes, had already passed through the Senate, and they were coordinating with the party whips to push it through the House.

"Paul will be your chief of staff," Redding announced. "I think you'd be best at keeping an eye on the political end of things, don't you agree? We'll let the young men micro-manage the field." He took a sip of coffee and crossed his arms, sitting back in the armchair. He let out a deep breath, as if admitting exhaustion, and glanced at his watch, indicating that he had other things to attend to.

Paul didn't have to think twice. This had been the culmination of years of study, and he knew this inside and out. "What will you call it?" he asked, pacing the room. He had his arms crossed, deep in thought, leaning against the wooden bookshelf.

"Farragut Center," Redding answered with vigor. He seemed much more excited about the name than one should be. Ted knew Redding was a history buff, holding a degree in American history.

"I'm sorry," Paul said, shaking his head and furrowing his brows. "I don't follow," he added, looking back at Ted, seeking help.

"The property we acquired overlooks Farragut Square in the district," Redding explained, taking another sip of coffee. "Slightly fitting if you ask me—presented with a roadblock, and we continue forward, damn the torpedoes or what have you." Redding chuckled.

*   *   *

Daniel Faron relished the idea of hitting the water by five-thirty in the morning. He had mastered the art of functioning efficiently on little sleep, and he rather enjoyed it that way. Located north of the district in Maryland, there was a small dock along the Potomac where Daniel had paid for yearly storage of his old single-man racing shell. Even on freezing winter mornings, he would drive from Bethesda to get a few vigorous kilometers in before heading to Langley. The solitude of being on the river alone appealed to him, providing an opportunity to be alone with his thoughts. The gentle flow of the morning river had a calming effect, regulating his mind. Although always a large man, Daniel didn't consider himself exceptionally skilled in rowing. Winning once during his college days was luck in his eyes. He believed his performance was a result of hard work and effort, compensating for his lack of natural talent.

Paul stood outside, rocking back and forth on the balls of his feet, waiting for Daniel near the dock along the shore. He had been diligently working in recent months. Grip Solutions LLC, a subsidiary of a complex network of companies established by Paul, operated in the shadows. They leveraged insider information through a back door in the markets, exploiting it for consistent funding. Paul had also recruited nearly a hundred employees to provide logistics support to the CIA. Their front corporation had become not only believable but also legitimate.

The cold frost on the ground nipped at Paul's feet through his shoes. The morning fog clung to the water, and the lazy Potomac dragged it along its surface. Deadened trees emerged from the mist on the far bank. Daniel was only fifty yards away, already steering the single skull toward the dock, cutting

9

through the water with the oars gliding across the surface. The boat made a soft washing sound as it approached, and Paul walked along the sloping grass toward the wooden dock. Daniel watched him approach but looked down at his feet instead of maintaining eye contact, trying to steady himself. By the time Paul reached the dock, Daniel had pulled the skull up to the side and was standing there, hunched over. "Daniel Faron, is it?" Paul asked, standing six yards away. Shivering slightly, he had his hands in his pockets, trying to fight off the cold. Daniel's focused expression changed, and the lines on his face turned downward.

"Yeah," Daniel cautiously replied, grabbing the boat by the gunwale and hauling it onto the dock. The water trickled back into the river.

"I'm Paul Irving," Paul extended his hand, and Daniel stood up to shake it. "Did you row crew in college?"

"Yes," Daniel replied, stowing the oars by the side of the boat.

"My old man rowed at Harvard. It's quite a sport,"

"What can I do for you, Paul?" Daniel asked, sounding exasperated as the cold air floated across the river.

"I was hoping we could talk," Paul said, speaking with a measured tone.

Daniel started carrying the boat uphill toward the boathouse. "What exactly do we need to talk about?" he asked, grunting under the weight of the boat. Paul followed behind, crushing the snow beneath his feet.

"I'm a friend of Ted Hawthorne's," Paul began.

Daniel placed the boat onto the metal racks and turned to face Paul, glancing at the dock and then at Paul with a deadpan expression. "Who did you say you were again?" He noticed a winter parka hanging nearby.

"I'm Paul Irving—" Paul started, but Daniel cut him off.

Daniel interrupted him. "--What is it that you do?"

"I work for an American company with contracts with the Agency. We're in the selected dispatches business. Apparently, we need a lawyer, despite Shakespeare's Dick the Butcher suggesting there aren't many lawyers out there with your expertise." Paul stood to the side as Daniel changed his sweater, seemingly unfazed by Paul's presence. Paul's speech had become staccato, losing his train of thought due to worry that Daniel wasn't properly listening. There were other lawyers at the Agency, many of whom would suffice, but Paul--and more importantly, Ted--wanted Daniel. He had been the lawyer Dunes had referenced, the one who knew how to navigate loopholes. Paul had done his homework, discreetly speaking to colleagues through third parties. Daniel wanted to take action and be involved in operations. That was Paul's carrot, and

The Collateral Dividend

when the moment was right, he'd dangle it. "I once worked for the CIA. Ask around Langley if you'd like."

Daniel sighed, stopped what he was doing, and stood up. He was tall, perhaps 6'4". "I'm flattered, Paul, but I'm not looking to move right now."

"I understand. The thing is, we need someone to help set up something we're working on. It would be more in line with what you've been wanting. I can guarantee you'd be in the room, part of the decision-making process. If you wanted, you could go into the field."

That stopped Daniel. He looked up from his backpack and scanned Paul's facial features.

"Ted Hawthorne thought you might be interested," Paul said, handing Daniel a grey business card with white lettering: Grip Solutions. "Check us out and give us a call, but if I don't hear from you by next week, I'll need to find another attorney." Daniel looked at him with a reserved expression, crossing his arms as they stood outside. Paul shivered while the door to the boathouse remained closed and locked.

"How did you know Ted?" Daniel asked after Paul had walked across the car park, a few spots away.

Paul closed the car door and walked toward Daniel. This was perhaps the most basic trick in the book. Paul had spent time in the field, as many senior administrators in the National Clandestine Service had. He had always been good at baiting and hooking potential assets, and recruiting was no different. "We work together," he said when they were closer.

"Are you in private intelligence?"

Paul shrugged. "Sort of." They were alone in the middle of Virginia, the cold making Paul's breath visible.

"What kind of work?"

Paul gave a coy smile, hesitating for a moment. He needed to be careful not to give away too much information. "We've taken the deposition matrix underground. Target identification, tracking, rendering, and removal have been moved out of the house," Paul looked at his watch. "I must go. But give me a call."

Daniel spent most of the morning thinking about Paul's offer, unsure of what to make of it. He wondered if it could be a ploy from a foreign country, if he was being targeted. He didn't dare mention it to anyone, as too much time had passed by noon for him to report the encounter without raising questions. He still had the business card in his coat pocket and examined its details after lunch. Looking out the window, he saw the interior courtyard of the new campus building, with a large copper monument where cryptographers attempted to decode it.

On impulse, he searched for "Grip Solutions" and had two system tabs open: one accessing internal files and the other pulling up an external website. He began scrolling through the information, reading that Grip provided technical and information support to the intelligence community. There were troves of internal classified files detailing their contracts. Grip wasn't a government entity, and the ownership and control details were redacted, which was unusual. Daniel had never seen such a thing before. How could a company have a contract with the CIA without disclosing its ownership? How could they ensure it wasn't foreign-controlled? Something seemed off. The group appeared large, with a few hundred employees, making it one of the moderate-sized contractors for the CIA. However, it had access to In-Q-Tel, the venture capital arm of the CIA, and was much larger than In-Q-Tel, with reported assets of nearly $1.4 billion. This wasn't just a CIA shell company; it was something else. Daniel wondered if the internal database had more information. He went down to the basement of the building, where computer terminals ran on a private network. Before entering the sealed room lined with a Faraday cage, he had to surrender all electronic devices. The network covered the entire agency's database, including restricted access information requiring additional codes for unauthorized users. Three years ago, there had been a transfer of $300 million from an account that he suspected was from a black ops budget. Everything seemed above board; it was simply a government contractor.

Daniel sat back in his lonely office chair, feeling stumped. Something about this didn't feel right. At least he wasn't being targeted by a foreign agency, he thought, finding some reassurance. But Paul's comment still bothered him, lingering in his mind throughout the evening. The idea of working in the field appealed to him. Daniel wondered if Paul was serious. Was there space for him to be in the field? He had trained at the farm but had never seen agency work overseas. He wanted to contribute to national security, but it felt like he was barely doing that anymore. He had become more of a transactional lawyer than an active participant. There was a time when he made decisions, and he wanted to be part of that again. It was dark when he went home around eight in the evening, deciding to call the number on the back of the business card. Paul answered almost immediately.

"I want to know more about it. Your contract with the Agency has a completely opaque structure. I've never seen that before."

Paul was coy. "If you're willing to join, I can promise you a well-paying job as an attorney. We can discuss your future contributions to other projects once you've joined," his voice trailed off, and Daniel remained silent.

"I'm sorry, but that's all I can offer you right now. The nature of these things requires you to be on the inside before we can proceed further."

"Is that a firm offer?"

"Yes," Paul confirmed. "We can discuss numbers if you're interested. We were thinking 500, but I don't think you're into that sort of thing," he tried to give the hard sell, but there was a long silence that made Paul a tad anxious. "This is your chance, Dan. If you want to be part of the legal side of fieldwork, I'm giving you that chance. If you want to do that and have the opportunity to see action, you won't find it anywhere else outside of DEVGRU, and based on your file, I don't think that's an option." Paul choked up on the proper phrase to use, avoiding calling it targeted killing over the phone, and then delivered the hook. "Why don't you stop by next week, and we can get started."

Silence.

"Sure," said Daniel. Paul had successfully convinced him. He would send Daniel the details tomorrow.

Daniel reflected on his own idealism, realizing that he was no longer the idealistic person he might have once believed himself to be. He liked to think that he once was, but deep down, he suspected it was a fallacy he told himself to suppress his long-held pessimism. What troubled him more was the fact that he spent time pondering these things, finding it silly. Dan and Paul had many things in common, having spent most of their lives thinking and being in academia. They both attended elite institutions, but Daniel was different. While Paul was slight, Daniel stood out with his size and physical endurance. Paul's experience in the field would likely be very different from Daniel's. Paul had been young, reckless, and had a short stint in the army. Before being sent overseas, he had trained at the farm, the Agency's secret training facility. He had never fired a shot in service and had most of his encounters with running intelligence assets through the Eastern Bloc.

That night, as Daniel lay in bed, he wondered where things would lead. He closed his eyes and lay flat on his back, finding it difficult to fall asleep. The coiled energy and insatiable thirst for an intellectual challenge made it hard for him to calm down at night without enough exercise. Part of him hated his own thoughts, but he wasn't sure if it was healthy or not to admit that. The idea of talking to a psychiatrist about it seemed daunting. It wasn't that he felt unwell; on the contrary, many of his past traumas, the childhood experiences that he thought could have potentially crippled his mental well-being, didn't seem to phase him. He felt well-adjusted.

Daniel's schedule had been sporadic over the past two weeks, which was how he preferred it. A severely regimented life unnerved him, but he never had difficulty filling his free time. However, lately, he found himself with more free time than before. His previous relationship had ended, a two-year affair that had slowly faded away, leaving him without the melodic routine of emotional and physical companionship. Daniel contemplated whether his distaste for routine had any significance and whether his constant moving had affected him. He knew he struggled to express and console emotions, but he believed he didn't lack them. Trying to clear his head and meditate, he focused on his breathing, although he wasn't particularly skilled at it. Before he knew it, the world melted away, and he drifted into sleep.

Daniel had spent a week looking through CIA files trying to better understand 'Grip Solutions LLC'. His research came up with nothing. Despite his best efforts, Daniel was meeting Paul with limited knowledge. They had arranged to meet at a coffee shop outside Langley at 11, but when Daniel arrived, he received a push notification from the phone's operating system, instructing him to go to an address in Arlington. This unexpected notification made Daniel nervous as he had never seen anything like it before, as if the phone maker's control had been overridden.

The building in Arlington was in an industrial park. Paul's car was parked near the warehouse entrance. It was a dreary afternoon, with a chilling wind. Paul was waiting by a steel door on the second floor, wearing his coat to shield himself from the wind. Daniel joined him and observed a biometric scanner on the door, which unlocked and led to a short hallway with another door. As they entered, the first steel door closed behind them, and the second door opened, revealing a converted office space.

Inside the room, there were two sofas, an armchair, a coffee table, and a desk pushed into a corner with a computer monitor. A TV mounted on the wall was playing the news. Ted Hawthorne, sitting in the armchair, stood up and greeted Daniel. Ted had gained weight over the years, but he still had a commanding presence. He gestured for Daniel to sit on the sofa and apologized for the secrecy surrounding the meeting.

Paul was also present in the room, sitting in the far corner to the side, which Daniel found odd.

As Ted continued talking, he used his hands to emphasize his words. He sat up straight, capturing Daniel's full attention, while his jacket rested on the arm of the chair.

Interrupting the flow, Paul matter-of-factly stated from behind them, "Grip Solutions is a front company. Internally, we refer to it as Farragut Center. We operate without oversight from the Agency."

Ted sipped his coffee and continued, "The question is, what's the point? We're here to handle selected dispatches."

"What does that even mean?" He remembered Paul mentioning it on the river. It sounded like a meaningless statement.

Disrupting Ted's flow, Paul interjected, "Our new euphemism for targeted killing." Daniel couldn't help but laugh, wanting to express his concerns about the dangers of targeted killing. However, he chose to remain cautious as Ted didn't seem amused.

Ted clarified their approach, "We'll use technology to augment human capabilities. Subtle, quiet. No drones." Unclear about his role, Daniel wondered what exactly he was supposed to do. "There's some finessing that needs to happen. We need your help in setting up the framework and decision-making process."

"If you're interested, there's also the opportunity to be in the field," Paul added, essentially implying that Daniel would need to resign.

"What does that look like?" Paul's request felt like a resignation ultimatum.

"We believe it's crucial for those in the field to have the capacity to scrutinize decision-making. They must apply their own deposition matrix, in real-time," Paul explained, referring to the database used to track, capture, render, or kill suspected enemies.

Ted chimed in, "We think you'd be brilliant at it," Ted said, but he knew Daniel would have reservations. Working in the field was not as easy as one might think, and there were uncertainties about what the field would entail. "Look, I'm not going to lie to you," Ted paused and cleared his throat. "There's a clear difference between endorsing a kill and doing it yourself." Ted tried to emphasize his point, but he wasn't sure if it had the desired impact. "Daniel, I want to be clear here. I didn't ask for your help or expertise in the legality of targeted killing, although we do need it. I asked for your help because we need a legal mind, someone with clear ideals of logic and process to think independently in the field. But it's not for the faint of heart. Do you follow?"

For Daniel, a lawyer in an armchair, the world was linear. Everything seemed to progress logically, from oil prices to regimes to temperature, rising and falling. He couldn't understand why it was unclear who the heroes and villains were or how moral considerations slowed things down. To him, the world was black and white, and he couldn't comprehend why that view would ever change. Before Daniel could speak, Ted nodded, raised his hand, and silenced him.

"Did you ever study Roman law in college?" Daniel shook his head. "There's an old Roman law called homo sacer that has baffled historians for centuries. It was invoked, they think, by oath-breaking and allowed a man to be effectively sacrificed by society." It sounded Hobbesian to Daniel. Ted had his arm rested on the chair's arm, coiled like a cobra as he formulated his words. "This form of law has been embedded into societies ever since. We have the duty to provide security. We want a lean deposition matrix, no bureaucracy."

"And what about due diligence?" Daniel interjected, biting the soft pad of his thumb.

Ted nodded. "It's a key process. It may have risen from the ashes of drone strikes, but it's not the successor. We won't be racking up hundreds of kills a month. These operations will have a personal touch. It's not intended to get out of hand or be a device to eliminate terrorist threats. It's clear national security. We're here to protect ourselves and, in the process, eliminate the gravest threats."

Ted knew Daniel for years but they were never more than acquaintances. He knew Daniel was eager to make a difference, to bring justice in his own way. The world was black and white to the young lawyer, and he was confident in his ability to differentiate between the two indefinitely. "I hope you know that we'll need to act abruptly for this to be effective. Some sacrifices will need to be made," Ted said.

Daniel acknowledged his understanding. The issue of leaving the Agency came up, but Paul reassured him, saying they would handle it. Daniel wondered if they had that much influence, but Paul's serious demeanor indicated they were not joking. When Daniel asked for some time to think, Paul replied, "Unfortunately not." Ted added, "We can give you a few hours." Daniel needed the time, and an hour later, Paul and Ted returned. Daniel made up his mind. "We're going to give you a medical check-up later. Paul will handle things with the Agency," Ted said, sitting down with a folder. "So, Princeton and then Yale. Where's home?" Ted asked casually, fiddling with a packet of gum.

"Boston."

"You used to hunt as a boy, shot clays and pheasants."

"I wasn't particularly good," Daniel admitted.

The Collateral Dividend

"Not according to the State of Massachusetts. Says here you were a top gun," Ted replied. Although not close friends, Ted was an acquaintance from the Langley halls. He probed, "Do you go home often?"

"Never." Daniel studied Ted's face, searching for any underlying meaning. Despite their lack of friendship, Ted seemed to possess intimate knowledge about Daniel. Would Daniel lie or tell the truth? Ted prided himself on his ability to read people, knowing that everyone harbored secrets. He was curious to see how Daniel Faron would react when confronted with his own.

Ted momentarily digressed, crossing his arms and reminiscing about his college days. "There are times when choices need to be made, even if they're unsavory," Ted abruptly stated. "Sometimes, it's better to have nothing to go home to." He glanced down at his notepad. "Ever done drugs?" he suddenly asked. While a question frequently posed by Langley, Ted wanted to be more specific. Taken aback, Daniel asked for clarification. "Have you been exposed to or taken brain-altering drugs or medication at any point?"

"Excuse me?"

"Just answer the question."

"No," Daniel replied definitively.

"And, uh, Princeton was your favorite of the two? What didn't you like about Yale?" Ted inquired further. Daniel struggled to explain, aside from mentioning the unwelcoming environment in New Haven. He and his colleagues despised it. He sometimes wondered if he would have been happier attending Harvard or even Columbia, despite not enjoying his time at Yale. But he never regretted the decision or looked back.

"I don't believe in looking back into the past. The decision must have made sense at the time, so why question it now?" Daniel said with a grin, emphasizing the importance of context.

Ted then probed why Daniel hadn't stayed closer to home, but Daniel evaded the question. Uncertain, he wondered if Ted knew the full story. Daniel laughed harder than Ted had expected, clarifying that his distance from home was never the issue, conveying it in a good-natured tone. Daniel questioned the necessity of their conversation, to which Ted replied, "It is." Ted glanced at his watch, signaling their departure. "We'll be back," he said, heading towards the door. "Wait here. Paul will return shortly to take you for the physical," he added before leaving the room.

Outside the door, Ted and Paul stood together. Paul appeared exhausted, which worried Ted. Paul had a tendency to push his limits. "You know, he must think we're messing with him," Ted remarked.

E.R. Wychwood

Paul shrugged. "Well, that's not entirely unfounded. How did you expect him to react?" He glanced back at the analyst behind the computer terminal, and a moment of silence ensued. A hand signal sufficed to allow them to proceed.

"At first? Not well," Ted admitted.

"I didn't think so either," Paul concurred. They waited for ten or fifteen minutes until Paul leaned forward and flicked a switch near the doorway. "I'm going in now," he announced, stepping out of the room and waiting for a subtle ticking sound to resonate through the hallway. It resembled a leaking faucet. Satisfied, Paul entered the room.

Daniel watched Paul walk in, taking note of his well-dressed appearance—a patterned plaid blazer, dark trousers, and an undone tie. Paul put on a pair of reading glasses, examined the papers in front of him, and asked, "What do you think?"

Daniel agreed, leaving the task of handling his resignation and transition from the Company to Paul. The details were not something Daniel needed to concern himself with. They would begin the process that day. "If you have any questions, now's the time to ask. We have a physical to complete before twenty past," Paul stated, glancing at his watch, indicating they were short on time. Things were moving rapidly, and Daniel felt a mix of illness and overwhelm. "I'm excited to get started, and I hope you are too," Daniel replied.

Nearly an hour later, as the hour was about to change, Paul impatiently tapped the nib of his pen on the pad of paper. He checked his watch and stood up. "Ted is waiting for us down the hall," he said, leading Daniel through the door and down the hallway, passing the elevator and entering a brightly lit white room. Paul closed the door behind them, and he guided Daniel to sit on the medical examination bed in the center of the room. Ted occupied a chair on the far side, next to medical supplies, rubbing his head as if soothing a headache. He was eating a freshly baked chocolate chip muffin, spreading warm butter thinly over it. Daniel couldn't help but notice the crumbs Ted was leaving all over the floor, which bothered him.

Daniel looked cautious and asked, "What kind of tests are these?" He glanced at the inoculator resting on a medical tray.

Paul shrugged, coming around from the far side and placing his hands in his trouser pockets, having removed his suit jacket and rolled up his shirt sleeves. "We're going to take some blood and give you a few inoculations. That's all," he explained. Just then, there was a knock on the door, and a young, frail-looking woman in a white lab coat entered, smiling at Ted and Paul before heading to the sink at the back of the room to wash her hands.

The Collateral Dividend

"The best trait one can have in this job is to be observant, to be aware of your surroundings at all times. The smallest factors can and will kill you," Ted stated abruptly, sharing a lesson woven into their training. The lesson didn't foster trust.

The nurse put on latex gloves, punctured the safety cap of the medical canister with the syringe needle, and drew it back to fill it. She then tapped it vertically, expelling any air bubbles. Once done, she removed the sterilizing cover of a second syringe and placed it down. Turning to face Daniel, she requested, "Do you mind removing your shirt, please?" Daniel stood up, complied, and hung his shirt over the back of the bed. The nurse used a sterilizing swab to clean Faron's shoulder and the nape of his arm, revealing a prominently visible vein beneath the skin. A vein ran the length of his forearm, disappearing and reappearing. "Are you allergic to penicillin?" she inquired, wanting to confirm. Daniel shook his head and glanced back at Ted Hawthorne, who discarded the remains of the muffin into the trash and cleared his throat. "You develop a sixth sense. You look at data, at anything, and you'll learn to derive meaning from it—information that could save your life," Ted continued, his words sounding rehearsed rather than spontaneous. "You learn to find linear paths amidst webs of data. You learn to route."

"Route?" Daniel questioned.

"It's like reading, but across both medium and message. We're going to train you to become very good at it. It won't be easy. Mastering routing will help you survive in the field," Ted explained, painting a rather pessimistic picture. Daniel couldn't help but wonder what they were all talking about.

Meanwhile, the nurse injected a needle into Daniel's arm, drawing a fair amount of blood. Daniel observed as she applied pressure to the puncture site, asking him to hold onto the cotton ball a bit longer. The blood had been loaded into a glass capsule attached to the back of the syringe. The nurse twisted it, separating the syringe from the glass capsule, and swirled it around before placing it in a basket.

Next, she injected a clear solution into Daniel's shoulder using the second syringe. Meanwhile, Ted continued talking, discussing the evolving nature of the enemy and how economics had become more dangerous than explosives.

Once the nurse finished packing up her supplies and ensured the medical tray was moved to the far side of the room, she went over to Paul and engaged in a quiet conversation in the corner. Afterward, Paul walked her out of the room.

E.R. Wychwood

Daniel turned his head, following the nurse's departure. He felt strange, with the room spinning around him, and began to feel queasy again. His fingers felt heavy, and he clumsily attempted to touch his fingertips together but failed. Feeling somewhat drunk, he swayed back and forth and noticed Paul stepping away. His vision blurred, and he found himself falling as he tried to climb off the table. "What the hell did you just give me?" he exclaimed, fumbling across the examination table and crashing into the medical locker. He vomited against the wall, struggling to stand. Daniel tried to support himself but found his arms unresponsive, and he fell hard. A sense of hallucination washed over him as the room spun rapidly, disorienting his perception of which way was up. He attempted to move, but it appeared as pathetic wallowing on the floor. Paul approached, and Daniel had the impression of him bending down. Paul checked Daniel's pulse, and Daniel weakly swatted at him, but his arms refused to cooperate. As Daniel's vision narrowed, the spinning and haze dissipated, leaving only darkness.

THE OLD HABITS OF MAN

It had been nearly two years since the last drone strike, the moment when Daniel collapsed to the ground, losing all memory of the subsequent three months. Now, after those two years, Farragut Center stood on its own two feet. However, sustaining itself went beyond mere financial stability. They were constantly on war footing, investing time and money into structuring the department internally to ensure that its size didn't compromise the quality of its work. Maintaining secrecy was paramount.

In the District of Columbia, the tides were shifting, and the uneasiness of approaching political changes could be felt near the Capitol. The Federal Communication Commission (FCC) was particularly buzzing with excitement. It was late winter, and the city had awakened from its slumber as the dormant feeling of changing seasons filled the air. Three months had passed since American Telecom publicly admitted its faltering state. The company was highly leveraged, and its revenues were declining. The events that followed mirrored those of RJR Nabasco—a tale of greed that drowned any hope for the company's survival.

News of American Telecom's plight first spread within the industry and the financial sector. All major competing firms had been warned. Philippe Gaillard received the news while attending a philanthropic event in the 18th district of Paris. Despite just announcing another fully funded school program, the news from New York brought him the greatest satisfaction of the day. Gaillard reached out to a friend in London, a young British man running a successful hedge fund with his brother. They were credit vultures, and Gaillard had done business deals with them before. He proposed the idea of taking on American Telecom, with the Brits acting as the front-runners. They would purchase the senior notes at a significant discount, forcing American Telecom into Chapter 11 bankruptcy. That's when Gaillard would make his move, taking over the clients, infrastructure, and continuing to provide telecommunication services. The Brits would receive a share of the profits and repayment of outstanding debt. Gaillard took the initial call with his British friends in the back of a school, underneath a stairwell, while Piere stood by the doorway.

After finishing the call, Gaillard returned to the event, but what was meant to be a twenty-minute call turned into a three-hour discussion. His wife was less than thrilled. Gaillard was obsessed with the thrill of deals, which had often driven him. Later that night, when he finally arrived at his office in La Defense, he could take definitive action. A term sheet was circulated to London before midnight, and lawyers were roused from their slumber to handle the proceedings.

While Gaillard would be spearheading the deal, his friends in London would play a crucial role in getting it started. There was little Gaillard could do until American Telecom entered Chapter 11 bankruptcy. He had previously attempted to acquire the group but was swiftly rejected by the board of directors. Now, he saw an opportunity to own it, and patience would allow him to secure it at a steeper discount.

Gaillard consulted his contact book, and it was nearly 6:30 PM in Washington. His next call was to his contacts within the FCC and the government, individuals he could rely on to facilitate the transaction, whether willingly or through coercion. The man from Ofcom had been one of Gaillard's contacts, but the murder case had gone cold, and Gaillard couldn't recall the man's name after two years.

Timing was crucial, as Gaillard emphasized when he finally reached Adam Stanley. Adam, a gaunt American with an eastern-seaboard drawl, had grown up poor. Gaillard had supported him financially, providing a scholarship for poor, talented students interested in telecommunications. Gaillard had groomed and mentored Adam, treating him like a son. They were friends, and now Gaillard subtly called in his favors. Adam would ensure that the FCC approved everything required for the deal. By the end of the month, Philippe Gaillard, armed with Gaillard Telecommunications' vast financial resources, believed everyone was aligned. The Brits had acquired most of American Telecom's senior debt at steep discounts and were pressuring the board to enter Chapter 11. They would also provide funding to guide the company through bankruptcy. It was inevitable that American Telecom would emerge from bankruptcy under new ownership.

Some of Gaillard's staff, particularly his legal counsel, found his approach foolish. Over dinner one evening, his legal counsel cautioned him, "You're relying too heavily on the Yates." Gaillard would respond, making his stance clear, "Buying American Telecom's debt ourselves is too risky. We're not a debt fund. Besides, exposing ourselves too much in the financial world could jeopardize our ability to tap into the debt capital markets again." Gaillard Telecom, the largest of its kind in Europe, was privately owned, but a significant portion of its debt was listed on the markets. Gaillard was wary of pushing too hard and potentially damaging their reputation as a safe and reliable entity. His advisors dared not question his tactics, and he had never raised capital through equity. Recently, following advice from clever individuals in London, they had begun raising capital through mobile-backed bonds—bonds backed by mobile phone payments from customers. Gaillard planned to use a similar approach to purchase American Telecom's assets and contracts out of bankruptcy. Control was paramount for Gaillard, and only his vote mattered within the company.

Gaillard met the Yates in London two weeks later in November, amidst the cool blue tones of Mayfair overshadowed by Westminster and Regent's Street. Their office, located near Savile Row, was housed in a nondescript building with a narrow frontage that expanded considerably once inside. For weeks, the lawyers had been diligently working on a memorandum of understanding governed by English law, reaching a point of no return, or so Philippe Gaillard had thought.

Then, things began to set into motion. Late one evening, after the markets had closed, the bankruptcy filing occurred. The *Wall Street Journal* swiftly picked up the case, featuring it on the front page of their website within an hour. It was a partially solvent restructuring, marking the collapse of American Telecom. The Yates seized the opportunity and purchased more of its debt at even steeper discounts. By the next morning, specialist news agencies focusing on distressed situations were reporting that the Yates would be offering a 'DIP facility' – a financing arrangement to be paid back almost immediately, facilitating the process.

Given their ownership of the majority of the $1 billion corporate bonds due in 2027, the Yates held considerable control over the proceedings. They were regarded as temporally and structurally senior, enjoying priority of repayment. The rest of the group's bonds were of lower ratings, mostly categorized as 'leveraged' or, as Michael Milken had once coined, 'junk bonds.'

The Yates had retained Ives Munro from Paul, Weiss as their lawyers, leveraging their longstanding friendship from their days at Eton and Cambridge. Paul, Weiss had a presence in both New York and London, making them well-versed in the ongoing bankruptcy process in the Southern District of New York, Gaillard's involvement was minimal, despite it consuming most of his free time. The Yates had asked him to remain in the background until he was needed, yet he maintained frequent communication with Adam Stanley, seeking internal updates.

Bankruptcies, especially on such a grand scale, were inherently complex. Most of the information Gaillard received was drip-fed through Ives at Paul, Weiss. During his morning personal training sessions on a stationary bike,

Gaillard would often call Ives, discussing his plans for American Telecom once acquired, highlighting the group's operational inefficiencies resulting from poor management, and seeking Ives' insights on the feasibility of a capital raise against AT's customer receivables for favorable borrowing on the US bond markets.

Gradually, Ives and his staff noticed Gaillard's increasingly erratic behavior. While Gaillard was known for his intense peaks and troughs, things felt different this time. On one occasion, he entered the office with an ebullient demeanor, nearly bouncing off the walls, proposing a $600 million donation to support inner-city children in Paris. He even announced plans for a dinner at Le Fouquet on Thursday, only to retreat to his office for the next 21 hours, immersed in planning the donation and bombarding everyone involved in the American Telecom transaction with emails from his phone. The dinner never materialized.

Meanwhile, in London, significant progress was underway. Paul, Weiss had promptly convened with Kirkland & Ellis to develop a restructuring plan. Kirkland, a dominant force in the bankruptcy circuit, had been appointed as legal advisors to American Telecom, a move despised by many, including Ives. Known for their aggressiveness and tireless work ethic, Kirkland posed a formidable challenge. However, the company's options were limited. Quercus Gate Capital Partners, controlled by the Yates family, held significant power. The Yates brothers, Hugo and Charlie, had backgrounds in finance, with Hugo's experience at Goldman, Sachs and Charlie's stint at McKinsey. Gaillard had always been frustrated by Charlie's lackadaisical approach to work, but it was at one of Charlie's infamous parties in Verbier where Gaillard had first met the Yates boys. The party, often associated with debauchery, attracted a diverse mix of attendees, including mysterious figures like "Richard," whose origins remained unknown.

The Yates brothers, resembling British Winklevoss twins, held commanding presence. Hugo, standing at nearly six-five, possessed a deep, hoarse voice earned through excessive alcohol consumption. Charlie, slightly shorter but equally striking, appeared more put-together despite his casual appearance. They navigated the office with confidence, and Hugo's disheveled look, unbuttoned sleeves, and perpetually untucked shirt added to his public schoolboy aura. Charlie, though less organized professionally, spent most of his days in sweaty cycle gear after morning rides, much to the annoyance of the staff.

Charlie's experience at McKinsey proved valuable, as he understood the workings and mindset of advisors, allowing him to facilitate communication with Quercus' transaction advisors. His ability to grease the wheels became apparent during their regular calls with Kirkland. Charlie emphasized their desire for clarity and the importance of achieving the right outcome rather than a specific one, which resonated with the company. They feared Gaillard, aware that their position would be precarious under his control. Gaillard, however, remained inconsequential to the Yates brothers, who comfortably sat in the driver's seat.

The lengthy and often unproductive calls continued. The boys received an odd remark from Gaillard's absence during a discussion about the value break. In distressed situations, the value break determined where the proceeds would stop if the company were sold. Breaking in the equity meant that all creditors would be paid, and shareholders would retain value, while breaking in the debt implied partial repayment of creditors and no value for shareholders. Gaillard firmly believed that the shareholders held no value, a stance he had expressed on previous calls. Uninvited to this particular call, Gaillard's absence went unnoticed.

During a subsequent break, Kirkland and PJT, the company's financial advisors, provided new numbers. The Yates brothers had to familiarize themselves with the updated information. In the following weeks, they revised their plan. Their focus shifted away from Gaillard; they no longer desired his involvement in running the business day-to-day. However, they still wanted to be compensated. Recognizing the marginal solvency of the equity, they proposed a payment structure involving cash and debt write-offs, commonly known as credit bidding. This plan required Chapter 11 filing, which would eventually alert Gaillard. The Yates brothers needed to prevent Gaillard from undermining their efforts. To facilitate their plan, they decided to offload Gaillard's sub-participating debts to Citibank's distressed desk. Gaillard learned about this development later that day, as Hugo explained it was necessary to avoid conflicts. If Gaillard wanted to acquire more debt, the Yates would assist him through the senior notes, with Citibank holding the debt in their accounts, allowing Gaillard to bear the financial risk.

The senior notes, subordinate to the Yates brothers' existing notes, would be paid second. However, the brothers had no intention of acquiring the senior notes. In fact, they planned to compromise them under their proposed plan. Though Sid, Quercus' trader, found their approach crass, he remained silent.

By December, Gaillard had invested considerable financial resources in preparing a bid. Over three hundred million dollars had been spent acquiring the senior notes and establishing licenses and infrastructure for operating the contracts obtained from American Telecom. However, as months went by, the bid process faced repeated obstacles. Issues with drafting the memorandum of understanding consistently emerged at the last minute, requiring additional tweaks. The Yates brothers seemed uneasy during video calls, suggesting something was amiss.

During one of their bi-weekly strategy calls, the Yates brothers, under the shared legal agreement with Gaillard, expressed their belief that preserving the business in its entirety would offer a greater value proposition. Consequently, they decided to part ways with Paul, Weiss, prompting Gaillard's frustration. Despite their previous agreement, the brothers viewed the situation differently. Gaillard couldn't help but think, "Those fucking Brits." He should have turned back and accepted defeat, but he remained convinced that the risk was worth the reward.

On September 17th, Adam called Gaillard with unfortunate news. The FCC would support a proposal by the Yates brothers to keep American Telecom solvent. Their plan involved acquiring the company and forgiving a portion of their debt, severely compromising the senior notes and negating Gaillard's deal. Gaillard's anger surged, but he believed there was still a chance. He proposed a tender offer and immediately began contacting management. With time running out and the filing set for the next morning, Gaillard insisted that they file a motion, forcing the court to consider his offer.

By the time the true extent of the situation became clear, Gaillard had lost precious hours. His management team, convinced that the company's shares still held value, engaged Rothschilds as financial advisors to facilitate the acquisition of debt and evaluate the group's shares. However, time was scarce. Gaillard decided to manipulate the numbers, convinced that no one would notice the difference. He even declared, "Not even the Wall Street Journal." And initially, he was right.

On December 10th, the motion countering the Yates brothers' proposal reached the court in the Southern District of New York, accepted by Judge Broker. It granted Gaillard a second chance. Gaillard argued that, with guidance from the FCC, the board was best equipped to determine which offer would ensure American Telecom's solvency. Judge Broker agreed, providing a glimmer of hope for Gaillard.

Late evening in winter, Gaillard's tender offer was sent. He had offered twenty dollars a share, but without a guarantee, the final price might be lower. Gaillard had been on a business trip in Western Europe when AT's board of directors responded with a receipt confirmation, surprising him. He called

The Collateral Dividend

Adam Stanley in Washington and waited anxiously at the end of the bed until the line connected.

Regretting answering the call, Adam Stanley felt the pang of hunger from skipping lunch, impairing his ability to think. Gaillard had helped him secure his role as a commissioner, and Stanley felt obligated to reciprocate. "You know I can't say what you want me to say," he whispered. "I think Quercus' offer is favored by the board." Stanley felt weak. The FCC held significant influence, and AT's board was no exception. However, due process was essential, and it made Gaillard uneasy. What troubled him more was that someone else had made a similarly competitive offer.

Curiously, Gaillard asked in a calm tone, "What's the offer?"

"The Yates brothers are offering eleven. It will be a credit bid with a guarantee," Stanley responded.

"Is the board currently in a meeting?" Gaillard inquired.

Stanley confirmed that they were. Gaillard reassured himself, "Then we should have nothing to worry about. Even if we lose, we have bought the debt – we will be paid eventually."

"I still believe the restructuring will happen. The sale will occur below topco," Stanley added.

Perplexed, Gaillard asked, "What does that mean?" It meant that his senior notes, issued by the parent company of American Telecom, would be worthless, rendering his $300 million investment reduced to just a few million. However, a financial loss was not fatal.

Stanley confirmed that they were. Gaillard reassured himself, "Then we should have nothing to worry about. Even if we lose, we have bought the debt – we will be paid eventually."

"I still believe the restructuring will happen. The sale will occur below topco," Stanley added.

Perplexed, Gaillard asked, "What does that mean?" It meant that his senior notes, issued by the parent company of American Telecom, would be worthless, rendering his $300 million investment reduced to just a few million. However, a financial loss was not fatal.

Adam Stanley sighed deeply, feeling exasperated. Approaching the American Telecom takeover required sensitivity. The company's sheer size granted it the power to make decisions even when insolvent. Gaillard's bid had surpassed numerous FCC hurdles—a foreign investor buying an American staple carried significant implications for the financial markets and the economy. Somehow, Gaillard had defied the odds, with the help of Adam Stanley practically in his back pocket. "We may have a problem," Adam eventually revealed. "They submitted a request for review of your FCC approval and privately expressed concerns regarding questionable business practices under your management."

Gaillard took a sip of water, placing the glass on the nightstand. He had already contacted his lawyer via email. Anger welled up within Gaillard; he wouldn't lose this bid without a fight. The young Yates brothers intended to crush him, and he knew it. They were wealthy, Oxford-educated, and wielded their influence confidently while running their father's empire. The world had watched them grow, and as chief stakeholders in numerous multinational corporations, their accusations carried significant weight. Gaillard imagined that they would say it wasn't personal, but that would be a lie—it was entirely personal. The brothers had once been granted access to Gaillard's books, and Philippe knew that a discerning mind would have discovered his money laundering and illegal deals. It would have required significant digging, but the evidence was there, buried beneath the numbers.

He had already contacted his lawyer via email. Gaillard was furious. He couldn't afford to lose this bid and be humiliated. The young Yates brothers were planning to destroy him, and he was well aware of it. They were young, wealthy, and skilled at leveraging their Oxbridge degrees. While running their father's empire was no easy task, they handled it with finesse. The world had witnessed their growth, and as chief stakeholders in numerous multinational corporations, their accusations carried significant weight. They might claim it was nothing personal, but that would be a lie. It was entirely personal. The brothers had once gained access to Gaillard's financial records, and Philippe knew that a keen mind would have discovered his money laundering and illicit deals. It would have taken extensive investigation, but beneath the complex numbers, the evidence existed.

Adam felt uneasy about the situation. It seemed like their game was up. He could no longer cover up Gaillard's questionable business practices. He had fought hard for Gaillard, and the takeover had turned into a fierce battle with violent bidding. "Philippe, they've raised concerns about moral hazard. They're pointing out questionable revenues from some of our subsidiaries," Adam expressed, his voice filled with apprehension. Gaillard remained silent, his eyes flickering as anxiety washed over him. "Philippe, the Board has informed me that they are rejecting your bids from now on, and the FCC intends to review your existing licenses."

The Frenchman leaned back, collapsing onto the mattress in one of the guest rooms where he had been sleeping, tucked under neatly pressed sheets.

His wife occupied a room down the hall. Philippe Gaillard gazed up at the ceiling, holding the phone to his ear, saying nothing. Adam could faintly hear his shallow breaths through the line. Was Philippe crying? Or was it just static interfering with the sound?

Gaillard seethed with anger, clenching his jaw and exhaling heavily through his nose. His successful expansion bid had crumbled, and the cutthroat bidding had left him heavily leveraged. He would lose millions, possibly even hundreds of millions. Gaillard found himself facing substantial financial losses. The AT bonds he had acquired to win the bid had plummeted in value. While the company had obtained some of the bonds, he had personally invested a significant portion. His mind raced, trying to assess the damage, but his finances were spread across various accounts and investments. He wouldn't know the full extent until he consulted with his accountant.

He buzzed for Piere, who had been sleeping in the adjacent room. It seemed no one could match Philippe Gaillard's work hours. "Is that all the news you have?" Gaillard asked over the receiver, his tone suggesting a state of shock. His eyes appeared glazed over. Adam felt anxious. He had been aware of Gaillard's business practices but had turned a blind eye because of their friendship. What Philippe did was his own business, and he had always reassured Adam that he would never engage in such activities in America. When Adam confirmed that he had no further news, Gaillard abruptly ended the call. Piere entered the room, having been awakened by the commotion. He sat in a chair near the vanity, dozing in and out. Piere was a man of few words, often mistaken for being mute by the executive committee at Gaillard Telecom. However, on occasion, he would speak. His voice didn't match his stature but wasn't effeminate either. He had become friends with Gaillard almost twenty-five years ago. Piere had served in the legionnaires and had lost part of his small finger and a portion of his shoulder during his service. Whenever he stood in a room, he would conceal his shorter finger with his hand or hide it under his armpit.

"We need to consult the accountant and discuss how we'll handle this," Gaillard said to Piere as he continued pacing. Piere mentally took note of the instructions. In the room, there was a wooden chair near the desk, which Piere grabbed by the arm and flung across the room, shattering the glass shower. Piere didn't flinch. Twenty years had made him almost immune to Gaillard's outbursts. Those familiar with Piere and his role understood that he was Gaillard's stabilizing force, his strength, and his composure.

"It's most upsetting that Adam couldn't do anything," Gaillard confided in Piere. The chair incident had awakened his wife, which affected his mood more than losing $500 million. They would find a way to recover the money, but Gaillard would have to spend more nights in the guest rooms if he kept upsetting her.

"Why don't we go to the study?" Piere suggested after Gaillard received a stern reprimand. Gaillard had been on the phone for the past twenty minutes, arranging meetings for the upcoming hours. The study would provide additional privacy. The room had been soundproofed and remained locked unless in use. Gaillard's paranoia had led him to have Piere personally sweep the room for listening devices on a daily basis.

The accusations of Gaillard's questionable business practices were true. "How could they have found out about our other operations?" Gaillard asked Piere, recounting their conversation. They had been meticulous, with Piere being primarily responsible. Gaillard wanted answers as to how the FCC could have uncovered their secrets. They had bribed or handled anyone who might have known. Most importantly, they had been extremely cautious about whom they disclosed information to. However, the secret had slipped out once or twice. A secretary who had worked with Gaillard Sr. had shared the story at a bar in 1984, but no one had believed her. Gaillard's father had served as a cryptologist and spy during the war for the Allies. That work had led to the establishment of a telecommunications company, but it was also how they expanded their market share. They had utilized client information, including recorded conversations, to exploit purchasing habits. They engaged in data mining, collecting and selling information for their own business interests. What had initially been an informal arrangement had transformed into a legitimate offshore enterprise involved in corporate espionage, data mining, and handling confidential information.

The Gaillard group had amassed a significant fortune by selling information discreetly. The French public revered Gaillard Sr. as a war hero and spy, unaware that they were being spied on by him and his son. Exploiting and selling information had become increasingly prevalent in the seventies, propelling the company to the top of the market in terms of account numbers. The Paris-based firm dominated Europe's phone lines. It was a dangerous and cyclical relationship. By exploiting client data, they attracted more clients, which, in turn, provided additional opportunities for exploitation. The challenge lay in pricing the data and ensuring that selling the information didn't raise suspicions of foul play. There were even insider trading benefits. Gaillard had evaded scrutiny through an array of complex offshore trading accounts. Occasionally, they had to mix false information with the genuine data. Sometimes market

The Collateral Dividend

stability required it. Gaillard likened their operations to Bletchley Park. If the British had utilized every piece of information decoded from the Enigma machine, the Germans would have realized they had been compromised.

Gaillard's desire for revenge consumed him. The next day, his accountant delivered an updated report, and the figures were disheartening. As the afternoon wore on, Gaillard found himself locked in his study, contemplating his next move. Piere, sensing his frustration, proposed the idea of eliminating Adam, recognizing the potential threat he posed to their operations. "Do it discreetly," Piere suggested, taking charge of the plan.

Simultaneously, Gaillard decided to instruct his lawyers in London to sue the Yates brothers for their deceitful actions. However, deep down, he knew that legal action alone would not suffice. True justice needed to be served by his own hands. The significant loss incurred by the trust fund weighed heavily on his mind.

His lawyers attempted to justify the losses, claiming that such setbacks were not uncommon in the realm of FCC bids. They advised Gaillard to be patient and suggested that he postpone the planned donation for several years. But Gaillard refused to accept defeat. He couldn't bear the thought of reneging on his promise, disappointing his wife, and tarnishing his reputation. The commitment had been made, and he was determined to honor it within the agreed timeframe.

Gaillard recognized that he had a limited window of two years to fulfill his commitment before any delay would expose his vulnerability. He was well aware that news of his substantial losses could attract opportunistic predators, endangering not only his life but also his company. The market would perceive his setbacks as a sign of weakness, inviting further troubles.

Following his meeting with the accountant, Gaillard realized that the question was no longer about recovery, but rather how quickly he could bounce back. The timeframe had shifted from years to weeks. But how would he achieve this daunting task? Gaillard pondered his options, considering his connections with questionable acquaintances from his past. It had been decades since his family had last engaged with these individuals. Piere, responsible for day-to-day operations, took charge of coordinating the recent hit on the man from Ofcom. Piere had a close friendship with a Chinese associate named Min, who operated a technology manufacturing company in Singapore. Min's company supplied most smartphones running on Gaillard's network. Piere suspected that Min might have ties to the Chinese government, possibly even the state intelligence service. At the very least, Min had unusual connections with the Chinese Ministry of State Security.

"Piere eventually mentioned that your father often used a Russian named Kroysgin," Piere said after brainstorming for an hour on the upcoming events. Gaillard had been unaware of the worn ties between his family and Vladimir Kroysgin, a former high-ranking officer in the KGB and now a wealthy Russian oligarch. Few knew much about him as he had faded into obscurity in the 1990s, although he had faced sanctions due to the war in Ukraine. However, his son remained unaffected. By that winter, Vladimir was in his nineties and on his deathbed, but the connections he could offer Gaillard were significant. Gaillard had a lengthy conversation with the elderly man, realizing that his business required more discreet members of the underworld for his ambitious plan. Surprisingly, the old man recommended his son, which conveniently reinforced the longstanding relationship between the two families. Gaillard found it to be a captivating narrative—a complex tale intertwining the fates of both families.

Gaillard learned that Sergei Kroysgin would be the perfect candidate for the task. Sergei had previously worked as a banker in London before fulfilling his father's wishes by serving the Kremlin. His British education had given him a passable but slightly flawed British accent—an era when Britain had turned a blind eye to the presence of oligarchs and their wealth. Most importantly, Sergei had received field service training, and Vladimir assured Gaillard that his capabilities were more than sufficient for any task at hand.

Although a nominal fee had been agreed upon, the primary motivation for the elder Kroysgin was the honor of assisting an old family friend. The most challenging aspect would be ensuring that the payment didn't trigger government sanctions. However, Gaillard's lawyers swiftly addressed this concern, and by the end of the month, Sergei had flown to Paris to meet Gaillard.

* * *

Sergei arrived late at the nondescript medical buildings, where security surprisingly seemed lax. Located on the third floor at the back of the building was a wing dedicated to palliative care. The staff treated him with a false deference, a respect he liked to believe stemmed from his own reputation. However, there were those who feared him, not for his own power, wit, or intellect, but for his father's influence. In fact, many here mistook Sergei for an ordinary, poor Russian immigrant who had fled to Western Germany after the fall of the Berlin Wall. Vladimir's stories about their past were all jumbled now, as the pain he endured made it hard for him to remember. Sometimes, as Sergei sat by his father's side, he wondered if they would have received better care had they stayed in Russia. But now Russia was nothing but a prison, and all the Kroysgins had escaped before sanctions were imposed, going into hiding. Sergei's sister, for instance, lived quietly in Greece. Occasionally, someone would stop him on the street, asking if he was related to Vladimir Kroysgin, but such encounters had become exceedingly rare. His father had always maintained a low profile, and though he had significant private influence within the Russian leadership, he was considered by many to be a demi-oligarch.

Sergei took pride in being his father's protégé son, but he had developed a nasty habit of succumbing to highly addictive vices. His father had never approved and had nearly disowned Sergei's sister when a London tabloid reported that she had been using drugs at a club during a term break. For Sergei, his vices mainly revolved around drugs and gambling.

By February of that year, Vladimir had been ill for quite some time, providing Sergei with considerable leverage to do as he pleased without his father's scrutiny. The Russian intelligence services had asked Sergei to leave nearly 18 months ago, and since then, he had been living lavishly in New York, unbeknownst to his ailing father.

Sergei knocked and peered through the door. Inside, stood a burly man, his 'brother,' a former FSB operative who bore a striking resemblance to Vladimir and Sergei. He had been retained to protect Vladimir and played the role of a devoted son, visiting every day and caring for his 'father.' When the door opened, the brother's fat hands withdrew from the deep pockets of his large coat, perched atop his broad shoulders.

Vladimir, out of breath, looked visibly deteriorated since Sergei's last visit. As if wallowing in self-pity, he motioned for his glasses and coughed weakly. Vladimir Kroysgin was a name that needed delicate handling in Red Square. The Kroysgins had been rewarded for their hard work during the days of communism, and Vladimir's position as the head of Russia's SVR had served to strengthen the waning power of Russian intelligence. He had always been a man of violent means, and the crises in Crimea and Chechnya had demanded a stronger service reminiscent of its predecessor, the KGB. Vladimir had secured his post due to his education and teaching at Saint Petersburg State University in the late seventies and early eighties. There was an old saying dear to the Kroysgin family's success: "treat all with the respect they themselves desire." This mantra had endeared the old man to people who eventually became quite powerful, and he had reaped the rewards ever since. However, Vladimir doubted whether his son had truly embraced this ethos.

As the younger Kroysgin entered the hospital room, he took off his jacket, placed it on the chair, and sat down, holding his father's weak hand. "Father," he said, "are you feeling well today?"

The senior Kroysgin took a deep breath through his oxygen mask, then weakly let the mask rest on his chest as his tired hands settled on his lap. "My son, how nice of you to visit," he gasped before coughing, his lungs strained by a deep, dry tenor.

Vladimir's ailing condition was not merely rooted in his body but also in his heavy smoking, which had led to emphysema, a slow death gradually approaching its inevitable end. Vladimir's delusions of continued command seldom resulted in international blowback. Although he continued to offer consultations from a distance for Russian intelligence, the service was now under the leadership of Mihkial Sokolov, who primarily focused on political operations and had saved both Russians and several oligarchs on numerous occasions. It was Sokolov who had orchestrated Vladimir's transfer to a hospital in Germany, forging Russian documents and utilizing agents within the German state to falsify immigration papers dating back to before the country's unification. According to the Germans, Kroysgin was Vladislav Balakin, a former Russian guard in East Germany who had trained as a plumber after unification. Forging the East German documentation was relatively easy, as parts of the German documentary system from that era had not yet been digitized. The more challenging task involved backdating the worsening diagnosis of emphysema over the past decade, fabricating decades' worth of German medical records, and setting up a flag operation to move Vladimir from one hospital to another. However, despite the complex steps involved, the process only required a few phishing attempts to gain access to the state medical records, a task that Russian hackers completed in just ten hours. Sokolov had been at the forefront of the cyber warfare being waged against the West, and compared to securing state secrets, medical records proved relatively simple.

All this effort had been made to smuggle Vladimir Kroysgin out of the country and evade sanctions. Initially, Kroysgin had reciprocated by assisting with operations on the other side of the sanctions. However, now that responsibility largely fell on Sergei's shoulders, although requests for such actions were few and far between. Sokolov did not entirely trust Sergei to do what was necessary, considering him nothing more than a drunk and a spoiled rich boy.

The Collateral Dividend

Vladimir lay tucked in beneath the covers, with the duvet neatly folded just past his knees. His frail frame seemed almost nonexistent under the covers. Laughing about his own impending death might appear morbid to some, but Vladimir had long confronted mortality head-on, having enshrouded his family within the clutches of death. "I need you to help a friend in France," he uttered, struggling to find his words and gasping for air. His cough sounded draining. "Ask..." He trailed off, and Sergei failed to catch the final words. "Casca?" The old man looked bewildered, any interruption of his train of thought enough to permanently derail it. Sergei attempted to redirect the conversation back to the topic at hand, but his efforts proved futile. The elder Kroysgin was no longer capable of engaging in coherent conversation or maintaining mental focus. He sat in bed for a long while, gazing across the room as if chasing his thoughts. It became increasingly apparent that further details could not be retrieved.

Sergei did not wish to become someone's lapdog. Perhaps his father was confused. "It's to repay a grave debt," his father had said before losing his train of thought completely. Sergei couldn't help but wonder what kind of debt could endure for generations.

The young Russian feared the unknown above all else. Above all, Sergei dreaded the overwhelming danger of disappointing his father. Vladimir had instilled in his children the imperative of displaying exuberant excellence, mirroring his own expectations. Like many Russian men of that era, Vladimir cared little for his daughter's achievements, but all of his children were to repel the notion of failure at all costs. Upholding their father's ideal of perfection had become both exhausting and habitual. Sergei's father's approval outweighed the risk of his own demise.

After nearly an hour, Sergei finally arrived at a hochhaus in Lichtenberg, Berlin. The building, an old apartment complex constructed by the Soviets in the 1970s, housed an elderly German woman who led a simple daily life. Inside one of the guest rooms, soundproofed nearly thirty years ago, sat an antiquated computer monitor. Sergei used the computer to contact Sokolov, their communication limited to text for anonymity and discretion. Occasionally, Sokolov would message him through social media platforms like Twitter, as they seemed uninterested in removing the pro-Russian noise that provided a distraction. However, there were instances when Sokolov insisted on secured communications. In the guest bedroom, Sergei hunched over the keyboard, facing a black monitor with white text while the cursor blinked at him.

E.R. Wychwood

His father had handed him a piece of paper with a cryptic message: "There is somewhere a noble family whose members fail each other..." Sergei anxiously awaited Sokolov's reply.

Mikhail Sokolov, in his cluttered and chaotic home, received the message on his phone and thought, "Fuck." The house resembled that of a professor, scattered with tidbits of thoughts, research materials, and books, preserving the progressive advances of discovery. Standing at the far end of the hall, Sokolov basked in the billowing light emanating from the windows behind him. In the living room, he packed a pipe with tobacco and used a gun-metal lighter to ignite a flame, taking three quick and successive puffs. Then he replied. Sergei watched as Sokolov typed, his anticipation growing. "Philippe Gaillard," the message read. "Instructions to follow. Standby." The message then transitioned into an automated response. Smoking his pipe, Sokolov furrowed his brow, realizing that it had been decades since Gaillard had called in a favor.

"Arche Café, 4 Temps le Parvis de la Defense. 15.30. Friday. Legend to be sent to Cairo Station for collection." Sergei had to seek clarification since he had been out of the field for too long. Cairo Station referred to the Berlin train station at Alexanderplatz. Things began to move swiftly. His cover would be that of a banker in Paris, mirroring his London training, thereby partially assuming his own identity. Throughout his life, Sergei had operated under a different last name than his father's to obscure any links between them.

"Be very cautious with all this. You'll have considerable freedom, but only because I hold your father, V.B., in high regard," Sokolov messaged, referring to Sergei's father. The young Russian had a knack for disappearing for months at a time, only reporting in once he had exhausted his funds. "He does cherish you, you know," Sokolov messaged before terminating the transmission. The screen went blank, and there was little Sokolov could do now to halt the momentum. Sergei believed that this mission would make his father proud. Furthermore, Sokolov had known that a day like this would come, that Gaillard would contact them, and utter that cryptic line. It would be incumbent upon Vladimir or, failing that, Sokolov himself to complete the task they had all begun fifty years ago. Soon, it would be over.

By the time Sergei flew to Paris and picked up the rental car, a lump had formed in his gut, creeping up to his throat. It felt so overwhelming that he feared he would lose his ability to speak. Quarter past three, and Sergei arrived in the La Defense district, finding a parking spot on the uppermost level of the car park near the café. The sun was shining, and from within the warm confines of the car, he sensed the light bringing a comforting warmth.

The Collateral Dividend

He sat in the driver's seat for a while, attempting to calm his breathing. It was then that he retrieved a handgun from the glove compartment and slipped it into the pocket of his trench coat. Sergei also took a powder tablet, allowing it to dissolve underneath his tongue. His eyes dilated, and a surge of energy coursed through him. Taking a deep breath, he got out of the car, closing the door firmly behind him.

Upon reaching the café, he chose a table on the farthest side of the outdoor courtyard and wiped the seat clean. Glancing around, Sergei considered it fitting for Gaillard to meet here, given that the company headquarters were merely a block away. However, he remained uncertain whether Gaillard would be the one to arrive.

The tablet's effects intensified, causing the ground to shift. It was not a clean batch. Sergei experienced another rush, feeling the blood pulsating in his temples. His attention became fixated on a puddle along the path, vivid images warping with the sky's refraction. Suddenly, he felt both alone and in sync with everything around him.

From the long courtyard, a tall man approached Sergei's right, his steps measured and deliberate. Sergei was aware yet detached. A euphoric sensation accompanied the bliss, overpowering any concerns. The puddle and the cobblestones seemed interconnected, intrinsically linked. Philippe Gaillard emerged from across the courtyard, with the wind pushing back his blonde hair, revealing high widow's peaks.

Sergei turned to face Gaillard. Taking a large gulp from his glass, Sergei noticed the unnerving stillness on Gaillard's face, emanating a sense of unease. If executed correctly, Sergei could shoot the man before anyone noticed. Gaillard was there to kill him.

In a swift and painless motion, Sergei rose from his seat, drew his weapon with practiced precision, and shot Gaillard dead. The man stumbled back and collapsed onto the ground. Sergei calmly turned away, walking towards the intersection. Chaos erupted as the sound of the gunshot echoed through the bustling square. He disposed of the gun in a nearby public wastebin.

Suddenly, Sergei found himself back in the café. Gaillard sat beside him, extending his hand and introducing himself. "A Kroysgin, I assume?" Gaillard asked. Sergei nodded, still disoriented. He shook Gaillard's hand and glanced around, trying to regain his bearings. Gaillard sensed Sergei's spaced-out state, observing his dilated, wide-eyed appearance. "Through my friend at the Kremlin, I've heard only good things about you. He says you live up to the Kroysgin name in every sense," Gaillard remarked, crossing his legs and leaning back nonchalantly in his chair. "You truly resemble your father." Sergei looked up at Gaillard, the pieces finally falling into place. He was back. "Gaillard, is it?"

Gaillard scrutinized Sergei's appearance, repeatedly assessing him. It was evident to Gaillard that the Russian was under the influence. The Frenchman nodded and said, "My friends call me Philippe," pausing momentarily. "You know who I am, so I assume you know what I do," he expected to bypass the formalities, but Sergei shook his head.

"I know in broad terms. I know that you are the chairman and CEO of Gaillard Telecommunications. I'm aware of your connection with my father through his work, and that both of you are billionaires," Sergei said, stealing a quick glance at the Gaillard logo on the building behind them. "I've been told that you have a close relationship with the Kremlin, which allows you to maintain telephone operations within the country."

Philippe chuckled. "Only broadly? Do you also happen to know about my fondness for Occitan poetry?" Sergei did not. "I do know that you're not as healthy as you claim to be," Sergei dryly remarked, his attention fixated on the watermark on his wineglass.

"That tells me more about you than what you know about me," Gaillard laughed again. "Now I see that you believe the rumors you hear, no matter how fake or absurd," he said. "Spoken like a true Russian, I might add," Philippe's strong French accent was unmistakable. They conversed in English, despite Sergei's knowledge of French. They had agreed upon English as the common language, as Sergei's French was not as fluent as it once was, and using it would have posed more of a barrier than a convenience. It was, however, passable. Philippe ordered a bottle of Bollinger, and they both waited for it to arrive. After tasting it, Philippe poured a glass for Sergei, gesturing for him to try it. However, Sergei interrupted him, uninterested in the pleasantries. He had tasted Bollinger before and found it to be mediocre champagne.

"I'm not exactly sure what you want from me," Sergei stated. Philippe tore off bits of fresh bread, dipped them in oil, and ate them while sitting with his leg crossed. He looked at Sergei with a quizzical expression and asked between bites, "Why do you think?" It was a genuine question, and when Sergei couldn't answer, Philippe answered for him. "You killed a Russian defector in London without being seen," Sergei immediately understood what Philippe meant. His body grew warm, and he became nervous. He had used Plutonium 210, and it hadn't been a pleasant experience. "Forgive me for admiring your work," Philippe added. "You killed a high-value Russian defector in the heart of perhaps the most surveilled city in the world. You're frankly the only one I feel I can trust for this. I know that you're not someone who kills for money. Your morals are higher than that. You'll kill for your father, but not for money. Those morals, I trust. Do you understand?" Philippe drank more wine, placing the glass on the table and leisurely stroking his mustache.

"About the favor," Sergei tried to redirect the conversation. "Some recent losses have put both myself, my company, and many of your father's oligarch friends in a precarious position. I've arranged to—let's say—manipulate the markets in my favor. However, there are people that need to be convinced."

Gaillard had no intention of explaining how or why those targeted were involved. He continued to drink his wine, clearly in no hurry. He simply wanted to enjoy the absence of rain and the fresh air for a little while. "Now, I need someone I can trust, someone who understands the world markets, and you fit both criteria," Philippe reached into his coat pocket and pulled out a pack of cigarettes. He tapped the package twice against his palm, removed one, and placed it between his lips. It was a traditional Gauloises from a pack of twenty-five, a brand he would consume in about a day and a half. He didn't possess a special lighter, instead lighting the end with a disposable one. He waited a moment, looking at Sergei, and took a deep, steady breath as the cigarette ignited. The smoke wafted into the air, providing immense relief. He felt at ease. "Do you want one?" he asked, and Sergei politely accepted. Sergei rarely smoked cigarettes, and the smoke burned quickly in his lungs. The French brand used a darker tobacco, imparting a strong kick.

"I'm sure you know of others who are willing to help," Sergei abruptly interjected, hesitant to become involved. Gaillard observed the Russian wasting the cigarette, letting it wither away in the wind. Gaillard placed his thumb on the end of his own cigarette and used the ashtray to shape the charred tip. He wanted to savor the moment. "No," he said, "not anyone who isn't also indifferent to money." He extended his hand to his leg and flicked the cigarette, shortening the ashes. "This requires a very specific skill set. Why hire two people when one person can accomplish the task just as well?" He took another drag on the cigarette, the sound of air softly escaping his mouth. "I've secured you a position at a trading desk in Switzerland. It's with an American firm called Mayer Klied. Have you heard of it?" Sergei nodded. It was one of the largest investment banks in New York. "I'll need you to work there. Eventually, you'll need to transfer to Manhattan, but not for a little while," Gaillard continued before Sergei could inquire further. "Switzerland plays a crucial role in all of this. This job must be done correctly. I will not accept failure, nor will your father. I am perfectly willing to overlook your little drug problem as long as you do as I ask. In fact, I'll gladly finance it if you keep me satisfied." Philippe handed the waiter his card, waiting for the bill to return. He signed it and then extinguished his cigarette, forcefully jamming it into the ashtray. Gaillard reached into his coat pocket for a business card and handed it to Sergei Krosgyn. Sergei glanced at the back of the card and then looked up at Gaillard, who grunted, "I'll see you at the train station tomorrow morning, 9 A.M. Don't be late. And get some rest, will you? You look terrible."

THE MAN FROM THE FCC

Adam Stanley tried to call out for help and plead for mercy, but the gag covering his mouth was fastened tightly. Helplessly, he looked at his captors, sensing a disturbing dullness about them. In a way, he knew he had brought this upon himself. Could there have been a way to avoid it? How could Gaillard, his friend of decades, do this to him? Perhaps it wasn't Gaillard but someone seeking revenge on him.

Bound to a chair in the center of the room, Adam noticed a tarp spread beneath him. A bloody wound on his head throbbed where he had been struck, rendering him unconscious for an uncertain amount of time. His desk had been ransacked with careful precision, leaving no visible signs of a search. The blinds were drawn back, revealing the glossy reflection of wet pavement outside.

Restlessly, Adam fidgeted in his seat, his hands securely bound with cable ties cushioned by foam covers. The room was dark, save for the stark light emanating from a distant lamp, offering limited visibility of no more than a few feet.

Approaching from across the room, the leader, named Lee, with his beady green eyes, paced in the darkness. He claimed they were sent by the FCC, causing Adam's heart to sink. He knew that meant Gaillard was involved. If Adam wanted to survive the night, he needed to present a convincing case. Lee, however, was a liar, deriving pleasure from watching others beg for their lives. Piere had orchestrated this attack, considering the involvement of Sergei too risky for their plans. Lee had little knowledge of Gaillard, having only heard Piere's voice on calls and received fragmented information to torment his victims.

With a lump of dread in his throat, Adam swallowed hard. Lee, removing his gloves, smiled while taking a seat facing Adam. It was clear he was not a local, likely a nomadic killer. Lee chastised Adam in a condescending tone, emphasizing that the FCC sought information on the brothers. He believed the files required for the application process were stored in the filing cabinet. Lee expressed his reluctance to tamper with the lock. Removing the tape from Adam's mouth, he folded it, sticking the ends together.

Gasping for air, Adam managed to utter, "Three-two-six-five, five-nine-six." Lee entered the numbers, triggering a fingerprint scan. He signaled his counterpart to move Adam closer so they could use his finger to unlock the

41

cabinet. As the lock released, Lee swiftly sifted through the files, selecting two adjacent ones before gently closing the drawer. They then switched off the office lights, guiding Adam down the hallway and into the back-loading bay near a strategically positioned surveillance camera. Adam resisted, prompting his accompanying captor to gag him once more and ruthlessly crush his hand in a door, causing unbearable pain. Overpowered, Adam's colleague began to scream.

Lee gazed at Adam and coldly commanded, "Now kill him." A Beretta pistol emerged from the biker jacket pocket. Grabbing Adam by the collar, Lee pushed him forward, causing him to stumble into the middle of the alley, directly within the camera's view. The loaded gun was raised and fired twice, striking Adam Stanley in the center of his chest with an upward trajectory. He collapsed, landing hard on the ground, motionless. Lee approached and seized Adam's wallet, watch, and other valuables before vanishing into the night with his accomplice, leaving behind the scene of a staged mugging under the orange glow of the alley lights.

*   *   *

THE MURDER didn't make the news until early the next morning when a delivery truck found Adam dead around 6 am. The intelligence community was caught off guard. Some suspected a targeted attack, while others speculated it was a failed mugging. Farragut Center remained oblivious to the situation, continuing with business as usual. The death of an FCC commissioner didn't seem to concern anyone. There was no sense of urgency.

Every morning, Daniel drove from the river at dawn, rain pouring the entire way. The rhythmic patter of raindrops against the windshield was oddly comforting to him. He couldn't recall when he started finding solace in the presence of water. It had a soothing effect on his mind, helping him maintain his sanity. For reasons he couldn't pinpoint, he found gloomy days more appealing than sunny ones.

Farragut Center was a seven-story building located on the corner of Farragut Square. The sixth floor had Grip's branding, with a reception desk at its entrance. Walking halfway along the floor, there was a glass door with a keycard checkpoint. Access required authorization from Paul or Ted, both of whom were notified whenever someone entered. During operating hours, one of them granted access. Once a week, Paul would disable the security systems, allowing a cleaner to tidy up the office space.

Beyond the second door, a staircase led to the floor above, where most of the plant machinery was located. A long, narrow hallway adorned with frosted glass led to an intersection branching out in a cross-shaped pattern. Hallways extended in both directions, offering views of the city below. Daniel's windowless office was situated down the hall, between intersecting corridors. He had decorated it modestly, with a few paintings, trinkets from his college days on his desk, and a rowing oar hanging on the wall. The computer terminal and office furniture were supplied by their friends at The Valley, a tech company in San Cupertino.

While many in the intelligence community considered Adam Stanley's death horrific but not significant enough to warrant immediate action, Brian Redding held a different opinion. That morning, he approached Ted with a sense of entitlement, recommending a deeper investigation. Ted didn't appreciate Redding's interference; it wasn't his place, and the fact that he knew it wasn't only added to Ted's frustration.

Ted called Paul from his car and arranged a meeting in the conference room. Paul relayed the message to Daniel and Avery, one of their senior analysts. Standing at the conference room doorway, Paul smirked at Daniel, who was putting on his well-tailored jacket. "Did you read the reports on the case officer in Venezuela I sent you last night?" Paul asked. They often exchanged notes on intelligence community reports found in Farragut Center's intercepted briefings. It was their way of keeping up with the current state of affairs.

"They're a bunch of reckless cowboys," Daniel replied, shaking his head. He had read the reports late the previous night during a bout of insomnia. His preference for gloomy days seemed to extend to his reading habits. He joined Paul in the conference room, rain streaming down the windows.

The CIA's involvement in South America had raised concerns among observers. A South American electronics manufacturer, in collaboration with a local university, had developed technology capable of jamming electronics and disabling wired devices. While initially intended for military and political applications, the criminal potential of such devices was evident. However, it wasn't the device development that interested Paul; it was the unsettling similarity between their product and one developed by The Valley, a multi-billion-dollar tech giant with close ties to Farragut Center.

Before Ted entered the conference room, Paul asked Daniel, "Are you still up for happy hour later?" Daniel gave him a nod in response. Ted joined them and took a seat at the head of the table, bringing four cups of coffee and a bottle of water for Daniel. "This morning, Adam Stanley was found dead in the alley behind the FCC building. The FBI will announce it as a homicide, most likely a mugging. Normally, this wouldn't concern us, but we've been advised to look into it. The autopsy suggests a professional hit, but the Bureau remains unconvinced."

"Naturally," Faron chimed in, earning a sharp look from Ted.

"We don't know who's responsible, but it doesn't seem like the work of a local syndicate," Ted continued, having searched through U.S. government files without finding conclusive evidence. There were no identifiable bullets, casings, or fingerprints. Forensic evidence was scarce. However, Ted did discover an encrypted timetable on Adam's phone. "Avery, start reviewing the information collected by the FBI. I don't expect much, but it's best to have something to start with." It always started with her. A significant amount of time was spent identifying persons of interest through keyword analysis and data mining. Farragut Center tracked assets using third-party sources, and one of their closest partnerships was with American technology firms. This collaboration aimed to enhance Avery's role as the sole responsible party for the entire signal intelligence process, with the assistance of massive servers downstairs that scanned for keywords and calculated probabilities. The community had long abandoned physical risk management, instead focusing on defending against the constant threat of terrorist attacks. In this age of risk management, everyone was treated as a suspect until their credentials proved otherwise.

Daniel leaned back in his chair with a somber expression, gazing out the window. Playing with his narrow orange repp tie, he remarked, "They wanted to send a message." Paul, seated across from Daniel, remained quiet, poring over the files on the table. With his rolled-up dress shirt sleeves and disheveled appearance, Daniel would have described him as unkempt. Finally, Paul chimed in, "I agree. It seems like they took something. The specific item may not matter as much as the fact that they managed to take it."

Ted, shivering from the cold outside, asked, "How soon can we expect to have a preliminary framework set up?" Paul provided a straightforward answer, stating it could be accomplished within a few hours if that was the desired timeline. The meeting concluded swiftly, and Daniel accompanied Paul back to his office, where they reviewed the security camera feeds from the previous night to identify any unusual activity. They discovered that a shipment had arrived at the back of the FCC building approximately thirty to forty minutes before Adam Stanley's estimated time of death. Paul traced the truck's route from the building to a local bar and then onto one of the main highways leading

The Collateral Dividend

into the city from Virginia. The resources and expertise required for such investigative work were beyond the reach of the FBI.

The shipment was evidently the killer's means of gaining access to the FCC. The bar's external camera captured a partial image of one of the men involved. Just to be sure, Paul ran the photo through facial recognition software. He suggested that Daniel visit the bar and see if the man was a frequent customer.

Near the end of the day, Daniel left for downtown. Everything seemed too straightforward, making him wonder why the FBI hadn't taken the same steps as Paul. He realized that Ted had tampered with the evidence, allowing Daniel to pursue the investigation unhindered. He parked his car outside the bar and waited for nearly thirty minutes until the winter sun had set, and the heavy rain had returned.

Daniel felt in his element. As the car lights dimmed, he sat there silently, observing the rain hitting the uneven road and pooling along the curb. It was bitterly cold, only a few degrees above freezing. The few pedestrians who dared to venture out were more concerned with staying dry than with the illegally parked cars along the curb.

On the passenger seat lay an open file folder with a printed photo given to him by Paul. It depicted a man in his late thirties—rounded face, compressed chin, and an off-kilter smile, worsened by uneven and yellowed teeth.

Daniel opened the car door, stepped onto the wet asphalt, and stood tall in the rain. He grabbed the umbrella from behind the driver's seat, popped it open to mask his figure, and closed the car door, muffled by the downpour.

Daniel opened the car door and stepped onto the wet asphalt, standing tall in the rain. He grabbed the umbrella from behind the driver's seat, popped it open, and masked his figure. The closing door was silenced by the downpour.

He had been waiting for nearly two hours and was feeling restless. Not wanting to stay until the bar closed, he decided to take a walk along the street. By one in the morning, Daniel found himself on a city street, going through the motions of smoking a cigarette. Standing across the way, he spotted a man and crossed the empty road to approach him. Cutting between two dormant cars, he reached the parallel curb and called out above the downpour.

"Excuse me," Daniel said, his authoritative tone cutting through the noise. The man turned around, and their eyes locked momentarily. Sensing the man's inclination to run, Daniel spoke firmly, "I know what you did." The man started to run, but Daniel swiftly deployed the umbrella, firing two metal prongs into the man's lower calf. The man twitched and fell into a nearby puddle. Daniel approached, removed the prongs, and emptied the launching canister from the umbrella.

Taking hold of the man's collar, Daniel pushed him against the aluminum paneling protecting a nearby storefront. "I'm looking for your friend," he stated, pinning the man against the wall. The man protested and resisted, but Daniel insisted, "There are two ways we can do this, and talking will be preferable."

The smaller man, named Dubois, claimed ignorance and asserted his rights, but Daniel applied pressure to his arm, prompting him to provide some information. Dubois revealed that his friend's name was Lee, a professional hired by Dubois' drug dealer boss. They had recently abandoned a delivery van outside D.C. in the mountains.

"Where can I find him?" Daniel inquired. Dubois mentioned that he was supposed to receive payment from Lee at the Budget Inn near Suitland. Daniel, considering letting Dubois go after their conversation, injected him with an autoinjector, causing Dubois to collapse. Daniel retrieved his umbrella and surveyed the alleyway before leaving, expecting the authorities to find Dubois and take him in for questioning. Lee was Daniel's true target, a sharp and elusive individual whom he desired to apprehend.

The rain muffled the sound of Daniel's car engine as he drove. The downpour made it challenging to see more than fifty feet ahead, and the once vibrant city of D.C. now appeared as a mere shell. After a few blocks, signs of active civilization began to emerge.

The Budget Inn was situated along a wide avenue on the outskirts of D.C. Daniel entered the lobby, manned by a single employee at that late hour. Climbing the stairwell to the upper floors, he walked down a long, empty hallway at the center of the building.

Daniel's breathing grew heavy as he approached the door. He unlocked it and stepped inside, the light from the bedside lamp casting a long silhouette. Moving cautiously, he surveyed the room, checking both the initial layout and the bathroom. Still wearing his raincoat, Daniel wiped water off the sleeves and examined the tired room.

Something felt off. He doubted that someone as skilled as Lee would leave sensitive documents unattended. The room lacked the usual burglar alarms he had come to expect. Perplexed, Daniel started going through the files, uncovering bill payments, fake credit cards, passports, and an FCC security clearance card.

There was movement behind him. Daniel tried to turn around. He felt himself pulled back and he collapsed to the ground. Lee, tugging hard on the

The Collateral Dividend

cable, had it tightly pressed against Faron's neck. If not for the scarf, the cable would have drawn blood. Lee stood far enough away to escape Daniel's flailing grasp. Gasping for air, Daniel struggled and gagged. Lee tried to lift Daniel off the ground by pulling the wire, but Daniel used the leverage to push back. Lee crashed forcefully into the opposite wall, winded. Daniel, still trying to catch his breath, stumbled and fell to the ground. Lee swiftly regained his footing and struck Daniel square in the neck, causing him to collapse against the side of the bed. Relentlessly, Lee continued his assault, hitting Faron across the face and in the stomach, sending Daniel tumbling across the room and crashing into a wooden writing chair. As he fell to the ground, Daniel desperately clutched at the desk. With a shift of his weight, he threw the chair, delivering a hard blow to Lee's broad shoulders, splintering the chair's wood.

Daniel followed up by kicking Lee's knee, causing him to buckle and fall to the floor. Faron seized the opportunity and grabbed Lee by the neck, but the wire lay just out of his reach. The two struggled briefly before Daniel lunged for the wire. Lee attempted to break free, but Daniel swiftly wrapped the wire around his neck, pulling it tight. Lee convulsed a few times, shivering for one last breath. There was a loud noise, resembling a glottal stop, repeating a few times until Lee's presence abruptly vanished. Life seeped away and then vanished entirely. Daniel found himself lying beneath a gruesome heap of blood and broken bones. Death felt unfamiliar to him. Despite his deep understanding of it, he knew nothing about its essence. The body that was once Lee bore no resemblance to its former self. Eventually, Daniel composed himself, pushed the body away from him, stumbled to his feet, and checked the room for any signs of danger. Breathing heavily, his hands bloodied and bruised, he stared at the lifeless body for several moments until the shock fully settled in.

His grey scarf was stained with blood, prompting Faron to remove it. As he did, memories flooded back to him, reminiscent of the first day of training. Vague recollections of being drugged resurfaced. Faron had believed those memories were from the initial months, but they belonged to the seventh or eighth month. Nobody had ever addressed that with him, nor did they seem willing to do so.

Faron held the scarf for a while, lost in thought. Memories surged forth, accompanied by a shard of glass from the shattered coffee table piercing the palm of his right hand. The glass protruded an eighth of an inch, but Faron felt nothing. It was an unusual sensation. He recollected hurting himself as a child when he cut his hand on a broken wine glass, experiencing intense pain.

E.R. Wychwood

Pulling out the shard, Faron examined his trembling fingers. Aware that he couldn't linger in the room for long, he stood up and searched the body. Lee's phone was in his pants pocket, and Faron scrolled through the contact list. Perhaps the call logs could provide valuable information. Afterward, he gave the room another thorough look, grabbed the files from the desk, and tucked them into his coat pocket. Lee had left the room in pristine condition. Faron spent ten minutes attempting to wash his hands in the sink, but no matter how vigorously he scrubbed, the blood seemed to persist.

Finally, he made his way to the rented car in the parking lot across the street using the stairwell. Once inside the car, he tried to catch his breath, attempting to detach himself from the recent events. It all felt mechanical.

Nearly two hours later, when the news arrived, they had organized a town car to pick up Faron from the car rental building. Paul, displeased at being awakened at three in the morning, had received the call, while Ted had retired to bed hours ago.

Faron had hoped to go home, to his own sanctuary, but it became clear from the moment they left that the black Ford Escape had been arranged to transport him back to Farragut Center. Paul had called Ted while Faron was on his way. They met in a briefing room upstairs where Paul threw off his jacket and scarf, pacing the room.

"How are you holding up, kid?" Ted asked, leaning against the doorframe.

"I've been better," Faron responded coldly, a tone that could have made Ted uneasy. Faron had suddenly become distant. "I want to start carrying a handgun, maybe something small like a .22. It would have made things a lot easier."

Ted wasn't sure what to make of that. Paul sat in the far corner of the room, arms crossed. "It depends on the situation," Paul interjected. "We don't want to leave behind much physical evidence. It's hard to do that when you've given someone a third eye."

"Maybe we should reconsider," Ted suggested. "I believe you have the discretion to handle it. If you want a handgun, we can work on arranging that." Ted had some ideas. They had utilized clever devices during their time at the CIA. "Why don't you walk me through what happened? Let's start with Dubois," Ted asked, noticing Faron's shifting gaze.

"Dubois sent me to Lee. Neither of them was very cooperative, obviously," Faron replied. "That was the job," he added snippily. It was evident to Ted that Faron was shaken. Daniel continued, "Dubois was a hired thug, low-level muscle for a local gang. Lee, on the other hand, was undoubtedly a professional." Faron smoothly reached into his pocket, retrieved the phone, and

The Collateral Dividend

tossed it onto the table. Information spilled out onto the monitor from the phone. A map occupied one corner of the table, alongside phone details. It was a disposable phone from a French company called Gaillard's. There were two calls to an unknown location, one to Canada, and five to Amsterdam. Faron looked up at Ted, opened a tab by pressing a red blip over Amsterdam, and a list of phone numbers appeared on the screen. He tapped the first number, and a name popped up: Patrick Finley.

"I want to see this through," Faron declared. Ted agreed, with the condition that Faron undergo a psychological assessment by a Langley shrink the following morning to ensure his emotional stability. In the meantime, they would attempt to retrieve Lee's files and bank records to gain a better understanding of the situation. Faron reluctantly consented, and despite being dismissed to go home, he couldn't sleep. Instead, he witnessed the arrival of morning by watching the sunrise through the crack in his blinds.

By the next day, Paul had traced nearly two million of Lee's money from a wire transfer in Amsterdam, handled by Patrick Finley. The account belonged to Groot Hoff Holdings, a company primarily dealing with hedge funds and investment portfolios. Paul had determined that the account owner was fictitious, created solely to facilitate payments for contracted hits. Meanwhile, Daniel Faron endured a grueling session with the Agency shrink, and an hour later, he discovered a white envelope on his car seat. Opening it, he found two blank passports, a plane ticket, and an iPad. He had also been prescribed medication to alleviate his restlessness, which now caused a throbbing headache at the base of his skull.

THE DEAD LINE

He never stayed in one place for too long. There was an anxiousness to it all that he didn't particularly like, and it would gnaw at him late at night and early in the morning. He had to be on the move, or else he would start feeling depressed and lethargic, his mind racing.

In the mornings, he would go for a run to help keep him alert for the rest of the day and maintain focus. Having his head of security with him wherever he went helped keep him sane. Socializing was a calamity for him; he found it draining.

With his shifting attention, Philippe Gaillard traveled frequently. He disliked public transport, so owning a private charter allowed him to travel as he pleased.

"Good morning," a figure at the door greeted, and Philippe turned his head to follow the woman as she walked across the deck. He glanced out at the green sloping hills that descended into the Seine River. The sky was divided by a dark gloom, and a warm breeze carried the scent of rain.

He stood up and smiled. "Good afternoon by now," he checked his watch. Pouring white wine into an empty glass, he extended it out and handed it to the woman. "To continued prosperity," Gaillard said, raising his own glass.

"- and good health," the woman replied. Philippe gave a flat smile and gazed at the sheer white cliffs peeking through the green landscape. He then sat back down, and the woman handed him a file folder.

"So, let's talk business," Gaillard said, crossing his leg and settling into the patio chair. A long glass railing ran along the deck. He skimmed through the files, leaned forward, and placed his glass of wine on the ledge.

"We're looking at 5% domestic growth thanks to our moves last quarter. That's up from the hit we took with American Telecom. Internationally, however, we've never been stronger. Min and his involvement have been invaluable for driving growth in China and the Asian markets."

They delved into the details of the business – numbers, growth, and challenges regarding crucial personnel that needed resolution for the week. They were exceeding targets but also going over budget. It was a topic that would be discussed later in the week during the executive committee meeting when Gaillard returned to Paris. The meeting was scheduled for the upcoming Wednesday, and Gaillard had two more days to enjoy the Normandy countryside. The woman then outlined the upcoming demands of the next fiscal

The Collateral Dividend

quarter. She was transparent; the next two years would be extremely tough. They had managed to fend off attempted buyouts for now, but they were not out of the woods yet.

Sliced bread had been brought to the table between their chairs. Philippe reached into the loaf and ate a buttered slice, thickly glazed. He cleaned the crumbs on a napkin on his lap. "What about our other revenue streams?"

"We had two hundred million in sales last year, and we're on target to maintain that this year, although not without sacrifices. Our revenue will be lower; the intelligence community isn't as interested in paying big bucks for SIGNINT client data anymore. Russia has expressed its discontent with our prices. Most of our profits are coming from Min and his company's growth. He has successfully exploited our client data to determine buying patterns and client needs in the region."

Gaillard nodded, reading through charts outlining revenue and sales numbers. "So everything in the kingdom is safe," Philippe concluded.

"Not exactly," the woman said. "I was getting to that part." When Gaillard urged her to cut to the chase, she mentioned Min's trouble. "The Valley is suing for patent infringements."

"Do they have a case?" Philippe asked. The woman shrugged but indicated it seemed like he had stolen patents. Gaillard cursed and shook his head. "I'd like the opportunity to speak with him this week or next."

"Everything's been finalized with Ralston," she said, as if moving on. "Amsterdam confirmed they received the payment, which was routed yesterday."

"That's good, then."

"It should be. But I have reason to believe someone may be trying to track this down."

"Why do you say that?"

"We erased the video footage before the FBI could review it, but Lee turned up dead in his hotel late last week."

Gaillard looked at her with a serious expression. "Do you think whoever did it knows?" The woman shrugged, and Gaillard continued, "Call up Patrick Finley. If anyone calls looking for him, tell them to contact us. Let's reach out to some local enforcers and see if they'd be willing to deal with anyone should the need arise." It had been carefully planned. "Marie," Gaillard suddenly called, and the woman turned to look at him. "I need you to keep me informed as much as possible. I want to micromanage this if it becomes an issue." The woman nodded. Gaillard had an obsession with things like this, which occasionally

51

drove her mad. He had hired her to be the organizer, to pull all the strings together, yet he consistently intervened and saw things through until the end. "Do you have anything else for me, my dear?" he asked, taking another bite of bread. She shook her head. "Splendid. Keep me in the loop, shall you?"

*   *   *

Daniel Farron Made his way across the boulevard with a short skip to avoid the puddles from the afternoon prior. He looked at his watch and popped his umbrella above his head to shield his pulled-back hair. It was wavy, dark and long enough that in Europe it looked like what the French called Cheveux Des Riches.

urning the corner, Daniel's mind raced as he found himself in the financial district, triggering memories of his father going to work in a suit and never returning. In school, Daniel's unchecked allowance had made him somewhat of a romantic figure—a well-dressed boy who rarely spoke but possessed a certain charm when he did. However, over time, drinking took its toll, transforming him into a stoic figure with flaws.

Daniel's attention to detail extended to his meticulously tailored suits. He believed that a well-dressed man could charm his way into nearly anything. His navy suit, with its unassuming style, conveyed a sense of being put together, though often overlooked. Daniel had mastered the art of blending in with the masses, utilizing his suits as both a cloak and a dagger. He purposely avoided wearing black, which he associated with a menacing, "g-man" appearance. Instead, he chose more discreet options, never wanting to appear suspicious. Sometimes, he relied on a jacket, a smile, and a sharp tongue to navigate past obstacles, assuming various roles such as a limousine driver or an executive heading home.

Less than a hundred yards ahead, the building loomed on the right side of the street. Across from it, a white van parked with the name "Grip Electrical Solutions, a division of Grip Solutions Incorporated" emblazoned on its side.

"Confirm that exterior cameras will be disabled in thirty seconds," a young man inside the truck tapped on a keyboard. "Asset is in play, visual confirmed."

"Green light," Paul, seated at his desk on the other side of the world, said with crossed arms and a ballpoint pen between his teeth. "Be quick, Daniel." Paul observed as Daniel walked with precise rhythm.

Daniel had meticulously counted the steps to the front door—thirty-five exactly. Without missing a beat, he entered the glass door and surveyed the

The Collateral Dividend

lobby. The high ceilings housed six teller booths, blocking the view of a safe holding deposit boxes along the far wall. Adjacent to a seating area was a help desk, and four elevator shafts stood on the far side.

Only two employees occupied the floor—a woman at the front desk and a security guard leaning against the far wall near the seating area.

"Can I help you, sir?" the woman asked, noticing Daniel's uncertainty. Daniel turned toward the help desk and leaned over the counter.

With charm, he inquired, "Good evening. I was wondering if Patrick Finley is still in?" Out of the corner of his eye, he noticed the cameras losing interest.

Glancing at her terminal's clock, the woman replied, "I'm sorry, sir, but the offices are closing for the evening. Perhaps you would like to return tomorrow? Shall I have him call you?"

"No, that's fine," Daniel responded nonchalantly, feigning disappointment. He hesitated for a moment before continuing, "Would it be possible to use your washrooms?" Leaning over the desk, he discreetly affixed a small metal magnet, resembling a screw head, to the back of the computer terminal.

"The bathroom is down the hall, just past the elevators on the right," the woman informed, already reaching for the phone.

"Splendid, thank you," Daniel smiled, moving down the hall until he reached the elevators. He entered the bathroom, leaning against the wall and awaited a response from the truck outside.

"Resetting the security feeds on a one-minute loop," the operator in the truck reported, causing a brief delay before the front desk's security feed reflected the modification. "You're clear. You've got fifty seconds." Daniel called the elevator and patiently waited for its arrival. The ride would take him up sixteen stories.

As the elevator doors opened, Daniel froze, his breathing heavy. He felt a familiar sense of panic, reminiscent of his childhood. Shaking himself back to reality, he stepped into the elevator car, aware of the camera watching him. The doors closed automatically, and the car ascended to the eighteenth floor. Gripping the side railing, Daniel remained tense until the elevator halted, and the doors opened, aligning perfectly with the floor.

The floor appeared dark, with faint yellow hues casting shadows on the rows of cubicles. A two-story neon sign from an adjacent building emitted the yellow light, which seeped through the glass walls of private offices, illuminating the cubicle labyrinth. Daniel approached the glass doors of the back offices, observing their secure installation and the industrial magnetic seal keeping them shut. Retrieving a roll of white tape from his pocket, he carefully applied it along the door's hinge and placed it between two panes of glass. Stepping back to the other side of the room, he took out his phone and used its camera to scan the QR code near the corner of the tape. With a quick double-tap, the glass shattered cleanly along the tape, and Daniel kicked it in, causing it to crash onto the ground. He crouched through the opening and examined the schematics displayed on his phone.

Daniel made his way down the far side of the offices, gun in hand but pointed down near his left thigh. "You should be approaching the office now, Daniel," the operator informed him.

Stopping at an office door, Daniel checked the name before tucking his weapon into his jacket pocket. Pressing against the handle, the door popped off its hinge with a soft sound, allowing Daniel to enter. The yellow light from outside cast dramatic shadows within the room. He pulled out a flash drive and inserted it into the computer terminal's side. Activating the screen, he placed his fingers on the keyboard, and a tracking system appeared. Memorizing the twelve-digit serial account key, he entered it into the query and pressed enter. The three-million-dollar account had been emptied through a money order the previous day. Daniel searched for information on where it had been deposited. The account had been closed, leaving no trace of the digital transfer except for transactions connecting it to another institution. It took only a moment to confirm that most of the account details were fraudulent.

"Have you found it yet, Daniel?" the voice crackled harshly, the sound amplified.

"Albert Jansen," Daniel responded, and the files were transferred to the USB drive.

A momentary delay preceded the operator's response. "We've got him. Reports directly to Finley, whose office you're in." They had arranged for Jansen's rendition that night, intending to secure and transport him for interrogation.

"Do we have what we need?" Daniel asked, his emotions cold.

"Should be," the operator replied, then paused. "Wait."

"What?" Daniel inquired.

"We're missing the confirmation of the money order cashing. There should be a paper trail somewhere," the operator explained, thinking. "Is there a filing cabinet nearby, Daniel?"

Daniel released a soft sigh, switched off the blue-hued computer screen, and surveyed the room. "What am I looking for?" he asked, effortlessly breaking the lock on the filing cabinet and pulling open the second drawer.

The Collateral Dividend

"It should be a recent confirmation," the operator replied. Daniel scanned the contents until he found the file he needed. He took the entire folder, ensuring the receipt was inside, folded it vertically, and placed it in his suit jacket pocket. Finally, he closed the drawer, locking it once again.

There was a shadow cast by two large figures on the far side of the hall, catching Daniel's attention before they approached. Quickly, he closed the office door and made his way towards the elevators. Taking cover just as the first bullet pierced through the cubicles, Daniel considered heading for the emergency exit, but it was too late. He swiftly pulled out his handgun, racking the slide to arm it. "Going dark," he whispered, and the transmission cut off. Pressing against the wall to conceal himself, he patiently waited for the first figure to enter his field of fire. As soon as it did, Daniel pulled the trigger. The weapon recoiled twice, and the figure crumpled to the floor, lifeless.

Faron repositioned himself and cautiously advanced down the hall, flanked by cubicles with tall walls. Daniel kept his weapon lowered, moving quietly through the aisles. His adversary continued to approach.

Daniel cautiously rounded the corner of an aisle before being unexpectedly struck by the figure. His gun slipped from his grasp and fell to the floor. Reacting swiftly, Daniel dodged the attack, knocking his assailant back and crashing through a cubicle wall in the process. As they tussled, Daniel managed to gain the upper hand, forcing his opponent onto his back. Seizing the opportunity, he kicked the rolling chair, causing his foe to lose balance and collapse.

Using the scissors from an office desk, the figure launched another assault, but Daniel skillfully defended himself, wielding the scissors like a seasoned boxer. Seizing the man's extended arm, Daniel forcefully slammed him into the corner of a nearby desk. Taking hold of the man's necktie, he tightened his grip until the man's breathing was completely obstructed. The figure struggled in vain, flailing his legs and arms.

The encounter ended swiftly and without bloodshed. Daniel wiped away the blood from his nose with a tissue and adjusted his jacket. He surveyed the silent office, the stillness mocking him. Glancing down at the lifeless body, then at his own blood-stained hands, he sat against the fabric of a cubicle wall, staring at the corpse for a long while before mustering the will to stand up. After searching both bodies, which yielded nothing of significance, he made his way to the emergency stairwell and exited through the back alleyway. Checking his watch, he realized he had thirty minutes to return to the hotel before a security check required him to report to Farragut Center. When he arrived at the hotel, he headed to the bar and ordered a drink.

"You look like hell," a voice from across the room remarked. Daniel turned around, wearing a somber expression, and looked at the man.

Without saying a word, Daniel turned back to his drink, gazing into the glass as he took a sip and set it down, slowly rotating it. "Good to see you as well, Henry. How are you?" he replied, his tone lacking enthusiasm. If someone didn't know better, they might have thought Daniel seemed disappointed to see the man. On the contrary, Daniel had reached out to him.

"Better than you, apparently. Christ, you look like your father," Henry Chattle remarked, now seated beside Daniel. He motioned for the bartender and ordered himself a coffee. "I'm glad you're here," he added, displaying a hint of affection, a rarity in recent times. Daniel glanced at his watch. "I have fifteen minutes before I need to check in," he said, sounding somewhat apologetic. Everything was tightly scheduled. Leaning back in his chair, he frowned, gazing into the distance of the room as the artificial light gradually overcame the evening gloom. The light from a streetlamp cast a heavy glow, draping over the various seating areas.

Rainwater trickled down the tinted glass, refracting the streetlights, and Henry's blue eyes shimmered as he glanced out the window towards the adjacent offices. "Who are your friends?" Henry asked, referring to the van parked outside. While Henry had limited experience in espionage or the intelligence field, he had a knack for keeping secrets and had navigated the intricacies of American policies and finances. Daniel increasingly shared his experiences with Henry during their occasional conversations.

Daniel smiled, aware that he couldn't reveal much. "What do you know about Albert Jensen?" he asked eventually. Despite the protocols, Daniel had confided in Henry, his surrogate father figure, though Henry slightly resented the toll it had taken on Daniel's personality.

"I knew you weren't here just for a vacation," Henry replied immediately, dismissing any other possibility. Shaking his head, he continued, "Never heard of him. Who is he?"

Faron shrugged, expecting no more from the response he received. He handed his guardian the document they had obtained from the bank. "He's a local banker. What do you make of this?" he inquired, as Henry examined the photocopy of the wire receipt. "Do you know where it came from?"

Henry, with ample experience in the banking world, studied the wire receipt and the swift code beneath the forged wire name. "Royal Dominion Bank," he

The Collateral Dividend

stated, pointing to the account number at the bottom of the document. "That's in Canada."

"Canada?" Daniel questioned, surprised by the revelation.

Henry nodded. "For a transfer of this magnitude to avoid suspicion, it would require a sizable account and an account manager overseeing it," he explained. Daniel handed Henry a second paper, containing a file on a scruffy-looking man with a soft chin. "What about him?" Daniel asked curtly, eagerly awaiting Henry's opinion. He had acquired the file along with the bank draft. The same account that had paid Lee had also paid this man on the same day, for a similar amount. It couldn't be mere coincidence. He sought Henry's insight.

Henry read the name, Patrick Finley. "You should stay away from this," he warned.

"What do you mean?" Daniel inquired.

"Patrick Finley? You don't know who he is?" Henry snorted, leaning back in his chair. "I suppose you wouldn't. You haven't been in the financial business as long as I have," he remarked, tidying the table. "Finley isn't a pleasant man. He's notorious for his harshness and has been accused of terrorist financing more than once."

"So he facilitates cover-ups?" Daniel deduced.

Henry nodded. "When companies need things 'cleaned up,' they turn to him. How did you stumble upon him?" Henry glanced at the file once more, then observed Daniel for a long while.

"You know your sister has been trying to reach you for weeks," Henry mentioned. Daniel had been explicitly instructed to avoid contacting anyone close to him. Ignoring her calls weighed heavily on him, for their safety, even though it left him feeling rather isolated. Somehow, Henry had slipped through the cracks, and he and Daniel maintained their connection. "What's the matter?" Henry asked, concerned.

"I had an episode today in an elevator," Daniel revealed, his voice tinged with trauma.

Furrowing his brow, Henry responded, "You haven't had one of those in years. Are you alright?" Daniel assured him he was fine. Henry sat there, allowing Daniel to process his thoughts. Daniel paid no attention, flipping open his wallet and gently running his hand over a wrinkled and stained photograph hidden inside. When Henry tried to catch a glimpse, Daniel swiftly closed the wallet and stowed it away. To Henry, Daniel's eyes were the last remnants of his humanity, but even then, as they stared into the distance, they concealed the underlying anguish. They were cold and gray. "What do you think caused it?" Henry inquired, genuinely concerned.

Daniel didn't have an answer. Henry shrugged and took a deep breath. "You know I'm always here to talk, Daniel," he assured him.

Taking the papers back, Daniel studied the listed files intently, frowning. "Do you have a pen?" he asked abruptly. Henry looked at him quizzically, then reached into his jacket pocket and handed Daniel a cheap blue plastic pen. Daniel circled a date on the papers, folded them, and returned the pen to Henry. "I have to go," he said hastily. "Will you be in Canada soon?" Daniel already knew that's where he was headed, and he secretly desired Henry's company.

"I can be," Henry replied. He wore a brown herringbone wool sports coat, resembling the old financier from Boston that he was. His hair was short, and it was evident that his once athletic frame had withered away. He pocketed the pen, grasped Daniel's arm, and said, "Daniel, I hope you realize there are things you can't sacrifice for the good of your country. Sometimes, you can never achieve a goal because some goals, by their very nature, are unattainable, you know." Henry didn't want Daniel to get hurt. "Just make sure you understand that what you're doing is morally right. There's only so far you can go before they ask you to cross one line too many."

Daniel smirked, concealing his emotions. He hesitated for a moment, then looked back at Henry. "I'll see you soon, Henry..."

*   *   *

Ted Hawthorne was in his element. Paul entered the room, followed by the psychologist who had interviewed Daniel the day before. Paul closed the door. "We combed through everything on his file," he said, glancing back at the woman seated across from him.

"And?" Ted looked at the woman, who glanced back above her glasses with squared shoulders. She took a deep breath, seemingly considering her words. "I don't know what you people do to them. And I'm not sure I want to know. In my professional opinion, it appears there is some form of behavioral modification. Let me stress that it is in no way healthy..."

Ted interrupted, addressing her as Doctor Acres to calm her angst. "I understand your concern, but whether behavioral modification occurred is not the issue. We brought you in for a readiness assessment to determine if he can perform his duties. Is he mentally capable of the cognitive tasks required?"

The Collateral Dividend

Doctor Acres took a breath, seated back on the sofa with her crossed leg and cradling a pillow in her crossed arms. Ted noticed her fiddling with her hands, a telltale sign of a smoker. There was a large file on the sofa beside her. She expressed an academic attitude in her tone, implying that Hawthorne and his team were playing with fire.

The Chief of Staff's eyes shifted to Ted, anticipating his response. When Ted failed to speak up, the Chief of Staff stepped in. "I'm sorry, but you know that won't happen. As much as I value your input, there must be some disconnect between what you're authorized to know and what we're willing to tell you."

Ignoring Paul, Doctor Acres looked directly at Ted. Her demands were stern and aggressive. "Mister Hawthorne, you are dealing with an emotionally unstable person you intend to use as a weapon. And unless you want the house of cards to fall, you will tell me what happened in training. Gentlemen, you called me; if you'd like me to provide my professional opinion, I will need everything."

Ted sighed and activated the computer, pulling up a file on the screen adjacent to the sofa. A mug shot of Daniel Faron appeared, along with detailed information. He waited for Doctor Acres to read the file and respond.

After reading, Doctor Acres let out a deep breath, adjusting her glasses and combing back her auburn hair. She looked sternly at Paul as if to say, '*boy, you fucked this up, didn't you.*' Then she said: "Certainly makes sense of some things," she said, referring to the information in the file. It took her a few moments to collect her thoughts. "Daniel is displaying signs of someone who carries immense psychological trauma. Don't you screen for these things? I didn't see anything on the file, but I suspect he underwent childhood trauma treatment. We are all a little 'off,' but what concerns me is that you may have undone some of this healing. If he was subjected to behavioral modification, we could be looking at a very volatile state."

Doctor Acres looked up at the screen again. "What may be occurring here is a byproduct of whatever you did to him. Not everyone can endure mental tinkering. I fear Daniel may only partially have unraveled. He's not insane or unstable, but he isn't entirely healthy," her voice trailed off. "I can't speculate on why. You know him much better than I do. What I would be interested in seeing is what exactly happened. I can tell you that he holds his hurt close, and it builds and eats at his conscience. If you're looking for him to abstain from executing those responsible for his pain, you are sorely mistaken." She skip a beat. "Why don't we talk about his previous traumatic losses?" she suggested.

Ted shook his head. "Not that I know of."

59

"Well, there certainly is something there, at least a memory," she insisted.

"Look, we conducted a psych evaluation when he came in. He was stable," Ted argued.

Paul, the most pragmatic of the group, interrupted Ted and extended his hand to calm the banter. "Everyone knows there's something wrong with him," he said calmly.

"The question isn't whether he had trauma, Ted. The question is what those traumas are and whether they're bound to affect what we're doing here."

"Well, he applied out of law school," Ted replied frankly.

"Where did he go?" Acres asked.

"Yale. After the farm, he requested covert action, wanted to spend some time in the field. By then, he was already working at Langley, and they didn't want him to leave," Ted explained.

Acres raised her eyebrows, adjusted her glasses, and cleared her throat. "I get the sense that most of the trauma had, at one point, been resolved. I think we're witnessing a regression. What exactly were you hoping to achieve?"

"The process is unique. We were looking for specific criteria and aiming to enhance them. Anyone can kill, but it takes a keen mind to remain invisible, to deceive a room. Critical thinking became a valuable skill here," Ted elaborated.

"Is he dangerous?" the chief of staff nervously asked, realizing the foolishness of the question. Acres didn't hesitate to point that out. Daniel was a man, not a weapon. The notion of danger in this context was entirely subjective, and Paul was treating it as if Daniel were some abstract object.

"I don't know, you tell me," Acres replied. "Is he a threat to the public and to you? It seems unlikely. At least I don't think so. Without knowing the extent of his endured trauma, we can't say for sure," Acres shook her head. "You boys know how to mess things up, don't you?" She looked at Ted. "I'd be interested to see how this progresses. He's certainly not a threat to anyone other than those in his way. And I don't think that's your plan." She paused for a moment, fixing her gaze on both men. "Fantastic meeting, gentlemen," she said with a touch of sarcasm. "Do keep me posted. Let me know if you need me to conduct further evaluations."

Paul took the initiative and opened the office door. Once she had left, he turned back, re-entered the office, and locked the door. He looked at Ted. "What do you think?"

Ted let out a sigh and shrugged. "Paul, I don't want to admit this, but I think we may have missed something. Would you take some time in the next few weeks to review everything again? And don't mention anything to Daniel,"

The Collateral Dividend

Paul checked his watch. "He's been on standby for ten minutes now, just waiting for our confirmation."

Ted sighed and looked at Paul over the rim of his glasses. He gestured towards the sofa where Acres had been seated. "As far as I'm concerned, he is capable of overcoming this hurdle," Ted said confidently. "He'd be a cold man if he didn't want revenge, and I think we've been foolish to believe he wasn't seeking it."

*   *   *

Paul had Avery comb through the finances that Daniel had obtained in Amsterdam. They had only scratched the surface but found a significant amount of information. They had identified someone who had received payment from the Amsterdam account and matched it with a phone call from Lee's phone. Paul needed some time to think and went into Avery's office before calling Daniel back and closing the door. He wanted to discuss their new target. Waldemar had received a payment from the account that morning.

Paul asked, "So, who is he?" feeling a bit embarrassed that they were considering eliminating someone they knew nothing about.

"Do you remember that murder years ago of the British government official?" Avery asked, and Paul shook his head, unable to recall anything particularly memorable about it. Avery began casually searching for a news article online. It wasn't crucial, but she felt it would bother her if she didn't show Paul. "Waldemar was suspected of being involved. He was the last person to see the official before they were killed. The British authorities could never establish a connection, so he continued with his work. He's a consultant, I believe. Anyway, he was one of the five calls to Lee. Do you think there's a connection?"

Paul crossed his arms and rested his index finger against his lips, deep in thought. "You said he's a consultant?"

Avery shrugged. "He's not directly involved in the dirty work, that's for certain. He became a sort of celebrity in the UK after all of this happened. He has some connection to royalty – a distant cousin of the Earl of Pembroke or something. There were rumors that he was quite rough with his lovers." Avery found the news article and, before showing it to Paul, sat up straight. The dots had connected, and she looked at Paul. "Paul, the official was on the board of Ofcom. This seems to be a pattern," she stated. Ofcom was the British equivalent of the FCC. It wasn't the first time that someone of Adam Stanley's stature had been murdered. Waldemar was probably paid for his assistance in equipping Lee with the necessary tools.

Paul came around the desk and examined the file. The young Brit went by the name Waldo, a nickname from his days at a British private school. He had retreated to Germany after the investigation in the UK, where his family resided, and he maintained a low profile, except for his extravagant partying with some of Germany's wealthiest individuals. The question remained: Why was he in Amsterdam? There was a particular nightlife in Amsterdam that couldn't be replicated anywhere else.

Paul was convinced. They had gathered enough evidence to send Daniel to clean up this long overdue mess. Paul recalled walking back to his office, thinking they could swiftly execute this operation. It seemed highly unlikely that the money had come from anywhere other than Canada, so the trail was rapidly approaching its end.

That's when the text message arrived. It appeared on Lee's phone, and the news illuminated the screen. They weren't entirely sure what it meant, but they knew it held significance. The message was deliberately cryptic. Paul attempted to read it aloud: "S'esmeron mielhs que l'aurs el fuec arden, on pus lo au totz hom qui be.ls en-ten."

THE INSIDER JOB

Daniel lay flat on his back, staring at the cold ceiling for what felt like an hour before he received a text message. Thoughts of home flooded his mind, triggered by Henry's presence. Placing the phone on his chest, he anticipated the vibration that would wake him when the message arrived. To his surprise, the text was empty. He dialed back the number and a female operator answered, her tone cold as Faron completed the security check-in.

"Transferring," the operator droned, and the line clicked. Faron patiently waited for the connection to be established. Finally, after going through the necessary protocol, his mug shot appeared on Paul's screen. The Chief of Staff pressed the illuminated yellow button on the telephone terminal to activate the call.

"Did you get the files?" Daniel asked as the line reconnected. Sleep remained elusive in the late hours of Amsterdam.

"We did," Paul assured him. Using the swift code, they had traced the bank associated with the money. The code allowed them to track the origin and destination of wired funds. While wiring money was a stealthy method, it was also lazy and relatively easy to follow. Any competent accountant could trace the trail of funds. "We traced the money deposited into the account you accessed by following the Institution number. It's a bank in-"

"Canada," Daniel interrupted.

"Yes," Paul continued. "Downtown Toronto. Our files indicate that it was withdrawn, but we're unsure of the destination." Depositing money into a Canadian account had elements of both brilliance and stupidity. The manner in which it was done suggested that tracing the funds might prove challenging. The sum involved was substantial, and if money could be laundered through one of the most secure banking systems in the world, Farragut Center needed to acknowledge the gravity of the situation.

"So what does he want me to do?" Daniel inquired, referring to Ted's instructions.

Paul studied the flight map displayed on the screen. A red line seamlessly traversed from Amsterdam to Toronto, digitally representing the movement of money across the globe. Starting in Canada, it passed through Amsterdam before branching out to various accounts and targets worldwide. They had identified only a few payouts originating from the Amsterdam account, but they anticipated discovering many more soon. "I'm arranging a charter," Paul said, providing Daniel clear instructions on how to dispose of his weapons before boarding the flight. They would send him to Canada and equip him with the necessary information to trace the origins of the money. Paul also urged Daniel to exercise discretion when choosing to kill. However, in the same breath, he explained why he was assigning Daniel to pursue Waldemar. He shared the details with Daniel, mentioning that Waldemar was staying at the Hotel de L'Europe in the city center. Paul omitted the fact that Waldemar was a British national and that the evidence against him was tenuous. "I want this to appear as an accident, Daniel. It requires more finesse than the mess you created here in D.C.," Paul said, his tone bordering on rudeness.

Daniel rose from his bed, walked to the dresser, and opened the drawer. Placing the loaded gun on the wooden surface, he declared, "I'll report back in an hour." Ending the call, he stuffed the phone into his pocket put on his jacket and buttoned it.

The hotel would have appeared stuffy if not for the multitude of contemporary furniture defined by hues of red, dominating one's eyes and drawing them across the room to the chaotic yet brilliantly assembled patterns. Daniel Faron sat near the back of the room, engrossed in reading a newspaper, The Guardian. He damn well hated newspapers. He believed that if he were going to read something, it should be a literary novel. Daniel found that he could learn a great deal from those sorts of things. His favorites were historical texts, but he certainly didn't have the time to read those anymore. And therein lay what Paul had so desperately wanted to capture. They didn't want someone capable of extreme feats of strength – they wanted a mind – and they had gotten a mind with all its idiosyncrasies and traumas.

Waldemar entered from across the street. He was well dressed, but there was a flash to how he wore his clothes and when.

Daniel watched Waldemar over the top of the morning paper, waiting for Waldo to walk down the hall to the elevator. Daniel could do this in his sleep. He was almost bored with his work. There was a melody to how things went, a wave-like pattern. Eventually, Daniel rose, folded the newspaper in half, placed it underneath his arm, and followed Waldo to the elevator, stepping into the car moments before the door closed. With a half-hearted smile, he acknowledged the elevator's accomplice and focused on catching his racing mind.

The lift doors opened. Daniel got off after Waldemar. Waldo went left, and Daniel swung to the right, strolling down the hall. Waldemar pushed the door open with his shoulder, pocketed the key, and entered. Meanwhile, Daniel had

The Collateral Dividend

looped back and was coming down the hall rather quickly. He stuck his foot in the gap of the door, covered Waldo's mouth, knocked the man back, and forced him to drop the money envelope onto the ground. Waldemar was startled and attempted to fight back, but Daniel threw him into the wall, causing him to fall hard on the floor.

Daniel locked the door. Waldemar was still lying on the ground, having hit his head on the way down. Daniel walked forward, took him by the collar, and shoved him onto the bed. Waldemar laid flat on his back. Daniel reached into his pocket, opened the bottle of dissolvable medicine tablets, and dumped the entire bottle onto the glass counter of the writing desk. Daniel drew his gun, pointing it directly at Waldo's head across the room. He still hadn't said a word. Daniel gave the room a once-over. It was a single room with a bed pushed up against the wall, flanked by two four-foot-tall windows adjacent to each other. Across from the door was a French door leading out to a balcony.

"Who the hell are you?" Waldemar asked, but received no response. Daniel moved to the fridge near the balcony and pulled out a travel-sized bottle of vodka. Waldo slowly rose, prepared to run.

"Sit down," Daniel said, drawing his weapon again and pointing it blankly at Waldemar. He then peeled the sealant off the back of the pre-cut tape he stored in his pocket, grabbed a handful of pills, and walked over to the bed. Waldo groaned and locked his jaw, but Daniel plugged his nose and squeezed his cheeks so Waldo could open his mouth. When Waldo gasped for air, Daniel rammed the handful of pills into his mouth and fastened the tape across his lips, sealing them shut. The drugs began to work after ten minutes, and Daniel removed the tape.

Waldemar swayed back and forth as Daniel cracked open a bottle of vodka. He poured it down Waldemar's throat, causing him to gag and spit up on his chest and the floor.

Daniel gave him a moment's break, then pressed the bottle against Waldemar's lips until the burning sensation became unbearable. He pushed Waldemar onto his back, staring at the ceiling. Faron searched the hotel room for any signs of his presence. Finally, he lifted Waldemar off the bed and carried him to the balcony. With a swift motion, he cut the cable tie binding Waldemar's hands and pushed him over the edge. Waldemar fell onto the roof of a car, causing it to collapse inward, shattering the windows and setting off the car alarm. He was dead upon impact.

Daniel resisted the urge to look over the edge. He closed one of the French doors leading to the balcony and wiped any sweat or residue from his prints on the medicine bottle. Faron picked up the cable tie and tape, smashed the vodka bottle on the ground, and then grabbed the envelope of money. The envelope contained two hundred thousand dollars, neatly bundled into four stacks of five-hundred-dollar bills. Faron tucked the envelope between the folded halves of the newspaper, exited the hotel room, and firmly closed the door.

He tried not to dwell on what he had just done. There was a stairwell on the far side of the building, which he took down to the lobby. He walked out of the hotel and down the block without looking back. Eventually, he found himself near a canal. Along the road, there was a quaint bar nestled against the canal wall. Daniel attempted to stop and order a drink.

He sat in a booth across from the bar, with a window overlooking the canal. Daniel remained there for about four drinks. At one point, he noticed the silhouette of a woman standing in the middle of the canal. She bore a striking resemblance to someone he once knew. Daniel stood up from the bar stool to get a better view, but by the time he did, the woman had disappeared. He sat back down, stared at his crystal glass, and rotated it before taking a sip. This wasn't the first time such a thing had happened. Occasionally, the sky would undergo a dramatic shift in color, as if subjected to heavy contrast. The effect would traverse the sky like a stream, racing across the clouds until it collided with the horizon.

Daniel didn't dare mention these experiences to Paul. He suspected that they were aware of his hallucinations, and he didn't want to be taken out of the field. Fortunately, the hallucinations had become less frequent over time. The initial months had been the most challenging, as everything seemed to blur. Adapting to the invisibility and loneliness only compounded the confusion caused by the sporadic hallucinatory episodes. Memories would resurface in fragments, but he could always distinguish between what was real and what was not, though it remained disconcerting.

There were moments when Daniel would go for a late-night drive. The streetlights would blur, and the details around him would sharpen. For a fleeting instant, he felt as if he could see the darkness with perfect clarity. The reason behind these occurrences eluded him. He feared it might be some psychosomatic ailment, which could explain his reduced ability to feel pain. However, he had yet to experience a heightened deprivation of any other senses or motor skills.

"I'm not sure I would call that discreet," Paul said immediately when they spoke on the phone twenty minutes later. Daniel Faron's food had arrived, and

The Collateral Dividend

he took a long sip of scotch. It was late, and the vibrant evening had grown silent. The city sighed as if exhausted.

"You wanted an accident," Daniel replied.

"I didn't want your work to be one," Paul rubbed his chin and gazed out across the square. His computer screen displayed a looped feed from a security camera across the street from the Amsterdam hotel. It had captured a glimpse of Waldemar colliding with the car, and Paul had been trying to derive meaning from it.

"What am I looking for in Toronto?" Daniel Faron changed the subject as he finished his smoked sausage and potato hash. He appeared bored, indifferent to whether they succeeded or failed.

"The money came from an account at the Royal Dominion Bank in Toronto yesterday. It was wired to Amsterdam, and Finley handled the funds. He converted it into cash or bank drafts and distributed them to other internal accounts before funneling the money into payable accounts owned by businesses in Turkey and a few other Mediterranean countries. As you know, Lee's money ended up in Turkey," Paul explained. "So we're dealing with a money laundering scheme here." He shared the account numbers and information on his screen and informed Daniel that he was sending him the details. "The Canadian account is unlisted. It's a business account connected to a trust, or at least that's what I gathered. The corporate contact is a Canadian working for a firm called Cartres."

"Never heard of them. Are they significant?"

"They own numerous firms, mostly managing offshore trusts. Their primary business is in the Americas," Paul said. Daniel inquired about the corporate contact.

"Christopher James Ralston. He worked for HSBC in Singapore for years." The alarming reality was that Paul had effortlessly obtained a significant amount of information on Ralston. The digital age provided access to an overwhelming amount of publicly available data. Farragut Center exploited this openness with ruthless efficiency, which even Paul found unnerving. "He's a managing director overseeing several offshore offices. He has previously worked in Guernsey and the Cayman Islands, building a substantial client base." Paul had gathered this information from a quick internet search. He had convinced Avery to delve into Cartres' corporate archives and attempt to access their private files. It had been a risky move, but they managed to find fragments of information. "He still serves as a fiduciary for some of his clients." This was where things became intriguing. Among the few accounts Paul had discovered, one appeared

67

suspicious. "I made a few calls to some acquaintances," he informed Daniel about the suspicious account. "No one seems to know whose trust it is. It's not uncommon for the industry to remain somewhat tight-lipped about ownership, but outright ignorance is relatively rare." The trust Paul had uncovered was of significant magnitude, one of the largest in the hemisphere. The fact that other managers were unaware of its owner made it even more suspicious. "Colloquially, they refer to it as Casca. It has been active for decades and has only had two managers. The previous manager died in a car accident shortly after assuming control." Trusts were inherently peculiar, and the name of this trust alluded to one of the first to attack Julius Caesar. It was a clever name for an account.

After ending the conversation, Paul sat back in his chair and scrutinized the computer screen. He pondered further on the trust located in the Caribbean. The entire situation seemed convoluted. Trusts were notorious for their secrecy, making it challenging to obtain information. Extensive digging was required. Paul began printing pages of legal documents, trying to familiarize himself with the world of trusts. His time at Harvard had left him with a small library, now stored in an office down the hall. To keep his office organized, he had started using a conference room nearby. Returning to his office, Paul sighed deeply, rubbed his eyes, and attempted to shake off his fatigue. The sun had long set, and he found himself staring at the harsh glow emanating from the computer screens. The cleaning staff would arrive soon, and Paul realized that it had been a while since he stayed at the office late.

Eventually, he stood up, turned on the lights, locked himself in the room, settled at the back, and stared at the computer screen running a tracking algorithm. He watched the ebb and flow of information in the world markets. Sometimes, during moments of intense chaos, Paul enjoyed going to a conference room, closing the blackout blinds, and sitting in the silence of the noise-canceling walls. But today was not one of those days.

* * *

In Toronto, he found a shipping container at the Toronto Port Authority. There was one near the back of the facility, bore the serial number: B-M-1986-0006-0017. Inside, he took a crate and then went to Henry's business near downtown.

He met Henry in the mezzanine. The older man smiled at Daniel and asked, "How are you?" Daniel quickly responded before they embraced, the hug lingering longer than usual.

They proceeded toward the elevators at the back of the lobby. To the side of their path, there lay a dead body. Was it Lee? His mouth hung open, his eyes clouded and vacant. Daniel turned to look at the body, but it suddenly vanished as if a film error had corrected itself. Daniel placed his hand over his eyes, squeezing the bridge of his nose, attempting to focus amidst the gripping anxiety in his heart. Pain seared through his hand, a reminder of the recent fight he had unexpectedly survived. It was the first time he had felt pain in a long while, but before he could fully grasp the sensation, it dissipated, leaving him feeling numb once again.

Even before stepping onto the elevator, Daniel felt sweat trickling down the back of his neck. Perspiration emerged, and his collar constricted, suffocating him. The building suddenly felt oppressively small, and fear washed over his face. Holding the elevator doors open with his free hand, he hesitated, keeping them available for a moment longer. Eventually, he made the decision to step out of the elevator car and faced Henry, who still stood inside. "I'll meet you upstairs," Daniel said. Elevators were like death traps; once the doors closed, they sealed the fate of their passengers should the power fail. Henry looked at him uncomfortably as the doors closed, separating them. Daniel stared at the stainless-steel doors for a moment. He then took the stairs.

"Another attack?" Daniel shrugged, trying to ignore Henry's question. "Would you like to talk about it?" Henry placed Daniel's glass on the bar table and leaned against the wall.

Daniel watched the rainy streets below as people went about their day. He moved past the bar, picked up his glass, and examined it for a while before adding more whiskey. He took two pills from the aspirin bottle Ted had given him and swallowed them, starting slow and then finishing the glass in one gulp. He forcefully placed the empty crystal glass on the counter. Seated at the bar, he asked, "Do you know Christopher Ralston?" A part of him wanted to go over to the sofa where Henry was sitting and lay on Henry's shoulder, as if he were a child again, but he felt irrational and emotional.

"Your father had considered using Ralston for your trusts," Henry replied. They sat in silence for a while. Henry wasn't sure why Daniel was trying to reject his past so comprehensively. "Is this Ralston guy involved in all of this too?" Henry asked, and Daniel explained their current situation. Henry wondered why Daniel was doing this. Daniel could never work again if he wanted to. Ralston seemed to be involved in a plot of great danger, and nobody was quite sure what it entailed.

"Do you think I could stay here for a few days?" Daniel asked, already assuming he could but feeling it rude to impose. Henry gave him a look and said, "You're welcome here as long as you need - you know that. You're family. You don't have to ask." He then headed towards the door, mentioning some work he had across the street. "Call if you need me or can't find anything in the house. There's more scotch under the bar." There was a moment of hesitation as he stood at the door, then he turned to face Daniel. "If you have some free time tonight, I'd love to have dinner. It's been a while."

Daniel nodded. "It has. I'll have to let you know." He waited for Henry to leave before taking the tablet computer from the front flap of the suitcase and placing it on the chair across from the bed. He unpacked his things, transferred the Canadian cash into the empty bag, and stowed it underneath the bed. He took the handgun out of the gun box and placed it on the duvet.

Eventually, Daniel turned on the tablet and sat in the chair. The cool light of the rainy city cast through the window, reflecting onto the tablet's screen. "Information you collected in Amsterdam outlined the money that paid off Lee originated in Canada," Paul's recording played. The file details appeared on the screen, allowing Daniel to browse through them with his fingers. It felt like an interactive lecture. Lines of red in various widths spread across the globe from D.C. back to Amsterdam and now Canada, signifying the movement of money they were interested in. Alongside the lines, a ticker tape of data scrolled. Zooming in, one could read the details of each transaction.

Daniel made notes on the tablet while shuffling through a read-out. "Albert Jansen was the administrator handling all business accounts managed by Patrick Finley. The business operates logistic consulting, so the rather large payouts we saw weren't unheard of. I have some people here looking through their older stuff to see if it gives us any leads," Paul said. "The money was laundered through a few dozen internal accounts and banking systems before reaching our dearly departed. It amounted to about five million American dollars and almost certainly came from a wire sent from Canada. We've determined that the account it originated from is connected to Christopher Ralston. It was likely actionable from a trust known as Casca, but this is purely speculative and needs confirmation. Furthermore, Ralston has a long history of working with trusts. These guys are experts at hiding money, making it difficult for us to track its origins." Paul had pre-recorded the briefing, allowing Daniel to interact with the information. "We don't want to blow this out of proportion, so we should

The Collateral Dividend

gather more information without arousing suspicion from Ralston or disrupting his business. If he's directly involved, we make it look like an accident and proceed accordingly. If he isn't, we move on." An image of Ralston, a full-looking man in his fifties, appeared on the tablet screen.

After a few moments of browsing, the video minimized back into the app. Daniel rubbed his index and thumb together in a circular motion, finding it soothing and helping him remain focused and calm. It occasionally helped with the hallucinations, or at least he believed so. He sat there for a while, lost in thought, before his phone rang.

"Have you read the file?" Paul asked. He was combing his hair and buttoning up a new shirt. A deep hunger called out, and he initially satisfied it with a tall mug of coffee. Ralston's role meant Daniel couldn't bully him around. Paul needed access to Ralston's files to determine the details of the trust.

Daniel took the briefcase and crossed the street. It was mid-afternoon, and the city's air carried a weighty mugginess. Traffic congested the streets. He walked until he reached the nearest underground parking and took the stairwell down to the bottom floor, nearly six or seven stories below. He disabled the cameras and waited until the area was empty. Spotting a Jaguar two-door coupe, he liked the idea of using it to move around the city. Placing the briefcase near the front bumper, he removed the license plates and replaced them with a different set. Leaving the bag on the floor, he grabbed his smartphone and a small device from his jacket pocket. Connecting the two devices using the docking port, he pushed the blank key into the car door and confirmed the command on the phone's screen. A soft thud resonated through the garage, and his phone screen displayed the word "CONFIRMED." He pulled out the key and opened the car door. With the door open, he replaced the posted VINs on the windshield and inside the door. He knew he was becoming needlessly paranoid, but Daniel had convinced himself that these precautions kept him alive.

Approaching Ralston's office on the twenty-third floor, Daniel realized there was only one way to approach this situation. Reluctantly, he decided to take the elevator after pacing the lobby for ten minutes, deliberating how to overcome his fear. When he reached the reception desk on the twenty-third floor, he asked if there was a way he could drop something off for Christopher Ralston. The painting on the wall appeared to be moving, causing Daniel to sweat. He requested directions to the nearest washroom.

The small washroom provided a moment of respite. Daniel closed and locked the door, looking at himself in the mirror and taking a deep breath. The

71

anxiety had been replaced by a searing headache, starting at the base of his skull and extending upwards. He tapped the sink, which turned on, and he washed his hands and cleaned his face. He took two more tablets.

When he came out, he handed the receptionist a business card from a gunmetal case in his jacket pocket. The card had Grip Solutions written in embossed lettering at the top, with his name listed as in-house counsel.

"I'm running a little late," he had said. "Could you give Mr. Ralston this? I'd love to speak with him about some business opportunities."

Each card had a signal that could wirelessly access networks within a limited range. It could hack into the company's computers if placed within a reasonable proximity. Inside the card was a small transmitter. The crucial point was that the card needed to remain stationary and would no longer function once bent. Daniel simply had to wait for Ralston to activate the hacking device by placing it within range of either his computer terminal or his smartphone – preferably both.

Soon after being notified, he received a call from Ralston. The link had been established, and files started pouring in. Daniel let the call go to an automated answering system and waited for Ralston to leave a message. It was at that moment the card went offline, and the transmission ceased. They had retrieved as much data as possible. Daniel hoped it would be enough. He was seated on a bench in the square between two bank office towers, waiting for the data to transmit back to Farragut Center.

"He's not as busy as I expected," Daniel remarked once the data had been transferred, and he scrolled through the next three days of Ralston's calendar. The phone contained a lengthy list of contacts – all of whom would need to be examined to determine the owner of Casca. Trusts were often shrouded in secrecy. They were difficult to regulate and equally challenging to track.

Paul had conducted some investigation. He had obtained Royal Dominion's banking logs through Avery. They had discovered the account from which the money had originated and determined that Ralston wasn't the one who had deposited the funds. "He's a young lawyer at the firm," Paul had mentioned, referring to Milos Nodaric, a heavyset man. Nodaric reported to Ralston. Despite his occasional absence, Ralston would email Nodaric assignments without checking if the young lawyer was even in the office. After reviewing the initial files, it became evident that Nodaric was both exploited and indispensable to Ralston's work. Although his profile was lower, he had access to many of the things Ralston was involved in, making him a viable target. The focus should

The Collateral Dividend

not shift away from Ralston, but Paul had broadened Daniel's perspective. Nodaric, the lumpy and careless yet sharp legal mind, was fair game.

Daniel gazed down the congested, bustling street. "What are your thoughts on all this?" he asked after a cursory glance at the files. Most of them were shallow documents drafted solely to comply with legal requirements. It was the first time Daniel had asked Paul to be completely honest.

Paul had just finished eating a yogurt capsule. He wiped his hands on a napkin and cleaned his face. "I don't like it at all," he replied. "I think we've stumbled upon something much bigger than anticipated. What worries me is that we don't know how deep this goes. We aren't even certain what we're dealing with." Paul remained unconvinced that it was their responsibility. However, Daniel pointed out that the account was funding potentially politically motivated assassinations, making it precisely within their commitment. "I trust you have things under control?" Paul glanced at his watch. "When is his lunch?"

"Twenty minutes," Daniel replied, uncertain of the location. He took a chance, hoping to secure a table and keep a close eye on Ralston. Later in the evening, he knew it would be much easier to follow Nodaric.

Paul grunted, utterly exhausted from lack of sleep. "I'm going to catch a nap," he said. "Contact Avery if you need any support from us here." It would be a long day, and he needed every opportunity to catch up on sleep he could get.

THE TRUST LAWYER

Daniel sat in silence as he finished his meal. Across the room, Ralston sat at a table, his arm casually draped over the back of the chair. In one hand, he held the lunch menu, while his reading glasses perched on the edge of his nose. Daniel observed from a distance, reflecting on the effort it took to secure a table in this busy establishment. He had even paid a substantial sum to the maître d' for this late lunch seating.

Another man eventually joined Ralston at the table, and their conversation seemed cryptic and filled with coded language that Daniel struggled to understand. Nevertheless, he diligently recorded everything, knowing the significance it held. Paul later played back the recording, running it through an algorithm in an attempt to decipher the hidden meanings, particularly related to trusts and beneficiaries.

After an hour, a third guest arrived, and Daniel, now on his fourth course, maintained order among the starters. In a subtle movement, he discreetly snapped a photo, which automatically uploaded to an encrypted cloud accessible in Washington.

"We've been monitoring these men for some time," Paul remarked to Daniel.

Curious, Daniel inquired, "Who are they?" But Paul chose to keep that information close to his chest. "We can discuss that later. Right now, we need Ralston's files," Paul instructed, and Daniel promptly took action.

As the day slowly transitioned into evening, Paul mentioned that he would try to go home for a few hours—an unusual occurrence in recent months. However, Paul felt conflicted, considering it a potential waste of time. The accounts they utilized in their operations had been funded through ad hoc creations, employing a complex scheme involving falsified accounts worldwide. The Farragut Center, much like the funds they were tracking, relied on this intricate web of financing. Though it all began with Adam Stanley, the situation seemed to be escalating rapidly. Adam had been acquainted with many individuals in the intelligence community, aware of the Center's phone monitoring activities on American networks. While he didn't know about the diversion of fees to fund Farragut Center, he was certainly aware of the movement of money. With Adam gone, the siphoning had to cease entirely, and Farragut Center operated under tight constraints. Unfortunately, this crucial information had not been communicated to Paul or Ted. Furthermore, the accounts they had been skimming in the Department of Transportation were gradually running dry.

Paul instructed Avery to contact him if any developments arose, setting his phone to notify him of any anomalies on the servers. As she stood in the doorway of her room, she observed Paul attempting to make a call, but the person on the other end didn't answer. Paul then returned home, entering with a bouquet of flowers, as was his weekly tradition. "I thought I'd find you here," he greeted Rachel with a smile, concealing the flowers behind his back. Leaning in, he kissed her on the cheek, pleasantly surprising her. When he revealed the bouquet, she smiled broadly, telling him he shouldn't have gone to such lengths.

"You're too much," she exclaimed, her smile revealing a touch of naivety and carelessness. Although she wondered what prompted his early return, such occasions were infrequent, making the reason less important. "How about we go out for dinner and a movie?" Paul suggested, his tone filled with opportunity. He felt an overwhelming happiness, a sense of comfort in how things were progressing. However, his reaction left Rachel feeling off-balance. Paul possessed a magnetic and divisive magnanimity, capable of setting the emotional tone of any room. His own feelings propelled interactions forward, regardless of others' sentiments. It was exhausting, and she pondered how long she would endure being hurt before giving up. Even in moments of bliss, where she felt his undivided attention, there lingered a bitter disappointment, a cutting edge that shattered her hope of never being hurt again. She knew that one day he would become consumed by his work, leaving her disappointed and forgotten. How many more episodes would she endure? These thoughts plagued her mind, yearning for discussion and resolution, for the ability to conquer their problems. However, their relationship remained fragile, and sometimes it seemed better to suffer silently, hoping her concerns would fade away.

Meanwhile, Daniel's curiosity about the unidentified men grew. He attempted to access files and run facial recognition software, but each search request was blocked. He briefly considered tracking them to uncover their identities but dismissed it as a waste of time. Suspicion filled Daniel's mind, sensing that there was much more happening than he had been told. Paul had always claimed to be forthcoming, but Daniel's keen memory retained countless details, meticulously cataloging them. There was a period when he had no recollection of being drugged for three months afterward. Occasionally, fragments of those memories resurfaced, but their foreign nature didn't raise any red flags for Daniel.

The Collateral Dividend

Daniel had left the television on, and the news played in a repetitive loop, updating him on the state of the world. One ongoing event was the beginning stages of a civil war in Greece, leaving Daniel to wonder how long it would endure. Henry entered the living room an hour later, surprised to find Daniel still awake. Placing his bag on a nearby seat, he walked over to the kitchen and opened the fridge. "Can't sleep?" he asked, though he suspected there was more to it.

"Still on the clock," Daniel replied softly, accepting the water bottle Henry tossed to him and opening it. The weariness beneath Daniel's eyes was evident as he gazed out at the city streets.

In the living room, a rare Persian rug adorned the hardwood floor. Henry, still wearing his shoes, wiped his boots on the rug before taking a seat opposite Daniel on the sofa. Reflecting on Daniel's childhood, Henry recalled the challenges they had all faced. "You can't bring back the ones you love. We all experience loss. It's how we cope with that loss that shapes us," Henry began, attempting to offer guidance. "Daniel, I always believed you wouldn't let anything overcome you. This loss wasn't your fault. But you can't let it consume you."

Daniel's tone turned somewhat cynical as he questioned, "Do you really believe that?"

"Yes, I do," Henry continued. "You either let it consume you or find a way to move forward. But you won't find true happiness if you don't accept it and work on healing. I thought you had overcome all the adversities, but I was mistaken. You're trying to bury something you haven't properly dealt with, and that's not healthy." Henry paused, contemplating his next words. Dealing with the loss of one's parents at such a young age was undoubtedly challenging. His gaze shifted across the room, locking onto Daniel. "When you were little, you were always the most sensitive of your siblings. Do you remember?" Henry asked, then continued, "You would get emotionally hurt so easily, as if your passion knew no bounds. You laughed the loudest, cried the hardest, and fell in love the fastest. Daniel, don't forget who you are just because it hurts less."

Daniel remained stoic, he was fighting back tears. "I'm not driven by my passion, Henry. I'm focused on my duty."

"It seems personal to be just a duty," Henry remarked, gesturing toward Daniel. "You won't truly succeed until you come to terms with this. I was thinking about it today at work," he added, often contemplating his children's well-being. "I suspect there's a trauma that resurfaced and brought back all this pain. We should talk about it." Henry suggested involving Paul, but Daniel wasn't keen on the idea.

At that moment, Daniel's phone chimed, interrupting their conversation. He checked it and stood up. "Where are you going?" Henry asked with an authoritative tone only a guardian could muster. It was late, and the city's downtown core was transitioning into a state of rest. Corporate employees had departed for the suburbs, while vibrant neon lights and pulsating electronic music enlivened the night. "And did you buy a car?"

"If you're up later, perhaps we can talk again," Daniel proposed, considering Casca as a lead. However, the account remained shrouded in mystery, with no listed owner or value. Paul didn't suspect Garcia's involvement and believed it was best to focus on the financiers and lawyers managing the accounts.

Daniel went into the other room. He took two tablets from the aspirin prescription given to him by Ted, hoping to alleviate the pain in his neck. The pain persisted. Determined to ignore the throbbing in his head, he found himself suddenly standing in the hallway outside Nodaric's flat. Daniel swiftly assessed his surroundings, drew his weapon, and attached the suppressor. With the gun ready, he heard a cry for help, envisioning Nodaric as a cruel and abusive man. The sound of music drowned out the scream, but Daniel's knew difference between pleasure and fear.

After a brief moment of hesitation outside the door, Daniel recalled a hypothetical exercise he had once discussed with Paul. However, he disagreed with Paul's opinion that interfering was the greatest sin, as he believed that circumstances sometimes demanded action. Daniel leaned against the door. Then, with a small device that resembled a 12-volt car converter, Daniel broke the lock with a sound that resembled a cracking whip. There was a long hall, and it led into the living room. A speaker had been pushed against the wall. Daniel thought about shutting off the power. There was a door to his right, and Daniel lunged into the room, and the wood along the frame splintered. A part of Daniel wished he could have unseen the impression of Nodaric – stark naked if not for the gold watch, dress socks and unbuttoned dress shirt. His tummy peaked out between the folds of the shirt – a white beach ball between blue. The girl was lying face down on the bed. She was completely naked. Her clothes were thrown about.

When Daniel tumbled into the room, Nodaric turned to face the door. He looked like a deer in headlights. He was beet red in the face. Daniel came across the room, took Nodaric by the shirt collar, and pulled back so that Nodaric

The Collateral Dividend

tumbled onto the ground in the living room. Karen screamed and ran into the bathroom.

Daniel then went to the living room. His shoulders had rolled forward. His tone had quickly changed. He was still holding the handgun, and it was pointed at Nodaric. He told the lawyer to sit down. Nodaric complied. He then pulled the trigger, and a bullet obliterated the speaker system, and there was a loud screech, and then the room collapsed into silence.

Interrupting Nodaric's attempt to speak, Daniel pointed the gun at his head and instructed him to answer his questions. Nodaric remained silent, prompting Daniel to inquire about Casca and its owner. The lawyer revealed that Casca was one of Ralston's accounts, but claimed ignorance about it. However, Daniel suspected that Nodaric knew more. He continued pressing for information, asking about the origin of the packages earmarked for Ralston, as well as other individuals involved in the trust accounts. Nodaric's responses were unfocused and indicated his intoxicated and high state. Growing impatient, Daniel learned that Casca operated as a corporation in Bermuda, with most of its assets stored in physical safes and servers. The servers frequently sent requests for Ralston to fulfill, and the true owner of Casca remained unknown to Nodaric.

As Nodaric swayed and struggled to catch his breath, he mentioned Ralston's role as the fiduciary, trustee, and director of the Casca account. The trust owned various assets, primarily paintings, and occasionally received sums of money. Nodaric recounted his visit to the Casca facility in Bermuda, noting the servers' heightened security. Feeling the effects of his actions, Daniel allowed Nodaric to put on some pants, removed the suppressor, and holstered the gun.

"Look I don't have any money here, just take anything you want dude," Nodaric pleaded.

"Shut up," Daniel retorted, pointing the gun at Nodaric's head. "I'm going to ask you questions, and you're going to answer them," he continued, waiting for a response. Nodaric remained silent. Daniel inquired about Casca and its ownership.

"That's one of Ralston's accounts," the lawyer replied.

What do you know of it?' 'Nothing.' Nodaric was swaying. He was both high and drunk, and the spins had begun to set in. They tried again. This time they would start slow.

What could Nodaric tell him about Casca?

Nodaric was unfocused. He started by telling Daniel some gibberish about bearer shares and how the owner frequently would send packages earmarked for

79

Ralston. Daniel asked where the packets came from, and Nodaric had said sometimes New York, sometimes Singapore. 'Have you ever met the man?' Daniel then asked, and Nodaric shook his head. Daniel then asked him if there was anyone else who worked on the trust accounts other than Ralston. Nodaric didn't know.

Daniel was losing patience. Nodaric was lying on his back, panting to catch his breath. He then tried to explain how trusts worked. Ralston was the fiduciary and the trustee and also held a directorship of the account. The trust housed a corporation known as Casca in Bermuda. It paid a fee to own a small property to accommodate a dozen servers and physical safes, which held most of the trust's assets. There was the occasional sum of money –although most were born in the company's accounts. The firm never reported a capital gain; most of the physical assets were paintings. Nodaric had once travelled down there to do an inventory, and he told Daniel that the servers seemed to be the most secure. Sometimes the servers themselves would give requests for Ralston to carry out. This was quite common. Who the actual owner was, Nodaric wasn't sure.

"Can I at least put some pants on," he said in a slur, and Daniel felt terrible for him for a moment. He removed the suppressor, put the tube into his coat pocket, and holstered the gun.

Daniel stood up, walked into the bedroom, and looked at the room's mess. He was taking shallow breaths. Nodaric had picked up his pants and was buttoning up his shirt. He looked at the back of Daniel and then at the door to the apartment not far down the hall. Nodaric felt a charge of energy. His heart started beating quickly. He could no longer feel his toes or fingers and moved toward the door while still wearing his pants. Nodaric opened the door. The hinge cried out, and Nodaric was now running down the hallway.

Daniel then realized what had happened, and he went for the door. Daniel came into the stairwell in a crash after Nodaric. He stared down the long narrow chasm between the stairs. Nodaric was six floors down. He was barefoot, and when he reached the lobby, he pushed out the door and started running south toward the rail line. All Daniel could think about was how badly he'd fucked up. He was standing out on the street in the dead of night. The fog had not receded, and in the distance, he could see Nodaric around the corner of the tunnel. Nodaric hadn't taken his coat or his phone.

Nodaric pushed feverishly through the greenish glass door of the train station. He then climbed the stairs onto the overpass that straddled the elevated railroads. Nodaric leapt onto the tracks and was vying with the oncoming train.

The Collateral Dividend

Daniel was standing on the train platform. A crowd had gathered to watch. Daniel looked down the length of the tracks and thought about going around and cutting him off on the far side. There was not enough time, and he risked losing Nodaric on one of the trains. Daniel hurdled onto the rail bed. The departing train hammered its horn loudly in a long, obnoxious burst. The train had begun to gain speed. Nodaric skipped in his footing, clasped hold of a nearby handle and pulled himself up.

Daniel attempted to follow, but the train had already gained too much speed. He hitched onto a train car near the back, at least four behind where Nodaric had boarded. The sealed door took a good measure of his strength to open, and once he had, he brashly pushed himself into the passenger car, where he collapsed to the ground.

Daniel could see Nodaric through the window of the interlocking cars. The cars were empty, and when the train submerged beneath a tunnel, the tinted hue of the lighting flickered on.

Nodaric was standing at the door leading into the next car. He tried to kick Daniel. Daniel lurched forward and tackled Nodaric. He had him by the pant leg, and Nodaric kicked Daniel hard in the face and then wriggled free just as the car pulled to the next stop.

Nodaric came out onto the platform. They were a few miles out of downtown. Nodaric's feet hurt. They were black. The gravel of the train tracks had cut the underside of his heels. His heart was beating fast. Nodaric looked back. He'd lost him, the thought. Nodaric had a house not far from here. When he reached the door of his house, he was heaving hard.

Daniel took in a deep breath and attempted to calm his jangled nerves. He only realised he was across the street from Nodaric's house. There were two police officers near Nodaric's front door, and they were standing there talking to one another. There was something peculiar about the way they were loitering there. Eventually, one went around the corner and walked on the sidewalk parallel to Daniel.

Nodaric took the duffle bag from the cabinet, slung it over his shoulder, and hurriedly made his way up the reclaimed wood stairwell and into the guest bedroom near the front of the house.

The officer who approached from the side was carrying a MAC-11, a small compact machine pistol that could unleash its thirty-two bullets in a split second. These were not legitimate officers, Daniel was certain.

Daniel examined the car key-shaped device made of black composite plastic. It had a small hole on its back and a button within reach of his thumb. It was an improvised gun, loaded and ready. He handled it cautiously and with measured determination.

He walked across the street, gripping the keyfob device tightly, lunged forward, and pressed it against the back of the man's neck, targeting his spine. With a mechanical 'pfft,' the shot pierced the man's skin, leaving a small puncture wound between the third and fourth vertebrae. The man fell headlong into a nearby bush, motionless.

Daniel reloaded his weapon and took the MAC-11 and moved for the doorway, his feet agile. As he turned the corner, he had a clear view of the impostors. Without hesitation, Daniel pulled the trigger, dispatching the second man. He reloaded. Nodaric was in the bathtub. He grabbed him by the collar, dragging him across the floor. Nodaric squirmed, leaving bloody footprints as he tried to resist. Daniel forcefully sat Nodaric in a chair, pointing the gun at him. The tall man adjusted his jacket on his shoulders, preparing for what was to come. Nodaric would talk, or Daniel would kill him. "I know nothing more," Nodaric insisted, but Daniel believed otherwise. He questioned Nodaric about the location of the Casca servers, and though reluctant, Nodaric eventually revealed the information. When asked about the payment to Amsterdam, Nodaric denied any knowledge. Daniel, growing more aggressive, asserted that Nodaric was aware, mentioning the money transfer made by Ralston to the bank in Amsterdam. Nodaric began to sweat, realizing Daniel knew more than Nodaric initially thought. The payable request had come directly from Patrick Finley, the Banker in Amsterdam, and Nodaric had been the one sent with the money.

With clearer thoughts, Nodaric remained seated as Daniel took a moment to compose himself before pulling the trigger. Nodaric's head snapped back abruptly, and he slumped in the chair, blood seeping from his third eye, staining his lap.

Daniel called for support and met them in the stairwell ten or twenty minutes later. They arrived in city worker uniforms. The house was cleaned and restored within an hour, and then the bodies were moved. Daniel accompanied them back to the apartment. The body was taken upstairs to be staged.

"Is everything alright?" Paul asked, glancing up at the other three suited men in the room.

"Someone knows we're here," Daniel stated.

"Why? What did you do?"

"I did what I had to," Daniel replied, lacking pride in his words.

"And what does that mean, Daniel?"

The Collateral Dividend

"He's dead, alright?" Faron casually sang.

The courtyard was empty as he briskly crossed it, heading towards the car. Before Paul could respond, Daniel clarified, "We obtained the necessary information from him, and he's dead. But we weren't the only ones searching for him."

"What?" Paul asked, picking up the receiver and standing up, no longer using the speakerphone. "Who the hell do you think you are?" He waited for the others outside his office. "How do you know he didn't have more to tell?"

"Paul, that's not the important part," Daniel began, clearing his throat. "Nodaric provided details on accessing the trust," he explained. "I'm not even sure if Ralston knows the account's owner. Are you familiar with bearer shares?" Daniel inquired, seeking confirmation.

"Equity security instrument, right? Allows an institution not to register ownership. Whoever holds the certificate owns the company," Paul recalled accurately.

Daniel explained that Casca had been set up, so its ownership was through bearer shares. 'Fuck,' Paul had said. It was going to be bloody well impossible to track that.

Daniel proceeded to recount what Nodaric had disclosed. Casca possessed a vast array of assets, mostly equities with the American brokerage firm Mayer Kleid. Additionally, they owned a few companies: Red-Arenque, a Central American manufacturing company; Imer Software, a software development company; and Fréteous Industries, specializing in freight shipping. The accounts also held a significant number of shares in American Telecom, some banks, and several Fortune 500 companies.

If Paul were to speculate, he would assume that Casca had been designed for market manipulation. The best way to find out was to access the servers.

Paul grimaced. "Certainly seems like a laundry list of unconnected companies," Daniel agreed. He couldn't help but think about Nodaric. He regretted killing him. It had been a gratuitous act driven by emotion. But then again, something had to be done, didn't it? It was a concept he had long grappled with in his old profession. Was justice a product of moral righteousness or merely a reflection of existing laws? One had to believe in a skewed concept of morality to justify preemptive actions.

"Why go through all this trouble to send it through Canada?" Daniel pondered. The revenue agency had limited prosecution resources compared to the IRS, and the nation's robust banking system made successful money laundering and subsequent international transfers possible. Paul was examining the GPS coordinates for the Casca servers in Bermuda. "I'll work on securing those assets. Sit tight."

"No," Daniel interjected. "If we take the money offline, it will alert whoever is on the other end. They've gone to great lengths to conceal the funds, and if we disrupt the operation, we may never uncover their true identity."

Paul hadn't considered that perspective. While leaving the trust intact posed risks, tampering with Ralston or the Trust would likely result in losing any trace of the mastermind behind it all. He had come to trust Daniel more than some of the analysts in the office. Daniel had proven himself to be exceptionally intelligent, surpassing others in his field. "So, where does that leave us?" Paul eventually inquired.

Daniel pondered the question for a moment. "Nodaric mentioned that the servers have been used to transmit trade orders. They must be connected to the internet. Why don't we attempt to hack into them and see if we can find any information that leads us somewhere?" It was nearly 2 am, and Daniel asked if there was anything else he should do before calling it a night.

Paul felt exhausted. An empty to-go salad container was sealed and placed at the far end of his desk. Next to it sat an empty clear smoothie mug, its plastic stained with traces of strawberry red. He instructed Daniel to get some rest and considered going home himself. However, the thought seemed daunting. He didn't want to disturb his girlfriend, and he convinced himself that it was best to spend another night at the office.

By the next morning, Paul felt the ache of sleeping on a cot. The ability to sleep anywhere was a young man's game, and espionage was too. Paul was only getting older. He realized the time of day as he sat on the edge of the cot. It was brutally early. With an expression of weariness, Paul stared at the barren wall across his office. Determined, he stood up, straightened his shoulders, turned on the office light, and opened the door. The day was already in motion. Paul glanced down the hallway, rubbing his face to shake off the remnants of sleep. The building's interior was a labyrinth of frosted glass walls, dividing offices from one another. Paul made his way down the hall until he reached an office with the words "SIGINT Analysis" etched into the frosted glass. Peering inside, he saw Avery sitting at her desk, chin in hand, engrossed in examining computer screens. He knocked before entering and closed the door behind him.

"So?" he inquired, taking a seat across from Avery. Her blinds were pulled down, blocking the morning light that streamed across the sky.

The Collateral Dividend

"The markets are moving, Paul," she began as they started the meeting. "The cell phone data from Ralston's device arrived from The Valley today. I've been working non-stop, trying to make sense of it all."

"Go on," Paul gestured, and Avery turned the screen towards him, pointing at a particular line of information.

"He made a phone call to someone in France," she said. "The southern coast, of all places." Tapping the keyboard, she maximized a tabbed window. "Someone contacted Ralston using encryption, making the line impenetrable. We can't determine what transpired or who dialed Ralston. But my immediate suspicion is that we've found our man. The fact that someone possesses such complex security encryption is concerning."

"Damn," Paul muttered, crossing his arms. "Can we find any information on the person in France? What about the companies I asked you to look into?"

Avery sighed and reached for the papers on her desk. She toyed with the pen in her right hand, contemplating her response. "I've conducted a thorough analysis," she began, determined to go through each company individually. She believed Paul was mistaken in dismissing them as pointless. These companies were wholly owned by the trust and were legitimate businesses. She reasoned that there must be a good reason for their existence. Starting with Fréteous, a small shipping firm from the south of France, she explained, "They have access to most global ports. Then there's Imer and Red-Arenque, which are symbiotic. Imer produces sixty percent of the programming for financial data vendors, while Red-Arenque manufactures the computer hardware used for stock market terminals."

Paul shook his head. "Whoever owns this operation is trying to seriously manipulate the markets. It's getting out of hand, and I can't predict where it's leading. But I heard you have something else for me." He attempted to shift the focus, leaning forward with crossed arms and a raised eyebrow.

"I do," Avery said, turning around in her seat to locate the file she needed. Adjusting her position, she pulled both sides of her black cardigan forward, as if warding off the cold. She handed the file to Paul, who pulled out the reports and held them from the bottom to read the top of the briefing. After reading it through once, he placed the paper on the table, a puzzled expression forming as if his eyes had misted over. Paul remained motionless, his gaze fixed on the woman across from him.

"The Greeks?" he finally voiced, attempting to grasp the rising policy concern. "The Greeks," he repeated.

85

E.R. Wychwood

"There's too much chatter for there to be no hint of political instability. We might be looking at a national-level collapse," Avery warned.

"Good work, Avery," Paul acknowledged. The possibility of a Greek revolution indicated an impending political dispute. Soon, Farragut Center would need to reach out and assess the pulse of the Greek nation.

"Morning," Dr. Acres greeted as she strolled around the table, took a sip of coffee, and glanced at Paul. The blank white mug left a circular stain on the desk, which she promptly cleaned with a tissue from a box behind the computer. "So, you wanted to discuss Daniel further?"

Paul nodded, placing a few file folders onto the table and pushing them toward her. Acres quickly scanned the files, then looked up at Paul. "Do you mind if I set up shop here and go through these?" she asked. Paul nodded, leading her down the hall to Daniel's office, where she could work undisturbed. "Swing by when you're done," Paul said, leaving her alone in the office.

Acres surveyed the room, taking in the paintings and trinkets placed around. A blazer hung on the back of the door, and she ran her fingers over the fabric. She sensed Paul's deep concern for Daniel. The two men shared a close bond, and she believed Paul felt guilty for compelling a friend to carry out such heinous acts. Moving around the desk, Acres took a seat and began reading the files. They were well-written, reflecting Paul's extensive academic background and brilliance. He had orchestrated a highly efficient intelligence operation, with interconnected staff producing some of the most effective intelligence products Acres had ever encountered.

However, what concerned Acres was the lack of safety measures or limits on field operatives who embodied Hobbes' Leviathan. Daniel was acting as a sovereign state, immune to consequences or repercussions. Daniel had arrived at this point through circumstances more complex than he was led to believe. He certainly wasn't the first choice for fieldwork at Farragut Center, not even the second or third. The files shed light on the criteria for potential candidates, primarily focusing on physical attributes. They needed to be attractive but not excessively so. Their jaw and cheekbones had to be just right, allowing them to appear drastically different depending on how they dressed, effectively disguising their nationality. Height and eye color were also crucial factors, with a preference for individuals around six feet two inches tall, deviating no more than two inches. Anything outside these parameters compromised a candidate's ability to blend in seamlessly. Light-shaded eyes, typically gray or blue, were desired, and colored contacts expanded the range of operational identities. Daniel fit the bill perfectly.

Of course, psychological prerequisites outweighed physical attributes. The files hinted at the use of severe behavioral modification techniques. Candidates were supposed to be stable, but the process itself was rigorous and dangerous. Critical functions of the mind were deliberately deprived and reformulated, and these modifications required minimal data sets to maintain accuracy. The program had learned the hard way, having unintentionally caused severe harm to two candidates before Daniel. It was cutting-edge scientific research, but also perilous. Conditioning played a significant role in the modifications, emphasizing logical thinking, making Daniel's law degree a natural fit. Drug supplements further accentuated specific patterns, similar to drugs used to treat attention deficits. They altered critical brain chemicals to enhance attention to detail and other mental faculties. Flipping to the back of the packet, Acres noted the involvement of one of her former colleagues, a Harvard emeritus professor who was renowned for his expertise in behavioral modification.

There were, of course, consequences to this, and Acres was fascinated by them. The most noticeable one was altered memory retention. Initially, everyone perceived this as beneficial, but Acres held a different view. The brain's limit on memory served as a defensive mechanism, allowing one to forget the bad and suppress painful memories to avoid depression or intrusive thoughts.

On her desk, Acres had a notepad with the words "Childhood trauma" underlined. Notes about being bullied and losing parents indicated a painful childhood. Daniel had been cryptic and evasive when discussing his past with Acres. She presumed that these traumas had resurfaced.

The documents solely focused on the direct physical effects of the drugs. It was not uncommon for candidates to experience reduced sensations. Coupled with susceptibility to depression, the inability to feel gave Acres an uneasy feeling. She opened the desk drawers and discovered a leather book among a messy pile of fountain pen ink canisters and office supplies. Intrigued, Acres found herself reading Daniel's notes and journal entries dating back nearly a year and a half. It raised concerns for her.

"When it comes to your operations, how crucial is he?" Acres asked upon returning to Paul's office, handing him back the files.

"Immensely. Why?" Paul inquired.

"Well," Acres began, "he's exhibiting symptoms of burnout and likely compassion fatigue. Both are extremely common in lawyers, and it wouldn't surprise me if he already had some of those before entering the field. It might be best for him to take some time away from work." She made the suggestion, suspecting it would be ignored.

"Are there any other alternatives?" Paul cautiously asked, trying not to reveal his ignorance of the suggestion. "What if we arranged frequent sessions with you for him? Would that help?"

"It may," Acres replied, observing Paul closely as if deciphering his thoughts. Paul gazed out the window, where the wind sighed and clouds moved steadily eastward. "We were never meant to kill people. I think you forget that. While some may deserve to die, if you're unable to grant either life or death, then you're not justified in depriving either," Doctor Acres stood up, put on her coat, and prepared to leave. Standing by the door, she kept her hands by her sides. "Again, if you need anything, let me know. It was a pleasure as always, Paul," and she let herself out.

Paul found himself overwhelmed. They had discovered access to Casca on the deep web, and the trust accounts were linked to an independent bank. The bank's outdated security made entry easy. "We're almost ready to access it," one of the programmers said, just before attempting to breach the firewalls. It proved relatively simple, a few lines of code, and Paul found himself staring at a manifest and ownership files.

Avery stood beside him, reading through the information and compiling a list of names. "Do you know who 'Min' is?" she asked. Paul shook his head.

"Wait," the programmer exclaimed hurriedly, stabbing at the keyboard. The server fought back. Caught off guard, the malware slipped through, and Paul's computer screen went black. "Shit," the programmer cursed, attempting to unplug the computer from the server, but it was too late.

The screens flashed a breach, and the computers began shutting down to counteract the intrusion. "What the hell was that?" Paul found himself asking, staring at the screen displaying a repeating emblem. "What does it mean?"

"It's a calling card," Avery said. "We've been hacked."

THE STRUCTURER

Daniel often skipped breakfast, oscillating between enjoying fried eggs and finding them repulsive. Instead, he would start drinking almost immediately after breakfast, when the pulse of his headache was no longer just a distant memory. The previous night had been horrid, and such nights were becoming all too common, just like the hallucinations he experienced. Daniel had finally mentioned it to Paul the night before, who didn't seem concerned and expected it to happen. "Did you try taking aspirin?" Daniel remembered Paul asking. The frequency of the images seemed to lessen when he took the pills that Ted had given him.

Without those pills, he would often find himself daydreaming with a vividness and accuracy as horrific as reality. When mixed with alcohol, their severity deepened, becoming ingrained in his off-duty activities, much like having breakfast or washing his hands.

On this particular day, Daniel found himself walking through a forest in late winter, where the bitterness of the season had encased the woods in an icy grip. The darkness of the late night was interrupted by slivers of moonlight that refracted off the snow, casting an eerie shade of blue over the forest. After wandering for about ten minutes, he decided to turn back. Eventually, he reached a clearing—a meadow covered in snow—that halted the dense chaos of the forest. This was the part Daniel hated the most.

At the end of the meadow, there was a sloping hill that led up to a vast courtyard situated between two red brick buildings with grey cornerstones. Daniel had arrived at the courtyard, where some older students who had been playing in the snow noticed him and approached. The group leader taunted Daniel, referring to his forest expedition and mocking him for potentially calling his sister. Another boy, standing to the side, claimed to have heard that Daniel's father was a terrorist and that's why he was killed.

Overwhelmed with emotions, Daniel began to cry, and when the boy pushed him, Daniel retaliated with a hard swing, knocking the boy to the ground. In a frenzy, Daniel continued to punch the fallen boy while the rest of the group surrounded them, chanting and wagering on the outcome.

Suddenly, a man's voice pierced through the chaos, silencing the commotion. A tall, thin man wearing a camel winter coat and a fedora emerged from the crowd. He took hold of Daniel's collar, pulled him away from the boy, and stood him up straight. He instructed the fallen boy, Lucas, to stand as well, then addressed the group, expressing disappointment in their behavior. He demanded an explanation of what had happened.

The group turned on Daniel, pointing fingers and skewering the truth. They accused him of attacking Lucas out of nowhere and tried to convince Mr. Pierce that Daniel was a freak and crazy. However, despite their accusations, the instructor turned to Daniel, who was cleaning his running nose, and asked for his side of the story. Daniel remained silent. Mr. Pierce then instructed the boys to return to their rooms and write an apology to Daniel and himself. He warned them of the consequences of lying to an instructor and dismissed their attempts to redeem themselves.

Keeping his hand on Daniel's shoulder, Mr. Pierce suggested they go inside for something warm. They headed towards the staff quarters, located in the building adjacent to the lecture rooms, connected to the chapel by a grand hallway with broad windows and high ceilings that took on a menacing atmosphere at night.

Inside the cramped office, tucked away to the side, Mr. Pierce cleared some space to sit, moving aside stacks of academic works and history excerpts that outlined Daniel's remaining semester curriculum. He poured himself a glass of scotch from the cabinet behind his desk and offered Daniel a choice between diet coke or trying some scotch, suggesting it might help soothe his wounds. Despite winning the fight, Daniel had a cut on his forehead. Mr. Pierce handed him a can of coke, proceeded to clean the wound, and asked if he was alright. Daniel nodded, and after tending to the injury, Mr. Pierce sat down in a chair across the room and crossed his feet. He then asked Daniel what had happened.

After a while of sitting in silence, Daniel mustered the courage to ask, "Is it true? You worked for the CIA?" Mr. Pierce responded with a big smile and a laugh, curious about how Daniel had heard that rumor. He confirmed that he had once done some policy analysis for the CIA but emphasized it was a long time ago. Daniel expressed his interest in the subject, and Mr. Pierce retrieved a book on the CIA from a shelf and handed it to him, suggesting he could keep it since he hadn't read it in years. This act brought a small smile to Daniel's face, a rare occurrence.

The conversation shifted to Daniel's father, Henry. Mr. Pierce mentioned that they talked often and revealed that he was a classmate of Henry's, along with Daniel's father. He explained that Henry had sent Daniel to Hellmuth College because he loved him very much, despite being critical of him. Mr. Pierce shed light on the difficulties of raising someone else's children, especially when they were much younger than him. He shared a personal anecdote about his own experiences as a boy, trekking into the forest after his father's death, and urged Daniel to understand that burying emotions could lead to a harrowing journey.

While they were engrossed in their conversation, the sound of a closing steel door jolted Daniel back to reality. He found himself seated in the leather chair, no longer lost in his thoughts. Daniel took another gulp of scotch, placed the glass on the coffee table, and stood up as he recognized the approaching footsteps. When Henry entered the room, Daniel went over and hugged him tightly.

"Is everything alright?" Henry asked as he finally entered the common room. He placed his keys and the stack of mail on the granite counter.

"I've just been thinking a lot," Daniel replied. It was noon on a Friday, and Henry had finished his week's work, planning to leave for Boston later that afternoon. He poured himself a scotch and joined Daniel in the living room. "Oh?" he inquired, curious about Daniel's thoughts.

"When we were kids," Daniel began, "I've been reminiscing."

"Are you thinking or seeing things?" Henry asked, aware of Daniel's past experiences.

Daniel sighed and took a sip of whiskey. The glass dangled from his fingers, swirling the liquid across the ice. "I'm afraid they're getting worse," he confessed.

"You need to be careful," Henry cautioned. "What if you can no longer distinguish between reality and illusion?"

"But I can, Henry," Daniel insisted, frustration evident in his voice. "You know, I used to pray at the chapel every day, hoping it was just a bad dream."

"I know you did," Henry acknowledged. "I sometimes wished the same. I must admit, I was more focused on my own fading youth than on what was necessary to nurture someone else's. I've always felt guilty about that. I was scared of messing up."

Daniel looked at Henry with anguish in his eyes. He wanted to say that it hadn't affected him, but that would have been a lie. Daniel rubbed his unshaven chin, the few days' growth accentuating his defined jawline. Henry tried to lighten the mood, comparing Daniel to a musketeer, which made him smile. "Do you ever wonder what it would have been like?" Henry asked, knowing he pondered that question himself. He wondered if the choices he made were the same his father would have made.

E.R. Wychwood

"Do you remember the first night?" Henry asked, aware that the memory was etched in Daniel's mind.

"You stayed the night. We hardly saw you twice a year, and suddenly Uncle Henry appeared and spent the night," Daniel recalled.

"I was terrified," Henry confessed. "I had just graduated from college. Suddenly, I had three kids and a multimillion-dollar company." He shook his head, reminiscing about that day. "Your brother figured it out before we even told you or your sister. He connected the dots at school." Henry hadn't thought about that in a long time. "When I told you that night, you..."

"...ran out into the forest behind the house, and you came back with a blanket. We sat there among the leaves, gazing at the stars, and cried until I fell asleep," Daniel interrupted, finishing Henry's sentence. "Henry, what am I doing?" Daniel's nose began to tingle, his eyes growing heavy and teary.

"This is no longer a question of legality, Daniel," Henry replied. "Regardless of whether it's legal or not, it's happening and will continue to happen. The real question is, do you believe it should be legal? And if you don't, why are you doing it?"

"I have an obligation. This is the right thing to do, and I need to see it through," Daniel affirmed.

"As long as you see the world in black and white, things will work themselves out," Henry stated. That was the problem—Daniel no longer saw the world as black and white. It had blurred into a monochromatic shade of gray. Daniel's phone buzzed on the coffee table, and he put his glass down to answer it.

"Good morning," Daniel greeted.

"We found a link," Paul said as he entered the office. The rain had set the mood for the early morning, and he threw his tan cotton trench coat, a gift from his girlfriend, onto the guest seat by the door. Sitting down at his desk, he tapped the computer screen to wake it up. The keyboard was hidden beneath the far side of the desk, and he rested his fingertips above the keys before logging in. "You should see a photo of him on your screen now," Paul continued. Daniel pulled the smartphone away from his ear and examined the photo. It depicted a British man with dark black hair parted down the middle. His temples showed signs of graying, and he had a prominent nose. Daniel thought he resembled a more severe-looking Eric Bana. Putting the phone back to his ear, Daniel asked, "His name is Mark Patel?"

"Yes," Paul confirmed. "We used a brute-force attack to access the trust servers. We obtained the names of several directors, but no ownership details."

The Collateral Dividend

"Directors? What do you mean?" Daniel inquired.

"It's a bit complicated," Paul began to explain. "We've identified a few individuals who have limited control over aspects of the trust. These directors are not the primary focus of Farragut Center's operation. The Trust was storing malware, which we synced with our servers. We're currently scanning to determine if any information was compromised. Fortunately, the hacker left his signature. Avery recognized it and managed to contact one of her friends at the NSA. They had been monitoring Patel for some time. Turns out, he works for Imer Software and is one of those anonymous hackers who often fights against the military-information complex. I believe Patel will know who hired him, even if he never met the owner of the Trust. Hackers don't work for people without vetting them."

"Is that all we have to go on?" Daniel questioned, now sitting on the edge of his bed with his arms crossed. "An assumption and a calling card? I'd feel more confident if we were certain Patel is responsible."

"It's been confirmed," Paul replied somewhat brusquely. "Avery did some digging. She traced two-thirds of a million to Patel's account, wired from the same Amsterdam branch that Lee's money came from. I want you to bring him in for questioning, alive. Patel used his credit card in Rome to book a room at the Hotel Stanza. Bring him in quietly." Paul sent Daniel an image of the hotel and added, "Patel is a British national, so be cautious. He works for Casca's software company based in Metropolitan London. The firm specializes in programming software for stock market terminals and government computers. Patel's expertise lies in firewalls and countering security measures."

"Do we have a flight arranged?" Daniel asked abruptly and with a touch of urgency.

"We're implementing changes to our policies, and there are some things you should know," Paul said. "This will likely be your final rendition. We want to focus on your expertise, so Ted and I believe it's best for you to exclusively handle renditions involving hard assets. The flight will be ready within the next hour. It will wait in Rome until you secure Patel."

"What about Ralston?" Daniel inquired.

"Ralston is under surveillance. He's left the country and is currently in Bermuda," Paul informed him.

"Why am I just hearing about this now?" Daniel questioned, feeling a bit left out.

93

"Not every field operation requires your involvement, Daniel. I have other assets in the field who are monitoring Ralston. We'll discuss it further once you've secured Patel," Paul concluded.

Daniel observed Mark Patel from across the street, leaning against a blue lorry truck. Patel continued walking along the street towards the Metro station, which was just a block away. As he reached the curb of Viale Manzoni, a black motorcycle pulled up beside him and abruptly came to a stop. Patel handed his messenger bag to the driver, who quickly sped off into the traffic. Patel resumed his walk.

Daniel had an autoinjector connected to the bottom of his watch, primed and ready. He approached Patel, swiftly grabbing him by the neck. In a hasty reaction, Patel attempted to push Daniel away. The narrow alleyway only allowed enough space for three people to stand side by side. As they grappled, Daniel struggled to keep Patel at bay, hoping to render him unconscious with the autoinjector. Patel fought back, gripping Daniel's neck tightly and using his leg to push him against the wall. With a free hand, Patel reached into his pocket and pulled out a switchblade, swiftly opening it. In a swing, the blade grazed Daniel's chest, and Patel followed up with a forceful kick, sending Daniel crashing against the wall and onto the ground.

Shivering, Patel slumped against the wall, trying to stay upright. His motor skills faltered, and he dropped the knife. Patel glanced at his trembling hands, then turned his gaze towards his attacker. Meanwhile, Daniel regained his composure, slowly rising from the floor after catching his breath. In the side street nearby, a grey van had pulled up, its side door opening. Overwhelmed, Patel collapsed to the ground, feeling his body convulse uncontrollably. A grey haze clouded his vision until finally, his eyes closed, he slipped into unconsciousness, and everything fell silent.

*   *   *

"What was the point of having money if one could not spend it?" Philippe pondered, reclining in his chair and gazing at the captivating horizon from the foothills of his ancestral castle in Normandy. A close friend, Christopher Ralston, sat beside him, privy to the darker side of Philippe's nature.

"My great-grandfather perished near here," Christopher mentioned, as they sat together, observing the swift movement of the sky. "In the Battle of Dieppe."

The Collateral Dividend

"You remind me of that every time we're here, Chris," Philippe dryly retorted, his attention fixed on the distant sound of a car crushing gravel. Checking his watch—a vintage Jaeger LeCouture, one of his earliest acquisitions as CEO—he realized the tardiness of their awaited guest. Philippe extracted a case from his pocket, swallowed two tablets, and remarked, "He's late."

"Philippe, he did mention that the flight was delayed," Ralston reasoned. Gaillard shot him a disdainful glance, and when an Asian man emerged onto the porch, Philippe chided him for his tardiness. Ralston cast a fleeting glance at the man, who wisely avoided any argument.

"Shall we begin?" Gaillard inquired as the Asian man took his seat after entering the room.

"Indeed," Ralston replied. "Min and I have discussed the necessary steps once we withdraw the funds from the markets." A plate of charcuteries was brought out and placed on the coffee table, enticing their appetites. Min, the hungriest among them, leaned forward and took three pieces of prosciutto-wrapped melon.

Gaillard raised his hand, halting Ralston, and then shifted his attention to Min. "What on earth are you doing?" he asked, while taking two pieces for himself and devouring them simultaneously, oblivious to social decorum. "Please continue," he managed to utter with a mouth full of food. Ralston had never witnessed Gaillard like this—reckless, impulsive, and lacking any filters.

"Why don't I walk you through how this will work," Ralston suggested, retrieving a tablet from his briefcase and handing it to Gaillard. "Finding someone to execute the trades will be your responsibility. I trust you have someone discreet enough to push the button." Gaillard nodded, assuring them of Sergei's competence and quick thinking.

"The trade orders will be pre-set. Once the markets close, the algorithm will bypass security protocols and execute the outstanding trades, generating profit by reselling the shares at market levels," Ralston explained. "The funds will be directed to an account I've established in Switzerland, then transferred through several other accounts in Guernsey, Bermuda, and the Cayman Islands." A stillness permeated Ralston's presence as he sat motionless, his face devoid of expression. He then began outlining the path through which the money would return to Gaillard. Their target amount exceeded three hundred million, posing challenges in terms of transfer logistics. Ralston grinned broadly, assuring Gaillard that they had devised a plan to retrieve the funds without losing a penny. While some taxes would be inevitable, Ralston had found a way for Gaillard to avoid most European taxes while remaining in the green. European banks were unsuitable for parking the money due to inflationary concerns outweighing interest benefits. Ralston proposed introducing the funds into the markets through Africa and Asia, where banks were less likely to scrutinize the origin of the money. Min, in this regard, played a crucial role, leveraging his connections in these regions.

"To make the money more manageable, it will need to be liquidated in £10,000 increments and dispersed across multiple businesses affiliated with one of your less secretive trusts," Ralston elaborated. "Each transfer will be £9,999 or occasionally two transfers of £5,000, adopting a randomized pattern to avoid arousing suspicion. Transferring ten thousand dollars typically triggers a report and internal investigation, while multiple transfers below the threshold are deemed acceptable." They had employed a randomizer to generate transfers ranging from £3,500 to £9,999.

Ralston pointed at the tablet, and Gaillard perused the extensive list of predetermined transfer amounts and requests. The level of intricate planning impressed him; none of this had been conceived overnight.

"Min will assist us in establishing contacts in Asia and Africa. He has friends whose connections will prove valuable," Ralston remarked. His forced charm now focused on Min.

Gaillard remained silent for a prolonged moment, his gaze fixed on the two men. Finally, he crossed his arms and asked abruptly, "Do you trust him?"

"Trust Klaus? Absolutely," Ralston assured. "He may be impulsive and brash, but he won't jeopardize the plan." Ralston sipped water from his tall glass, continuing, "Besides, his role isn't pivotal in all of this. Austria merely serves as another tax haven, cheaper than hiring someone else to handle the tasks Klaus can undertake."

"What are the details of his estate?" Gaillard inquired, catching Ralston off guard. He wondered what Gaillard meant, and the answer arrived bluntly—Gaillard wanted Klaus eliminated. He was serious. Gaillard's trust in Klaus had been shattered; he had heard rumors of Klaus betraying him, an unforgivable offense.

"I can arrange it however you wish—or however Klaus wishes," Ralston replied. Gaillard instructed him to ensure Klaus's demise discreetly, preserving his assets and maintaining the illusion that Klaus was alive. "Who is the person who introduced you to those individuals inside Farragut Center?" Gaillard turned his attention to Min, his piercing gaze focused. Was Gaillard referring to Ezra? Min could think of no one else who fit the criteria. Ezra had helped Min establish valuable connections within the closely knit community. Some

The Collateral Dividend

individuals within Farragut Center, on the non-operational side, had discovered their illicit activities abroad. Min revealed that instead of exposing them, they managed to convince these individuals to aid Gaillard's cause.

Their hack of Farragut Center yielded minimal results, a mere handful of terabytes acquired swiftly. However, whistleblowers divulged a wealth of classified data, convinced that releasing it was the right course of action. This data would enable Gaillard to amass a fortune, aiding in both dismantling Farragut Center and profiting from the information.

They were on track. Gaillard proudly announced his intention to donate a sum exceeding one hundred million euros, diverting part of the laundered money in 10,000-pound increments to direct donations. "I want him," Gaillard declared, stating his desire for Ezra to act as the intermediary. Gaillard elaborated on his reasoning, emphasizing Ezra's background in the intelligence community and his proficiency in recruiting assets discreetly. Gaillard sought someone to assume Klaus's identity, possessing all the necessary qualities without succumbing to greed or pride. Professionals like Ezra knew how to maintain discretion. When well-compensated and provided with clear instructions, trust and subversion were non-issues—a quality Gaillard esteemed.

Min assured Gaillard that he would facilitate the introductions. The relationship served another purpose—to bridge the gap. Min held strong connections with Ezra, which Gaillard lacked and never intended to establish. This triangular relationship was fragile, and tracing the money and communication paths would prove challenging. That was precisely Gaillard's objective. He didn't want a linear path; the deliberate backtracking and inefficiencies were designed for his benefit.

THE CASCA TRUST

In Daniel's opinion, London's reputation as a rainy city was exaggerated. He remembered it rarely raining there, certainly not like the torrential downpours back home. Seattle was the real rainy city. The charter had arrived late, and with the help of the pilots, Daniel had transported Patel into the city. London served as the hub for Farragut Center in Europe. Paul had chosen a discreet property on the outskirts of the metropolitan area, nestled in a manufacturing district where nobody would pay much attention.

The storage facility, located near the Thames, was an unassuming one-story building with blacked-out windows and a garage door that appeared untouched. Inside, there was a small kitchen, two single beds, and a cramped living room occupying the front portion of the space. Past the bathroom door, a heavy steel door led to a long room. Faron carefully carried Patel into the middle of the room, placing him on the chair near the stainless-steel desk.

They searched through Patel's belongings and discovered another message: a note written on cardstock paper with a fountain pen. It read: 'uoill ades e mon chan, C'un sirventes prezan Vuoill far; mas him no.is cui Q'ieu ja cel avol brui, Q'anta e dans Mi par e volpillatges, Qand ja.is part bols lignatges Ni l'uns a l'autre faill.'

Daniel took more pills to ease his throbbing headache, applying pressure to his temples. He noticed the bruises along his shoulder and hands, feeling slight discomfort but no significant pain. The blood from his chest wound trickled down his arms, staining them red momentarily. Collapsing, he sat in the shower, questioning the morality of their actions. After enduring months of violence, he now faced a moral dilemma. He had used a suture kit from the kitchen to clean the wound on his chest, observing it in the mirror. The pain was absent, an eerie realization.

In the adjacent room, Daniel found a garden hose and filled a large plastic tank with three bags of ice from the freezer. He ensured the water was freezing cold, testing it with his hand. Turning on the sound dampeners, the room fell into silence. Placing a chair behind Patel, Daniel spent the next hour and a half on his phone until Patel regained consciousness.

Mark Patel jolted awake, feeling disoriented and trying to make sense of his surroundings. He found himself in a dimly lit room during the early hours of the morning, uncertain of the time. The throbbing vein in his temple echoed with each heartbeat. He struggled to stay alert, to think clearly and be aware of his surroundings, but his focus had already slipped away. Pain surged through his body, particularly in his sprained knee. Realizing the predicament he was in, he thought to himself, "You're a bloody idiot." His days of hacking government servers seemed to have caught up with him. Glancing at his hands, he discovered they were handcuffed to the chair.

Mark Patel didn't simply awaken; he jolted upright, feeling disoriented. He surveyed his surroundings, struggling to identify the objects in the dimly lit room. Was it morning, with the sun just rising, or was it evening? Time had become elusive to Patel. A throbbing vein in his temple pulsated with each heartbeat, hindering his attempts to remain alert and aware of his surroundings. His focus had already slipped away.

A surge of pain shot through his body, reminiscent of a rapid pulse, as he attempted to move his sprained knee. Patel berated himself, recognizing his own foolishness. It seemed he had been playing with a loaded gun rather than an empty one. This was his day of reckoning, he thought. They had finally caught up with him, those he had antagonized by hacking into government servers. He strained to examine his hands, only to discover them handcuffed to the chair between his legs, spread apart.

"Good morning, Mister Patel," Daniel finally spoke in a dry tone, rising to his feet and sauntering towards the seated man. "Welcome back home to London."

"If you think trying to scare me will serve any purpose, mate, you're mistaken," Patel called out, attempting to crane his neck for a better view of Daniel. "Don't you think my friends can find me here? You can't detain me without cause. I'm a British citizen."

"Oh, really?" Daniel retorted. "You're a terrorist."

"A terrorist?" Patel repeated, bursting into laughter. "I'm a libertarian. Do you believe in what they have you doing?" He glanced back at Daniel over his shoulder, a knowing smile playing on his lips. "You must be Daniel, no?" Patel's remark left Daniel silent, his heart gripped by a pang of unease. How did he know? "Oh, come now, you aren't the only ones who know how to use a bloody computer," Patel continued. "Did you not know? Cloak and Dagger is quite amusing. I wonder who came up with that." He paused, relishing the wide smile adorning his face. Patel had a knack for getting under others' skin.

Daniel felt an intense urge to deliver a powerful blow to the side of Patel's head. The hack had caused a breach of sensitive information, and the nerdy

Patel had undoubtedly witnessed more than he should have. It remained to be seen whom else he had shared the information with.

A buzz at the door signaled the release of the security lock, and a man entered, carrying a worn-out briefcase. Daniel struck Patel hard in the back of his head, causing Patel's long black hair, parted down the middle, to fall forward.

"Good morning," the interrogator said, shaking Daniel's hand. Neither bothered with introductions. He draped his coat on a nearby table, placing his briefcase beside it. "Has he said much of anything?"

Daniel shook his head, crossed his arms, and studied Patel, trying to decipher the enigmatic man.

The interrogator patted Daniel on the shoulder, indicating that he would take over. He walked towards the seat, pulled it from across the room, and positioned it in front of Patel. Seating himself, he laced his fingers and rested his hands on the table. "So, welcome home, Mark," the interrogator said, surprisingly calm, cool, and collected. He then swiftly retrieved a stack of files from the left corner of the table. "Listen, I don't expect you to be surprised by what we found on you. I'm sure there isn't much electronic data to be had."

"You're right. There isn't," Patel replied.

"Yes, well, electronic data isn't our primary interest these days," the interrogator stated. "In fact, you'll find an extensive collection of physical data that certain people were more than willing to provide us. For instance, the internet never mentions your daughter." The interrogator smiled, a sly expression on his face. "She's in Cannes, in case you were wondering." He looked down and handed Patel a photograph.

"How did you get this?" Patel asked, surprised. He hadn't seen his daughter in years since his wife had left.

"Mark, we aren't here to make things difficult. We all have our desires, and we are willing to share the details about your daughter if you provide us with what we need," the interrogator explained.

"You're blackmailing me," Patel retorted.

"Now, Mark, need I remind you that your wife and daughter left you? The court deemed you emotionally unstable and denied you visitation rights. How did that make you feel?" The interrogator knew he had found Patel's weak spot. Leaning in, he gave a thin smile, speaking softly as if sharing the latest gossip. "Now, I've heard that you are privy to some highly sensitive information," he announced, feigning fascination.

Patel remained coy. "And who told you that?"

"Mister Patel," the interrogator said with a smile, attempting to charm his way into Patel's psyche. "If we kissed and told, we wouldn't be able to maintain this excellent symbiotic relationship, would we?" He raised his hands apologetically. "So, are you willing to cooperate with us?"

Patel thrust his chin out, a mischievous smile gracing his face. The interrogator leaned in, his gaze fixed on Patel. "Go fuck yourself," Patel retorted.

The interrogator's grin flattened. "Well, you have two options. Listen carefully," he addressed Patel in a harsh tone, ensuring he had the man's full attention. "Either you cooperate with us, and I will offer you asylum in the United States. We may even resolve the legal dispute concerning your daughter. Or, we extract the information forcefully and leave you to the wilderness, where your employers will likely dispose of you. Take your time to think about it, and when I return, I expect your answer." The interrogator walked towards the door, leaving Patel alone in the room.

Seeking some rest, the interrogator set up a secure link to Washington. In the observation room, a television screen displayed a webcam image of Ted Hawthorne seated in his office chair, with Paul occasionally leaning in from behind.

Daniel and the interrogator remained silent, each occupied with their own thoughts. Daniel sat in the corner, twiddling his thumbs, while the interrogator picked up a hardcover book. After a brief moment, he inquired, "What are you reading, Daniel?"

Daniel closed the book and placed it on the desk. "Oh, nothing," he replied dismissively.

The interrogator glanced at the book, reading aloud its title, "Implications of Behavioral Modification for Cognitive and Neuroscience." He raised an eyebrow. "Are you a doctor?"

"What?" Daniel responded, caught off guard. He pointed at the book. "No," he replied, standing up. "Where were you coming from?"

"Hamburg," the interrogator answered wearily.

"How did it go?" Daniel inquired.

"Well," the interrogator sighed, "if we're being honest, it went downhill quickly." The aftermath of a botched operation carried an inherent sense of danger during an interrogation. The room buzzed with intense energy, often leading to mistakes. Daniel spent most of his time sitting in the back, his brow furrowed, fixating on the grain of the wood. An aura of isolation surrounded him, and it was evident that Daniel had recently become aware of this isolation.

Meanwhile, the relentless music kept Mark Patel awake. The interrogator finally turned it off and entered the room, sitting directly in front of the British programmer. Patel's head bobbed up and down, his eyes struggling to focus. Occasionally, his head would nod, only to be jolted back to awareness by the clanking of his handcuffs. The interrogator observed this cycle before leaning forward, snapping his fingers, and slapping Patel's cheek. "Mister Patel," he said firmly, "are you going to remain silent or make this easier on yourself?"

Patel squinted, attempting to rouse himself from his groggy state. He strained to focus his vision and shake off the remnants of sleep. Two burly men stood near the door, and upon a signal from the interrogator, they unlocked Patel's handcuffs and released him from the chair. Overpowering him, they led Patel toward a water tank that Daniel had set up earlier. One of the men held onto Patel's neck, keeping it steady. They dragged him to the edge of the tank and forcefully pushed his head into the water. Cold water rushed over Patel's face, robbing him of his breath. He wriggled in an attempt to rise to the surface, gasping for air, but one of the men used his body weight to pin Patel down. Struggling violently, Patel's thrashing body and the strain on the man's face added to the discomfort of everyone present. Daniel found himself torn between wanting to help the men and wanting to stop them.

Eventually, Patel could no longer hold his breath. The frigid water stung his face, and his chest felt ready to burst. Unable to contain it any longer, he released his breath in a flurry of bubbles. Just as he reached his breaking point, they pulled him out of the tank. Patel spat out water, fell to his knees, and lay exhausted on the floor. His face was cold, his fists clenched, and he fought to catch his breath.

The interrogator stood in front of Patel, squatting down to meet his gaze. "Mark, this won't be easy if you refuse to cooperate. Why don't you tell me about your work?"

Patel cleared his throat, rolling onto his side. "I haven't done anything wrong," he replied between breaths.

The interrogator walked over to the table and retrieved a folder and a photograph.

"You hacked into private government servers through a trust in Bermuda that owns your firm," the interrogator barked aggressively. "What can you tell me about the trust?"

"I know nothing," he replied, gritting his teeth as he aggressively inhaled through his nose. The interrogator signaled to the two men standing nearby. Patel crawled across the floor, and one of the men stomped hard on his hand.

The Collateral Dividend

Patel was then dragged up and forcefully plunged headlong into the tub of water.

Time seemed to stretch endlessly. Patel's sanity was slipping away as he lost count, fully aware of his grim fate. He wasn't prepared for what came next.

"This is becoming tedious, Mark," the interrogator shouted. "Tell me about the trust. Where is the money coming from? How did you breach the government servers?" Mark waved off the questions, his hands braced against the tank's frame as he stared into the water, struggling for breath. His black hair was soaked, obscuring his face.

"Six months ago, I was approached to create an offensive firewall," he finally confessed.

"By whom?" the interrogator inquired.

Patel shook his head. The interrogator took hold of Patel's arm, yanked him off the tub, and wrestled him to the ground. It was a brutal struggle, with Patel resisting and attempting to break free. Finally, he crashed hard onto his back, hitting his head on the floor, and blood began to flow. The interrogator straddled Patel, his gaze shifting to the men, instructing one of them to hand him the cloth from the side of the tank.

At the bottom of the tank, there was a large faucet that could be rapidly turned on and off, fully opened or closed. "Come and hold him down," the interrogator commanded, before moving around and placing the cloth over Mark's face. He twisted the faucet open. The noise reverberated, resembling the desperate struggle of someone drowning. Daniel wore a grimace, his expression soured. Mark Patel's head thrashed violently, his attempt to escape the icy water that felt like a slap on his face.

"Now, walk me through the firewall," the interrogator demanded.

"It was designed as an offensive measure," Mark replied.

"Explain, Mark. What do you mean by offensive?" the interrogator asked, reaching into his pocket. It was growing late into the night. He pulled out a power bar, unwrapped it, and offered a piece to Mark.

"The server contained built-in malware. The plan was that when someone tried to access the server, the malware would embed itself into their hardware," Mark revealed.

"And what does the malware do?" the interrogator inquired.

"It grants temporary access to your servers, access to everything," Mark explained.

The interrogator fed another piece of the power bar into Patel's mouth, the loud chewing filling the room. Patel had not eaten in nearly two days, and he

103

sighed with relief. The bar lacked flavor, but it provided nourishment. "What happened to that information?" the interrogator asked, aware that Patel had delivered it to a driver in Rome, intended for the account owner. Daniel suspected it would be used as collateral. The owner of the Trust was well aware that Farragut Center was pursuing them.

"You see, Mark, I find it hard to believe you have no idea who owns Casca," the interrogator leaned in, peering at Mark, his expression tinged with a faint smile. "Because you're not the kind of person who takes a job without researching the employer," he continued.

Mark shook his head, his movements limited. He felt as if he had swum a marathon.

Once again, the tub slid over Mark's face, and the cloth held him down as the water flowed over him. The sound of gurgling, drowning noises drowned out the interrogator's angry tirade.

The mask was removed from Mark Patel's face. "You know you'll pay for this in hell," he muttered.

"Who do you think you are, trying to be Kohlberg?" the interrogator asked, placing the towel over Mark's face and turning on the tap again. "Did you perform any other tasks for these people?" he asked. Patel nodded weakly, his energy fading.

"Tell me about it," the interrogator pressed.

Mark wore a dry expression. "Imer programs stock market terminals, right? They wanted something capable of disrupting the entire network, a built-in mechanism to halt trading and then authorize and execute artificial trades at predetermined levels. You following?" Mark spoke rapidly.

"What do you mean?" the interrogator inquired.

"Imagine you send an order to sell at five dollars, and then something forces the exchange to shut down. The software is designed to authorize your order at a different price, either taking the share itself or redistributing the difference. It all appears as a system error, and nobody suspects a thing," Mark explained.

"So, who bought it?" the interrogator asked.

Mark Patel laughed. "I don't know," he replied.

"But you do," the interrogator retorted with a sly smirk. He wanted Mark to reveal everything, to play the game of cat and mouse. It required the interrogator to ask the right questions at the right time, subtly extracting the information they needed. This task demanded finesse, patience, and an intuitive sense, but today the interrogator's instincts were failing him.

The Collateral Dividend

Mark Patel chuckled, clearly eager for another round of the game. "Of course, I bloody well looked into who wanted to hire me. I'm not careless," Mark teased. When the interrogator pressed for a name, Patel suggested it was only fair for them to sweeten the deal and provide some incentive.

"No," the interrogator replied, circling Patel and kneeling on the opposite side, leaning in close and speaking softly into Mark's ear. "You lost that privilege a long time ago, long before we wasted all this water on you."

"Philippe Gaillard," Mark uttered.

"The French billionaire?" the interrogator asked, slightly taken aback.

"Well, my friend, I don't know if he grew weary of his French Ligue 1 team, but he certainly possesses the ability to make things happen without lifting a finger," Mark stated.

"Do you know what he's planning?" the interrogator asked calmly, unapologetically.

Once again, Mark laughed, having caught his breath. He appeared more animated now. "Do you have any more of that power bar?" he inquired, and the interrogator allowed him to sit up in the chair, handing him the remaining bar. Mark chewed while speaking, admiring it in his slightly trembling hand. He then looked up at the interrogator with a deadpan expression. "He's not one to be embarrassed, you see. He's the kind of person whose emotional state can't be easily tampered with. China is less fragile than his ego, so to speak. He's after someone specific. Why request a program with such precise specifications? There are simpler ways to steal a few hundred million," Mark explained.

"It seems you've thought this through," the interrogator remarked.

Mark nodded, glancing down at the cable ties that restrained him. "Would you?" he asked, adopting a kindly tone. The interrogator wanted to see where Patel was going with this.

"Of course," the interrogator responded, instructing one of the men to cut Patel free. The man produced a switchblade, releasing the cable ties from Mark's ankles and then his wrists. Mark rubbed his sore, bruised joints and looked up at the towering man. He offered a warm smile. "Cheers," he said gratefully.

The large man stood beside the chair, bending forward to retrieve the broken cable ties from the floor. Initially, he dismissed it as a trivial matter, but then abruptly fell silent. He emitted a few garbled syllables, followed by incoherent groans that reflected pure bodily pain. Patel, seated in the chair, had a handgun in his possession, concealed on his inner shin. Acting swiftly, Patel seized the weapon and aimed it forward. With a clean shot to the lower jaw, the bullet pierced through the man's head, causing him to collapse before Mark, who struggled to rise to his feet due to his injured leg. Mark, now upright, directed his aim towards the second man positioned to his left. The gun discharged twice more, hitting the second man in the chest, resulting in a spurt of blood and a lifeless descent to the floor.

The initial gunshot had jolted Daniel to his feet, drawing his attention away from his reading in the corner of the living room. As he moved closer, his determined stride propelled him towards the door. In the meantime, Patel, limping across the room, brandished the gun towards the interrogator, firing two rounds. Sensing Daniel's approach, Patel fired another shot, aiming to intimidate him. Peering around the door, Daniel, with his gun held firmly, precisely calibrated his aim and squeezed the trigger. The recoil caused the gun to jerk, and the assailant crumpled to the ground.

Advancing cautiously, gun at the ready, Daniel surveyed the scene. Patel lay on his back, a bullet lodged in his neck, his head swaying from side to side as he gurgled on his own blood. Desperate, he sought the gun just out of reach. Daniel, responding decisively, pulled the trigger, causing Mark's head to recoil violently against the floor, ending his struggle. The room fell into an eerie silence, broken only by Daniel's gaze sweeping across the lifeless bodies. He then approached the lead interrogator, who had suffered gunshot wounds to the chest and arm. Kneeling down, Daniel pressed towels against the wounds to stem the bleeding. The interrogator's breathing grew labored, producing the unsettling sound of wet, raspy gasps. Daniel stared at the wounded man, who eventually reached out and clasped Daniel's hand. Contemplating the gesture for a while, Daniel lifted the interrogator's body from the ground and cradled it in his arms. The interrogator rested his head against Daniel's chest, finding solace as the pain began to ebb away. In that moment, Daniel recognized the profound human need for compassion, even in the face of grim circumstances. He held the interrogator, understanding that although everything wasn't currently alright, there was hope for eventual resolution.

Whispering his name, the dying interrogator revealed, "I'm Noah." Coughing up blood and shedding tears, he teetered on the brink of death, his face drained of color. Daniel replied with his own name, observing Noah's consciousness fade away as his head went limp, leaving no doubt that he had passed. Still cradling the lifeless body, Daniel needed time to comprehend the events that had unfolded. There was an odd intimacy in holding the dead, a connection to Noah that he hadn't experienced in a long while.

The Collateral Dividend

Late that night, a flight awaited Daniel's departure. He drove to the airport, watching the moon traverse the sky while he lingered outside the hangar. The stark contrast between the moon and the sky intensified his sense of solitude.

The following day, Daniel arrived at the office at his usual time. Paul greeted him as they met at the stairwell, offering him a diet coke and inquiring about his return home. Daniel nodded, recounting the comfort of a hot shower and a restless night spent reading Charles Sanders Peirce's writings in his living room. Curious about Paul's experience, Daniel posed the question, prompting Paul to mention that he had slept in for the first time in a while. Expressing a desire to discuss something, Daniel piqued Paul's curiosity.

In Paul's office, as Paul settled behind his desk, he gestured for Daniel to take a seat in the adjacent chair. Daniel conveyed his struggle with determining whether they were truly doing what was right. Paul swiftly assured him, emphasizing their righteousness and attempting to ascertain if Daniel questioned his own moral standing. Sensing the inadequacy of this line of inquiry, Paul adjusted his approach. Daniel's expression grew coarse, accompanied by a shake of his head. His gaze drifted toward the window across the street, and he responded dismissively, "No, I'm just not convinced we're doing what's right."

Paul took a deep breath, determined to reinforce their just cause. He held a pen in his hand, gesturing pointedly toward Daniel. "The heroes and villains can sometimes blur, but I assure you we're doing the right thing," he declared, though Daniel's discontent ran deeper, rendering him incapable of discerning the distinction between the two sides. To him, it seemed that uniforms were the only apparent difference. His dissatisfaction lingered.

Moving on, Paul handed Daniel a photograph, urging him to scrutinize it. The image portrayed Philippe Gaillard, a fair-skinned man with a hint of pink on his cheeks and a faint birthmark between his blonde eyebrows. Gaillard's long hair, parted to one side and swept over the opposite temple, gave him an eerie resemblance to a Nazi SS officer—a slender, ghostly figure emanating a stringent Aryan aura. Paul provided background information, explaining that Gaillard's father had established Gaillard Telecommunications in the 1960s, making it a significant player in the French market. Gaillard's telecommunication services catered to nearly six hundred million people worldwide, holding exclusive contracts with Singapore, Macau, Hong Kong, and expanding into Africa. What intrigued them the most was Gaillard's successful entry into the British market two years prior, securing over thirty percent control.

E.R. Wychwood

Seated with one leg crossed, Daniel delved into the documents, his curiosity piqued. "Educated?" he asked, to which Paul nodded, confirming Gaillard's extensive academic achievements. "He attended Insead for his MBA, pursued a master's and undergraduate degree in electrical engineering at SciencePo. Quite a formidable rival for your Princeton/Yale combination, wouldn't you say?" Daniel shrugged, seemingly unfazed.

A knock on the door interrupted their conversation, and Avery entered, taking a seat beside Daniel. She shared intriguing information about Waldemar, who was connected to the British telecommunications watchdog killing—a case that Daniel had handled in Amsterdam. This incident had occurred three months prior to Gaillard's entry into the British market.

"So, Waldemar and Lee had the same role—to eliminate an official within the regulatory body to facilitate Gaillard's market penetration," Daniel reasoned, struggling to believe the audacity of the situation.

"Exactly," affirmed Avery. She continued, poring over her notes, while Paul regarded Daniel with a determined gaze, holding a pen in his hand. "The ownership of the trust remains elusive," he stated firmly.

Daniel sarcastically responded, "So, we're acting on a hunch?"

"No," Paul asserted authoritatively. "Avery has gathered as much information as possible on Gaillard. He's our man, Daniel, and I need your support on this."

Daniel glanced at Avery, who handed him a file. Absorbed in its contents, he pondered the situation. "Casca is intriguing. Ownership is tied to bearer instruments, but limited corporate authority has been granted to specific individuals. Gaillard has close connections to all of them. Some may be insignificant, but targeting the big fish seems prudent," Avery explained.

Daniel contemplated the complexity of the task at hand. Gaillard was a multi-billion-dollar company, and Philippe Gaillard himself wouldn't casually roam the dark streets of Paris without protection. Paul inquired about the involvement of other companies in the situation.

Avery hesitated momentarily before responding, "We're uncertain about their exact role. However, Gaillard and these companies conduct extensive business with each other. They have access to the stock markets, but demanding the removal of their market terminals based on a hunch is not feasible. Approximately thirty percent of the active terminals in the world are affiliated with them. We lack the resources and manpower to ensure each terminal is clean." Avery paused, considering mentioning Mark Patel's hacking skills. Instead, she added, "Mark Patel was a skilled hacker, and although we couldn't

The Collateral Dividend

find much online about him, we discovered that his work for Gaillard was done on a freelance basis. Gaillard likely created a pathway for his involvement within the coding."

"What about Adam Stanley?" Daniel inquired, his memory tracing back to the origin of their investigation.

"There's no evidence of any encounter between Gaillard and Stanley," replied Avery. "I'll try to access the FCC's internal reports later today and see if there's any relevant information."

Daniel nodded, his thoughts swirling as he furrowed his brow. Avery affirmed his point, saying, "Absolutely."

"And Ralston?" Daniel pressed further.

"Even if he wanted to help us, he wouldn't be able to disable the trust permanently," Avery explained. "Besides, targeting him wouldn't lead us to Gaillard."

"I'll discuss it with Ted later to ensure it aligns with our policies and the politics on the hill," Daniel said, pausing for a moment. He scowled, a blank expression on his face.

Avery acknowledged his concern and proposed their plan. "In the meantime, Daniel, let me explain how this will work. Avery will establish connections between Gaillard and the market-tampering allegations. If the evidence is credible and Gaillard poses a lasting threat, we'll send you to take care of him."

Daniel then raised an important question about the breach in their servers. "Do we know the extent of the damage Patel caused?"

"We're handling it," assured Paul. "Leave it to us."

"Alright," Daniel said, standing at the doorway with his hands crossed comfortably in front of him. He looked at Paul expressionlessly. "Is there anything else you need from me?"

"No, but stick around the office, would you?" Paul requested as Daniel walked out of the room and down the hall.

Later that day, Avery returned to Paul's office after several hours of investigation. The setting sun cast an orange glow across the room as she entered with a smile. "We may have found something," she said, inviting Paul to the conference room where she had been working. The room was bathed in bright light, and digital information adorned the multi-touch surfaces of the walls and conference table. Paul felt overwhelmed, his mind racing to keep up with the visual deluge after a long day staring at a screen.

"Do you remember when we discussed Waldemar's involvement in the Ofcom murder?" Avery asked, trying to refresh Paul's memory.

Paul nodded, intrigued. "What am I looking at here, Avery?" he inquired, rolling up his sleeves and stepping closer to the table, his angular face revealing a hint of curiosity.

"These two murders are eerily similar," Avery explained. "Both disguised as muggings."

"So they're connected?" Paul questioned, sensing there was more.

"Absolutely," Avery confirmed. "When American Telecom went under, Gaillard tried to acquire their assets and commercial license through a hostile takeover."

Paul waited for additional details. "But?"

"But a British firm beat Gaillard to it," Avery continued. "They outbid him, and the board accepted their offer. The British firm then liquidated A-T's assets, causing the share value to plummet. Gaillard took a heavy loss."

"How significant was the loss?" Paul inquired.

"Enough for him to seek revenge," Avery replied.

Paul nodded, crossing his arms and thoughtfully covering his lip with his index finger. He examined the scattered pieces of information on the table. "What's your plan, Avery?" he asked, his mind slowly grasping the brilliance of the idea.

"Let's inform Whitehall and provide them with the evidence we've gathered," Paul suggested, eager to hand off the operation to someone else.

Paul nodded, crossing his arms and subtly covering his lip with his index finger. He paced around the table, meticulously examining the scattered pieces of information. "What the hell are you planning?" he asked, almost rhetorically. His gaze fixed on a photograph of the owners of the British firm, and he released a deep breath. "Let's contact Whitehall and provide them with our findings. It's best to let them handle Gaillard," Paul eagerly suggested, wanting to pass off the unconventional espionage work to someone else. It was a realm outside his preference.

"I disagree with you, Paul," she responded in a frank tone. "Handing this off would be detrimental. I don't believe their lives are directly threatened, especially the boys. Gaillard is more cunning than resorting to outright killings. He revels in inflicting legal damage, particularly in the financial realm. His satisfaction lies in crippling others within the bounds of the law," she explained.

Paul sought clarification, "What are you suggesting?"

"What I'm suggesting is that Patel had already realized this," she stated. "He wasn't a fool. Patel couldn't comprehend why Gaillard would need a program

The Collateral Dividend

specifically designed to target accounts. Neither could we, initially. But now we know that Gaillard intends to use it to exploit the vulnerabilities of those boys."

Confused, Paul asked, "What do you mean?"

"Nothing is more gratifying for a banker than to ruin their adversary and watch them struggle to handle the aftermath. Gaillard understands this well. He won't engage in blatantly illegal activities that can be undone in courts or markets," she explained.

"But don't the shares need to be available for Gaillard's program to work?" Paul questioned.

Avery gave a subtle smile, appreciating Paul's sharp mind. She found his obsession with work intriguing, wondering if it had affected his personal life. "Absolutely," Avery confirmed, glancing at the door as Daniel entered the room. She motioned towards the conference table, where a computer tab displayed a digital storage file. Avery opened the file and selected a document, pushing it across the table. Paul intercepted it, finding a photograph of a woman in her twenties—Isabel Yates.

Clearing her throat, Avery began, "This is Isabel Yates, the youngest member of the family. I believe she's of great interest to Gaillard and most susceptible to blackmail."

Daniel grunted and exchanged a bored look with Paul. "So we contact the authorities to ensure her safety?" he suggested.

Avery shook her head, "She has been in Zurich for almost three weeks, with no intention of returning home."

Curious, Paul inquired, "Why did they have a falling out?"

Avery suspected a betrayal had caused the rift. "The Yates family has a complex legal structure. Each of the three siblings holds a third of the corporation's shares, which encompass most of their assets. Normally, when control over these assets is sold, they must offer the shares to the other siblings before considering third-party buyers—unless bankruptcy is involved," Avery explained.

Paul sought further clarification, "How does bankruptcy affect it?"

Daniel interjected, "If someone goes insolvent, their assets are held on trust. Typically, the assets are liquidated to repay creditors, leading to a forced sale to the other siblings."

Avery added, "Additionally, there's a clause that triggers an automatic transfer of the shares to the other members for one pound."

111

E.R. Wychwood

"Essentially, they can transfer the shares for free," Avery confirmed. Paul furrowed his brows, his pen tapping against his lips. "So, what does this mean for us?" he asked.

'Six months ago, Gaillard acquired a £50 million debt from the Royal Bank, which the Brothers owed. It appears that they were already operating on a precarious financial footing, and when the markets dipped amidst the Brexit rumors, they fell into arrears. Unlike their sister, who had invested most of her wealth outside the business, the Brothers had injected a significant portion of their assets into their ventures. While they could potentially raise the required funds, such a substantial amount would put several of their companies at a severe economic disadvantage.'

"So you're telling me that a family with billions to their name can't scrape together £30 million to settle a bad debt, and now they're facing liquidation?" Paul questioned, a mix of disbelief and curiosity evident in his tone.

"Essentially," she replied. "They find themselves in dire financial straits. They lacked the necessary liquidity."

"Then, as long as Isabel assists, this shouldn't be a problem for the brothers. The trust could sell off a smaller subsidiary, resolving the issue," Paul suggested, awestruck by the vast disparity between the debt and the total value of the brothers' assets.

"That's the predicament," Avery explained. "All three siblings share a portion of that debt. When the Royal Bank faced debt-equity problems, they discharged a significant portion of their loans. The brothers were explicitly picked up by Gaillard, but someone else acquired Isabel's debt."

"Who?" Paul inquired.

Avery offered a fleeting smile. "Patrick Finley," she revealed.

"Groot Hoff," Paul recalled, referring to the bank Daniel had visited earlier in the year.

"After that, the debt seems to vanish," she added.

"How is that possible?" Paul queried further.

"They might have colluded," Daniel proposed, considering one possibility. "Or Gaillard might have struck a deal. Perhaps he waived the debt in exchange for a legal transfer of shares, subject to a condition precedent that the deal is finalized at Gaillard's discretion." He glanced at Paul, whose expression conveyed a mix of slow realization and sudden understanding. Avery, not being a lawyer by trade, sought clarification. Daniel tried again. "The shares cannot be transferred until Gaillard decides. If he takes the brothers to bankruptcy court, it would nullify the condition, allowing the assets to be transferred to Isabel, and Gaillard would seal the deal."

"Surely he can't be that brilliant, Daniel," Paul cautioned, skeptical of Gaillard's supposed brilliance.

Avery sided with Daniel, sensing Gaillard's hand in the deal. It was underhanded, convoluted, and above all, technically brilliant. "He's acquiring a multi-billion-pound business virtually for nothing," she remarked.

"Well, apart from a £60 million loss on the loan, plus whatever fees they pay," Paul added.

"Most importantly, he regains control of American Telecom," Avery confirmed. "That's why Isabel becomes a target of significant interest for both sides. If you're the brothers, you need her to help refinance and settle the debt under Gaillard's control. And if you're Gaillard – orchestrating this purchase deal with her – all he needs is a winding-up order to succeed."

"But surely such a deal wouldn't hold up in court," Paul pondered, still absorbed in the scenario Daniel had painted.

"Perhaps it could be challenged on grounds of undue influence, but even then, the most she would likely get is an equitable remedy. By that time, Gaillard would have made a fortune, and paying her off would be a minor inconvenience," Avery reasoned.

"Being willing to settle, even below market value, seems contrary to what we know about Gaillard so far," Paul pointed out.

"Paul," Daniel interrupted, "that's where I believe you're mistaken. This is primarily about control, not money. It's a matter of pride. Gaillard is fine as long as the Yates stay in the game, but he wants them to suffer and he desires American Telecom."

"Daniel is correct," Avery defended.

"So it would be wise for us to investigate further," Paul said, receiving a nod of agreement from Avery.

"I've discovered additional information regarding the companies under Casca," Avery shared. "Several shipping orders have been placed between Singapore and Athens in the past three months. These orders were financed by Casca's guaranteed banking debts. I bring this up because of the recent unrest in Greece that we discussed."

"Do we know what they've been shipping?" Paul inquired.

"No," Avery replied, shaking her head. "Although there is a shipment waiting to be transported at the port in Singapore."

"Where are they headed?" Paul probed.

113

E.R. Wychwood

"There are two destinations. One is Athens, and the other is a port along the coast of India."

"Let's shut down the entire operation," Paul asserted firmly, crossing his arms with a dry frown on his face.

Daniel leaned against the window frame, arms crossed, shaking his head. He pushed off the wall and approached the table. "I disagree," he abruptly stated, catching Paul's attention. "He knows who we are, and we're onto him. But he's toying with us. That means he's either overconfident or foolish, and either way, we need to exploit that. If we shut everything down, he'll realize we're closer than he thinks, and we'll only be left speculating about his plans. We'll lose him for good. I believe he underestimates our willingness to take him out in broad daylight. However, what's more valuable is maintaining our advantage through ignorance."

"What do you suggest, then?" Paul inquired.

"We should go after him asymmetrically. First, we disrupt his overt dealings with the Greeks, and then we clean up before targeting everyone involved with Casca," Daniel explained, gesturing as if envisioning people standing in a line. "We start with the girl. She's our way in. Then, we eliminate them one by one. Once Gaillard is isolated, we can expose him to the authorities."

Paul nodded. "That should give us some leverage in case they gather any counterintelligence."

"Exactly," Daniel agreed.

"And what if they go dark? What's our plan then?"

Daniel didn't have an immediate answer. "We bait them," he eventually replied after acknowledging the flaw in the plan. He proposed letting Gaillard steal the money, using it as a means to track and identify all those involved. It would require Avery to work on tracing the money as it left the markets, reaching out to her contacts in the intelligence community. Daniel acknowledged that a substantial amount of money would be lost, potentially affecting the economy, but he believed it was worth the risk.

Paul felt confident in their early agreement. He had been monitoring the two men who had met with Ralston in Canada for a while now, information he kept from Daniel. "Let's proceed with that," Paul said. "Avery, make sure to contact your associates at the NSA. I have a colleague running an intelligence collection program that might be useful."

Turning to Daniel, Paul asked, "What do you think?"

Daniel pouted, pondering the situation. "Pretty girl. Do we know why there was a falling out within the family?"

The Collateral Dividend

"You ever watched a documentary on the Kennedys?" Avery interjected with a relaxed tone, earning a sarcastic look from Daniel, being a Boston native who had undoubtedly seen them. "Something like that," she said, hands in her trouser pockets, her thin frame draped in a mauve-green cardigan.

"So, how do we earn her trust?" Daniel furrowed his eyebrows. "A girl burdened with so much baggage won't easily fall into the arms of any charming man."

"Oh, certainly not," Avery retorted, making a snide remark about Daniel's confidence in being the field agent. A mischievous grin hinted that she had a solution to the problem.

"I've prepared for a situation like this," Paul leaned forward in his chair. "We've spiked a cologne with pheromones that stimulate oxytocin, the hormone associated with bonding and social cues," his voice trailed off.

"—and orgasms, if my memory serves me correctly," Daniel interjected cheekily. Paul shot him a look.

"Just ensure you regulate yourself with the pills we'll provide. It'll keep your hormone levels in check and prevent blind trust issues," Paul continued, momentarily considering the potential effects of the spiked cologne in his own life before dismissing the thought. "This might prove useful," Paul said, burying his personal musings. "I want you to get close to her. Find out if she's involved, and if she is, take her down." Paul's arms were crossed, his tone matter-of-fact. It would only work if Daniel could follow instructions, manage his medication, and remain impartial. "Can you stay objective throughout this operation?" he asked, a legitimate concern.

Daniel nodded, questioning further about a cover story and rules of engagement. "I'll send the details to your package in Zurich and work on increasing your expenditure account balance. Use the charge card we provided you." Daniel then left to gather his belongings, ensuring his suitcase was stocked at the office for such occasions. The door closed, and Paul turned to Avery. "Let's reach out to some contacts in New York, set him up with a job, create a cover for him."

"Of course. What are you thinking?" Avery inquired.

"Let's list him as an analyst on the payroll of an investment firm, Cable Schwartz," Paul suggested, requesting a passport from Langley to be created with deliberate wear and tear. "He'll wear colored contacts, perhaps blue, for added distinctiveness. We'll modify the photographs and print the credentials. I want to provide him with some travel history, but an older passport without any stamps would raise suspicion. So, let's forge trips to Hong Kong, London,

115

Bermuda, and Guernsey. We'll also create a fake bank account, contact list, and wallet. We'll send all of this to Zurich and leave it at the designated drop location for him." Within moments, Daniel's entire life since law school had been meticulously reconstructed into a grandiose fictional narrative that seemed too extraordinary to be false.

"Have you had a chance to examine those poems?" Paul asked, and Avery looked up from the conference room table.

"Yes, actually," she replied, opening a tab on the multi-touch surface, waiting for the file to load. "They're troubadour songs."

"A what?" Paul questioned, realizing his initial assumption was misguided.

"Old Occitan lyrical poetry," Avery explained, having spent hours researching them. As they were written in Occitan, they needed to contact a literature professor at Warwick University in the UK.

"Like a sonnet?" Paul proposed, feeling somewhat foolish for the comparison.

"Sort of, not exactly," Avery replied, choosing not to correct him further. "The passages we've gathered are excerpts from different poems. The first one we intercepted, the text message sent to Lee's phone, was particularly intriguing. It's been refined better than gold in the burning fire, and those who listen to it understand it well." Avery looked up at Paul. "Any idea what that could mean?"

Paul furrowed his brow and shook his head, his mind consumed by the implications. "What about the others?" he inquired, pulling up the notes containing the messages Daniel had retrieved from the body in Amsterdam and another from Patel.

Avery glanced at the notes, then shifted her attention to the email chain exchanged between her and the professor in the UK. "Ah, this one is rather intriguing," she remarked, beginning to make sense of it after a second reading and closer examination. "We found this one on Patel, but when we consider it in the context of the one in Amsterdam, it starts to unveil a deeper meaning." Clearing her throat, she pointed her finger at the screen to follow along with the words. "I ask for, and my singing; because I want to compose a grand sirventes," she diverted from the text momentarily before continuing, "that's the type of poem this is. But let no man think that I conceal base dissension in my songs or elsewhere since I think it is a shame and harm and waste when there is somewhere a noble family whose members fail each other."

Arms crossed, Paul raised an eyebrow. "Alright, what does the second one say?"

The Collateral Dividend

"That's where it gets interesting. Just remember that last line," Avery replied. She looked up at Paul, her eyes filled with intrigue. "Justice doesn't admit that one should reject family in times of war. Still, his relatives do it. I believe he's trying to guide us. Considering what we know about Isabel, it seems as if he's using the text to refer to her."

Paul pondered for a moment. "How does it relate to the first text?"

"I don't know," Avery admitted, her voice trailing off. "Why would he be helping us?"

Paul shook his head, a hint of suspicion in his eyes. "He may be luring us," he reasoned. "It's best not to have Daniel engage with him. I fear Gaillard might be setting us up, waiting for Daniel to strike while the spotlight is on, exposing Farragut Center."

While Avery busied herself with finalizing voicemails and business cards, Paul attended to other operational matters. A satellite was deployed in high orbit solely for visual surveillance purposes. Paul had a habit of frequently checking the relay feed, often more than necessary. The advancements had reached a point where he could use his phone to monitor the relay periodically throughout the day, even in bed. The dull glow of the phone screen seemed out of place, yet its seamless integration into the mobile device made it enticingly convenient. Those close to Paul, aware of his actions, often overlooked his occasional inappropriate behavior.

The seemingly invisible alliance between Farragut Center and the tech giant known as The Valley was no coincidence. Paul's exceptional achievement was convincing them that, in exchange for unrestricted and free access to technology, Farragut Center would help them evade inconvenient American laws. The Valley provided the technology, allowing them to delve into client data without government restrictions, while Farragut Center gained access to The Valley's global consumer devices and assets network. It was a mutually beneficial arrangement, devoid of morality and legality, yet maintained with the tacit approval of government regulators as long as national security was preserved.

Perhaps these relationships catapulted Farragut Center into the clandestine epicenter of the American intelligence community. However, analysis presented its own set of challenges. With Avery overseeing the entire SIGNINT department, they heavily relied on filters and pre-digested data, making it quick but occasionally unreliable. Paul's greatest advantage stemmed from the symbiotic relationship he had forged, ensuring mutual success over the years.

E.R. Wychwood

"We've got them," a young man exclaimed from the doorway, prompting Paul to rise from his seat and join him.

Paul followed the man into a secondary office down the hall, taking a seat at the conference desk near a large computer screen. "What do we have?" he inquired.

"The assets are moving to intercept," the man informed, his arms crossed as he stood near the back of the room. "Thirty seconds." The screen focused on a section of shoreline along the Indian Ocean, several miles south of the Indian-Pakistani border. A boat docked with the word "Fréteous" emblazoned in white letters on its hull. Nearby, a group of vehicles had left trails of thick Arabian sand, forming a cloud of dirt. The dusty ripples spread like a blanket being drawn to cover the blue expanse of the sea.

"Confirm the target; do we have a green light?" The room filled with the sound relayed from the asset on the ground. A small photo of the operative speaking appeared on the screen, followed by a confirmation of his authority. The man glanced at Paul, waiting for confirmation, a hint of hesitation in his tone. "There are confirmed U.S. citizens on the ground, sir," he reported.

Paul nodded, his gaze fixed on the briefing packet. Fréteous had recently arrived from the Port of Singapore, carrying a shipment of arms. Paul's plan was straightforward: to ensure everyone was on the same page. Gaillard's funding of ultranationalists had to cease immediately, and they would coordinate and impersonate the CIA to achieve that objective.

Regarding Gaillard's financial dealings, Paul believed it was best to handle it similarly to their approach with Casca. Although the element of surprise had been lost, Paul wanted to maintain complete control. He felt that the only way to apprehend Gaillard and dismantle Casca was to allow Daniel to take the lead systematically. "Take them out," Paul commanded after a moment of contemplation. A small group of operatives hidden in the foliage flanked the sheer cliffs, opening fire and eliminating nearly all of the targets.

"Nice kill, keep shooting," one of the surveillance operators confirmed via telemetry. After the firefight subsided and the smoke dispersed, the assets emerged from the trees and descended the sandy slope towards the lifeless bodies. The kills were confirmed, and photographs were taken to document the operation.

Collateral damage had become an inherent part of their vocabulary. With the task complete, Paul nodded in satisfaction, patting the surveillance operator on the back. "Good work," he commended. "Wrap it up and arrange an extraction

The Collateral Dividend

plan. Don't hesitate to involve Langley. They know who to contact if they discover anything significant on that ship."

For a brief moment, the telemetry feed faltered. Suddenly, the overlaid display vanished, and the satellite's angle underwent a drastic shift. "Did you do that?" the surveillance operator questioned, glancing at his colleague, who shook his head. "Get the boss back in here. We've encountered a situation."

Paul swiftly returned to the room, his face displaying concern. He looked up at the screen, trying to comprehend the unfolding events. "Is it a drone malfunction?" he queried, attempting to assess the magnitude of the situation. "What the hell is that?" one of the operators exclaimed upon witnessing a white streak cutting across the telemetry, culminating in a dazzling burst of light near the ground operatives' location. The source seemed to originate from the adjacent cliff. "We're losing altitude on the drone," the operator stated, as the camera angle rapidly descended toward the ground. The pilots frantically attempted to regain control, resetting the systems, but their efforts proved futile. The drone crashed hard on the perimeter of the operating area, its camera and systems shorting out.

"What the hell just happened?" Paul demanded, his question met with silence. He pondered the likelihood of this being an accident, but the odds didn't seem favorable. His immediate course of action was to instruct the assets on the ground to recover the drone's data. However, before they could do so, they came under sudden and violent attack, leaving Paul and the CIA blind. The CIA scrambled a crewed aircraft to confirm their fears an hour later. The mission had failed, resulting in 100 casualties out of 100. Almost an hour after the local assets failed to be extracted, a memo arrived across the servers. Paul sought answers, but he knew the solution wouldn't come immediately. It was likely to take months before they made any progress. "I want this investigated," he declared to a group of employees gathered in his office. "I want to know the whereabouts of that drone and what happened to it. I want answers by the end of winter."

*　　*　　*

Sergei Kosygin had been toiling away for long hours, his sleep growing scarce. The relentless work had a way of dragging on, blurring days into months. He had always excelled with numbers, using it as a convenient cover for his true whereabouts during his time in Russia. The narrative woven around him portrayed him as a German national in Hong Kong, a disguise he had adopted in London, Hong Kong, and now Zurich, where he went by the name Yuri. The compliance officer at the Zurich office showed little interest, failing to question whether Sergei was under sanctions or of Russian origin.

In this realm of offshore finance, the line between onshore and offshore money blurred. Sergei reveled in the luxurious lifestyle, not merely for the wages it provided, but for the exhilarating pace it offered. The Zurich office, a satellite of the Manhattan firm, catered mostly to German and Swiss clients, focusing on trading fiduciary accounts and safeguarding investments. Although Sergei had been occupied with projecting future earnings for several average-sized accounts over the past four months, his work had garnered attention from the senior leadership in the team, opening doors for him. One such opportunity presented itself as an invitation to a charitable fundraiser held at the home of a managing director—an annual gala known to yield fruitful results for both the charity and the bank.

On the Monday before the party Sergei received a message from Gaillard. They agreed to meet on Wednesday night. Sergei thought Gaillard odd. He was eccentric and erratic. Sergei had given up asking questions or trying to understand why Gaillard did things.

While having dinner at a 24-hour diner near his apartment, Sergei felt a haze of intoxication envelop him as he absentmindedly played with his food, his mind adrift. Across the restaurant, Gaillard sat with a newspaper, his gaze fixed upon Sergei. It had been months since they last spoke, except for the occasion when Sergei was asked to poison a senior investment team member in Zurich. Slowly but surely, he had administered cholesterol pills to the unfortunate victim, until one day his heart could no longer withstand the strain, giving way to a fatal explosion within his chest.

Sergei glanced up from his plate, scanning the diner, until his eyes met Gaillard's. Recognizing the silent cue, Gaillard folded the newspaper, rose from his booth, and walked over to Sergei. "What do you want?" Sergei asked, his tone tinged with reluctance once Gaillard settled into the seat across from him.Gaillard mentioned hearing about the upcoming party, to which Sergei simply nodded. Gaillard continued, "It sounds like fun," again receiving a nod from Sergei, who buried his head in his neck as he continued to eat. Gaillard leaned in abruptly, placing his hand on the table and gripping Sergei's jaw, forcing him to meet his gaze. Gaillard wore a wide smile as he stated the obvious, "You're high."

"Listen, friend. I don't tell you how to live your life, so don't tell me how to live mine," Sergei retorted, his tone eccentric, his eyes wide and piercing.

The Collateral Dividend

Gaillard shook his head, reclining back in his seat, his gaze wandering into the distance. He handed Sergei the newspaper and cryptically uttered, "I need him dealt with."

Curiously, Sergei asked, "Why?"

Gaillard maintained a straight face, his jaw muscles rippling, as he took a deep breath. "Just deal with it," he said, abruptly standing up and leaving the diner. A black town car awaited him outside, and with Piere, his head of security, opening the back door, Gaillard got in. The winter air was heavy and damp as the car pulled away from the curb.

Gaillard picked up the telephone installed in the armrest, placing it to his ear. "Marie," he greeted, crossing his leg comfortably and observing the city through the tinted windows. "Any new developments?" he inquired, referring to his assistant who managed most of his business schedules.

"We're being told they have Patel," the woman on the other line responded hurriedly. Philippe remained silent, his chin held with pain evident in his eyes. His gaze followed the traffic. "And what of the information?" he asked calmly, his voice measured and courteous.

"He reached the courier before they reached him, but only just. It included access to Echelon security networks," Marie explained.

"Could you elaborate on that for me, Marie?" Gaillard requested, maintaining his calm demeanor. "We now have access to the American security network and have identified who's chasing us," Marie confirmed. She expressed confidence in remaining ahead of Farragut Center and outlined her plan to do so. Gaillard, after pondering for a moment, responded, "I'd like to be more aggressive than that. I want to lure them. They tried to kill me, and I won't let their manipulation go unpunished. When they come after this drone, I want them to face the harshest enemy. Let me think about how we'll hide this information and get back to you. We need to be careful not to leave a trace."

"Of course. We have friends holding onto the drone. I'm sure they would welcome the media attention," Marie noted. "Part of the list includes some rather dangerous people. A few of them are closing in."

"Why don't we set them up to fail?" Gaillard suggested, maintaining an oddly calm demeanor. He focused on maintaining consistent breathing. When he finally mustered the strength to speak, he had fully contemplated the information. "Perhaps we send another gift," he proposed.

"Tzavaras would like to speak with you as well. We lost a shipment in the port of India," Marie informed Gaillard.

121

E.R. Wychwood

Gaillard had already seen the email. There was a bottle of water on the car's armrest, and he unscrewed the lid, holding it to his lips as he propped the phone between his neck and shoulder. He took a sip, keeping the water in his mouth for a moment before swallowing two tablets. Placing the water back down, he inquired, "Can he talk now?" Marie assured him she would patch him through.

"Monsieur Tzavaras, I just heard the news," Gaillard greeted when the line clicked on. "I can assure you that this is only a minor hiccup. You and your party retain the full support of our media capabilities." Gaillard actively modified search engines to suppress the atrocities committed by Tzavaras. The man on the other line hesitated, stating that more needed to be done. Gaillard seized the opportunity, his small beady eyes gleaming as he waited for Tzavaras to finish his rant. "I'll tell you what, Alekos. I have an opportunity for you, so listen carefully," Gaillard said, rolling up the glass divider between the front and back of the vehicle. As the divider sealed shut, the car fell into silence.

Sergei Kroysgin met a few co-workers at a local tavern down the street. They had dinner and consumed copious amounts of drinks before heading to the party. In the bathroom stall, Sergei did a rail of cocaine to counter the overwhelming adrenaline and trauma. It was during this moment that he reviewed his calculated plans. Among the attendees was a Saudi Prince, whom Kroysgin knew well. Both Gaillard's reasoning and Kroysgin's relationship with the Prince remained clouded. Neither of them was willing to readily admit the truth. Thus, it fell to Sergei to kill the Prince, discreetly.

By the time the group arrived, in a buzzed stupor, the party was already in full swing. Gaillard had already made his way around the party once and was savoring his second glass of wine when he noticed the visibly intoxicated Sergei stumbling into the main room. Their eyes briefly locked, and Gaillard could tell that Sergei had been heavily drinking. Sergei settled comfortably in one of the busier rooms adjacent to a grand piano, within earshot of the Saudi Prince. He sat there, sipping wine, patiently waiting for the Prince to enter the room, while positioning himself near the washrooms. Sergei finished his drink, placed the glass on the piano, stood up, and crossed the room. An autoinjector rested in the outer pocket of his coat, and he walked toward the washrooms, feigning drunken stumbling. Both Sergei and the Prince exchanged a long, uncomfortable gaze.

Gaillard sat across the room, watching this interaction with a passive expression that made him appear dull or fatigued. Gaillard couldn't quite discern the emotion, but during their subsequent discussion at the hotel, Andre asserted with conviction that they were in love. He speculated that Kroysgin was the

The Collateral Dividend

Prince's lover, and anyone observant enough could see it. Gaillard wasn't entirely convinced but pondered the possibility. He knew there were several things Kroysgin had kept hidden from his father and family, making one wonder if that was one of them.

Kroysgin stood just a yard away, pen cap removed, autoinjector loaded. He accidentally collided with a group of people just before reaching the Prince, using the collision as a distraction to swiftly inject the Prince. The needle's sharp pain merged seamlessly with the chaos, unnoticed by the Prince, who was too preoccupied with Kroysgin's drunken antics.

The drug took effect slowly, with the first hints of nausea arising over the course of ten minutes. The Prince's breathing grew heavy, and as he staggered toward the piano near where Sergei had been seated, he steadied himself against the solid wooden frame. Attempting to clear his throat, he locked eyes with Sergei one last time. Fear vanished from his face as blood drained away, and he collapsed onto the piano, causing the wood legs to crack as the instrument crashed down with a cacophony of sound. Lifeless and breathless, he lay on the ground. A collective gasp filled the room.

Sergei remained shocked by his own actions, sitting motionless for a while, gazing at the collapsed body. He allowed himself to be carried by the shifting crowd, bypassing the onlookers. The party soon spilled out onto the street, and Sergei slipped into an adjacent alleyway. He walked until he reached an unfamiliar road, where he found a bench and took a seat, staring at the ground. He had been crying for about ten minutes before he realized what he was doing.

He found himself far north, along a canal of the Sihl River that narrowed through the downtown core and emptied into Zurich Lake. Zurich always struck him as a peculiar city. It emanated a cold and structured aura. The Swiss architecture displayed great beauty, with classicist and baroque buildings seamlessly blending in the wealthy districts of Zurich. Yet, in winter, there was an unmistakable lack of greenery. The city felt lifeless and grey.

THE ECHELON PACKAGE

Daniel Faron arrived in Zurich that week, early in the morning. It had been nearly six months since they began tracking Lee on that cold spring night in Washington. Now, winter had set in, bringing bitter cold to Europe. Espionage was a slow and cumbersome process, but after months of investigation, Farragut Center was ready for its final move against Gaillard.

The flight had arrived ahead of schedule, so Daniel waited around until he received a locker number in the S-bhan terminal beneath the airport. His headaches had been getting worse, gradually crippling him. The faces of the team members played out before his eyes, almost as if they were physical objects in the room. He couldn't push those images out of his mind. Seeking relief, he found a fountain, drank some water, and tried to clear his head. He felt like he was losing control.

The bag he carried was heavier than expected, but he managed to lug it onto the train and then took the subway south to downtown. Zurich appeared dark and dreary. When he had left the airport, it was still before dawn, and the city by the lake lay dormant in the cold slumber of winter.

In his new line of work, Daniel had occasionally found solace in his accommodations. Isabel, with her extraordinary wealth, had made it necessary for Daniel to play the part. He disliked the idea of staying in a foreign and unkempt room, but fortunately, that wouldn't be the case today. In less democratic countries, he had spent nights sleeping in ditches.

The hotel stood as a grand square building with an impressive stone facade, its tall narrow windows exuding elegance. Daniel had visited Zurich once as a child, but they hadn't stayed at this particular hotel.

Exhausted, Daniel collapsed onto the duvet-covered bed and closed his eyes. Deep circles marked the fatigue beneath his eyes, and weariness consumed his body. He managed to sleep for an hour before waking up drenched in cold sweat at a quarter to eight. Sitting up, he stared at the cream-colored wall across from the bed. His gaze shifted to the duffle bag resting on the hotel room floor. It contained new identification cards, a passport, date of birth, home address, and profession. Daniel was being handed a new life.

He pondered this new persona. While he remained cautious, most of his information stayed the same. The most exhausting part was the tremendous amount of time required. The person whose passport he held looked like

The Collateral Dividend

Daniel, but he was not Daniel. He was a fictional character, an idea. Yet, Daniel had to become him. He had to think like him, act like him, even sleep like him. Patience wore thin with this endeavor. Eventually, many of the creative mannerisms Daniel adopted became permanent traits.

"Our friend is in town," Paul informed him later that morning. He shared details about Ralston, who was in Zurich for work. "He's meeting a client at a nearby restaurant. The client has ties to Casca, so we hope it might provide more information about the trust."

"Do you know where?" Daniel asked, and Paul sent him the information. "I'll call you back," he said before getting dressed. He put on a navy blue single-breasted suit and descended the stairwell to the lobby.

The restaurant exuded luxury. Daniel could filter out the background noise and focus on the peculiar individuals in the bustling dining hall. Ralston sat across the room, his napkin resting on his lap as he buttered a loaf of bread. Accompanying him was an Asian man whom Daniel didn't recognize from any briefings or files. A third person, a young blonde German boy, sat with them.

Daniel began his evening with a generous pour of scotch, kick-starting the night. As he sat there, nibbling on bread, the three men engaged in conversation. Ralston was known for his cautious choice of words, while the young German boy appeared less guarded, piquing Daniel's interest for future interactions.

"So, how's Sirventes?" inquired the Asian man, assuming Sirventes referred to someone specific.

"Bitter as always," replied Ralston with an eccentric tone. "He's curious about the shipments. I mentioned that you were working on greasing the wheels with a customs officer."

The Asian man nodded, a gesture unnoticed by Daniel. "I've heard Sirventes is working on creating an opening. Once that's accomplished, everything will fall into place."

Before Min could discuss his work further, Ralston was interrupted by a raised hand. "No," Min interjected confidently, cutting Ralston off. "I don't believe we need to. It's under control," he added. "If Gaillard has an issue with it, he can approach me directly." A prolonged silence followed, and the men redirected their attention to their food.

"Well, that's certainly one way to put it," Ralston remarked after allowing a few moments of silence to ease the tension. "Klaus, I'll need your authorization for several transfers later this month. Sirventes has a few tasks he wants completed before the big show next winter."

E.R. Wychwood

Leaning forward, Klaus grumbled, "He never stops with this nonsense. First, he wanted me to hold onto that information stolen from the Americans, and now he wants it sent to Min. Sirventes seems disoriented, Christopher. He doesn't know which way is up anymore."

"Sirventes took you under his wing, boy. Without him, you'd have squandered your parents' wealth. So stop behaving like a child," Ralston scolded sternly. "I've learned not to question these matters. Sirventes possesses intricate knowledge, and more often than not, that knowledge alters the situation."

"He's ill, you know. Everyone suspects it. His mind is slipping," Klaus declared, slapping Min's arm and seeking confirmation from the Asian man. Min, however, continued eating, paying no attention to the exchange.

"I assure you, he's fine. He knows precisely what he's doing," Min reassured, ending the discussion.

Shortly after finishing their meal, the group dispersed. Two men headed to the washroom while Ralston went upstairs to take a nap. Ralston's excessive eating and subsequent slumber only amplified his rotund figure. Daniel took advantage of the moment and discreetly planted a button-shaped tracking device in Klaus's winter coat, patiently waiting for him to leave.

As Daniel washed his hands, Min emerged from a bathroom stall. Their eyes met in the mirror, and Daniel offered a polite smile. He handed Min a washcloth for drying his hands. "Have you ever seen 'Rebel Without a Cause'?" Min asked unexpectedly.

"Once or twice," Daniel replied, slightly taken aback.

"It's one of my favorite movies. So quintessentially American—reckless yet concise. I'm not sure if anyone has told you this before, but you bear a striking resemblance to James Dean," Min remarked.

Daniel chuckled, saying, "Oh, really? No, I've never been told that."

"It's a wonderful hotel, isn't it?" Min remarked, seeking Daniel's agreement. Daniel nodded, adding, "Just traveling. How about you?" Daniel now focused directly on Min, a sense of unease settling over him. Min's penetrating gaze seemed to pierce through him, as if he could see Daniel's corroded and burdened soul lingering on the edges of his eyes.

"Business," Min eventually replied, scrutinizing Daniel's face intently. He had seen it before, not in the movies, and now it was etched in his memory.

Feeling his heart pound in his chest, Daniel approached the bar and signaled the bartender. "Three doubles of Lagavulin 25 on the rocks," he ordered, a sour taste lingering in his mouth. The room spun around him. Taking out a small case, he poured two pills onto the bar counter. His drink arrived, and he swirled the amber liquid, contemplating it.

*   *   *

"Are you drunk?" Paul asked when he called later that afternoon.

"No," Daniel lied, his gaze fixed on the snowfall outside. The bitter winter night imbued the air with a cold, stale feeling. The city transformed into a winter wonderland, with colorful shingles in every imaginable pastel extending as far as the eye could see, disappearing behind the foothills.

Daniel recounted the details of the dinner to Paul. After Daniel finished speaking, Paul responded with a pensive "hmm." "Do you think Min knew who you were?" he asked.

"I don't think he would forget me," Daniel replied.

"That may cause issues," Paul voiced his concern. "Well, nothing we can do about it now. I'll start looking into the other character—the German."

"What about Sirventes?" Daniel inquired.

Paul was already well-informed on the matter. Sirventes was linked to the person behind Casca, and Gaillard remained his strongest suspect. "That too. Check on Isabel, and do try to maintain some sobriety, would you? I don't think she'd be too receptive to someone who reeks of a Scottish bar."

"Is that all?" Daniel asked.

"Unless you have anything else," Paul suggested, prompting Daniel to remain silent. "We'll speak later then," he concluded, ending the call.

'So I've been digging on Gaillard,' Avery said, standing at Paul's office door. She held a briefing paper in a file folder and handed it to Paul as she entered the room.

Paul raised his index finger, and Avery fell silent. A yellow light on his desk blinked, and he pressed the button. 'Ted.'

'I'm just about to head to the hill,' Ted responded.

'Got a minute?' Paul asked, and Ted told him to come down the hall. 'You can tell him instead,' Paul said to Avery, and he walked with her down the aisle. They entered the office, and Paul introduced her to Ted. 'She's the best,' he said almost dismissively.

'Avery, it's a pleasure,' Ted said with a full smile. He paused, then asked, 'Now I'm just about to go and brief the D-N-I. Is there anything that I should be aware of?'

E.R. *Wychwood*

Avery had a few things, but she decided to start with Gaillard. 'He's taking drugs, and lots of them. I haven't been able to determine why, but they don't seem recreational.'

'Medicated?' Ted questioned.

'Possibly. If we continue our investigation, we may be able to find some answers.'

'Can we set up an Echelon package to keep tabs on him?' Ted asked politely.

Avery gave a thin smile and shook her head. 'He's terrific at scrubbing his devices. They've become very effective at blocking tracking signals. He's essentially digitally invisible to us.'

'We suspect he's trying to cover his losses,' Paul interjected. 'He pledged a cool hundred million to a French housing charity a year ago, and I suspect he'd like to save face and not back out of the promise.'

'So this is pride motivated,' Ted observed.

'Mostly,' Avery replied, and Ted seemed to scoff. 'Gaillard is quite active with the Greek ultranationalists as well.'

'Really?' Ted was intrigued. 'Why is this the first time I'm hearing about Greek ultranationalists?'

'Separatist ultranationalists, actually. They've only recently started to gain ground – nothing worth noting just yet – but certainly on our radar,' Paul explained. He felt it necessary to interject and defend his judgment in not informing Ted earlier.

'What's the sense in supporting that?'

Avery shrugged. 'It's not explicit. It comes from the Casca account. Fréteous is under investigation for illegal arms smuggling. Rumor has it they were involved in runs to Libya during the civil war,' Avery said, glancing over at Paul, who subtly shook his head to indicate that Ted did not know about the lost drone. 'But that's not our primary concern. I think a bigger issue is whether or not Patel was lying. Suppose Gaillard possesses malware that tricks the markets into diverting equity wherever he chooses. In that case, we could be facing a serious economic attack. However, it's still unknown where or how he plans to execute it.'

'Then there's the question about the poems,' Paul added, and Ted grunted. 'He's playing with us, Ted. He knows exactly who we are and what we're trying to do.'

Ted let out a deep breath. 'So what am I telling the D-N-I? That we have a potentially psychotic billionaire looking to get back at some kids who angered him?'

The Collateral Dividend

Paul shook his head. 'That's only half true. Gaillard is a passionate man, driven by pride in his actions. He may not act within the confines of the law, but seeking revenge will be legal for him. You must convey the delicacy of the situation and outline why we are pursuing him. He knows how to reach us, Ted. If we let him roam without consequences, we could end up on the front page of the Times.'

By the time Ted left the office, he was already running late for a meeting less than a mile away. Paul and Avery returned to one of the conference rooms down the sunny hallway. They turned off the lights, closed the blinds, and sat in the room's darkness.

There was a peculiar approach to this task that was both absurd and necessary. The unfortunate reality was that Paul needed Daniel to get close to someone who was incredibly guarded and cautious. To both men, it was a game, a puzzle that needed solving. As shrewd as it was, the game was their livelihood, and it had one rule: one could actively manipulate and utilize others' emotions but must never be caught having emotions of their own. Paul didn't have time for the inherent danger of emotions. As he once put it bluntly, emotions altered logic, hindering rational choices. It was detrimental to business.

Daniel had checked into the hotel early and had spoken with the concierge about the local nightlife. After unpacking his things, he had dinner alone around seven. He then discussed the next steps with Paul.

'Isabel is staying with a friend,' Daniel said. When he inquired about how to initiate contact, Paul proposed an idea. He had friends at Whitehall who had done some digging as a favor. Coincidentally, the friend Isabel was staying with had recently worked for MI6 in Germany. 'Her name is Catharine,' Paul said. Daniel switched to speakerphone and watched the video feed on his phone. 'She helped MI6 establish a connection with Klaus, a German contact of Gaillard's. Not much came of it, but she played a significant role.'

'How does she have the connection?' Daniel asked, not wanting to be introduced to someone who didn't have a good rapport.

'They are old family friends. We don't know much beyond that, but they've maintained consistent contact over the last decade,' Paul explained. They had convinced Catherine to host a party, which she described as an intimate gathering. However, she seemed to envision an extravagant party with suits, dresses, and free-flowing liquor. 'There's something intimate about large parties,' she had told Paul, recognizing it as a line from "The Great Gatsby."

Paul managed to coordinate Daniel's invitation, eliminating the initial barrier of conversing with a stranger. Now, it was up to Daniel.

129

E.R. Wychwood

The ball started rolling around nine when Isabel arrived, providing an opportunity for Catherine to mention that she should meet one of the other young guests from New York.

It was approximately ten when Daniel arrived at the apartment. Catherine greeted him at the door, and they exchanged kisses on the cheek. After swiftly scanning his surroundings, Daniel followed her into the main living area. The apartment spanned multiple floors, with a grand, two-story living room that opened to a balcony, offering a breathtaking view of the Swiss Alps.

Daniel poured himself a scotch and followed Catherine up the stairwell to an open space overlooking the living room. Catherine leaned elegantly against the railing, took a glass of chardonnay from the nearest tray, and waited until Daniel stood close to her. She enjoyed the feeling of being flirted with, and Daniel played along. Catherine placed her hand on her hip, wearing a long, gold-sparkling gown that accentuated her slender figure. She posed, leaning across the railing and observing the conversing crowd below. 'She's over by the piano,' she said, gesturing with her glass. 'Shall I introduce you two now?' Her curiosity about the reason for their meeting slowly gnawed at her. At one point, Catherine asked Daniel directly why they needed to meet, but he only smirked and remained silent. 'We'll go over there in a minute,' Catherine said, sipping her drink and observing the room as if overseeing a drunken herd of sheep.

Daniel took another sweeping glance around the room. He immediately recognized Isabel from afar. Although he had seen numerous photos of her, there was a brief moment of unfamiliarity. She had light blonde hair with a hint of strawberry, usually styled either pushed entirely to one side or parted neatly down the middle. Today it was down the middle. Her distinctive eyebrows reminded him of a young Brooke Shields or Jennifer Connelly.

Isabel wore a bored expression and a forced smile, but underneath it all, there was still a genuine smile. For some reason, Daniel found it incredibly attractive.

Catherine glided into the living room, exuding an air of elegance. Isabel, on the other hand, sported a romper that reminded Daniel of something Churchill might have worn during the war. He mentally noted that he could use that joke later. A nearby door led to the balcony, and Catherine playfully took Isabel by the waist, inquiring about her enjoyment of the night. "You're no fun anymore," she teased, reminiscing about the riots they had orchestrated in their younger years. College at St. Andrews had been a blast, but those days were long gone. It was time for them to grow up, or at least for one of them.

The Collateral Dividend

Catherine promptly introduced Daniel, leaning in to whisper a series of side remarks. Daniel had been a friend of Catherine's father's family and had graciously hosted Catherine during her visit to New York a few years ago. He was quite the character. Did Daniel recall that memorable night at the Club Piano? What a blast it had been. Daniel played along, now drinking at a quicker pace to calm his nerves. While he had been gazing at the night sky, the vibrant square of yellow light emanating from the skyline seemed to morph into unfamiliar shapes. He tried to refocus, offering a polite smile and summoning enough charm to sustain a steady conversation. Truth be told, he wasn't in the mood for this right now.

After the obligatory introductions, Isabel inquired, "What brings you here?" Daniel, attempting to echo her sentiment, replied, "Well, large parties aren't exactly my cup of tea either. But it beats sitting alone in a dimly lit bar, drowning my sorrows." His dry tone elicited a laugh from Isabel.

"Feeling pathetic, are we?" she bantered. If only she knew, Daniel thought. He seemed like a good sport, and there was something thoughtful about his demeanor. It was as if he had borrowed James Dean's looks, with a touch of harshness in his face. Occasionally, a glimpse of what Isabel believed to be the soul of a good man would flash before her, only to vanish, replaced by a distant glaze in his eyes.

"Are you here on vacation?" he asked, putting on a show that seemed to be working.

"Sort of," she replied sheepishly, a hint of embarrassment on her face. "I needed a break from the busyness of life." Daniel couldn't agree more.

Eventually, their conversation shifted to another couple engaged in a heated discussion across the room. "What do you think they're talking about?" Daniel playfully inquired, leaning forward to match her height.

Isabel, an avid people-watcher, observed, "Probably the fact that he was just caught eyeing that girl over there," gesturing toward another woman nearby. "Although I have an unfair advantage," she continued, "I know both of them. They're horrible arguers. It's pretty much all they do, that and have sex." A faint smile crossed Daniel's face. Isabel's tone of voice had a pleasant and soothing quality to it, making almost anything she said sound delightful and warm. Perhaps some of that was due to her elusive British charm. "You know, I studied psychology at university," she mentioned. "You'd be surprised at what you can learn about someone just by observing them."

"Is that so?" Daniel chuckled. "What's my story?" He took a sip of scotch, grinning.

E.R. *Wychwood*

Isabel's gaze momentarily dropped, and she looked into the distance. "Well, that's not fair. I already know you," she retorted.

"Barely, really," Daniel replied. "Or did they teach you mind-reading in your classes?" It was a feeble comment, but it made her laugh. Perhaps it was the wine.

"No, I'd probably hurt your feelings. You might find out for the first time that you're not funny," she quipped, followed by a laugh. Daniel appreciated her sharp wit and quick thinking, which added a touch of wicked timing to their exchange. "Well, you work too much and drink a lot," she observed, gesturing towards his glass of scotch. Daniel could sense that it wasn't a vice she wholeheartedly endorsed. So, he assured her that he rarely drank, setting down the glass and making a conscious effort not to touch it again. "Other than that, I don't know, you're very hard to read," she remarked. "Not that I'm any good at it. I half expected the course to teach us how to sit in big armchairs, but most of it was just partying."

"I used to create stories about people while watching them at the train station with my sister," Daniel shared. He knew that the only way to broach the topic of family was to bring up his own, even though it brought forth memories he would rather have kept buried. A wave of stress washed over him.

"You have a sister? Is she older?" Isabel inquired.

"Yes, she's older. I also have a brother, but I was always closest to her," Daniel shrugged, unsure of the exact reason. "Maybe it was the circumstances. We're close in age, and she was like a mother in some ways. We would help each other break curfew when we were in school," he chuckled.

"I have two brothers. They're twins," Isabel mentioned, her eyes scanning the room. She rocked back and forth on the balls of her feet. "They can be real jerks." Daniel nearly spit out his drink. "But we did have fun during ski season, which is partially why I'm here." Daniel hadn't seen his siblings in years, and he hadn't even spoken to his brother in nearly three years.

"Do you miss them?" Isabel asked.

"Well, of course," he replied, his voice trailing off. "Nothing in particular happened; it's just... it isn't feasible anymore. We've grown so different, and you know how work is," he said, with a tinge of regret.

"Nothing's ever feasible unless you make it that way," Isabel commented, always the opportunist. "I think a lot of my friction with my brothers comes from work. There's more to life than just work."

Daniel let out a sigh. He didn't like to think that he was at fault, but deep down, he knew he probably was. He considered reaching out to one of them,

The Collateral Dividend

although contacting Henry had become increasingly difficult these days. "So, two brothers. Jerks," Isabel laughed. "The biggest jerks," she emphasized. "Please tell me you're not a finance lad in a Patagonia vest who rowed crew." Daniel winced. "Distressed debt. I don't have a vest, but I did row crew at Yale." Isabel took the wine glass, dramatically placing it on the coffee table. "Well, nice to meet you," she said, mimicking the actions of preparing to leave. "That's all I've got. Screw me, then, I guess." Daniel lightly touched her arm, signaling for her to stay. Once she achieved the desired reaction, she picked up the wine glass and took a big gulp, surveying the party. It was reaching its peak—a roaring bash.

"I have two brothers who excelled at everything. My dad was quite the influence on all of us. He emphasized the importance of family, but it was very much his way or the highway. So..." she gestured to the room, indicating the difficulty. "But I do love them," Isabel said. "We're all very close. There aren't many secrets between us," she added, the statement seeming somewhat hypocritical to what she had said earlier. It appeared that she had a complex family dynamic and harbored some resentment towards it.

The ebb and flow of the room's sound reverberated, causing both of them to be mindful of their volume. "Do you want to get out of here for a little bit? Maybe grab something to eat?" Daniel asked, almost two hours later, as it became evident that neither of them enjoyed the party.

"I'd like that," Isabel replied, smiling. She suggested a place down the street that was still open. The brisk walk would sober them up a bit. The Swiss winter winds were harsh but bearable, making the walk enjoyable. When they were seated at the restaurant, Daniel declined to order another drink. He asked Isabel if there was anything she wanted, but she politely declined. She was never much of a drinker. It was at that moment that Daniel interrupted their conversation.

"I'm going to get some oysters. Will you join me?" he asked.

Isabel examined him for a moment, checking if he was serious. "You're very slick, you know," she teased.

"I'm really not," Daniel said sheepishly. "You never gave me your assessment."

"Obviously, you're a bit of a twat banker who raids businesses and went to Yale like Daddy wanted. And you're going to charm me tonight and disappear onto some dating app by noon tomorrow," she said, playfully bantering. She didn't mean it, but the mention of her father hit Daniel hard. He struggled to swallow it. "Obviously," Daniel replied sarcastically. "I'm actually here for a while, and I'm not really into short flings. They feel awful."

"I agree," Isabel concurred. "So, what vibe do I give off? How would you read me? What do you see?" She leaned her arm on the table, resting her chin on her palm, and adjusted her position so that when she smiled and looked down at the table, her mouth rested against her wrist.

"A beautiful girl," Daniel said frankly, his tone calm, catching Isabel off guard. He leaned in closer. "Alright. You went to Cheltenham or something, grew up in Kensington or Putney," he said, cutting through the details. "Then St Andrews, and now you live in Clapham with all the other blonde public school girls—no, wait, you're in Marylebone. Despite what your friendship with Catherine would suggest, you'd rather go to a restaurant for an early night than go out to a private members' club."

Isabel leaned back, visible surprise on her face. "Are you stalking me? I feel personally attacked," she laughed. "You missed the obvious guess of Chelsea. And it was St. Paul's Girls', not Cheltenham. But you're right, I'm in Marylebone."

Daniel paused for a moment. "I haven't quite figured out what you do for work yet," he admitted.

Isabel burst into laughter again. "I'm in finance."

Daniel's mouth opened and his eyes widened. 'As if you were giving me shit for that.' He exclaimed.

"It takes one to know one," She said. "I have to admit, I can't quite place where you're from. You sound international."

"Boston," he said assuredly, "perhaps it's a good thing I don't have the accent," he added with a grin.

"But you do have one," she replied. "It's almost mid-Atlantic. Very old-timey. You sound like FDR."

"I hope that's a compliment."

"It is. Not grating like Californian," she said, attempting an American accent. It wasn't particularly good.

"So you're here for business," she redirected, trying to bring back the topic that had long since waned.

"I am, unfortunately." Her lips pursed, and her chin rose as if the sliver of information was enlightening. "What type of business brings you so far from home?" She said it in a flirtatious manner.

He hesitated, examining the glass of water before speaking. "I work for a company based in New York. We mostly deal with international work as middlemen, involved in various sectors, primarily finance and insurance. Currently, our focus is on securities. We have some contacts here that we're

The Collateral Dividend

looking to terminate." Daniel carefully measured his words, feeling awkward about lying to Isabel. He tried to phrase it in a way that wasn't entirely false. "Unfortunately, I seem to be the bearer of bad news."

"Tell me if I'm being too blunt, but I sense that you're running away from something."

"Who isn't running away from something? I'd like to meet that person," she replied cheerfully. For a tense moment, he worried that she might have taken offense at his comment. She brushed her hair aside and looked at him. "Family, London, work, perhaps. All sorts of things. I had the opportunity to leave and not worry about going back. There are very few chances like that in life, you know. It would be a shame to look back and regret not breaking free from the routine. I think I'd regret not living life with the spontaneity that comes from living day by day." She thoughtfully considered her decision to leave London, trying to reason why it was a valid choice. She wasn't certain he would find it remotely interesting. She had thought it through and focused on making the most of her life, with this year being one filled with selfish and unstructured choices.

At that moment, the oysters arrived. They each had a few, and Daniel leaned forward, unable to shake the feeling that there was something dangerous about her. "This might sound silly, but there's something about you that draws me towards you," she said. Daniel thought she still seemed guarded, even cautious, but her words and mannerisms were bold and straightforward.

"That sounds terrifying," he said with a charismatic grin, laced with whiskey and charm. "Should I start running away now?" he playfully asked, and she laughed, smitten yet slightly embarrassed.

"No, no," she replied sheepishly. "I didn't mean it like that at all. There's just a sense of familiarity with you," she said, almost awkwardly. The idea of getting to know someone felt awkward, but not in this moment. "I probably sound even more insane."

Daniel shook his head, looking down at his hands as he fiddled with the water glass. "Not at all," he said.

"How well do you know Catherine?" he asked, shifting the conversation to a mutual acquaintance. Catherine's family had been long-time friends with Isabel's family. They would often visit Catherine and her family in the heart of the Alps, venturing across the channel to Western Europe.

"Well, I'm glad she insisted," Daniel said, smiling now as he took a sip of water. "Maybe she had a hunch."

"Perhaps," Isabel agreed. The waiter approached to clear the table, and Daniel leaned back in his chair, finally taking notice of the dining room. They were the only customers remaining, apart from the staff. Daniel glanced at his watch. It was nearly midnight, yet he didn't feel tired. Looking out the dining room window, he pondered their next move. "What do you think about heading back soon?" he asked, and Isabel nodded.

"Are you staying in town long?"

"I am," he admitted, acknowledging that he already missed the comfort and familiarity of home, which a hotel lacked. Isabel explained that's why she chose to stay with Catherine; she couldn't stand being alone in a hotel room, especially for the duration of her stay.

As they approached the exit, the party was still in full swing, with drunken guests retreating and the staff leaving for the night. Only Daniel, Isabel, and Catherine remained. They settled onto the sofas and engaged in a conversation about world politics for a while. Eventually, Catherine drifted off, curled up on the nearby sofa, covered by a luxurious cashmere blanket, still fully dressed in an expensive couture dress worth more than most people's mortgages.

The night grew darker, and a sense of familiarity hung in the air, like a heavy winter fog, creating moments of attraction. Time seemed to slow down, and both were uncertain how to proceed, how to make the first move. Perhaps due to the drinks consumed or the lateness of the hour, Daniel felt more enchanted than ever.

He desired to kiss her. There was something about the freckles on her face, the delicate features of her cheeks, and her kind eyes that warmed him. He felt disarmed by her witty smile and welcoming green eyes. The conversation lulled, and neither had anything else to say. Acting on impulse, Daniel leaned toward her. When their lips met, there was a subtle intake of breath, and for a moment, everything felt weightless.

After a brief moment, Daniel leaned back. Their eyes locked, and no words were spoken. Isabel leaned forward, her arms wrapped around his neck, and kissed him passionately. "If it's all right with you, I'd like to do this again," he managed to say between kisses, with their lips barely apart.

"Uh huh," she nodded, biting her lip gently. Her head leaned forward to kiss him again. "Perhaps tomorrow." Daniel agreed.

However, he knew he couldn't rush into this. He was torn between the intensity of the moment and what was logical. But this was a hurried, frenetic passion. Isabel began to undress him, but when she was down to her bra, Daniel paused and looked over at Catherine across the room. "Perhaps we should go

The Collateral Dividend

upstairs," he suggested. Isabel was kissing his neck, her hands exploring. She nodded. "But I really shouldn't stay," Daniel hesitated. Isabel shook her head. "I think you should." She got up from the sofa and took his hand.

The events that followed became a blur for Daniel. Exhaustion consumed his mind, and he couldn't recall whether he brushed his teeth or how they ended up in bed. Nevertheless, when he woke up the next morning, sunlight streamed through the window, and his arm was asleep under her head, with the duvet nearly stolen from him.

As Daniel glanced around the unfamiliar room, he wondered how he ended up in situations like this. A woman stood at the door, walking over to the bed with a friendly smile, giving him a needle in the arm. Two more figures accompanied her, grabbing Daniel's arms and leading him towards a water tub on the far side of the room. He attempted to resist, but he was overpowered and fell headlong into the tub.

* * *

He woke up drenched in sweat, glancing at the clock on his bedside table. It was quarter to seven. The vivid and haunting images from his dreams lingered in his mind. Getting out of bed, he inserted his earphones and made his way to the bathroom down the hall.

"Good morning," Paul greeted, checking his watch. It was nearly 1 am in Washington, and exhaustion marked his face. The city square lay before him, an empty black void surrounded by hazy orange orbs of city streetlights.

He inquired about any progress, though Paul already knew the answer. "I suspect we may have to spend a few months here," Daniel admitted. "If she's hiding something, I doubt she'll be forthcoming."

"Philippe Gaillard has retreated to Paris for now," Paul shared regarding business matters. "Approaching year-end, and if our suspicions are correct, he's facing significant losses. It wouldn't surprise me if he isn't afraid of hostile takeovers or even bankruptcy."

"Does that imply Isabel's innocence?" Daniel asked, his gaze fixed on the drawing table with a suit draped over the chair.

"No, not at all," Paul clarified. Fatigue consumed him, the type that accompanies prolonged inactivity. It was a sleep-deprived weariness. "We still have several persons of interest in Zurich. As far as we know, there's nothing to suggest that any one of them won't approach her." Daniel's heart tightened with anxiety, fearing such an outcome.

137

"What about the other business?" Daniel's tone turned cold as he scowled into the distance.

"We've been tracking Klaus. He's returned to Germany, so he's no longer a priority for you," Paul explained. "However, he's been having frequent phone calls with a trading desk in Zurich. Are you familiar with Sergei Kosygin?" Daniel shook his head. "Well, he's a Russian banker working at Mayer Kleid in Zurich. We'll keep an eye on him. You might receive messages regarding local assets. I suggest you contact them," Paul cautioned, emphasizing the danger of the situation. "I want you to be cautious in all this."

"And why is that?" Daniel attempted to interject, but Paul ruthlessly interrupted.

"Do you still experience visions?" Paul inquired, his tone bordering on condescension. It seemed as if he considered the visions an exaggerated reaction. "I've spoken with Doctor Acres. She would like you to reach out to her whenever they occur." Daniel attempted to object again, but Paul refused to entertain it. "If you plan to spend more time in society, we need you to act normally. I can't risk you shooting someone based on something you thought they did."

"I can always distinguish between reality and imagination," Daniel insisted.

Paul dismissed the importance of Daniel's ability to differentiate. Playing the role of the "bad cop," he concealed the fact that he had never intended to pull Daniel out of the field.

For the first time in months, Daniel abstained from alcohol. The collective hangover had felt unbearable, and upon recovering, he found himself immersed in three weeks in Zurich. Almost every day, he saw Isabel. As the three-week mark approached, he trudged through the bitter February cold, heading to her apartment. It struck him that he genuinely cared for her, a feeling that no longer felt contrived. Daniel simply existed in her presence. This realization scared him. Upon reflecting, he recognized that moment as a profound happiness, one that accompanied the delicate stages of falling in love. It terrified him because falling in love was never part of the plan. Yet there he stood, trying to extract secrets from someone while unwittingly falling for her. What a precarious situation indeed. There were moments when Daniel believed that Isabel shared the same sentiments. Just as he grew comfortable with their relationship, she would vanish for a day, ignoring calls and texts, leaving him puzzled. Then, out of nowhere, Isabel would return, leaving Daniel to wonder what had transpired. He dared not bring it up, fearing unnecessary conflict.

The Collateral Dividend

As always, Daniel arrived late, knocking on the door and leaning against the frame, waiting for her to answer. When she did, he gave her a crooked grin, stepping into the room. He placed his hand on her neck, planting a kiss on the four corners of her mouth. The door closed behind him, plunging the room into momentary darkness. Their lips parted, and Daniel rested his head against hers, embracing her tightly.

"Ready to go?" he asked, standing by the door with his hands in his coat pockets.

She leaned forward, kissing him again before walking towards the nearby closet to retrieve her coat. "You're late," she teased lightly, slipping into her wool-lined rubber boots and picking up the keys from the coffee table near the door. Not one for hats, her ears turned bright red when the winter wind nipped at them.

"What's that saying about good things coming to those who wait?" Daniel held the door, waiting for her to exit before closing it snugly.

"I don't think tardiness falls under that criteria," Isabel retorted. She locked the door, buttoned up her coat, and remarked, "Where are we headed?" as they stepped onto the street. Snow had fallen rapidly in Zurich, with crushed sand lining the sidewalks and snowbanks piled against the doors. The bitter cold kissed exposed skin, robbing the winter sky of color. Daniel despised winter.

"There's a restaurant in the first District near the river that I'd love to try," he suggested, knowing she would be receptive to the idea. He proposed they walk there.

"Do you ever wonder what life will be like when we're older?" Isabel abruptly asked, turning to look at him. She wedged her fingers between his arm and held on tight before returning them to her pockets. Daniel inquired about her meaning, and she elaborated, "Don't you wonder how you'll be ten years from now?"

Daniel hadn't given it much thought. It was difficult to imagine himself in his current profession, as it lacked a linear trajectory. There was no corporate ladder to climb, no ultimate goal to reach. The topic unsettled him. Would he be able to leave cleanly? Was a clean exit even possible? "How much older are we talking about, dear?" he questioned.

"Ew," Isabel reacted. "I definitely don't love that. 'Dear' is such an old-person pet name." Daniel already felt old. They both did. "I have thought about it," she eventually responded. "I don't feel old until I reflect on my university and school days—suddenly, it was a decade ago." They had been seated at the restaurant table for a few moments.

"And what have you concluded?" Daniel asked.

"I always thought by now I'd be settled down, though I've realized that my settling won't be in London," she revealed, briefly glancing at her phone and reading a text message. She pondered the message for a while, losing her train of thought. "Um," she uttered, interrupting the conversation. Placing her phone in her purse, she apologized sheepishly, "I'm sorry, I completely forgot what I was going to say. It was a message from my family, well, mainly my brothers. I probably shouldn't have looked at it."

Daniel sensed an opportunity. "I didn't know you had brothers. Would you like to talk about it? What was the message about?" His tone was deliberate, precise, and almost militant.

Isabel let out a deep sigh. "My siblings don't understand. They don't understand why I'm here. They'd rather have me back in England, contributing to the family."

"Why are you here then?" Daniel pressed.

Isabel found it difficult to provide a simple answer. The reasons were more complex than she cared to admit. She missed home, and there was always a lingering ache of longing. She hoped that one day the convoluted and prideful forces that had driven her to the east would resolve themselves. She wanted to be in Zurich, skiing in the Alps, away from London and its familiarity, yet she also yearned for home. Home felt distant, enveloped by nostalgia. The positive memories of days gone by held greater power than any negative ones. "You look tired," she observed.

"I've been having nightmares," he confessed openly, knowing that there was no point in hiding it. His feelings for her were so intense that he appeared overwhelmingly passionate. At times, this worried her, but most of the time, it simply exposed his emotions.

"Are they about the same thing?" Isabel inquired.

Daniel shrugged, saying, "Sometimes." He wasn't sure if he wanted to delve into this topic any further. "Can we head back?" he asked after a long silence. Anxiety had been building up within him. It was evident to Isabel that he was distressed. He seemed on the verge of tears, struggling to hold back his emotions.

"Of course," she agreed. "Is everything alright?" she asked once they had returned, and he gazed around the room, his eyelids heavy. His vision was blurred. Daniel looked at her with wide eyes, his gaze resembling wet sandstones.

The Collateral Dividend

"Um," he stammered, "I don't know," and he closed his eyes tightly, trying to prevent uncontrollable tears. Isabel crossed the room, and Daniel melted into her arms, unable to explain why. He considered himself pathetic, wilting before her like a feeble flower. Part of him wished to remain sitting there, while another part didn't want her or anyone else to witness him in such a state.

"Is this about the nightmares?" Isabel asked after a moment. He was cuddled beside her on the sofa, trying to hold his composure, but it was of little use.

"I don't know," he replied, almost childishly. The dynamic felt backwards to him. He was insecure, vulnerable, and exposed. His nerves felt raw.

"Take deep breaths," Isabel said, and he apologized because he felt like he had ruined their night out. Isabel dismissed the idea. "Nonsense, we can sit here as long as you need," she reassured him. In the past month, there had been dozens of occasions where she had needed him in the same way.

"I think...," he swallowed hard, fighting back tears, "I'm messed up, Isabel," he said frankly, his eyes beginning to water.

"Of course, it's true," she tried to assure him. "You aren't a bad person. Everyone goes through these types of things."

"I don't know," he said regretfully.

"That's fine," she said, "because I know." The two sat in silence until Daniel felt calmer. "Are you feeling better?" she asked after twenty minutes.

"Yes, thank you," Daniel said, sitting up and looking at her. He caressed her neck. "You didn't have to stay here with me."

"Of course I did. You're important to me."

"It scares me that I'm as into you as I am because... I love you, Isabel," he said, catching himself off guard and unsure how to react to what he had said.

"I do, too," she replied almost without thinking. But as she began to think about it, she fell into reticence and awkwardness. The sudden realization that she was in love terrified her. She didn't know how to react, and running away seemed like the only way she knew to deal with such a frightening feeling. The intimacy made Isabel anxious. The idea that she had become so close to someone outside her family so quickly was stressful.

This wasn't the first time she had experienced these overwhelming feelings. Every so often, she would feel consumed by anxiety and have to take things step by step. It was a crippling sensation she had only hinted at a few times, and Daniel felt helpless. He wished there was a way he could help her, a way to connect and protect her. Isabel had made it clear that closing herself off was her way of coping. "Just don't forget that I'm always here for you," he told her, sitting up and drying his puffy eyes with his hands.

141

E.R. Wychwood

As Daniel's phone rang, he retrieved it from his coat pocket and stared at the screen. After a moment, he pressed the lock button and let the screen go dark. "I've got to go," he apologized, standing up abruptly. Isabel seemed shocked by his sudden change of tone and sat on the sofa, looking surprised. Daniel put on his coat, and when she asked if everything was all right, he stopped fiddling with his coat collar, walked over to the sofa, extended his hand, and held hers. He kissed her on the lips once, then again with more intensity. He smiled. "Why don't we plan to have dinner tonight?" he suggested genuinely. "I really enjoyed today." She smiled back and told him she couldn't wait.

"Okay," Daniel said. He kissed her once more, stood back for a moment, and almost awkwardly waited until he realized he needed to leave.

Daniel felt selfish. He hadn't been able to focus on anything other than Isabel for weeks. Memories of their time together would interrupt his thoughts, making it difficult for him to concentrate on his work. His profession suffered as a result, a messy mix of excessive drinking, pain, and infatuation. But infatuation wasn't the right word; he knew it was something much deeper. Paul had always dismissed the term "obsessive," and Daniel preferred the alternative definition that aligned more with passion. "Everyone is obsessed about something," Paul often said. "It's part of human nature. The mind can't be indifferent about everything. It will select something and allocate all its resources to the chemicals released by that positive feeling. We all obsess about something; it might as well be something good."

Daniel found himself obsessing over Isabel. Thoughts of her consumed him constantly, and that frightened him. He wasn't accustomed to being vulnerable. He had always prided himself on having perfect control over trust and relationships, caring less, leaving first, and trusting the least.

Curiosity tingled within him as he found himself seriously considering a relationship with Isabel. He wondered how it could work, if at all. He also wondered what Paul would think. Eventually, he let go of the fear of others' opinions and focused solely on his own happiness. Why should he be bound by history? Why should his actions forever shape policies and memories without allowing him to shape his own destiny?

Isabel sat on the sofa, gazing out of the window, watching the bustling city pass by. For some reason, perhaps due to her own reservations or Daniel's sudden presence, she doubted if this was truly what she wanted. Was it making her happy? If her relationship with her mother had been better, she might have considered reaching out for advice. However, their relationship lacked the care

The Collateral Dividend

and affection beyond the mundane friendship of a mother and daughter, overshadowed by bitterness and a sense of professionalism.

She felt guilty for the seemingly blissful life she led in Zurich, far removed from the chaos of her family. Trouble brewed back home, and the realization that life went on without her was a stressful concept to grasp. Furthermore, the mounting pressure on the firm to hand over management intensified the torment from the extended family. The vultures were circling, waiting for their chance to strike.

Daniel contemplated dinner. It had been nearly three and a half months in Zurich. Philippe Gaillard continued his global travels, and Paul struggled to keep track of him. Gaillard seemed to move with an invisible cloak, appearing only sporadically. Whenever they made progress in tracking him, he would vanish.

On a late April morning, Paul got out of bed, wearing nothing but a pair of briefs. He went to the closet door, selected a suit and a shirt from the row. "Are you going to the office now?" a woman asked from the bed, wrapped in a cocoon-like embrace of a white duvet.

Paul turned around, looking at her as he tied his tie. "We have some assets abroad that need attention. I'll be back within two, maybe three hours," he explained, moving closer to the edge of the bed. He could sense her displeasure. "Rachel, I have an obligation here."

"Can't you delegate this to someone else? When you took this job, you promised that you wouldn't have to work as much. But to be honest, you work even more now," she said, getting out of bed and heading to the bathroom to start her day. Paul stared at the closed bathroom door, feeling the tension.

"Honey, I... I don't mean to work as much as I do, but I have a responsibility to these people. I promise this won't last forever," he pleaded.

Rachel opened the door, standing in the frame. She shook her head. "I don't think you even realize you're lying," she said with an acidic tone.

"For Christ's sake, Rachel, these are things I can't delegate," Paul retorted.

"Whatever, Paul. I don't know if you remember, but we made plans for dinner at my mother's six weeks ago. If you can make it, great. If not, I suppose that will be fine too," she said, her disappointment evident.

"I'll be there," Paul assured her. He made his way to the bathroom, with its white tiles and cool-toned walls. "You're important to me, you know that?" he told her as she put on a set of earrings.

"Then start showing it, Paul. Because frankly, I'm tired of you not trying and constantly telling me that you will," she replied.

E.R. Wychwood

Paul arrived at the office shortly after ten. He had ruminated over the conversation with Rachel throughout the drive, leaving an uneasy feeling in his stomach that lingered throughout the day. In Zurich, the sun began its descent, casting warm hues across the city. The bright shades of blossoming foliage painted a vibrant picture, awakening the senses. The sun's rays broke through the clouds, bathing the naked windows in a brilliant orange glow. The air outside felt cold and thin, accentuated by the clear blue sky.

Ted, who rarely appeared outside of regular work hours, entered Paul's office unexpectedly. Paul was surprised to see him. "How's it going?" Ted asked, casually inquiring about various missions worldwide. "What about Zurich? How's that going?"

"Good," Paul replied. "We're working on narrowing down the individuals involved. One of the targets is being sued by Silicon Valley for patent theft."

"Should it affect our operations?" Ted questioned, unaware that it already had.

"No," Paul responded, shaking his head. "I don't think so," he added, swallowing hard.

"And what about Gaillard's activities in Greece?" Ted inquired, still oblivious to the leak. Paul had effectively concealed the evidence, working to pinpoint the source. "Any progress on that?"

"It's a work in progress," Paul reassured him. "Is there anything else I can help you with?"

Ted shook his head. "Nah, that should be fine. Sorry to interrupt. I didn't expect to find you here on a Sunday. I just wanted to grab some briefing notes for a meeting with Redding tomorrow."

"There's no such thing as a break, sir," Paul replied, nodding. "But be sure to leave early today, all right? You've been here too much."

Paul assured him that he would, and once Ted left, he closed the door and picked up the phone. As the call connected, Daniel answered, his tone harsh and dismissive. "Did I interrupt anything?" Paul asked.

"No," Daniel replied from the back of a cab, gazing out onto the bustling street. The city flowed with a pace, moving forward with lurching steps.

"How are things there?" Paul inquired.

"Slow," Daniel replied. "She interacted with Sergei Kroysgin, but I caught a glimpse of a letter from Mayer Kleid addressed to her at the apartment."

Paul sat up, keen to know its contents. "What did it say?" he asked.

Daniel admitted he didn't know. "All right, I'll see if Avery has anything from their internal servers," Paul suggested, considering the possibility that the

The Collateral Dividend

family banked with their firm. "That could be useful. Do you have anything else for us?"

"No," Daniel responded. He hadn't been particularly productive during his time there. Paul let out a deep sigh. "Daniel, it's been nearly four months. We need to start seeing some results. We're spending too much money for you to be there doing nothing."

"I need more time. Something is happening here, and it pertains to us. Besides," Daniel said cheerfully, "I'm on my way to see our contact now. I'll call you in an hour." He ended the call and turned off his phone, not considering the significance of Paul's surprise at the meeting he had mentioned.

Paul sat at his desk, frowning. He hadn't set up any meetings for Daniel in months. Farragut Center had no resources in the region, and he was puzzled by what Daniel had meant. He attempted to call Daniel back, but his phone was switched off. Despite his ability to remotely activate it, Paul decided not to interfere. If Daniel had spoken with CIA assets without Paul's knowledge, calling him back could jeopardize his cover.

Daniel's drive down to the meet took half an hour, but it was evident he was running behind schedule. He felt lethargic, a consequence of his habit of lounging around and doing nothing most nights. This sedentary lifestyle had taken a toll on his physical condition, as his figure had slightly shifted, and he was no longer in the peak shape he once enjoyed.

As darkness began to descend, Daniel opted for a cab ride to Leonhard Street. The quietness of the early evening allowed eerie figures to loom in his mind. He walked along the narrow asphalt sidewalks for a few blocks, where trolley wires hung overhead. Seeking a moment of security, Daniel entered a nearby pub and settled at the back, keeping a watchful eye on the door for about ten minutes. No one arrived, so he decided to preserve his sense of safety by making his way through the kitchen, exiting via the back door, and entering an alley that spanned the length of the block, connecting two parallel streets. The deserted streets prompted Daniel to scan both directions before heading back towards the river. Aware that Isabel would likely wonder about his whereabouts, he switched on his phone and sent her a text, inquiring if their plans for the night were still on.

Unbeknownst to Daniel, a man stood with his back turned against the alley wall, his shoulders hunched. Although Daniel noticed this figure, he thought nothing of it, perceiving the man as a lighter and homeless individual, weighing at least twenty pounds less than himself. As Daniel drew within four yards of the man, he observed the man dropping something that appeared to be lightweight. Curiously, Daniel bent down, retrieved the item from the ground, and extended it towards the hooded and shivering figure.

At that very moment, the figure lunged forward, swiftly revealing a concealed blade hidden within the sleeve of his arm. The blade pierced deep into Daniel's abdomen, a wound that should have elicited searing pain. However, Daniel felt nothing more than a numbing sense of shock. Stumbling backward, his hands became drenched in deep red blood, which saturated his shirt. Overwhelmed by the injury, Daniel collapsed onto the nearby ground, gasping for breath. Grasping the knife firmly, he tugged at the figure's arm, pulling him down as well. The pain was absent due to shock, yet Daniel's motor functions became erratic and unreliable.

Dislodging the knife from his abdomen, Daniel let it fall to the ground while the figure toppled over. Daniel, now sprawled on the floor, began to lose blood rapidly. His body had succumbed to shock, rendering him unable to perceive pain. Amidst intermittent bursts of pain that abruptly surfaced, Daniel tightened his grip around the figure's neck, strangling him amidst a pool of blood along the alley wall. In this disoriented state, Daniel's attempts to cease his hallucinations proved futile.

Removing his coat, he assessed the wound with a determined gaze. Daniel unwrapped his scarf and pressed it against the gushing wound, attempting to slow the flow of blood that appeared as dark as night. Struggling to prop himself against the wall, Daniel could no longer feel his own face. The pounding in his head matched the rhythm of his racing heart. His trembling hands betrayed the horror of his actions or perhaps the blood loss itself. Daniel's gaze shifted from the lifeless body to the empty street.

Nausea overwhelmed Daniel, and he retched against the side of the brick wall before slumping against the alley's surface. Crawling until he collapsed outside the alley, he lay on the roadside, covered in sweat, with blurred vision. He sprawled out in an attempt to cool down, feeling as if he were intoxicated. Rolling onto his side, he experienced bouts of dry heaving, accompanied by a profound dizziness as the lights along the street swirled like ethereal orbs.

Within an hour, Paul received word of the incident. As his phone regained connectivity, it detected Daniel's diminished heart rate. Being the only one in the office, with another hour before he needed to meet Rachel, Paul made repeated attempts to contact Daniel but to no avail. Determined not to succumb to emotions, he reminded himself that regret was unprofessional, despite his strong friendship with Daniel. This served as a poignant reminder of the ever-present specter of death.

The Collateral Dividend

Struggling to focus on himself, Daniel fought to maintain a clear mind, but exhaustion repeatedly sent him collapsing onto the asphalt. His vision wavered in and out, and he was uncertain of his level of consciousness. Coughing up blood, he received assistance to the sidewalk, where he leaned against the wall. Overwhelming weariness enveloped him, and the weight of his eyelids beckoned him towards sleep. In mere moments, he closed his eyes, and the world faded into darkness.

*   *   *

Sergei awoke in a restless blur, finding himself on the loveseat. He took a nervous breath and surveyed the room. He was in his rented apartment, which came furnished—a critical factor in his decision. Sergei had no desire to bother with selecting his own furniture.

He gave the room a thorough once-over, trying to recall if he had returned home at a decent hour. The organized atmosphere felt foreign to him. Clearly, he hadn't cleaned it himself. Everything seemed new—the furniture and even the smell—unlike what he remembered from yesterday. But it was the result of a heavy night of drinking and snorting cocaine. A line on a mirrored plate rested on the coffee table. Sergei leaned forward, credit card in hand, and refined the line, preparing to indulge. A cut plastic straw awaited him, and he inhaled deeply through his nose. The room resonated with the loud weeping sound of a long snort, and Sergei's throat cleared as if he had been punched in the gut. He tilted his head back, wide-eyed and buzzing, emitting grunts as his body adjusted to the jolt.

Sergei examined the luxurious carpets and seating areas. Two sofas in shades of red and gold stood directly in front of him. A chandelier hung from the ceiling, and the balcony extended from the living room to his bedroom, offering a captivating view of the city to the south. Just then, his phone vibrated on the coffee table. He moved over to it, picked it up, and answered, "Hello?"

"Good morning," Philippe Gaillard greeted softly, getting straight to the point. "I need you to pay a visit to someone for me tonight. It must be done quietly. He is involved in a rather sensitive profession."

Sergei, still hungover and barely feeling anything, attributed it to the cocaine. A burning sensation in his throat had begun, and he longed for another line. "Do you have the details?" he asked tensely, as if he had been holding his breath.

E.R. Wychwood

"I have already sent them to you," Gaillard replied. "I need you to leave something for him, written in his own hand. Can you manage that?" Sergei assured him that he could. "Good. Now, regarding another matter—there will be an opening at the firm in New York in a few days. I want you to apply for it. Understood?" Sergei assured him once again that it would be done.

As the sun set, Sergei knew he had an hour. Exiting his car, he approached the hotel entrance and made his way down a narrow hallway. Making sure no one was around, he skillfully picked the lock, entered the hotel room, and positioned himself near the writing desk. He waited for the couple, who were immersed in their evening activities after dinner. Sergei focused on calming his breathing, then retrieved a tablet of MDMA, letting it dissolve under his tongue. He resisted the temptation to snort cocaine, as doing it in the hotel room felt unprofessional. He wanted to hold onto some semblance of moral restraint.

When the couple returned to the hotel room, flicking on the lights, Sergei pointed a gun at them, instructing them to lock the door. He then gestured for them to sit down, positioning himself across from them. He stared at them intently for a while, waiting for the ecstasy tablet to take effect. Gripping the husband's shoulder tightly, Sergei applied pressure until he yielded. Sergei forced the man to hold the gun, and when he couldn't resist, Sergei shot him in the head. The wife screamed. Sergei took hold of her waist, pointed the gun at her, and led her into the bathroom. His intoxication prevented him from fully comprehending his own actions. He callously forced her into the shallow water, where she drowned. Returning to the main part of the hotel room, Sergei placed the gun in the man's hand, making slight adjustments to the body before blood patterns set. He surveyed the scene he had orchestrated, feeling the early signs of nausea creeping over him.

It was messy, but the staging adhered to the old-school methods of the KGB. Sergei continued to stage the rest of the room strategically, placing the wife's skin under the husband's fingernails and carefully trashing the room, weaving a narrative. Sergei was skilled at this. He thought to himself that he should have been a detective in another life.

After shaking for approximately ten minutes, Sergei managed to bring himself down from the high, reaching a functional state. He then used an emergency stairwell to exit into the alley after dealing with the security camera.

"How did it go?" Philippe Gaillard inquired, ensuring the line was secure before asking Sergei to provide a detailed account.

"It's more than just taking a life. It chips away at a part of you," Sergei responded almost callously. He seemed indifferent. "In fact, it erodes a man until only a hollow shell remains." Sergei wasn't a compassionate man. He was solely concerned with his own well-being and making his father proud.

"Well, sometimes someone must die," Philippe Gaillard stated matter-of-factly. "Did you leave the handwritten note?" he asked, and Sergei closed his eyes tightly, his hand pressed against his forehead. He had forgotten, but he wasn't about to admit it to Gaillard.

"Of course," Sergei assured him, and then inquired if there was anything else Philippe wanted to discuss.

"No, my friend. Get some rest. You'll hear from me in the coming weeks," Philippe replied, reclining in his bed with the covers up to his chest. He wore reading glasses and held a book in his hands. Philippe ended the call.

It was now eleven thirty. Philippe took his pills and burrowed deeper beneath the sheets. Rolling over, he switched off the lamp, instantly plunging the long room into a blackness as abrupt as a moonless night. Lengthy and distorted shadows cast from the city streets crept in. Philippe gazed out at the city for thirty minutes until exhaustion overpowered his remaining alertness. He turned to face the fireplace, closed his eyes, and drifted into a dreamless sleep.

THE GREEK

He went by Alekos Tzavaras and was feared by the Greek authorities. His rising appeal in the political theater resulted from years of economic slumps. The Eurozone had left the Greeks on the curb, along with the Spanish and Portuguese. Like children in the schoolyard, the Europeans had devised the term 'PIGS' years ago, and Alekos likened the EU's view of them to precisely that. There was a great deal of discrimination in the term. To him, it was both humiliating and insulting, implying they were swine, somehow of a lower caste than the rest of the European collective. Alekos laughed. They had set his nation to fail. The Greek government was on the verge of collapse – funds were being cut left, right, and center. The Greeks were a proud people, and Alekos passionately believed in the glory of Greek history. This was the center of the world, the origin of great memories and even better philosophical minds.

They called him an ultranationalist, but if that's what they called someone who preferred the Greeks to return to their former glory, then that's what he was. He likened his vision to that of a harsher Socrates. Some at the university had laughed, others applauded Alekos' absurd yet brilliant weaving of narratives and fantasy. One of his favorites was to skewer the old Greek epics and draw in Michel Foucault's "Il n'y a pas de hors-texte": there is nothing outside the context.

The foreigners who had strangled Greek politics for years were ignorant of history and its lessons. The irony was that if one looked far back enough, Alekos himself was not even a Greek native; his cultural embrace of Greek mythology downplayed this fact. He often went by Ares, a name used for its symbolic meanings and to protect Alekos' close friends from harm. Being a radical was challenging, and an idea was much more difficult to destroy than a man. But his critics would cruelly call him Erebus, the god of darkness and shadows, for his shallow thoughts and actions. Those in the foreign community likened him to Ares, the Greek god of violence, vengeance, and war. It was also a nod to his close allies in the north of Africa. Despite all this fanfare, Alekos had seriously threatened Eurozone peace. Alekos knew how the nations worked. He had mastered the art of politics in Greek democracy before resorting to more crude measures. He held resentment toward the cause of his native land's collapse. It had fallen far from where it once was. When asked why he reverted to violence, he would quickly reference John Locke's "Two

The Collateral Dividend

Treatises of Government": "Whenever legislators endeavor to take away and destroy the property of the people or to reduce them to slavery under arbitrary power, they put themselves into a state of war with the people, who are thereupon absolved from any further obedience."

Despite the succinct nature of his thoughts and his long history as a pseudo-academic in the halls of Greek mythology, Tzavaras was unkempt. He was no academic, not in the slightest, and it was an insult to those who were that he claimed to be.

Ahead of him stood a woman. With intense grey and empty eyes, he approached her. Kneeling in front of her, he gently held the nape of her chin, forcing her to meet his gaze. His voice, tainted by a harsh Greek accent, sent shivers down the woman's spine. "Tell me once more," he demanded, "how did the Germans find us?"

The woman wept, closing her eyes, avoiding the sight of the monstrous man. His pale skin looked lifeless as he gave a thin smile. "You betrayed us, didn't you?" she screamed. He silenced her with a forceful kiss, attempting to calm her troubled cries. "Hush, my love," he whispered. "What were you thinking? Did you want us all to die, or were you simply foolish?" His anger erupted, and Tzavaras, struggling to regain composure, closed his eyes and took several deep breaths. "If she has nothing to tell us, then kill her."

"No, please..." she wept, desperately seeking mercy from their leader. "I don't know what you want."

He turned and backhanded her across the face. "Silence! Do you think I enjoy this?" he snapped curtly. It was a rhetorical question. With a nod, a nearby man pulled the trigger of a handgun, and the woman slumped forward, like a prisoner of war executed in cold blood.

Tzavaras then shifted his gaze to another man in the room. "Dispose of the body," he dismissed casually before checking his watch. Time was running out. A map hung on the far side of the room. Alekos approached it, leaning on the table, tracing the highlighted lines that cut across the city's narrow streets. The abandoned office building baked in the approaching summer heat, rendering the overhead fans ineffective against the sweltering conditions.

Looking across the room, Tzavaras smiled at his young nephew. As the young man approached, Tzavaras draped his arm around his neck, allowing him to study the layout. "Nephew, what are your thoughts?" Tzavaras inquired once his nephew had examined the plan.

His nephew's eyes remained fixed, unwavering. Picking up a marker from beside the assault rifle on the table, he drew a thick red line with his right hand.

"There shouldn't be much resistance on the south side," he stated, placing a blueprint on top of the map, studying it intently. Crossing his arms, he pondered the best approach for their mission. Unlike his uncle, Elias had studied Physics at the University of Athens. "It would have been easier if we had the promised equipment, uncle."

Tzavaras shook his head. "Don't mention it. I know better than anyone how much we needed those resources."

Curiosity getting the better of him, Elias asked, "If you don't mind me asking, where did they go? I thought we had a benefactor."

"We did," Tzavaras replied sharply, his voice resonating with depth. "But sometimes plans go awry. They will try to stop us at the doors. Make sure you don't kill anyone who doesn't resist. We can't afford the media turning against us."

"Ensure you secure the doors once inside," Elias reminded him. Tzavaras gave a thin smile, placing his hand on Elias' back. His nephew was learning quickly. "Uncle, what about police positioning here and here?" Elias pointed at the alleyways that offered superior firing positions.

Tzavaras chuckled, stepping away from his nephew. He picked something up from a cardboard box on the floor and tossed it at him. "I'm sure it won't be a problem." A harsh grin stretched across his face as he waited for Elias to notice the three gray blocks connected by thick black wires—explosives. Elias understood Tzavaras' plan. The message had to be spread by any means necessary. In war, the one who controlled the message controlled everything. "You know, Elias, when I was a boy in Athens, my mentor, a philosophy professor, warned for years about the impending financial collapse and the recklessness of our nation. He is no longer with us because he couldn't do what was necessary. Our proud nation cannot fall into the hands of others. We are at war, and we will not lose."

"Uncle, we're running out of money to finance this. We can barely afford to feed ourselves," Elias interjected, only to be abruptly cut off.

"Elias, your father didn't leave you and your mother, nor did he die in vain. If what you say is true, I will reach out to our friends abroad to see if they can help," Tzavaras said firmly. "Now, come. Let us go to war." He picked up the assault rifle from the table and slung the strap around his neck.

Leading his nephew to the stairwell, they descended into the parking garage where two black sedans awaited. Tzavaras settled into the front seat, placing his weapon between his feet, the barrel peeking through his knees. Leaning back, he glanced at the passengers in the back seat as they left the parking garage and

The Collateral Dividend

ventured onto the city streets. The cars sped away, heading east for several blocks until they reached the city center, where they came to a halt.

Tzavaras stepped out of the vehicle first, inhaling deeply the dry Mediterranean air. He swiftly eliminated the police guard standing near the building's entrance. Taking control of the lobby, he held his gun high, firing a three-round burst. Before the civilians could take cover, Tzavaras's men unleashed a hail of gunfire, killing the receptionist and security guards. Blood stained the glass door that safeguarded the studios and offices. Tzavaras motioned for his nephew to lead. They shattered the glass, promptly neutralizing the guard, and scanned left and right. "This way, uncle," Elias pointed to the right, indicating their search for a television computer terminal. Tzavaras proceeded down the hallway, veering left to enter the control room near the entrance. Once inside, he fired shots, ordering everyone to the ground. "You, come here," he commanded, pointing his gun at the nearest television operator. The man, trembling, cautiously emerged from behind the terminal and approached the armed men. Tzavaras produced a flash drive, allowing his gun to dangle from his neck. "Plug this in. Broadcast it on all your stations," he instructed, the operator hesitatingly looking to his manager, who silently shook his head.

Tzavaras drew his handgun, aiming it at the manager, then turned his attention back to the operator. "Broadcast it on all stations. Now," his eyes bore into the operator. The manager gave a signal, but this time, Tzavaras didn't hesitate. He pulled the trigger, and the gun's successive clacks echoed as the manager collapsed onto the desk and then to the floor. Tzavaras faced the terminal operator, who cautiously approached and took the flash drive. Moving to the terminal, he plugged it in and typed commands into the computer. The numerous screens in the background flickered, transitioning from black to active displays. Tzavaras appeared on every screen, deliberately edited to mimic a hijacked video. The feed jolted intermittently, accompanied by varying volume levels that captivated the viewers. Tzavaras smiled wanly. "Thank you," he uttered, cleanly shooting the operator in the head and letting his body crumple to the ground. "Everyone else, out of the room," he ordered. The remaining television operators hastily vacated the room, leaving through the doors, which were subsequently locked with a heavy chain. Satisfied with his work, Tzavaras found a rolling office chair from the back of the room, sat down, and crossed his legs. Leaning back, he gazed at the screen with a faint smile.

Acknowledging his slight vanity, Tzavaras had accepted it as part of life. The people of Greece deserved a better leader, and he aspired to be that person.

153

"Greece was once a proud nation, a nation that led the world through innovation and free thought," his voice resounded through the room as their hijacked video played. Tzavaras rose from the chair, surveying the room and finding contentment in his actions. On the far side of the room, there were more doors, and they exited through them, securing the doors with a heavy chain. Tzavaras checked the placement of the explosives near the structural supports in the main lobby. Satisfied with the arrangement, he switched on a hand radio and descended downstairs to the waiting vehicles parked in the back alley near the emergency exit.

"We have been used, the scapegoats of an economic crisis that America deserved. The global economy brought profit to many nations but raped countless others," Tzavaras's voice crackled through the radio. "We are capable of much more and need not remain beneath the thumb of our European oppressors. They consider us inferior, no better than bugs. Coercion leads to enslavement, and our government's surrender has made us slaves. We must reclaim our nation with the iron fist that once dominated the Mediterranean world. We will rebuild and destroy those who wish to keep us in poverty."

Tzavaras paused as an explosion erupted in the distance, followed by another and another. Demonstrations were taking place across the city, with blue flares illuminating the night sky—the symbol of the ultranationalists, a sign of the nation's support. "I call upon all the people to take to the streets and show this government whose nation this truly is. I urge you to judge our leaders, who have led us down this path, with extreme prejudice."

Turning off the hand radio, Tzavaras observed as the city streets rapidly descended into chaos. A faint smile played on his lips. It was time.

*   *   *

By all accounts, he should have been dead. Daniel had drifted in and out of consciousness. One of the bystanders who had found him attempted to make a phone call, and the unread text messages from Isabel indicated that she was the first person to be contacted. An ambulance arrived within an hour, but he had lost a significant amount of blood. He was barely coherent, and when his weak pulse became apparent, the first responders worked to stabilize him.

Daniel's next memory of consciousness occurred nearly two days later. As he awoke, he glanced down at his feet and noticed the presence of Paul Irving near the foot of his bed. His heart rate quickened, and the steady, consistent beep of the heart rate monitor accelerated. Isabel, who had been sitting beside him, sat up and placed her hand on his shoulder. Daniel reached out and grabbed her hand, relieved to see her.

Back in Zurich, the image of Paul vanished from Daniel's mind. He looked at Isabel, and she softly greeted him, stroking his head. Daniel let out a deep breath, resting his head against her torso. When asked how he was feeling, he couldn't provide a definite answer.

"I... I don't know," he replied, looking up at her. "God, it's good to see you," he added, feeling as if someone was clutching his heart.

The doctor entered the room, addressing him as Mr. Finch. The doctor, a short and stocky man with greying hair, informed Daniel that he was lucky to be alive. He inquired if Daniel remembered what had happened, to which Daniel nodded and recounted the attempted mugging. The doctor expressed concerns about scarring in his lungs and reduced sensations during testing. Daniel asked for clarification, and the doctor explained that he should have passed out from the pain within ten minutes but instead passed out due to blood loss. The doctor prescribed pain medication, cautioning Daniel to take them only if necessary. He also mentioned that representatives from the Kriminalpolizei wanted to speak with Daniel about the incident.

One of the shorter men from the Kriminalpolizei entered the room, wearing a harsh expression. He closed the door and took a seat, expressing apologies for bothering Daniel. They hoped to gather information about the incident from him, but Daniel admitted that he couldn't recall many details and wouldn't be of much help in identifying the assailant.

"I'm not sure if you're aware, but the man we suspect tried to mug you is dead," the other man stated, pen in hand, ready to record any information Daniel might provide. Sensing their suspicion and knowing better than to incriminate himself, Daniel remained silent, waiting for them to ask the necessary questions. His mind raced, realizing that his cover might be compromised, and he could potentially face investigation and trial for murder. While he had a valid defense, the prospect of being incarcerated for weeks or months loomed.

Shaking his head, Daniel truthfully replied, "No, I'm sorry, I didn't see anything."

The shorter man requested that Daniel stay within the country while the investigation continued and encouraged him to share any recollections if they surfaced. Daniel looked to Isabel, extending his hand to hold hers, seeking comfort and support.

E.R. Wychwood

In the bright room, Daniel struggled to focus on his hands, let alone objects three feet away. After experiencing a dreamless night, he felt slightly better the next day and requested discharge a few days later. In the meantime, he drifted in and out of consciousness, and Isabel sat beside him, filling pages and pages of a notepad with writing.

"Doing work?" he asked in one of his bouts of consciousness.

"No," she replied, "just writing." Daniel asked what she was writing, and she told him she wasn't sure. But when she was stressed or anxious, she would either write or go for a jog. "But running would mean I'd leave you here alone, and I don't want to do that."

Daniel's eyelids were heavy and folded. He gazed over at her while she was seated in the chair. It was very thoughtful of her to stay with him, but he would be here for at least another day. He would be fine, but she needed to remember her own priorities as well. "Go for a run. It's not like I'm going anywhere." It was one of his periods of wakefulness. Every so often, he would awake in a cold sweat, haunted by the specters of past kills.

Eventually, Daniel called Paul, who was seated on his brother-in-law's sofa watching a baseball game when the call came in. He sat up suddenly and went to the back door, standing out on the porch. "You wouldn't believe the amount of work it took me to fix what you did," Paul said once they had exchanged greetings. He leaned on the railing and watched the city of Baltimore cycle through its mid-day.

Daniel then recalled what had happened. He sat up in bed, swung his legs around, and let them dangle off the edge. Starting from the beginning, he recounted the events to Paul. Paul waited until he had shared all that he could remember. "We went looking for you after things didn't seem right. Don't worry, we masked the killing. One of the bystanders was one of ours. By the time he got to you, too much blood had been lost." Paul picked at his earlobe and glanced back into the house where Rachel was standing at the glass door, looking at him with a harsh expression. Paul signaled to her to give him a moment, then turned back around to watch the city.

"How did this happen?" Daniel asked when they had finished discussing the implications for the operation.

Paul let out a deep sigh. He had some idea, and Avery had gone over the messaging system. "Well, I suspect the access to our networks is a result of the Patel hack. We are experiencing anomalies elsewhere as well." Paul informed him that until further notice, they would not use texts as directives. This breach was not just affecting their services, but also The Valley's. It was a bigger issue, as it meant that information was out there that could cripple everyone involved. Paul had a better understanding of what Gaillard was up to. Gaillard had their numbers, and if he was smart, he would wait until Paul sent Daniel after him. Somehow, Gaillard would evade death and catch Farragut Center with their pants down. Their lowest moment would be when Gaillard struck.

"I think we should take him out," Daniel suggested.

"No," Paul rebutted. He wanted to tell Daniel that he was acting like a bloody idiot. "He's waiting for us to do something stupid. If we're going to get him, we need to be sure that none of this other data is out there." Paul stood by the door with his hand on the handle. "I've got to run, but keep me posted," he told Daniel, ending the call and going back inside.

By the time Isabel got home and changed, she was quite happy with the decision to go for a run. It helped clear her mind. The fresh lakeside air was cold, and with each breath, she felt renewed.

Daniel was a charming man, someone she trusted greatly. But was she ready to settle? There were a few occasions when she had caught him in little white lies, and for some reason, they greatly bothered Isabel and affected her self-esteem. He was always cautious about his phone and possessions, but was it because of his profession? He spent too much time with her for it to be another woman, didn't he?

As Isabel ran hard now, her breathing heavy, she cut through a park, along a narrow path, and over a bridge to a pathway that ran along the river. "You need to be careful," she said to herself, and her breathing became irregular, triggering a wave of grief. Talking to herself helped maintain her sanity. She had been thinking hard about it all. "You love him, don't you?" she asked herself, but there was hesitation. She couldn't pinpoint why she was afraid, but the fear lingered. It felt as if he was more invested in the relationship than she was, and that seemed unfair. "You're only going to hurt him," she told herself, running even faster now. "I came here selfishly. I have done nothing to help myself grow."

Isabel slowed to a walk beside a park bench, clutching the back of it while supporting her body by holding her knee straight. She sucked in the air, exhausted. She was angry with herself for dwelling so deeply on these thoughts. Standing tall, hands on her hips, she took deep breaths. "I can't keep going on like this, undecided. He's important, and I love him, but this can't happen now," she said, trying to sound definitive. She attempted to control and dictate her feelings, but she knew it was naive.

E.R. Wychwood

Daniel contemplated revealing the complete truth to her, but he couldn't. He didn't want it to end in heartbreak, and for some reason, it felt like it would. He'd hated it. His father had come into his room. "Good morning," his father had said well before the sun cast its light strips through the window. He had coughed a response. "How are you feeling Daniel?" his father brought his leg up and he sat on the side of the bed and his torso lanced forward so that his arm supported him and he could embrace his son. He first placed the back of his hand onto Daniel's forehead to check is temperature and then went through the toils of giving Daniel medicine. "Mum and Dad must to go to Los Angeles, we'll be back early next week, alright?" he had leaned forward and pushed back Daniel's hair from his forehead and he gave him a kiss. Daniel had rolled to face his father and draped his small arms around his dad's neck and hid his face in his neck.

"I love you, Daniel. Now go back to sleep," he again kissed Daniel on his forehead. The memory had haunted him and Daniel sat up in a cold sweat and stared at the foreign room. He was back in Zurich – far from Boston – far from the memory of his father who was but a ghost of his past.

A week later, Daniel had recovered from his injuries, although he couldn't feel the pain from the healing wounds. Isabel had been running more frequently, sometimes disappearing for hours or even days, leaving Daniel wondering. He often thought about Henry, his mentor, and felt a desire to ask him about matters of love and commitment. However, the passage of time had created an unbridgeable gap between them.

Daniel's thoughts were in disarray. He felt uncertain about what was right and wrong as he grew older, unable to distinguish between the two. The world seemed to be a spectrum of gray, obscuring its varying truths. Gradually, he and Isabel started arguing, and she saw it as a reason to slow down or possibly end their relationship. The weightiness of their relationship seemed to anchor them, dragging them down.

"What do you think about all this?" Daniel asked as they watched the news, a segment about the CIA catching their attention.

"Just because they aren't getting caught doesn't mean they've changed. A leopard never loses its spots," she replied, her tone tinged with bitterness, surprising Daniel. He wondered why she held that belief, but she seemed uncertain herself, shrugging in response. "I don't know," she said, nestling under his arm and looking up at him. "Do you think they should be doing that?"

"I think if they've betrayed the government or pose a threat to people's well-being, then using force to protect citizens is justifiable," Daniel replied. Since

The Collateral Dividend

being stabbed, he had neglected shaving, a small act of defiance and laziness. With his beard and grown-out hair, he resembled more of an Italian soccer star than a banker.

Isabel laughed. "Spoken like a true American," she remarked, unafraid to voice her disagreement. She was unabashed in her opinions, and Daniel found it immensely attractive. "I don't know; I just don't think revenge is something that should be endorsed. The violence of it all is corrosive. It eats away at people, you know? I've seen my brothers take down men, and for what? It's no way to live."

"And what about justice?" Daniel inquired.

"There's a quote in French, 'Il n'y a pas de hors-texte' – there is nothing outside context," Isabel replied thoughtfully. "I believe everything has a way of working itself out, even things we think have gone catastrophically wrong. For me, justice is not revenge." Her tone held deliberate conviction. Isabel was unapologetic, brash, and honest, qualities that drew Daniel to her.

For the first time in a long while, Daniel felt he could trust someone other than Paul or Henry. He envisioned a future with Isabel, and they had even discussed the possibility of her joining him when he returned to New York. Most of the time, she liked the idea. However, occasionally, her past would resurface, reminding her of the turmoil and chaos that had engulfed her life in England. Daniel could sense these moments when she grew quiet and still, anxiety washing over her face like a cold, stale draft.

It took nearly a month or two for Daniel to fully recover from his injuries, leaving behind only a deep scar. By then, he had been in Zurich for almost seven months, and a shift was palpable in his relationship with Isabel. They had reached a point of stasis, where they had to decide whether to move forward or end things altogether. Still, they lacked the crucial information they needed.

He continued to maintain the lie that he worked in the financial district, spending some time in and around the office complex each day, perhaps attempting to convince himself that his deception was not despicable.

But what troubled him more were the recurring nightmares that jolted him awake in a cold sweat. The dreams had become increasingly vivid, leaving him sitting on the edge of the bed, head in hands, while Isabel tried to calm him down.

Early on, Isabel had suggested he see a psychiatrist, prompting Daniel to regularly call Dr. Acres in Langley to discuss his dreams. Dr. Acres had recommended increasing the dosage of the drugs prescribed by Farragut Center, something Daniel was hesitant to do. Yet, there was comfort in Isabel's presence, and their interactions solidified their already intertwined bond.

"What do you think about all this?" Daniel floated the question to her while they were watching the news, which featured a piece on the CIA.

"Just because they aren't getting caught doesn't mean they've changed. A leopard never loses its spots," she had said, her tone tinged with bitterness, surprising Daniel. Why did she think that? He asked, but she was unsure, shrugging in response. "I don't know," she said, nestled underneath his arm and looking up at him. "Do you think they should be doing that?"

"I think if they've betrayed the government or threaten the well-being of people, then I see no reason why force shouldn't be used to protect citizens," Daniel replied. He hadn't shaved since he was stabbed; it was an act of defiance and laziness. With his grown-out hair and beard, he looked more like an Italian soccer star than a banker.

Isabel laughed. "Spoken like a true American," she said, unafraid to express her disagreement. She was unapologetic in her opinions. "I don't know; I just don't think revenge is something that should be endorsed. The violence of it all is corrosive. It eats at people, you know? I've seen my brothers cut down men – and for what? It's no life to live."

"And what about justice?"

"There's a quote in French, 'Il n'y a pas de hors-texte' – there is nothing outside context. I think everything has a way of working itself out, even the things we think have gone catastrophically wrong. Justice, at least for me, is not revenge," she said with deliberateness. Isabel was unapologetic, brash, and honest, and Daniel found it immensely attractive.

For the first time in a long time, Daniel trusted someone other than Paul or Henry. He could see a future with her, and occasionally, the idea had been floated that when Daniel was sent back to New York, Isabel would come with him. Most of the time, she quite liked that idea. But every so often, she would find herself pulled back into her past, reminded of the turmoil and chaos that had withered its way into her life back in England. Daniel could often tell when these fits occurred because she would go very quiet and still, and anxiety would wash over her face like a cold, stale draft.

It took nearly a month or two more for Daniel to fully recover from his injuries until all that was left was a deep scar. By then, he had been in Zurich for almost seven months, and there were the first hints of a shift in his relationship with Isabel. They had reached a point where they either had to move forward or end things entirely. They still did not have the information they needed.

He had maintained the lie that he was working in the financial district, visiting the office complex at the beginning and middle of an eight-hour period each day, perhaps to convince himself that lying this way wasn't despicable.

But what vexed him more were the constant nightmares that would wake him in a cold sweat in the dead of night. They had become much more vivid, and on more than one occasion, he had sat at the edge of the bed with his head in his hands while Isabel tried to talk him down.

Early on, Isabel had suggested he see a psychiatrist. Though he initially resisted, he began regularly calling Dr. Acres in Langley to talk through the dreams. Part of Acres' recommendation was to increase the dose of drugs prescribed by Farragut Center, something Daniel was hesitant to comply with. However, the fact that Isabel was there brought him comfort, and their interactions seemed to strengthen their already tightly intertwined bond.

When Isabel slept, it seemed as if she barely breathed. Sometimes, he would wake and watch her, wondering what she dreamt about and what she thought about him. Sometimes, near the end of the month or after a long time apart, she would come across as cold and distant. He caressed the top of her head.

The idea that he had done something wrong began to creep into his mind, and he worried that perhaps she had discovered his lies and intended to leave him. No, that wasn't it; Daniel was a very good judge of character. He hadn't slipped up in his own lie, of that he was certain, but the doubt remained.

Daniel had to accept that there was another possibility – one he had been avoiding acknowledging with every fiber of his being. Perhaps Isabel's distance was because she was lying to him. Was it possible that she was hiding her involvement in the plot to steal money from her brothers or her involvement with Gaillard? It was something Daniel feared more than anything. He had a fear that his trust had been turned against him, and he had been made a fool of – that he had not only been duped into loving someone who didn't love him but that they had used that love to crush him.

"Not everyone is a pathological liar like you, Daniel," he said aloud to himself, as if saying it out loud helped solidify the thought. But these pervasive thoughts rotted his mind. That was the problem; they undermined everything he did and clouded his thoughts. It was what made him such a good spy. He couldn't trust that others were being truthful with him. He couldn't trust them, no matter how deeply he desired to do so. There was this gnawing feeling that a fragment of truth was always being withheld. He observed decisions being made with alternative priorities. Perhaps it was because he felt insecure about his past, with such disdain, that the future was plagued by fear, especially the fear of trust and its offspring.

*　　*　　*

Sergei had nearly killed himself. He was certain that he had done one too many lines of cocaine the night before and had become too aggressive with an escort. The memories of that night flooded into his head all at once. He felt silly, stupid for the mistake he had made, and for his recent behavior. As the morning sun cast strong lines across the living room floor, he covered his face with a pillow, attempting to fall back asleep. Restless and hungover, a combination that often went hand in hand, Sergei struggled to find peace.

A loud knock on the door shattered the fragile tranquility, followed by the crashing sound of the door being forced open and the splintering of wood. Sergei got out of bed, his world spinning, but he managed to focus enough to grab the gun from the table and point it forward.

"Are you packed?" Philippe Gaillard's voice echoed from the living room. Sergei reluctantly put the gun down and collapsed onto the bed, feeling ill. He did a bump of cocaine in an attempt to regain focus and cleaned the residue from his nose. Gaillard remarked, "I see you look quite ready to go," glancing at his watch. "I know your flight leaves this evening, but I was wondering if you'd care to join me for lunch. Why don't we talk?"

"This moment?" Sergei asked, collapsing onto the sofa and closing his eyes, nursing a glass of vodka against his forehead.

"Of course," Philippe said, taking a seat in a chair and scanning the apartment. "What do you have to drink here?"

"There's some wine in the fridge," Sergei gestured weakly toward the nearby kitchen. Piere was already there, pouring a drink for Philippe Gaillard.

"Sergei, it is ten in the morning; I am not an alcoholic," Philippe shamefully remarked as Piere handed him a mug of coffee. Taking a long sip, Philippe let out a deep breath. "Sergei, when you get to New York, there is something I will need you to do at month's end. We're going to place an algorithm into a market terminal and head office. You will need to activate it and initiate the market orders. It will prompt several margin calls and a handful of booked orders. You can continue working there for as long as you desire afterward, but I would prefer a minimum of a month."

"Are they orders from your account?" Sergei asked, his suspicions aroused.

The Collateral Dividend

Philippe Gaillard chuckled. "No, my friend," he replied with a broad grin. "Once you activate the algorithm in the terminal, the program will take care of the rest."

Sergei couldn't help but ask about lunch. He knew there was always a catch.

"We've had some new developments that are... unsettling," Gaillard said, pushing himself off the counter and walking toward Sergei. He handed a photograph to the Russian, a face Sergei recognized but couldn't place. Gaillard's phobias had spiraled out of control, and even Piere couldn't keep them in check. Sergei was tasked with dealing with Klaus, an emphatic figure, spoon-feeding him blowfish poison disguised as seafood. "I'd love to show you something," he had been instructed to say, bringing Klaus up to his apartment. The encounter was awkward, but fear of Gaillard kept Klaus from questioning it.

"How well do you know Gaillard?" Klaus eventually asked, after they both had a smoke. The air smelled faintly of Gauloises. "He's going insane, you know. You must know this," Klaus said, trying to elaborate, but Sergei was unaware of what Klaus was talking about. "He's sick, Sergei. A sick old man who's gone insane. Don't you find this all a bit crazy?" Sergei hadn't given it much thought. To be honest, he hadn't really considered the purpose of it all. He hadn't pondered why Gaillard had brought him here or what his motives were. Sergei tried to push such thoughts aside. The pay was good, and he was far away from the prying eyes of his father and the service. As long as Gaillard allowed him to remain employed by the bank, Sergei felt free from expectations and pressures—a powerful emotion.

"Sick of what?" Sergei asked, his face contorted with repulsion, as if the idea disgusted him to the core.

"Oh, it's true," Klaus insisted. "We need to run, Sergei, before he makes an impulsive decision and kills us all." Klaus suddenly felt violently ill, worse than ever before. He knocked over a nearby glass table, collapsing into the washroom, his head hanging over the toilet. Vomiting became violent, as if trying to expel an evil spirit from the depths of his body. Soon after, Klaus began to vomit blood, convulsing on the ground.

Ezra Cohen stood in the doorway of the washroom, gazing at Klaus's lifeless body. Sergei stood beside him. They would need to clean up the mess and find a way to dispose of the body so that it no longer resembled Klaus. Ezra had already taken on Klaus's mannerisms, studied him day and night, and erased all online images of Klaus, replacing them with photos of himself. The same had been done with physical photographs. Klaus's close friends were either no longer in contact or were convinced that Ezra was the young German. Coincidentally, they looked quite similar—both tall blondes who appeared to be the same age, despite Ezra being nearly fifteen years older.

"Is there anything you need from me?" Sergei asked, checking his watch. His suitcase had been brought to the front. Ezra shook his head. Minor details remained before Ezra fully assumed the role of Klaus. There was nothing else Sergei could do.

THE HIGH TIDE

Paul arrived early, looking exhausted, and followed his usual routine. After a shower, he had a bottle of Huel, dressed, and took the metro to a location a block south of the offices. By then, it was nearly six-thirty, and he often made a stop at the local coffee shop for a muffin and a large coffee with three creams. Paul was typically one of the first to open Farragut Center and often the last to leave.

His day typically began by reviewing security and intelligence briefings for the President. A staffer from Langley would bring it down and place it under guard until Paul arrived. After reading the brief, Paul would dispose of it in a burn bag later in the day. By quarter to seven, he settled into his office, and within an hour, he had already gone through four meetings with various divisions, ranging from signals intelligence to support staff.

The smooth operation of Farragut Center relied on all its moving parts, and Paul was responsible for ensuring operations abroad ran efficiently. The Director of National Intelligence (DNI) had always been cautious about delving into the inner workings of Farragut Center, and perhaps it was for the best that he remained uninformed. This was how things operated, and everyone else was content with that arrangement. The DNI believed in smooth functioning, efficiency, and achieving the best possible results. It required meticulous and tedious bureaucratic planning to allocate the limited resources provided to Paul. He liked to think of himself as a mastermind, a revolutionary within the intelligence community's special access programs.

By noon, Paul shifted his focus to field operations. He had another meeting with Dr. Acres, the psychiatrist from Langley who had prepared a psychological report based on Paul's extensive daily reading. When asked about Daniel, Paul mentioned that he appeared more confused than before. Dr. Acres considered it a curious case, suggesting that Daniel's moral dilemma and self-reflection might stem from his interactions with Isabel. Paul inquired further, prompting the psychiatrist to explain that she had observed similar effects on PTSD victims. In her sessions with Daniel, she noticed significant improvements in his character and morals. Paul confirmed that Daniel still experienced hallucinations, leaving Dr. Acres concerned about Isabel's involvement and the potential for a positive outcome.

E.R. Wychwood

Paul was uncertain and saw Dr. Acres out before making his way back to his office. On the way, he stopped by several other offices to get updates on routine matters. While standing in his office, he asked a colleague about the progress on a crashed drone investigation.

"I was planning on discussing it with you after lunch," the colleague replied. "We were able to track the drone's data storage for several miles across the border using information from local cell towers. It was a tedious process, but we managed to uncover a few things."

Paul pressed for more information, knowing he had to brief the Director of National Intelligence within the hour. He preferred handling the situation internally, but the involvement of the CIA, NSA, and DOD meant Farragut Center would likely play a limited role. Through the DNI's office, they would only establish guidelines and ground rules.

"The drone contained encryption algorithms used in intelligence community surveillance protocols," the analyst explained. Paul stared out the window for a while before sitting down and playing with the pen on his desk. He asked the analyst to clarify the situation.

"The security algorithms failed a few months ago, allowing access through our servers. However, physically possessing control of the data in those drones gives the possessor access to the entire network."

Paul rubbed his temples. "But you mentioned we know where it went."

The analyst nodded. "We know at least the initial destination," he clarified, realizing the difficulty of tracking its subsequent movements. Tracing a money trail would require extensive and painstaking work. It became crucial to retrieve the data swiftly and efficiently before it fell into the wrong hands. Farragut Center treated this incident like an outbreak, fully aware that it could spread rapidly.

"Where did it go?" Paul asked, already reaching for the classified packet handed to him by the analyst. He opened it, examining the photograph and briefing packet.

"Port of Sudan," the analyst replied, pointing to the marked location of the drone hardware.

Without hesitation, Paul started signing the authorization page, handing it back to the analyst. "Contact Director Dunes. I want to coordinate a mission to retrieve this data," he said abruptly, observing the young man leave his office. "How soon can we deploy assets to the area?" Paul crossed his arms and leaned back in his chair.

"Next week seems likely," the young man responded.

Paul nodded. "Perfect. Make it happen.

*   *   *

When they met for dinner that evening, something was amiss in her eyes—a hint of disappointment and despair. They stumbled through half the meal, and finally, Daniel placed his fork down on the stark white table setting. He gazed at her for a long while, interrupting Isabel's polite eating. She glanced down at her plate when she noticed his stare.

"What's the matter?" Daniel asked, his concern evident. He couldn't shake off the feeling that something was wrong. He wondered if he was succumbing to the classic beauty and beast syndrome, where his fear of losing her could consume them both and push her away. The knowledge that he had manufactured artificial feelings added to his unease. There were moments when he forgot to take his medication, and he might have inadvertently consumed substantial levels of oxytocin. The line between real and fake emotions had become blurred. Daniel acknowledged that he was suffering, and his attempts to alleviate his fears only seemed to exacerbate them, like a looming beast casting a long shadow of fear over his days. He visualized this beast as a cloaked figure, a harbinger of doom, sucking the joy and passion out of their relationship, dragging him into a cycle of eternal regret. The image of the figure dissolved as the room came back into focus, and the billowing curtains resembled the figure's tall capes in the wind.

"You've been acting different since you came here," Daniel finally broke the silence, sensing the need for an explanation.

"Nothing," Isabel assured him, her focus on the quinoa salad. She wished he could accept her words at face value and stop prodding further.

Daniel felt frustrated. He attempted to engage her in conversation, but a seemingly impenetrable wall stood between them, souring their moods and imposing a stubborn silence that weighed heavily on both their chests. Sighs and cautious glances followed, intensifying Daniel's suspicion that their relationship had reached a breaking point, although he couldn't pinpoint why. Despite a lingering passion, the air felt stale and devoid of life. Doubt overshadowed his thoughts, and he struggled to make sense of his own emotions.

They had originally planned to continue their evening with a late dinner, but Daniel insisted on addressing the issue. They found a park bench where they could talk it out.

"This is silly," Isabel huffed, crossing her arms and turning to face Daniel. Her facial lines furrowed, and her hair blew in the wind as she wrestled with how to express herself. Despite her efforts, the words failed to convey the depth of her feelings. "I can't do this anymore," she suddenly blurted out, her composure faltering. Daniel tried to offer comfort, unsure if it was the reaction she desired. He questioned if he had unintentionally caused her distress with his unfiltered honesty.

She loved him, but there were more things to consider. "You've made me immensely happy over the past few months," she had said frankly. As she mustered forward, her train of thought seemed rehearsed. This decision hadn't been sudden; it had been burrowing into the back of her mind for a while. "I'm not emotionally ready for the type of commitment that this is leading to." Daniel had gotten underneath her skin, and dealing with that responsibility was unnerving. It felt stressful, tiresome, and she wanted to escape that feeling.

She had told him that ending things wasn't easy, not just because telling someone it was over was hard, but also because she genuinely cared for him. But it was more than that, and Isabel didn't have the heart to explain it to him.

While wounded, Daniel's concern remained focused on her. It felt pathetic, his own helplessness. But perhaps, amidst the pain, a seed of altruism sprouted—a departure from his usual worry-filled thoughts. He wasn't certain what to make of it.

"I don't regret any of it," she finally said. Daniel had his arm draped across the side of the bench, watching as the wind swayed the nearby trees. The sky had turned gloomy, and there seemed to be an inconsistency in the direction of the wind.

At the beginning of the conversation, Daniel had contemplated telling her the truth, all of it. In retrospect, he was glad he hadn't said anything. He felt foolish for having those feelings. Had he been played? Was this, as Isabel insisted, a case of the right people at the wrong time?

It put him in a precarious situation. He was now obligated to keep tabs on her, tracking her movements for both her safety and national security. How awkward it was to keep Isabel under surveillance when the original plan had collapsed under the weight of unforeseen circumstances. Nobody had anticipated that the beautiful woman from London would reach an emotional impasse, especially when the threat to her safety still lingered.

The night felt hazy, and everything he did seemed unfamiliar. The world and its activities stung like an open sore. It felt as if he had awoken in a daze, suddenly confronted with the harsh reality that he didn't trust many people. He

The Collateral Dividend

found himself crying without knowing why. Occasionally, more often than he cared to admit, he found himself talking as if someone were there, but it was only him.

"Now's not a good time," Daniel had replied to the morning briefing from Paul. Despite getting up and going about his day, he found himself slumped on the sofa in sweatpants by nine-thirty, lying around until midday.

Regardless of whether it was a good time or not, they needed to talk. "We have something that I think may interest you," Paul said urgently. "Something's happened—Gaillard has disappeared," Paul said, his mood sour. Paul had been eating an apple, pacing his office with an almost nervous twitch. He then asked Daniel if he had received the package from Farragut Center.

The package had arrived that morning, but Daniel hadn't opened it yet. He glanced over at the package resting on the table near the bed. "I'm looking at it now," Daniel replied casually. "What do you mean, disappeared?" he asked, hearing Paul bite his tongue.

"We've lost him entirely. He had a meeting with Sergei Kroysgin this morning and took a charter out of Zurich this afternoon."

"Where was it headed?" Daniel asked. That was the problem—they didn't know. "What about Sergei? Do you think he'd know?"

"Possibly, but he'd never talk," Paul surmised. "Besides," he continued, "that would be too direct, and I suspect it would force Gaillard to go underground completely." Daniel interjected, telling him that such an event might have already happened.

"What would you like me to do?" Daniel asked, and much to his surprise, Paul told him to do nothing. "Sit tight," he said, knowing full well that Daniel would do something. It was almost a test—they had run out of leads.

For the first time in a long time, Daniel had formulated ideas about what could be done. It would be a good distraction, going beyond Paul's authorization.

Paul knew more than he let on; he believed it was best to let things play out before deciding to act. "How are things otherwise?" Paul eventually asked, and Daniel let out a deep sigh. They were over. "Well, Christ. Why would you do that? We needed you to remain in contact with her, not stop seeing her just because it wasn't working," Paul was in a sour mood. He simply didn't understand. Daniel didn't think it was necessary to explain himself or the hurt. What was the point? Sympathy was of no use to him.

What a silly thing to do. The plan would have ensured he could keep hanging around, and somehow Daniel had messed it up. Paul wondered if

Daniel had even considered the consequences of his actions while screening the third phone call this morning from home. Sometimes he wondered if Rachel even realized he was working. He would see her when he got home.

Avery had accomplished in a short time what would have taken Faron months in the field. They now knew the key players in Casca—Gaillard, Min, Klaus, and Ralston. It was still unclear how each one fit in, and Paul wanted more information. It wasn't until midafternoon that Paul had a chance to grab a bite to eat, ordering Chinese food and eating it at his desk while watching the server cycle through the near limitless transactions that had gone through Casca.

Daniel found himself having trouble sleeping again. He would toss and turn for two hours or so before lying flat on his back, attempting to clear his head of racing thoughts. Conflicting ideas surrounded his linear thoughts, spinning and circling until he addressed them one by one.

Daniel wondered if Paul already knew about Isabel. A part of him believed that Farragut Center was already aware. There was little they didn't know about him, although he still had pockets of information that remained his own secrets. In the twilight of the night, he no longer desired the openness of his life. There was a point when his intimacy with Farragut Center had been encouraged. Daniel had liked the idea that everything from his shoe size to allergies was known by the Center. Initially, it made him feel safe, as though they were always looking out for him. Now, with his thoughts circling like vultures, Daniel wasn't sure he wanted to lead an open life. Did they really need to know his undergraduate GPA or his dating habits after college to reinforce national security?

He felt hollow. "You'd be a pretty cold bastard if you didn't feel hurt by all this," he told himself. Yet, he couldn't forget that the memory would be etched into his mind.

By half-past one, he sat up at the end of the bed, hiding his head in his hands, deciding he needed a walk. The street was long and narrow, with shrubbery growing along the curb, dividing the narrow sidewalk from the road. Park benches were scattered every few hundred yards, allowing people to sit and gaze at the delicate buildings with grey plaster and red shingles. He walked past Catherine's apartment, trying not to stare up at the windows but failing. Something seemed amiss—the windows appeared fogged and smeared, and all the curtains were drawn shut with the lights on. As Daniel approached the building's entrance, he noticed the door seemed broken. He tried to ignore it until he was almost entirely past the building lobby.

The Collateral Dividend

    It was then that he stopped, turned, and fully faced the door. Daniel walked over to it, pulled the handle, and the door, which was usually tightly sealed, flew open, emitting a long and tiresome whine from its hinges.

    If his mind had been somewhat calmed during the walk, it certainly was no longer. Part of Daniel wished Isabel would be out, and it would only be Catherine inside, smoking a joint. He hoped for a rational explanation for all these coincidences.

    By the time he reached the top floor, Daniel walked down the long hallway and craned his neck to the left, trying to catch a glimpse of Isabel's apartment door. "If nothing is out of place, there's no use in stopping to say hello," Daniel told himself. He didn't particularly want to answer why he was pacing around Isabel's front door. Standing outside someone's door unannounced felt amiss and unsettling.

    At the end of the left hallway stood a door, battered and scratched, its handle emerging from the shadow of the doorframe. Daniel, three yards away, felt his breath escape him. He glanced down the hallway and then back at the door, his hands buried deep in the slip pockets of an old winter coat. Pressing against the door, Daniel slowly pushed it open, allowing a thin strip of light from the atrium to seep through the crack into the hallway. With a gentle touch, he widened the opening enough to slip past the frame, ensuring the door closed softly behind him.

    From his coat pocket, Daniel retrieved a handgun and disabled the safety, realizing it had been almost a year since he last fired a weapon. The narrow hall led to a dark living room, gradually revealing itself as the walls peeled back. It was a scene of desolation. The upturned sofa lay torn and tattered, its fabric pillows in shreds. Broken glass from mirrors, vases, and lights covered the floor like crushed powder. The fireplace had burnt out, its mantle devoid of any belongings, now littered with dirt, leaves, and trinkets of various shapes. Shattered pottery, torn furniture, missing or shattered televisions, and cracked photo frames strewn across the room hinted at a violent intrusion. Even the Van Gogh paintings that once graced the walls had met a similar fate— one cut from its frame, another torn with a broken lamp thrust through its canvas.

    A sense of danger enveloped Daniel as he made his way to the far end of the living room, peering into the small reading room that led to the kitchen. Bullet holes marred the thick wood paneling of the bookshelves, and he gingerly ran his finger along one of them, identifying them as nine-millimeter rounds. Books lay scattered on the floor, and near the window, Catherine's lifeless body lay in a disheveled heap on the love seat. A bullet had pierced her head, splattering the room with crimson. Her wide-open eyes betrayed no emotion. Overlooking the street, the closed blinds shielded the scene, while the nearby stereo blared alternative indie rock. Daniel located the terminal, reducing the volume to a manageable level, allowing his thoughts to resurface. Catherine, an innocent victim, deserved at least a small gesture of decency, and so he gently closed her eyelids.

Ascending the stairwell, Daniel systematically checked the rest of the house to ensure it was empty. Isabel's room, though devoid of personal belongings, remained intact compared to the rest of the ransacked house. It appeared methodically packed rather than ruthlessly torn apart. Paintings and books were absent from the walls and shelves. The floor lay bare, and the stripped mattress bore a diagonal cut. A thought crept into Daniel's mind—had he been deceived?

Returning to the living room, Daniel fixated on Catherine's lifeless form, struggling to come to terms with the overwhelming loss. The ringing of a cellphone shattered the silence, and Daniel reached for it, watching it tremble on the table. On the screen, an unfamiliar message appeared: "La lengua vir on la dent mi fa mal e.l cor vas selhs ont hom no.s pot jauzir; so so.l baro malvat, cuy Dieus azir, que an baissat a pretz son sessal." Daniel surveyed the room but found nothing amiss. The secluded street outside remained empty.

Suddenly, a bullet tore through the balcony window, ricocheting off the doorframe and embedding itself in the ceiling with a hiss. Daniel swiftly dropped to the ground as a barrage of shots shattered the glass, obliterating the remaining fragile remnants within. Crawling towards the door, Daniel wedged his attacker's gun between the door and its frame, disarming them. With a powerful shove, he knocked the assailants to the ground, fired into the doorframe, and made his escape through a back exit.

Removing his phone from his breast pocket, Daniel dialed a number, stumbling onto the sidewalk as he crossed the road aimlessly, his mind lost in turmoil. There was no need for words. Paul, having witnessed everything through a satellite feed, expressed relief at Daniel's safety and ordered his recall from the field. "A charter is waiting for you," Paul informed him. "Try not to dwell on it. After all, you can't expect her to stick around after you ended things," Paul added, oblivious to the fact that Daniel had not brought their relationship to a close, nor did he intend to correct Paul anytime soon. "Unfortunately, we still can't confirm her involvement," Paul continued. "But we can't be certain she's not," Daniel retorted, a lump forming in his throat, creating discomfort. Raindrops fell longingly, tracing lines on the narrow, weary street as Daniel gazed into the distance.

The Collateral Dividend

"You can't dwell on the past; it's unprofessional," Paul asserted matter-of-factly. Exhaustively scanning all public flights within a twelve-hour window, they found no matches for Isabel's whereabouts. Expanding the search criteria, they attempted to trace the travels of Philippe Gaillard, hoping to locate Isabel indirectly.

A week passed before Avery tracked down Gaillard's Gulfstream, enabling them to trace his movements using the tail number. Tracking was never a challenge for Paul; the difficulty lay in executing preemptive actions. How would they apprehend Gaillard? Paul considered using market money as bait, fully aware that it would entail significant losses. Yet, he never questioned whether it was the right decision, opting to keep it to himself, not even divulging the plan to Daniel or Ted. Paul would rather be seen as incompetent than have his values questioned, for a moral dilemma plagued their mission, although neither Paul nor Avery had any qualms about it.

Eventually, they reached out to their partners at The Valley in a final attempt to assess the extent of the damage caused by the breach. While the verdict was still pending, discussions shed light on previously overlooked information. The Valley had initiated a lawsuit against Min and his firm for patent infringements, and it became evident that the breach at Farragut Center had repercussions rippling outward.

They discovered that Gaillard's travels had become more frequent, far exceeding his previous patterns. Paul noted his charitable contributions, a noble gesture tainted by the illegal acquisition of funds. "Daniel," Doctor Acres addressed him from across the table in his office. Lost in thought, Daniel sat back in his chair, a bottle of scotch in hand. Acres, concerned for his well-being, admonished him about his excessive drinking, her tone authoritative and unapologetic. Daniel glanced at the remaining gulp in his glass, yearning to consume it, to seize it across the table.

With a deep breath and a strained smile, Daniel met Acres' gaze. He thanked her for taking the time to meet him and abruptly asked, "Do you ever feel overwhelmed?" His tone grew solemn, revealing the months of sleepless nights and relentless hallucinations that plagued him. His chosen profession had slowly eroded his mental stability, and the terrifying realization that his actions possessed both great evil and great good gnawed at his core. The line between the two blurred, and distinguishing them had become unbearably challenging.

Daniel then confided in Acres, expressing his deep concern for Isabel and the overwhelming responsibility he felt for her disappearance. He suspected she had run away, stumbling over his words as he tried to articulate his love for her.

Despite his hesitations, the truth remained evident. Acres, skilled in reading people, perceived his attempt to hide the depth of his feelings from himself and others.

"Perhaps it's best to take some time," Acres said, jotting down a note on her pad. Daniel, in facing his own demons, was becoming one himself. Destroying the things that haunt you carries the risk of self-destruction, she warned him. There was great danger in that.

"Is it too absurd to believe that things like this always have a way of figuring themselves out?" Daniel pondered.

"Not at all," Acres defended. "But you have to believe in it before it can protect you." Her tone was prudish.

"Do you think it's worth looking for her?" Daniel asked Acres.

"Perhaps eventually. Professionally speaking, I think she made the right decision. You need this time to grieve, to grow," Acres advised.

"But what about her safety?" Daniel voiced his worry about Gaillard potentially reaching her. He hadn't told Paul about the text message or the ensuing gunfight. All that had been said was that she was gone, and it seemed that no one was really looking for her. Daniel suspected they were more focused on finding her after the money had been stolen.

"Daniel, I think you're trying to distract yourself here. There are serious things going on that you need to address. Resolving this matter is of minor importance compared to dealing with Gaillard and the mental and physical traumas you're trying to overcome," Acres observed. She realized that Daniel was using the search for Isabel as a diversion. After a few minutes of silence, her tone softened, and she asked a poignant question that shed light on the situation. "How do you think she felt about you? Without overanalyzing," she inquired, acknowledging the insightful nature of a woman's perspective. Acres initially had hesitations, but she found a great deal of depth in Daniel's thoughts and his cold, shrewd demeanor.

Lost in thoughts of Isabel, Daniel sat in his chair, missing her dearly. He wondered where she was and what she was thinking. The idea of her thinking about him seemed outrageous, yet he couldn't help but think about her. He questioned if there was something he could have done to change things or if his actions had caused her to become distant and cold. He had no answers, only fragments of details that deepened his worry and intrigue.

"You're a very passionate man," Acres commented, bringing Daniel back to reality. They were back in the office, with Acres sitting across from him in a conference room chair. It was evident from his distracted expression that he

The Collateral Dividend

had lost focus. "That's not to say it's a bad thing, Mr. Faron. Your emotions are intense. I've noticed a pattern. When you're supposed to feel something or recall a memory where you should feel something, your mind tries to connect images to that feeling. It attempts to fix itself by sending images," Acres explained.

Daniel exhaled deeply, running his hand through his thick, long hair, occasionally bothered by its presence. He swallowed hard, struggling to find words to respond.

"Are you still experiencing hallucinations?" Acres inquired, and Daniel nodded.

"It never stops, really. What happened in my head is not something that gets better," Daniel admitted frankly.

"Not by itself," Acres optimistically countered, but Daniel didn't believe it. Over the past two years, he had realized that his preference for remaining single was a fallacy. In his unburdened mind, he longed for the companionship he nostalgically remembered from his parents. He had only witnessed the good times and was unaware of the challenges they faced. The idea that he could have a happy life like theirs had quickly shattered, leaving him feeling broken.

"We're trying to track down who's responsible, and it's all for what?" The words were spoken in a slow and measured drawl. There was no rush in the speaker's tone; instead, he seemed calm and content, lost in deep thought. "For what, huh? To protect some idea? I'm not even sure what that idea is," Acres asked, seeking clarification. Daniel leaned forward, his finger tapping the table for emphasis. "What I'm talking about is that there are things happening out there that you have to either ignore or embrace simply because they serve some ideal," he said, his voice tinged with cynicism. "I'm asked to make judgments about who lives and who dies. Is that based on determinism? Rationalism? 'Il n'y a pas de hors-texte,'" he smoothly uttered the phrase, followed by its translation: "There is nothing outside context." He continued, "But what good is that if context is subjective? Acres, how am I supposed to know if what I'm doing is something I can live with?" His words reflected a sour mood, as if a feeling long pent up inside him had suddenly snapped. Daniel had been grappling with these thoughts for a long time, and he wondered how Paul would have reacted if he had shared them. Probably with a sarcastic remark like, "Are you a philosopher now?"

"I think that's something you'll always struggle with. But you came here for a reason, didn't you? You must have believed in something," Acres replied, prompting Daniel to reflect on his initial purpose. She then asked him to share that reason. It was time for him to decide if he still held onto that belief. Daniel remembered. They were here for justice—or at least, that's what he had thought. But were they truly seeking justice in its purest form, or had it become a distorted version that Daniel could no longer recognize as an ideal?

By the time Acres left, Daniel had immersed himself in hours of backlogged operational reports from his frequent field service. Despite his independent role in the field, he was held accountable by Brian Redding, the Director of National Intelligence, who maintained strict oversight. Farragut Center faced constant threats of closure or financial instability. Ted, displeased with the black-and-white approach evident in many reports, had raised the issue, only to be told that it was how Daniel perceived it. This simplicity had started to blur, leaving Daniel struggling to grasp the true nature of their actions in Zurich.

After three weeks of searching, they had engaged in lengthy discussions with their counterparts and eventually located Gaillard in London, dealing with settling accounts. This had made the Director of National Intelligence nervous, leading to a tense exchange during their weekly meeting. Seeking clarity on the current state of affairs, Redding asked, "So what exactly are you saying?" Paul reasoned that Gaillard was playing with them, as they had encountered five ghost sites across Slavic Europe without finding him. Paul reached for a file folder containing five letters left for them, including a recent one sent to Daniel's phone, which nearly got him killed. "Two of them seemed related—they mentioned relatives and betrayal. When taken in context, I'm inclined to believe they were pointing us toward Isabel," Paul explained, contemplating Gaillard's intentions. He continued, "I think he wants us to apprehend her. I believe he wants us to make a mistake, either by killing or capturing someone carelessly, so that he can retaliate."

The DNI furrowed his brows, finding it hard to believe that Philippe Gaillard was truly that malicious. Even if he were the type to seek revenge on the Yates brothers, where did Farragut Center come into play? This was something that Paul didn't know, and it seemed illogical and senseless, which bothered him the most.

They had veered off-topic, but Paul brought them back to the main issue. Referring to the most recent poem he had sent, Paul said, "My tongue ever turns to the aching tooth, and my heart turns to those who can't enjoy." Paul believed this line related to Daniel and his losses. "Such are the wicked barons, whom God hates, who have been scrimping on their dues," Paul continued, reading aloud and attempting to analyze the idea for Redding.

"Is the girl, Isabel Yates, safe? Or has she been kidnapped? What's the deal?" the DNI asked, seeking clarity.

The Collateral Dividend

Paul let out a deep sigh. He didn't know for sure. They suspected that Isabel had left suddenly, embarking on another nomadic journey around the world for fun. However, they couldn't ignore the fact that her old roommate had been murdered and the presence of a poem convinced Daniel that Gaillard had her under his control. Earlier that day, Acres had shared this information with Paul in confidence, advising him not to mention it to Daniel. Acres had violated client trust, but it was for a justifiable cause.

"What do you think?" the DNI inquired after Paul had considered various possibilities.

"I think Daniel knows Isabel better than anyone here, but he's also emotionally involved," Paul replied. "Whether she's involved or not, Gaillard has his eyes on her, and that's more than what we currently have."

"So, are we tracking her or Gaillard?" the DNI questioned.

"We're trying to," Paul sighed. "Gaillard has been frequently traveling through Europe, more often than in the past year. We suspect he's planning to make a move in the markets within the next week. I'm sending Daniel to oversee the transaction in New York through a trading desk with Cable Schwartz. They're cooperating with us, and in return, we'll notify them before the crash."

"How does Gaillard intend to shut down the markets?" Redding asked, aware that market shutdowns were rare occurrences.

"Gaillard has been in extended contact with Alekos Tzavaras," Paul explained, displaying a photo of Alekos Tzavaras on the screen. Redding leaned back in his chair, gazing out the window. The conference room overlooked 17th Street. "I suspect Tzavaras is involved somehow. He blames us for the Greek fiscal crisis, and I believe they want to retaliate and use it as a distraction." Paul continued, showing a video of the Greek ultranationalists in action. War had broken out in Greece, plunging the country into chaos.

"Are these threats credible?" Redding inquired, concerned about the potential for a terrorist attack and the extent of the damage they could cause.

"Absolutely. Tzavaras trained with Gaillard's head of security during their time in Chasseurs Alpins. His experience in mountain terrain and urban warfare is evident in combat. He has created highly trained commanders. Whatever market closure Gaillard plans, if Tzavaras is involved, it will likely involve making a profit. The Ultranationalists are running out of funds rapidly," Paul explained.

"Keep an eye on it, and I'll ensure Homeland Security is on alert," Redding instructed. He then shifted the topic to the information leak involving the drone.

Paul sighed, recalling the embarrassing discussion. He explained to Redding how Farragut Center had been hacked, causing programming issues. They had collaborated with The Valley to rewrite a significant amount of code, and aside from a few terminals down the hall, all infected hardware had been isolated and removed. "When Casca accessed our servers, they obtained a considerable amount of data, which allowed them to occasionally override Valley's commands," Paul admitted.

Redding nodded, remembering Paul's previous explanation. "I recall it took down a surveillance drone," he said, and Paul confirmed his recollection. Redding expressed his concern, asking, "So, what are we dealing with here?"

"The data they retrieved from the hack wasn't mission-critical. However, while searching for the data, they stumbled upon information from the drone," Paul clarified, his voice filled with unease. He couldn't believe it had come to this. Rocking slowly back and forth in his office chair, he continued, "Large aspects, if not all, of the drone's data seem critical to the sustenance of this program. If it falls into the wrong hands, even a politician with a grudge could bring us and The Valley down. Our tech partners trust us to maintain confidentiality."

"Of course," the DNI acknowledged, aware that the firms had willingly partnered with Farragut Center and any accidental betrayal could be catastrophic. He gazed out the window, observing the steady rain and listening to its patter. "What do you need from me?" the DNI asked straightforwardly, crossing his arms and reclining in his chair.

"We located the information in the port of Sudan. I'd like to deploy assets to retrieve it," Paul requested.

"Absolutely," Brian Redding agreed. "Contact Director Dunes at the CIA. He'll provide you with assets if you need resources beyond your command."

Just then, there was a knock on the door, and Avery stood in the doorway. She apologized for interrupting but mentioned that one of the contaminated computers stored down the hall was acting up, and it was something Paul should see. When they reached the room, the computer screen was black, occasionally flashing between black and white before turning completely gray. Numbers appeared on the screen, soon replaced by white letters. Paul realized that the zeros represented spaces between words. The text read: "Mas d'ome.m meravill fortmen, Que sap mals e bes au-tressi E sap com va.l cars al moli...

The Collateral Dividend

Que.ill mermes son cozen El anar: d'autrui o de si A gran regart ser e mati, et es tot jorn en balansa."

"What does it say?" Paul asked, and Avery admitted she couldn't read it. A few hours later, she received a response from the professor, and she read it aloud while seated in Paul's office, holding the computer tablet and looking at Paul and Daniel. "Are we all ready?" she asked, but neither of them responded. "Right, so it says: 'But I greatly marvel at how a man who knows bad and good equally well and knows the way of the world would lessen his smarting pain by journeying abroad: either for himself or for others, he is worried morning, noon, and night; and he is in danger each day,'" Avery recited. She put the computer tablet down and looked at Daniel, then at Paul.

Daniel regarded Paul and suggested that the message might be about him. "He's telling us he thinks we can distinguish good from bad, that I'm traveling abroad for someone else's ideas and am in danger because of it," he explained softly.

"Don't be ridiculous," Paul responded, although he sensed the truth in Daniel's words. "He's toying with us, trying to get inside our heads." Paul paused, deep in thought. Perhaps this had something to do with the impending heist, he speculated. "This message isn't related to the previous one."

Daniel then brought up another matter, using the tablet to write down the words from memory. The text appeared in Times New Roman font on the screen. He asked Avery about the dialect, and she clarified that it was an old Occitan poem.

"I've seen this before," Avery informed them, searching through the files on the computer tablet. She found the file from the British Ofcom case, where the Ofcom representative had written a note in what seemed to be his own handwriting. It contained the text of this poem: "My tongue ever turns to the aching tooth, and my heart turns to those who can't enjoy." Avery explained that back then, it could be interpreted as a phrase indicating someone paying attention to a thorn in their side. "So he's implying that he's directing his harsh words towards those who bother him and showing sympathy to those who comply," Avery added, deconstructing the literal meaning of the phrases.

Suddenly, Avery realized that the two messages connected. The message sent to Farragut Center linked to the end of the statement sent to Daniel and the Ofcom representative. Sitting back in her chair, she exclaimed, "He's sending us a veiled threat disguised as a challenge."

Paul frowned, disliking the situation. He turned to Avery and asked, "Do we have any information on Tzavaras?"

E.R. Wychwood

Nodding, Avery replied, "His son arrived in New York under a false name a week ago. They've paid off a few members of the Port Authority and coordinated with key activists for a demonstration in downtown Manhattan tomorrow. The NYPD expects it to occur near the World Trade Center, north of the security checkpoints."

"What is he planning?" Paul muttered, staring at the map of lower Manhattan on the conference table. He stood up, examining the areas where the demonstrations were expected to take place. "Do the authorities know that Tzavaras has bribed these people?" he asked audibly.

"No," Avery answered.

Paul nodded and made a decision. "Redding has given us the green light to track down that information in Sudan. Let's act swiftly. In the meantime, Daniel, head to New York and oversee the demonstrations. Let Tzavaras take the money, but ensure no civilians get hurt. Once we're certain we can trace the money, eliminate Tzavaras."

* * *

Robert Kowalski was exhausted, drenched in sweat, and desperate for a refreshing bath. The scorching desert heat only made matters worse. Collapsing onto the ground upon entering the room, he lay flat on his back, as if seeking relief from the sweltering air. Sand had infiltrated every inch of his being, from his khaki gear to his boots, his clothes, and even his beard. The relentless sandstorm was unforgiving, and Robert couldn't help but wonder why they had been sent into such harsh conditions. Clearly, someone in Washington had made a serious mistake.

After meticulously cleaning his semi-automatic carbine to protect it from the sand, Robert leaned it against the far wall. Through a small window near the closed balcony, he could barely make out the city block across the street using his infrared goggles from the table. It was evident that they were dealing with an arms dealer who valued his privacy.

The sandstorm severely limited Robert's visibility, making it difficult to see beyond ten yards. Under normal circumstances, he would have had a clear view of the Red Sea from this room. However, the inhospitable desert obscured everything in its path for miles.

"It's blistering hot out there," grumbled the first figure, his voice tinged with frustration. Robert recognized him as Mason Harper, a seasoned operator with whom he had worked for years on "Capture/Kill" missions as Army Special Operators. They were both well-versed in these types of operations.

Robert glanced at Mason, noticing his thick beard and slicked-back hair that set him apart from the typical operator. The second figure entered the room, leaning his rifle against the wall near the door. He was the youngest of the group, known for his quiet demeanor. Robert had yet to learn his name.

Mason joined Robert in the room and loosened the side flaps of his combat vest. He removed the chest rig with both hands and collapsed onto the cot. Robert sat up on the floor and tossed Mason a bottle of water. Mason cracked the lid, gulping down its contents until the bottle was empty.

They had received briefings twice, once in the U.S. and then again before their insertion into Sudan through a dark and dreary port. The CIA had provided them with a safe house near the target's residence, but they had been waiting for over a day, hoping for clear weather and favorable conditions. With time running out, Robert felt they would soon have to take their chances.

"This weather is terrible for such an important mission," Mason grumbled as he started putting his combat vest back on.

"You think there's more to this?" Robert asked, speaking to Mason off the record. It was rare for them to have such candid conversations. Their inability to discuss their work had its hidden blessings. Mason's eyes flickered, and without saying a word, they communicated more than words could convey. There was always a secondary agenda, and this scenario was no different. Policymakers in Washington had limited coercive power that manipulated Langley.

"What about Section?" Kowalski, standing across from Mason, cradled the rifle and waited for a moment before looking at the youngest of the three men. "Should he meet us at checkpoint Alpha? He's established a weak satellite uplink with Langley." Mason paused, gazing out the window towards the outlying sand dune, a quarter mile beyond the targeted compound. He could barely make out the ten-foot concrete wall surrounding the building.

Kowalski nodded, clipping the stock of his rifle to his chest and adjusting his shegmah to cover his face. "As long as this doesn't spiral into a fucking shit show like Syria, we should be fine," he said, his voice muffled beneath the layers of fabric. Langley was never one to deal in absolutes, and under Robert's watch, they had been lied to about the objective's location on multiple occasions.

Robert had lost a few operators in Syria while securing high-value targets. After the fighting subsided, the region fell into a state of controlled anarchy, infested with notorious criminals. Among them were shady targets that Langley had been tasked to secure by an unknown governmental body. The agency leading today's operation was the same, which made Robert nervous. It was known as Farragut Center, at least on the few citation forms he had glimpsed, and it rarely proved to be wrong.

They were in a building with a terrace on top, and an exterior stairwell led to the sand-ridden streets facing the north of the targeted compound. Kowalski took point, using his thermal goggles to navigate the surroundings, barely able to see his hand extended in front of him.

Robert scanned the building's top, noticing a figure waiting patiently for the green light. Kowalski, looking down and across the empty street to the compound walls, let his weapon hang between his legs and drew his handgun, pressing up against the wall.

"Offset target, thirteen hundred Zulu," crackled the harsh voice through the radios. Kowalski looked up at Mason, giving him a broad, exaggerated visual signal. "Two tangos on the inner perimeter," he said, referring to enemy combatants. "Storage is fifteen yards from entry," Mason confirmed in a hoarse and soft voice that barely penetrated the battering winds. Kowalski waited for confirmation before Mason adjusted his hands on the rifle, calmed his breathing, and turned off the safety. He pulled the trigger, the recoil shaking his body, and took down both militants with precise shots. Mason reloaded. "Tangos down," he confirmed.

Kowalski swiftly moved, pointing his handgun as he walked across the courtyard. He reached the first militant lying face down in the sand and dragged him towards a cluster of bushes against the corner of the main building. The youngest of the three did the same for the second body and waited for Mason to set charges on the steel door leading to the storage rooms.

Section, please confirm if we're ready to secure our objectives," Kowalski informed the second team, but received no response. He repeated the request, growing concerned about the tight timeline they were on. Waiting for plus-two minutes on the operational window, he realized they had to act independently. Positioned against the adjacent wall, Kowalski turned away as Mason produced a folded square aluminum charge. Once it detonated, breaking the door's hinges, silence fell.

Leading the way, Kowalski kicked the door open and kept his gun aimed down the hallway. Swiftly turning the corner, he maintained his weapon's downward position to cover his movement. The room he entered was an office adjacent to a canopied storage shed at the back. Two militants sat at computers, and Kowalski swiftly opened fire, killing them before they could react.

The Collateral Dividend

Mason joined Kowalski in the room, going straight to the first lifeless militant and lifting his slumped face off the keyboard, causing the body to collapse on the floor. From his pocket, Mason retrieved a jumper drive and connected it to the terminal's hard drive. This wireless link connected to the encircling aircraft from Langley, ensuring operational continuity. Unbeknownst to them, it also marked them as expendable assets. On the other side of the room, Kowalski repeated the process with the remaining computers, while their third accomplice rummaged through the filing cabinets lining the far wall. Papers began to scatter, soaked in the blood pooling in the center of the room.

Keeping a close eye on his watch, Kowalski felt the pressure of time as they neared their deadline. It struck him as odd that Section had not made contact, but he attributed it to the unreliable technology caused by the sandstorm. Meanwhile, the youngest team member opened the door leading to the storage facility, revealing stacked military containers. "Shit," he exclaimed, capturing the attention of both Kowalski and Mason. By the time they reached him, he had already opened one of the containers and was examining its contents—files about some of the world's wealthiest individuals. Kowalski began photographing the files, voicing his surprise, "We weren't supposed to find anything like this, were we?" Mason shrugged, acknowledging their lack of information. "Who wants it back?" he asked rhetorically.

As time grew short, they had to move swiftly. Using a digital camera, Kowalski documented the serial numbers on the set of boxes. Meanwhile, Mason completed his task in the computer room, and with the final crate, he set his weapon on the ground, pocketed a wad of cash, and stashed it in his rucksack to bring back to Langley. He also tucked a smaller stack, approximately thirty thousand dollars, beneath his bulletproof vest. Surprised by Mason's actions, Kowalski questioned him, only to be ignored. Clearly, Mason intended to take a personal share in addition to the mandatory sample they were supposed to return. Taking the lead, Kowalski moved through the storage area and out the back door.

With extraction three kilometers south, they had to increase their pace and make an aggressive push. Exiting through the back door, they hurried down the central corridor before turning into the third hall on the left. Kowalski held his gun at his cheek, precisely dispatching the nearest militant with two shots to his back. The man collapsed with a thud. Kowalski shifted his position to cover their rear while Mason, burdened by the heavy rucksack filled with money, rounded the corner and joined him outside.

E.R. Wychwood

Their cover had been blown, and stealth was no longer an option. Despite the screaming winds and swirling sand, Kowalski could hear the calls for the house's occupants to arm themselves—a sound he didn't appreciate. Mason checked his watch, rolled over, and struggled up the sand dune. Time was running out, so he unclipped the harness keeping his rucksack secure and pulled the cord, launching the bag into the air. Sprinting at full speed, they couldn't afford to focus on anything else.

"Big fish, confirm extraction at kilo-six," Mason transmitted over the radio, stumbling over another sandy ridge. The youngest team member had already been killed in the courtyard during a firefight they were ill-prepared for. Mason, short of breath, attempted to request an alternate extraction, but the operations officer, under strict orders not to respond, remained silent. The infrared screen, measuring no more than seventeen inches, displayed the circling MC-130E Combat Talon, a large rotor-winged aircraft above. Their extraction plan involved deploying a balloon and having the MC-130 swoop down, snatching the tethered harnesses, and swiftly evacuating the operators. However, due to the blown cover, all extraction solutions had been canceled. The first balloon had already deployed, and the operators' primary extraction balloons flashed on the infrared screen. It was evident that Kowalski and Mason still hoped for extraction, but their government had abandoned them.

Kowalski kept running, clutching the client list containing personal information on some of the wealthiest individuals in the country. The extraction balloon, tethered to his waist, trailed behind them. Mason, having exhausted his pistol magazine by firing at the incoming militants, tried to flee but was struck, collapsing to the ground. Robert, though injured, couldn't afford to stay still. He discarded his rifle and fought the pain. There was no time to retaliate; they needed to escape. Through all channels, he desperately cried, "Expedition-one requesting evac!" As the sandstorm cleared and visibility improved, he looked up at the sky but found no sign of rescue. Frustrated, he raised his middle finger to the circling MC-130. If they were lucky, they wouldn't survive the week. If unlucky, they would be left behind for months, enduring torture, starvation, and thirst. They had completed their mission and were now deemed expendable, a sacrifice necessary to protect the sensitive information.

THE LOOSE END

Daniel arrived at the outskirts of the city at around 5:15 in the morning. The sun had not yet risen, and the previous evening's limelight illuminated the falling snow. He parked his vehicle in the airport parking lot and made his way towards the city. As he walked through the LaGuardia terminal, he observed the constant flow of yellow cabs coming and going in the roundabout.

The weather was bitterly cold, and the grey sky made it appear even colder. It had been a while since Daniel had seen the East River, which isolated the island of Manhattan. He took the overpass to the terminal, passing through the cold and slushy sidewalk under the overhanging portico.

It was mid-February, and the increasing volumes in the markets indicated that Gaillard, someone Daniel associated with revenge and meticulous planning, would soon make a move. Gaillard seemed fixated on exacting his revenge on the same date he was betrayed, and Daniel believed it was a suitable date to prepare for.

Daniel hailed a nearby yellow cab, a crown victoria with an advertisement for a Broadway show on its roof. He got into the backseat, and as the cab pulled away, he stared out of the window, lost in his thoughts. They drove past the Robert Kennedy Bridge, and Daniel could see the progression of the Manhattan skyline, from the public housing in the north to the towering glass buildings near the New York Harbor in the south.

New York City had always held a bitter taste for Daniel, perhaps because it was where he had lost his parents, casting a dark shadow over the vibrant city. The offices of Mayer Kleid and Cable Schwartz, the firms associated with international turmoil, were located at the new World Trade Center. Daniel had a feeling he would soon be forced to visit there. He had received limited information from Paul, indicating that Sergei had recently started working there and was doing well.

Philippe Gaillard, aware of the looming threat from Farragut Center, had taken precautions and avoided spending too much time in New York before the big heist. The plan was designed in a way that Farragut Center would have to track Gaillard worldwide to even have a chance at capturing him. Gaillard knew that the agency, bound by political morality, would be unable to take the necessary actions for his capture. To strengthen his operations, Gaillard had infiltrated the intelligence community, keeping his illegal activities hidden beneath the surface.

Isabel's authorization numbers for trading had been stolen in the months leading up to her departure from Zurich. She was then lured into a secluded life in Greece, unknowingly living as a captive. Gaillard's man kept a watchful eye on her, and despite that, Tzavaras, another player in Gaillard's plan, attempted to seduce her.

Despite their occasional disagreements, Tzavaras and Gaillard formed an effective team. Gaillard, through Sergei, would handle the theft of funds, while Tzavaras would coordinate the terror attack. Gaillard's work in Zurich diverted the world's attention to the threat of resurging violence in Europe, which suited Tzavaras' intentions.

Tzavaras and Gaillard had met in Europe, in the city where Isabel was staying. Their plan was reviewed at Tzavaras' old family home. Elias, Tzavaras' nephew, would orchestrate a bank heist in Manhattan, causing the markets to shut down and assets to be frozen. Meanwhile, Sergei would execute trading using a smuggled market terminal. Elias would then escape through the demonstrating crowds and leave the United States with the help of Ralston and Sergei, heading towards Canada.

Philippe hadn't stopped moving since. He would constantly pace the room, and his sense of politeness had completely vanished. He was taking three pills every four hours, which were dreadful to swallow. His planning and critical thinking were finally coming together. When he took the elevator in the hotel in Austria, he had a brief conversation with Piere, which turned out to be one of their shortest ever. He had been waiting for...

"Mister Gaillard, how nice to see you again," Tzavaras stepped into the room with a swagger. He was a harsh man who knew how to manipulate people. His voice was rough but strangely calming, creating an unsettling sensation. These contradicting qualities worked surprisingly well in unison. Tzavaras seemed to slither across the room, his short, greying hair swept to the left in a Caesar cut.

"Alekos," Philippe stood up and turned to face the dangerous man, "I see you have found your way around the city." He looked at his own security personnel who had traveled from Greece along with Tzavaras. "How's the girl?" he asked, addressing his man softly. The tall man nodded, and with Philippe's approval, they moved on. When Philippe extended his hand for a formal handshake, the Greek initiated it but only briefly.

Tzavaras had his jacket undone and casually took a seat on the sofa, resting his arm on the back. Two or three young Greeks in suits stood near the door, all of them bulky, the muscle of the operation. "So," he said, raising his arms, "where is my equipment, Mister Gaillard?" He was direct and to the point.

Philippe smiled; he appreciated a man who could hold his own. The Frenchman had no time for beating around the bush and even less time for lies. "There is a parking lot off North End Avenue in New York. I have arranged for your vehicles to be parked there. Everything you require will be in the back."

"How many vehicles are there?" Tzavaras's intense gaze and his unassuming approach could have been mistaken for a threat if Philippe didn't know any better. Despite his upright posture, Tzavaras appeared slouchy, resembling an invertebrate as he moved around the room. Philippe likened him to a venomous centipede, which unnerved him. It wasn't that Tzavaras was physically slimy or dirty, but rather his persona, though seemingly welcoming, left strong undertones of disgust and spinelessness—an unpleasant aftertaste.

"Three," Philippe paused briefly. "I'm certain you won't need more than that; they're bullet-resistant."

"They won't be spending much time in them anyway," Tzavaras said, crossing his legs. "When will I get my money?" His tone was bland, but it carried a thinly veiled threat if the correct answer wasn't provided.

"As soon as the job is done," Philippe replied. "You can keep the stolen money as well, if you'd like." He waited for the atmosphere in the room to settle. "How is our house guest?" Gaillard casually asked about Isabel.

Tzavaras's posture on the sofa changed as he shifted his weight and leaned forward. He cocked his head to the side, and a withering smile emerged across his thin lips. "She is a beautiful girl, Mister Gaillard. Such a feisty young woman—I want nothing more than to crush her," he expressed desire for her but knew not to interfere with Gaillard's affairs. "I think she couldn't be happier," Tzavaras said, proud that the beauty of his country's backwater lands had been recognized.

"I've arranged to have Manhattan's CCTV system accessible through our communications network," Gaillard said, gesturing to his head of security who came over with food and a tall glass of wine. Gaillard unapologetically snacked on oysters, occasionally slurping one so loudly that Alekos would lose his train of thought. "So you will have the opportunity to watch and direct your nephew from the comfort of Greece."

Tzavaras thought it was wonderful. Then he discussed with Gaillard how the events should unfold. They had made a deal. Gaillard would fund Tzavaras' takeover of Greece and, in turn, persuade his friends at the French State Department to endorse the new Greek state. In exchange, Tzavaras needed to create some chaos. Gaillard had no doubt that Tzavaras would find the task enjoyable. However, with his hands full in Greece, Alekos Tzavaras believed it would be best to send his nephew instead. Elias was excited and had planned a bank heist in lower Manhattan that would generate revenue while fulfilling Gaillard's demands.

Eventually, Gaillard sat back in his chair and looked at Alekos frankly. "So, what do you need from me?" he asked after a long and uncomfortable pause.

Tzavaras was confused, unsure why Gaillard was asking that. "My understanding, Mr. Gaillard, was that my nephew was going to help you shut down the New York Stock Market."

"Ah, yes," Gaillard said, as if reminded of everything's semantic structure. "My apologies."

"A Mister Ralston has provided me with information about future payments but has yet to tell me whether I should open an account. I will need to know soon."

"He hasn't told you yet?" Gaillard asked, downing his glass of wine without any social awareness.

"Not yet."

"Dieu Merde," Gaillard exclaimed, slamming his hand down onto the corner of the armchair. "The next time you see him, I want you to kill him," Gaillard said impulsively, breathing heavily, and his face turning all the colors of a royal flush. Piere came forward, standing by his side, and extended his hand, offering Gaillard two pills and a glass of water. "Perhaps you should think about that for a little while longer," Piere suggested, but Gaillard grew even angrier. "How dare you," he told Piere, standing up from his chair. "You will do it, is that clear?" Gaillard then collapsed back into the chair. Piere tried to communicate to Tzavaras to ignore Gaillard's directive, placing his hand on Gaillard's shoulder while offering the pills again with his other hand.

"Is there anything else you need from me, Mr. Gaillard?" Tzavaras asked, noticing Gaillard's confusion. Piere shook his head behind the chair, but Tzavaras waited until Gaillard looked up at him and shook his head. "Have a good day," he said, walking away, not exactly sure what he had witnessed.

Philippe Gaillard took the pills and drank the water. Piere moved to the other side of the chair and took a seat there. Gaillard's wife stood in the doorway, and Piere sat up so she could see him. She entered the room, parallel to Piere, and held Gaillard's hand.

"He had another attack," Piere said to Gaillard's wife, who rubbed Philippe's hand until the drugs took effect. The attacks were becoming more frequent.

The Collateral Dividend

"You don't look well today," Gaillard carelessly remarked to his wife, and no one said anything. After ten minutes, Gaillard's eyes returned to the room, and he appeared normal again. His face turned red from embarrassment when he recalled what he had done. He looked up at his wife and began to cry, holding her hand and resting his forehead against hers.

"They're increasing in frequency," Piere informed him once Gaillard had regained his composure. Gaillard's wife asked what could be done. Piere wouldn't have known if not for the phone call he had made to Gaillard's doctors back home. "They've made modifications to the drug," he said, having done his research in preparation for this moment. "The doctors believe your dementia can be slowed by doubling the dosage and taking it every hour." Piere was told that this would prolong the degradation for a little over five more years. Eventually, Gaillard would require palliative care.

Gaillard looked scared, holding his wife's hand tightly and then kissing the back of it. "It's alright, darling," he said. "Could you excuse us for a moment?" Once his wife had stepped out of the room, he looked at Piere and then down at his folded hands resting in his lap. "How long?"

"A conservative estimate would be three years before, even with the drugs, you would be unfit to manage the business. With the drugs, we can completely inhibit the symptoms for up to two years, after which their effectiveness will gradually decrease," Piere explained.

"We need to discuss succession," Gaillard said. "Piere, you have been with me from the very beginning. I appreciate all that you do." Gaillard's voice trailed off. He looked up at Piere once more and told him that he wanted to meet with Maria again this week if possible.

*   *   *

For the first time in a long while, Sergei Krosgyn found himself enjoying his work environment. Money flowed among the bankers like swift currents. The gluttony and bravado of Wall Street's old era had never truly perished; it had merely gone underground. Sergei yearned for that culture. Late nights fueled by cocaine and early mornings engaged in stock market trades were what he lived for. Being far away from Moscow and his father only added to his delight.

The family business had ensnared him long ago, but he had never looked back. He now discovered that his thoughts no longer revolved around his father's disapproval. However, Sergei realized that he was still entangled in the old addictions that had once consumed him. Within a matter of days, he found a place in Chinatown that catered to his specific needs, thrusting him into the heart of a drug culture. He had assured Gaillard that he had quit cocaine entirely, but the wily Frenchman knew better.

Clear and concise orders were given, and Sergei was expected to adhere to them meticulously. The markets would open at nine-thirty, but after only an hour of trading, an armed robbery nearby would force a shutdown, placing lower Manhattan under lockdown. It was during this chaos that Sergei would carry out his task. Precisely at ten-fifteen, he had been instructed to execute an additional set of twenty trades using a flash drive in a designated market terminal down the hall. Then came the decisive blow. Encrypted within the flash drive was a dormant program that would only activate when connected to the correct hardware. Among the trading floors, there was a market terminal located just down the hall from Sergei's office. Plugging the flash drive into this terminal would initiate a ghost algorithm, triggering a sequence of automated trades. Subsequently, it would prompt the user to access secure networks, bypass security protocols, and execute trades to maximize profits. The funds would then be liquidated and channeled through a labyrinth of randomized Mayer Klied accounts before being dispersed worldwide and eventually settling into a predetermined account. Through this elaborate process, the money would find its way back to Philippe Gaillard.

Sergei had pondered his role in this intricate scheme. His father, whom he suspected was afflicted with a deranged illness, had shown a strange approval of the proposed idea. He had informed Sergei that it would make him immensely proud. Above all else, that was what Sergei had always yearned for. Even with his reservations about his job in New York, he couldn't muster the courage to do what he believed was right. The attack would proceed as planned.

THE HEIST

"I've had Avery and our financial experts comb through Mayer Kleid's accounts related to Sergei and Gaillard," his voice trailed off. "Gaillard has a small number of assets with them. Internal memos show they knew what they were doing during the crash – sold all their assets to the Greeks."

"So, if someone were to inform some very hostile Greeks that their current economic climate is partially because of these guys, it wouldn't bode well. Fuck."

"This may complicate things for us," Paul said. "I need you to keep an eye on Elias. We'll contact you once you're allowed to intervene." Paul addressed Daniel, and by the time Daniel arrived in Lower Manhattan, he sat in the park and observed the city moving around him. He wasn't sure how he would react when they reached the September 11th memorial. When they finally arrived and saw his parents' names on the granite, he wasn't exactly sure how he felt about it all.

Mayer Kleid occupied nearly fifty thousand square feet on the fiftieth floor of One World Trade. Cable Schwartz had three floors of space just below.

Near the memorial, a man stood staring up at the office tower with a handgun holstered at his waist. Daniel followed the man for nearly thirty minutes until he reached the far side of Wall Street, where three grey electrical service vans were parked end to end.

Alekos Tzavaras monitored the security feeds from hijacked CCTV cameras in Europe.

Elias Tzavaras sat in the front seat of the leading van, watching the city. He knew extraction would be difficult, but once Tzavaras held power in Greece, they could negotiate his extradition if he were captured.

A block away, their target was a retail banking branch at the base of a national financial institution. While Elias' uncle initially suggested targeting Mayer Kleid, Elias believed it was best to target someone unrelated. The physical notes to be stolen had no connection to what they were actually stealing. It was a diversion, a stunt. In Europe, Alekos had already planned riots in various cities throughout Greece and abroad, demanding a snap election. They were scheduled to break out within the hour, and once word spread, the markets would decline, causing the Dow Jones to slide. The intention was to force the markets to slide by ten percent, which would halt trading for an hour.

If the riots failed to trigger a shutdown, Elias would rob the building, and its proximity to the stock market would force a complete halt.

Elias smoked a cigarette slowly, allowing it to burn at a measured pace. Occasionally, he would step out of the car, stretch, and look down the length of the road. He would then walk over to the parking meter and renew the timer.

Elias stood on the curb, leaning against the back of the truck in his heavy cotton, dark blue jumpsuit and technician's belt. He rested his shoulder against the stenciled lettering 'Reach Electrical' on the side of the vehicle. A power transformer on the near side of the road had been opened, and one of Elias' men had attached a clamp to a cable.

"What is the signal?" one of his men asked Elias after he finished a phone call with his uncle.

Elias gave him a harsh look, mirroring one that his uncle had nearly perfected. It was a look that cut through a man's confidence and made one's skin crawl. "We're still waiting for the green light. Waiting for word from London. Twenty minutes," he replied.

"And if we don't hear anything?"

"Then we move in twenty minutes," Elias responded bluntly, with little patience for stupid questions. He glanced up at the street CCTV hanging from a building thirty yards ahead, wondering if anyone was watching him. He considered giving the camera the finger, but it seemed like inviting unnecessary attention. Elias stood out on the street again, watching one of the men tinker with the thick cables. "How much longer?" he asked, and the man stopped what he was doing and turned around.

"This is the right transformer," the man assured. They would need to wait for the green light, and then they would cut the entire grouping leading into the building. Elias had been told to disable the alarm system, which would trigger a request for support. At that point, Elias and his men would arrive, present falsified documentation, and gain complete access to the building with a few limitations.

From his family estate in Greece, Tzavaras sent the green light. The markets had been open for nearly two hours, and the rioting and protests in Europe had failed to cause the desired significant dips. Elias checked his phone at eleven. He took one last deep breath of smoke from the cigarette and flicked it onto the street. "We're moving," he declared, placing his hand on the back of the man kneeling on the ground. The man cut the cable, closed the box, and down the block, the first floor of the building plunged into darkness. The phone call came through ten minutes later, and Elias rerouted the call from the back of the van, assuring them they would be on their way.

Elias glanced up at the surveillance camera. His uncle had told him that he would be there in spirit, watching their every move through those CCTV cameras and communicating with Elias through a sat-phone. Elias stepped onto the street and climbed into the van's cabin.

The building faced Bryant Park. The street began to fill with protesters, and within thirty minutes, the police had been called but were overwhelmed by the surge of people. By then, the vans had pulled up. There was an underground tunnel leading to the building, serving as an access point for supplies. The vans rolled forward, and Elias pointed at the ramp. The driver turned slowly, and the van descended the steep entranceway. The number of people was astonishing, and the cars were barely moving.

Elias' car was the first to reach the loading bay. Armed security guards and a police officer greeted them at the bank's basement entrance. Elias took charge, introducing himself and presenting his false documents. They were informed that the security systems, particularly those linked to the vaults, were out of order. Elias frowned and crossed his arms. "Why don't you show me?" he suggested. The security guard offered to take him upstairs to the command center. Elias shouldered his tool bag and gestured to the elevator. The guard, clad in a thick black bulletproof vest and heavy black pants, led him to the third-floor security room. It was a large, disorganized space with banks of computer terminals and a large screen on the far wall. The room buzzed with noise, but none of the screens displayed anything noteworthy, except when the computer operators switched to feeds of the main branch lobby or the upper office floors. Elias placed his bag in a corner, informing them they might need access to it later, and left it there for when they finished downstairs. The security guard requested to inspect the bag, but all he saw was a pile of tools. He then gestured to the door.

The vault downstairs was not as impenetrable as they had anticipated. The cash was not placed under strict security once inside the vault, and it lacked die packets except in designated areas. The heist was Elias' brainchild, and he wasn't willing to take any chances. Several of his uncle's supporters were formerly senior members of the Greek National Bank security, which proved advantageous. Elias stood at the edge of the gaping vault door, with security measures and gates lining the aisles leading to it. Cameras, armed guards, and gates would have turned it into a firefight if they tried to force their way in.

The Collateral Dividend

There was a computer panel near the front of the heavy door, and Elias accessed the run-file by plugging in a pre-set program.

Elias looked at the vault door, walking into the first part of the room with his hands in his trouser pockets. The paint on the heavy tempered steel door was thick and chipping. Elias glanced back at the security guard who had accompanied him through the building. They had thoroughly researched their targets. Elias had requested all the information Gaillard had on anyone involved with the cash. "How are your kids?" Elias asked casually, surprising the security guard. Elias explained that they had met years before on a previous work order and had discussed the guard's daughter and son. The guard, not wanting to appear rude, confirmed that he remembered. Elias then got to work, removing the paneling from the side of the vault and manipulating the cables with a laptop and an electronic pen-like device.

After about forty minutes, the team started drilling into the walls and disabling the alarm timers. The security guard leaned against the vault door and asked, "How's it looking?"

Elias gave a wide smile, picked up the large tool bag from the ground, and looked down the length of the vault at the security guard, who stood near the door with his hands hooked into his belt loops. "Would you help us clean this up?" Elias asked, gesturing to the scattered tools in the dusty room. The guard moved forward, and Elias reached into his waistband, pulling out a gun and shooting the guard dead. The man behind him continued drilling. "Go get the others," Elias instructed, stepping out into the main room and killing the remaining guards.

The other two vans arrived in the underground parking lot. When the security guard approached, the passenger in the front van rolled down the window and shot the guard, who shivered and collapsed to the ground. The back doors of the van opened, and more of Elias' men emerged, entering the building and proceeding to the basement. The main treasury was two floors below the street, in a large concrete room with thick steel paneling and rows of safety deposit boxes. An inner gate and a security camera were near the top door, but they had already been irreparably damaged.

The bag left upstairs had been emitting a gas for ten minutes—a colorless, odorless gas that seeped from the tools until the entire room was filled, causing the men inside to choke on their own tongues.

Elias glanced at his watch. They had already collected nearly five million dollars in cash, stowed in technician bags, backpacks, and suitcases. They moved the money to the back of the van or near the elevator. Elias put on a

195

mask, loaded a machine gun, and went up to the bank lobby. Holding the weapon, he shot a bank customer who attempted to run towards the nearby door. He then gave the guard at the front desk enough time to reach for the alarm before killing every bank employee. Accompanied by two other men wearing suits to differentiate themselves from the technicians, Elias locked the doors and kept away from the windows, waiting for what would happen next.

* * *

Daniel observed the unfolding events from the courtyard across the street. The stock exchange, merely a few hundred yards away, had shut down as news spread of a bank robbery. On his left, a protest was rapidly spiraling out of control, while on his right, the heist was underway. Standing up, Daniel made his way to the far side of the building, navigating through the crowds heading north. As he reached the vicinity of the sloping ramp leading underground, he retrieved his gun. With a swift motion, he slid the housing forward, arming the weapon. Daniel aimed it toward the ground and cautiously advanced through the underground parking lot, keeping his focus ahead. Two ultranationalists who had remained near the vans came into view. Daniel closed in, ensuring he was within range, and fired five shots, swiftly eliminating both assailants. The first man took a direct hit to the chest, crumpling to the ground with a thud. The second, positioned near the passenger's door, attempted to retaliate but failed. Daniel's precise aim found its mark, striking the second man high in the clavicle. He collapsed backward, gasping for air.

Driven by instinct and training, Daniel moved purposefully across the room, his gun still trained ahead. He ascended the stairwell, swiftly turning the corner and venturing deeper into the heart of the building. His gaze fell upon lettering adorning the far wall, and he read the directions it provided. However, his attention was soon caught by another set of lettering, which read "MARK PATEL." Daniel attempted to read the font again, but the hallucination had vanished, leaving him perplexed.

Coming to a halt at the corner's edge, Daniel spotted two of Tzavaras's men down the hall. With clinical precision, he turned the corner and swiftly dispatched both adversaries. He hadn't bothered to attach a suppressor to his weapon, and in retrospect, he questioned whether it was the wisest choice. The two men slumped back, as if stumbling over their own feet, before crashing forcefully onto their backs.

The Collateral Dividend

In his office, Sergei found himself alone, the markets closed. He sat there, fixated on the computer screen, contemplating the nature of his actions. Retrieving a small vial from his pants pocket, he removed the top rubber stopper, pouring a small amount of fine powder onto the fleshy part of his hand. Leaning down, he brought his nose to the powder and snorted sharply, experiencing an instant rush. As he leaned back in his chair, the effects took hold.

The closure of the markets had plunged the trading floors into chaos. Amidst the cacophony of screams and shouts, Sergei closed his office door and proceeded down the hallway. From his vantage point, he overlooked the sunken trading floor, where pandemonium reigned. Paper flew through the air, people scurried in every direction, and the deafening clamor of phone calls filled the space. Sergei descended a stairwell onto the trading floor, making his way toward the trading desk of a young trader, who sat transfixed by a market terminal displaying error notifications. Seating himself at the terminal, the effects of his high growing stronger, Sergei struggled to focus on the objects before him. Resting his hands in his trouser pockets, he absentmindedly toyed with a small USB stick, no larger than an inch. Hitting the keyboard, he maximized the error notification display. Pressing four buttons simultaneously, the screen flashed, revealing an authorization command. Sergei stood up, straightening his tie, but the action only exacerbated his disorientation. Placing the USB stick on the table, he extracted a piece of paper containing a series of numbers, which he entered into the command prompt. Stooping down, he inserted the USB stick into the port, connecting it to the linked computer. Reclining in his chair once more, he stared intently at the screen, his leg twitching against the floor in rapid motion, causing his shoelaces to clap. He waited, counting seconds that stretched into minutes. Yet, nothing happened.

Suddenly, a loading screen materialized, the empty progress bar filling rapidly within seconds. Lines of code cascaded across the screen, thousands upon thousands of entries automatically recording into the computer. After a minute or two, the coding ground to a halt and vanished. The screen turned black, plunging the room into darkness. Simultaneously, all the computers in the room crashed. Silence enveloped the space as everyone looked around in awe. After a brief pause, the computers and lights flickered back to life, and Sergei stood up. Wiping his fingerprints clean, he pocketed the USB thumb stick.

Returning to his office, Sergei halted at a colleague's door and inquired about the ongoing situation. "Patel is brilliant," Ralston had once praised Sergei. "He's doing exceptional work. He'll be one of the few to emerge unscathed. Gaillard values loyalty. As long as you don't give him reason to suspect betrayal, you'll make it out alive." Sergei pondered whether he had performed his duties adequately, though he often found himself too intoxicated to discern the difference. Staring at his reflection in the window's mirror, he wondered if Gaillard's mental state had deteriorated to the point of delusion, haunted by Klaus's parting words, which still echoed despite the distance in space and time. "He's lost his mind. You must realize this. You have to escape," Sergei mused, his gaze fixed upon himself.

Gaillard detested loose ends and despised venturing into unplanned territory. It seemed unlikely that Elias would escape New York alive, and that's exactly how Gaillard wanted it. He desired Alekos to witness it firsthand, to experience Elias's demise with the same intensity as if he had seen it himself. Gaillard craved Alekos's suffering, not out of a wish for him to endure pain, but because he understood the transformative power of anguish—it would sharpen Alekos's focus and make him susceptible to Gaillard's manipulation for Gaillard's own benefit.

Alekos observed the city's turmoil through computer screens, while nearly five million dollars had already been loaded into the back of a car. With the market crash, Alekos knew he wouldn't have the luxury of conversing with his nephew, forcing him to sit in the darkness of his room, fixated on the computer screens.

The protests outside had overwhelmed the emergency services, and the panic that led to the closure of markets had not spilled over onto the streets. Elias positioned himself near the stairwell, watching as the NYPD assembled outside. Descending back downstairs, he discovered the lifeless bodies near the vans. Although Elias yearned for a hunt, time was running out. "We leave in five," he instructed one of his men, while ordering two others to accompany him. Together, they ventured into the building in search of the killer. However, upon reaching the basement vault, they only had enough time to grab a bag full of cash.

Meanwhile, Daniel engaged in a firefight with two men on the opposite side of the building. As he turned the corner and took aim, the empty hallway sneered back at him. The vault had been emptied. Daniel sprinted down the corridor, lunged into the stairwell, and swiftly ascended the stairs. The door led him out fifty yards behind the vans. Stepping out from the doorframe, he took aim and fired three rounds. He pulled the handgun's lever, causing the magazine to drop to the ground. After reloading, he fired two more bullets. One struck the passenger and the driver, causing the driver's head to jolt forward, collapsing onto the horn. The car accelerated and collided forcefully with a nearby pillar.

The first loaded truck swiftly departed, skipping onto the street and veering eastbound toward the rendezvous point—an alleyway in the dense and narrow east end of Wall Street. Elias had changed his attire, donning a sweater and jeans, blending in with the protestors outside. Elias, accompanied by the last two remaining collaborators, returned fire at Daniel, who sought refuge behind a shipping crate.

Elias emptied an entire magazine into the concrete wall, leaving it riddled like Swiss cheese. On the far side of the loading bay sat a grey German-made BMW sedan. Elias approached the vehicle, opened the driver's side door, and started the engine. He reloaded his weapon.

Daniel swiftly maneuvered across the loading bay, crouched but moving with purpose. Rising above the top of the shipping crate, he fired once more, causing another of Elias's colleagues to collapse. The final collaborator had already reached the sedan and fired shots above the shipping crate. Daniel reloaded, and as he reemerged, the sedan lurched forward, maneuvering around the loading bay and onto the city street.

Daniel broke into a sprint, reaching the city street and veering left. He ran down an alley, then crossed a large plaza teeming with protestors and police vehicles. Another alleyway awaited him, and he continued until he stood in the middle of the road, with the grey sedan just a dozen yards ahead, heading north. The protestors had diverted attention from the rear entrance, forcing the vehicles to move slowly until they were out of the area. No one suspected a thing. Elias revved up the car's engine, and it accelerated, unhindered, along the open road, heading north.

Daniel gazed down the road and momentarily watched as the car peeled away. The street lay silent. He drew his gun and squeezed the trigger three times. The resounding shots echoed, enveloping Lower Manhattan in silence. The first bullet struck low, hitting the back of the trunk with a thud that resembled a rock striking the car. The rear windshield shattered, causing Elias Tzavaras's head to lurch forward. The vehicle swerved and collided dramatically with the rear of a lorry. The frame crumpled and lay in tatters on the city street. Deep scratches marred the car's sides, exposing the peeled paint. It rolled over, coming to rest inverted, crushed, and shattered in the middle of the street. Daniel lowered his gun, fixating on the wreckage for a moment until the wail of police sirens jolted him back to reality.

E.R. Wychwood

Alekos Tzavaras witnessed the crash unfold on his computer. As the car came to a stop, a surge of rage overwhelmed him, unleashing a deafening scream. Elias's death ignited a fury in his eyes and cast a heavy, dark shadow upon his soul, as black as coal. All Alekos desired was to know everyone Daniel loved and to end their lives.

THE BLOWBACK

The President was abruptly awakened by a jolt to his arm. He rolled over and got out of bed, looking up at the man standing over him. This was a regular occurrence, and although sometimes tiresome, it was something he had signed up for long ago. "The phone, sir," said a tall man dressed in a black suit, standing over his bed. He waved the man away, and the figure disappeared through the door, taking a seat in one of the foldable chairs just outside the room. There was a newspaper on the chair beside the figure, and he picked it up, glancing at the page he had been reading moments before.

The call was connected. "Yeah?" he asked, rubbing his face. MKI stock had plummeted. Market trades, occurring within milliseconds following the attempted robbery, had shorted a laundry list of key futures on a frightening scale. The world markets reacted accordingly, and then there was a second shock as Galliard pulled his money back out, causing a flash-crash of speculation. Soon after, the President had been briefed, and they had spent the next week trying to stabilize the dollar and bond market as a result.

"Mr. President, we may have a situation," the man on the other line said, almost immediately, his tone grim. He was in the back of a car.

The President was still waking up. "What do you mean, a situation?" Everything had accelerated rather quickly. Within the span of a day, CIA operations in Sudan had destabilized. Farragut Center and Gaillard had made off with billions from savvy trades on the markets.

Paul and his colleagues had been referring to the events as "attacks" or "heists," but the reality was that the trades were legal in the loosest sense, and that was what made them difficult. It was this fact that bothered the President the most, and he had suggested multiple times that the SEC charge MKI for inducing the flash-crash. At least then they could blame the entire thing on the Russians. However, that option had its own problems, and there were those, including Ted, who had convinced the President otherwise.

Paul wanted nothing more than to nail Gaillard for his crimes, and he somehow felt that they would need to, regardless of what the public knew or didn't know. Gaillard had gone an entire month in complete and utter silence. And then, a blistering firestorm knocked Farragut Center back and put it in trouble. Gaillard's unrelenting attack had been unforgiving. Gaillard had begun paying debts and donating large sums of money, and Paul could only suspect that the money had come from the markets. They had still not heard or seen Isabel, and Gaillard continued with his unimpeded life of leisure and business as if he had never lost any money or ordered any killings. There were times when even Paul found himself questioning whether they had targeted the right man. For nearly the entire time, Daniel had failed to report back to Washington. He had stayed in Boston for a long time but purposely failed to explain where or what he had done. "A long overdue vacation," he had said and nothing more.

In the end, the intelligence community imploded, and Paul had kindly asked Ted to try and appease the President and explain the cause. Ted was faced with the difficult situation of attempting to explain how all this had come to be.

"Sudanese rebels streamed the execution of two CIA operatives online," Ted said hurriedly. They had barely managed to reach the videos in time, but the damage was already done. All major news agencies had caught wind of it, and discussions about the catastrophe had already begun. Rumors were circulating that riots had erupted outside the embassies in Khartoum, Somalia, and Egypt, reaching an unprecedented level during the President's administration. When the person on the other end of the line informed the President of the news, there was a monumental pause before confirming that operatives on the ground had verified it.

"Has Brian been notified?" the President asked anxiously.

"No, sir. It just happened moments ago," Ted admitted, his eyes fixed on the video playing on a screen inside the car.

The President rubbed his eyes and focused on the screen. He recognized the first face but couldn't connect a name to it until Kowalski's operational briefing appeared at the bottom. Although he couldn't pinpoint where he had seen the face before, he unmistakably identified him as a CIA agent. As the President watched the video, Kowalski was the first to be displayed. He was carried in, hands tied, head hanging low, and a burlap sack over his head. Kowalski was thrown into the room and pushed to the floor, landing hard on the concrete with his knees taking the brunt of the fall. His body slumped forward, indicating that he was merely a shell of his former self. The room was empty, if not dirty, and the camera concealed itself behind a flood of light. Heavy curtains covered the high windows of the industrial room, and in the distance, the sound of trucks shifting gears and accelerating could be heard. Next, Robert was presented. He was tied up, covered in grime and blood, with a broken nose and blood streaming from the corners of his eyes to his chin, crusted around his beard and neck. He collapsed in front of the camera, lying face-first on the floor until a masked militant behind him used the collar of his jacket to pull him up.

His head hung low on his chest, and when the camera zoomed in, his hair was used to keep him upright. "We know where they are, and we're working on strike capabilities," Ted candidly stated. If they still had drones, this would be the time to use them.

Someone behind the live stream camera began speaking. "These men are American spies," the man said. "They were trying to alter the world, steal money, and destroy a legitimate African business because it competed with American capitalism." The rhetoric was insignificant; it was the graphic footage that mattered. The man then asked in English, "Why did you come here?" Kowalski remained silent, his vulnerable neck exposed to the camera. Another figure emerged and mercilessly beat Kowalski. The human body could only endure so much, and eventually, Kowalski collapsed and wept. Covered in blood, his fingernails had been slowly removed one by one, savoring the pain of each. It was Langley's mandate to sever all connections between foreign operatives and the United States, but the militants knew who had come knocking. The video was excessively graphic, and even as a former Naval surgeon, the President felt nauseous. The video continued. Amid Kowalski's screams, they removed two of his fingers. A large, dirty, and worn blade was presented to the camera. They forced Kowalski to lay his hand flat on the ground, but he tried to clench it and pull it close to his chest, desperately pushing away. Two men held his hand flat, and a hammer struck his wrist, shattering the bone. Then they severed his fingers. Nearly ten minutes later, after Kowalski appeared exhausted and beaten, the execution took place. He looked defeated, abandoned, and prepared for slaughter. They brutally, painfully, and slowly beheaded him using a machete that appeared duller than a kitchen knife. The sound was loud, gut-wrenching, and seared into the President's memory. He turned off the feed, and the person on the other end informed him that the second execution had been preceded by a call for justice—to weaken and destroy those who had interfered in foreign affairs for so long. It was fear politics 101.

"How exactly did this happen?" the President asked once Ted had finished explaining the situation.

There was a long silence on the other end. "Why don't we discuss this in person, with the chiefs of staff?" Ted suggested. He was in the back of a black sedan already en route, currently stopped at a red light a few blocks north of the White House. Ted looked out the window at the quiet D.C. street, rain pouring down and streetlights reflecting off the damp summer road. They drove beneath the pillars of light, and a thin mist lingered close to the ground, avoiding the calm evening breeze wafting in from the Potomac.

By the time he arrived at the White House gates, the clearance for his passage hadn't reached the guards yet. Being an old and familiar face there, he was granted access anyway. To an onlooker, it might have been surprising to see a former CIA deputy director still maintaining Yankee White clearance, but the truth was that Ted ran this town.

The black town car pulled up under the overhanging portico of the West Wing. Rain fell horizontally, creating a stark contrast between the sheltered space beneath the canopy and the exposed area beyond. It was like the difference between night and day. Ted exited the car and was greeted at the door by a Secret Service agent standing next to the Marine Sergeant guarding the entrance.

"Mister Hawthorne," the Secret Service agent said, extending his hand. "Welcome back to the White House." Ted smiled and patted the man's shoulder with his other hand.

"Good to see you, Miles. Busy morning?"

Miles led Hawthorne into the entrance of the West Wing. "You could say that. It's been a hell of an early morning for him," he replied, leading Ted past the security checkpoint in a brisk manner. They bypassed the checkpoint entirely, and the security officer sitting there stood up, watching them pass. Miles guided Ted down the hallway and down the stairs into the basement. At the door to the situation room, another serviceman stood, swiping his keycard at the checkpoint and opening the door for Ted.

"He's waiting for you inside, Mister Hawthorne," Miles said before leaving Ted to enter the room alone.

Ted walked into the room and looked at the President, who was seated in the chair closest to them. On the other side of the conference table, not far from the President, sat the Director of National Intelligence, Brian Redding. Brian gave a subtle nod to Ted, who responded in kind. Today was not a day to flaunt one's allegiances.

Ted took a seat and placed a file folder on the table. The large screen occupying the entire surface of the table lit up, prompting a security login. President Watson was the first to speak, his charisma undeniable. He waited until the room fell silent, then turned to the Chair of the Joint Chiefs of Staff, who sat across from several other advisors called in on short notice. It seemed like no one in the room was fully awake yet.

The Collateral Dividend

"So let's review," the President said authoritatively, crossing his legs and leaning back in his chair. He looked at Ted. "What exactly happened here, Ted?"

Clearing his throat, Ted began to explain. "One of our surveillance drones was taken down through an electronic hack. As a result, some of our assets embedded in a Sudanese rebel group inadvertently leaked information. We've retrieved the drone and the data, and our operatives were sent to recover more information." Ted paused briefly, then used the screen on the table to display a briefing.

"Yesterday, our operatives initiated Operation BLUEGLASS. The project was led by a four-man team of CIA SAD operatives. These assets were inserted three miles inland from Port Sudan and were to travel to a compound just outside the city limits." Ted maximized a map of the region, outlining the operational plan. A red band highlighted the area on the table, repeatedly displaying the words "TOPSECRET//SPECIAL ACCESS REQUIRED – BLUEGLASS."

"The compound is controlled by former Sudanese Army Colonel Ali Omar Kutu. He's involved in slave trade, extortion, and arms dealing. He's a high-value individual within an extremist group loosely connected to our other Islamic friends in Syria and Iraq." Kutu was a prominent target on various U.S. target lists. "Our assets were targeting stolen information that could potentially bring down the entire intelligence community."

"What happened to the information?" one of the Joint Chiefs asked. The room grew visibly tense, and Ted looked at Brian, knowing he would face the brunt of the backlash.

"We managed to secure fragments of the data. However, more importantly, we've been able to determine where else the data went," Brian explained, displaying the file on the table. There was a mixed reaction of relief and apprehension in the room. No one called an early morning meeting for good news. "Unfortunately, the operatives were captured and killed. The Sudanese rebels executed them via a live stream online."

The President's voice grew intense as he asked, "So what the hell happened? And what exactly is the information?"

"It is our understanding that the SAD operatives Robert Kowalski and Mason Harper failed to maintain operational security. The clearance provided to the extraction aircraft extended only three kilometers away from the facility and denied extraction under blown security directives. In such a case, the operators were supposed to extract at a checkpoint, three kilometers out to sea."

205

E.R. Wychwood

"Now, how exactly do we plan to explain this to the media? It's not like we could talk our way out of this – we left men behind," one of the idealistic advisors for the President said, but Ted quickly dismissed his rebuttal.

"Excuse my interruption," Ted said, picking up immediately. "I don't tell you how to best coordinate elections, and I suggest you don't try to tell me how to best avoid wars." Ted had grown into his role as a bureaucrat. When asked for clarification on his comment, he simply let out a deep sigh, smiled, and said, "This wasn't some operation where the dead came home. They were informed of the risks and what was needed if we wanted to see this through. We need to handle this very carefully. The information relating to this and the Special Access Program is still at large. I can imagine, with the way Congress is, that they will want to hold hearings about this. We cannot afford for the stolen data to become public. It's critical that we distance ourselves from what it actually was."

"What exactly was it?" the Secretary of State asked cautiously. Her predecessor had fallen on a splintered sword when the drone programs had gone awry. The current Secretary of State was not keen on repeating the same mistake.

Ted responded immediately, "What it was – was an operation pertaining to security threats of the highest level. Colonel Kutu has, and does, harbor high-value insurgent targets. The assets identified what we're calling the client list: a rather extensive list of some very influential people. We aren't sure for what purpose Kutu possessed this list. However, the fact that he had the list temporarily means that some very serious people have been given access to purchase some very serious threats to national security. We sent these guys in there with the objective of tracking who the sender was and where the content was going," he paused for a moment, "so yes, Miss Secretary, these men knew full well that if operational security was breached, the cavalry wouldn't be coming over the nearest hill." Ted spoke in the frankest of tones. They had spent months on the operation, and only partially discovering what they had been looking for was perhaps worse than not finding out at all. Furthermore, Ted had lost two good men. He needed to downplay the importance; in this business, some information was better than none.

"Are we aware at all of the purpose of this 'list'?" the Secretary of State queried again.

Ted sighed, "Well, here's our problem: one of the assets deployed his emergency balloon, which successfully extracted the paper files retrieved from

The Collateral Dividend

the facility, but the files were only partial. Due to the sandstorm, we're only looking at what we believe to be half the story."

The President watched the room converse around him until, after several minutes of banter, he interjected. "The issue at hand is not the morality, legitimacy, or conduct of the operation. Ted will be asked to explain that later. What concerns us is how we deal with the leak, who's responsible," he took a pause, "and beyond that, where do we go from here."

The room went quiet for a long while, and Ted looked at his laced hands. "I'm told the NSA was able to secure the streaming before it received too much traffic. The news has already gotten a hold of it. They're wondering why we were in Sudan to begin with," and with good reason.

"I agree with Ted," the Director of National Intelligence concurred. "We need to take care of this, and the best way to do so isn't to ignore it. We need to bury this quickly."

The President didn't like what he was hearing. He knew that asking one of his cabinet members to sacrifice their political careers for good would be necessary. He ran his hands through his hair and then looked at Brian Redding. "Who would you suggest we throw under the bus, Brian? I assume certainly not you."

Brian laughed and leaned forward, then glanced at his notes. "Well, we certainly can't crucify someone who isn't willing to take the fall. But it should be someone in this room."

In the far corner of the room, the Director of Central Intelligence, Gregory Dunes, had remained quiet for most of the meeting. Dunes was a small man with high cheekbones and a long, thin face that made his forehead appear even longer. He cleared his throat and waited until the room gave him the desired attention. His rare moments of speaking always commanded everyone's willingness to listen. "I'll claim responsibility," Dunes declared.

Ted responded with concern, "Greg, you—" but he was interrupted by Dunes.

"It's no secret that Kowalski was CIA, and I'm more than capable of outmaneuvering Congress," Dunes stated firmly, having already made up his mind. His endurance was waning, and he believed he had just enough left in the tank for another two years. "Let them try to crucify me. I've never been afraid of some wood and nails. Besides, they can scrutinize our books all they want – they won't find anything connecting back to the operation." The room seemed to concur, and despite Ted's reservations about letting his friend take the blame,

207

he didn't have many options. "But it better be worth it, Ted. I'm not dying on the cross for a few rumors."

"It isn't," Ted assured, but it was imperative that they find out what was in the files. They needed to act on the information they had been provided.

"So where do we go from here?" the President asked again, his arms crossed.

Ted took a deep breath. "This presents a two-tiered area of concern. Operators could extract the data from the computer terminals found in the compound. There were regular money payments coming in and leaving shortly after. We suspect that the client list is a target list. It's part of the information that was lost in a hack last year. I think the best course of action is to retrieve it before dealing with those responsible."

"You mentioned we lost half the list?" the President's chief advisor inquired, emphasizing their concern for press security.

Ted sighed and adjusted himself in his seat. "They couldn't recover the entire list, but we were able to trace the video feed of the torture. The leaked data has the potential to seriously jeopardize our overseas operations. I believe, Mr. President, you were briefed on this by the DNI earlier in the week," Ted said, adopting a tone reminiscent of the President's.

The advisor nodded, taking notes on his pad of paper before pressing further. "So, did we gain anything from this operation other than bad news?," he directed the question directly at Ted.

"We destroyed the facility soon after the videos were streamed. Both Brian and I agreed that reducing it to ashes was preferable to allowing another warlord to roam freely," Ted nodded toward the Director of National Intelligence. "Before that happened, we managed to track shipments from the targeted site to other overseas assets."

"To where exactly?" the advisor leaned forward eagerly, filled with excitement.

Ted smiled faintly and activated a subsequent file, projecting it onto the tabletop. He looked across the room at the advisor over the rim of his glasses, observing as the room followed the visual interface displaying the money's shipping path. "Colonel Kutu, the warlord, used some of the money to cover freight costs."

"Singapore," the President exclaimed, his surprise evident.

Ted nodded, and the screen transitioned to a new interface. "The Special Access Program has some information about an ongoing operation related to the market crash last week."

The Collateral Dividend

"Mr. President, I would love to have access to that data for my department in relation to that operation," one of the advisors expressed, seeking approval from the President. Ted shook his head.

"We're collaborating with the SEC on a private investigation that involves the FBI, channeled through Director Dunes's office," Ted explained, aware that the analyst was curious about his identity. "We are narrowing down those responsible, but it seems this information is an attempt to undermine us."

"It seems like they're doing a good job," one of the advisors remarked, and Ted chose to ignore the comment. Paul had stressed the importance of not revealing their hand — making Gaillard the target couldn't be made public outside of Farragut Center. The program's secrecy relied on its ability to remain invisible and mysterious.

"There needs to be delicacy in how we approach all of this," Paul had told Ted during the briefing. They needed to catch their target without him being armed and ready; that meant taking the information offline first.

"We're working on something. We were able to track where the intel is headed," Ted stated, and when someone in the room asked where, he shook his head. "I won't disclose that. You wanted us to separate ourselves from the intelligence community to enhance security and efficiency. Trust me, we're doing exactly that."

The President's breathing had calmed, and he appeared composed. After a prolonged period of thought, he nodded, knowing that the slip-up in Sudan would weigh on them all for months. He then looked up at Ted. "Keep it quiet this time, get what we need, and do what you have to do," he said, prompting everyone in the room to stand up and prepare to leave.

THE CACUS BELLI

Daniel Faron stood at the door, looking across the room with a tired expression that hinted at underlying exhaustion. Having taken numerous flights from around the world, his body had yet to adjust. Paul met Daniel at the side door and quickly walked him towards Ted's office, filling him in on the details. With a half-smile, Daniel greeted Ted before collapsing onto the sofa in the room, releasing a deep breath. Though his suit appeared worn, its quality made it acceptable.

From his slumped position, Daniel's tired eyes gazed at Ted, conveying a sense of weariness. His mood seemed indifferent as he regarded Ted, a young man who had entered the later stages of his youth.

"Long flight, I see," Ted remarked, moving around the desk to stand seven yards away. The District of Columbia was covered in a thick morning fog, obscuring the view from Ted's office. Daniel estimated the visibility to be no more than fifty yards.

Daniel merely grunted in response. He had caught one of the last flights out of Hong Kong the previous night, and despite the city's glamorous lights and infrastructure, he knew that ultimately Hong Kong was no different from anywhere else. When he had met Paul at the door, it had been one of the few times they had seen each other in weeks, and Paul appeared as though he hadn't slept during that time. Daniel suspected he probably hadn't, considering Paul's memory foam cot stashed behind his office door, which he likely hadn't left for at least a hundred consecutive days.

By the time Daniel reached Ted's office door, he had already been fully debriefed. "We had an asset in Sudan who caused quite a commotion this morning," Ted explained, bringing Daniel back to the present moment and away from his sleep-induced haze. "It has raised some unexpected issues," Ted hesitated momentarily, searching for the right words, "larger than we had anticipated." Leaning forward, he handed Daniel a folder wrapped in red tape, marked with the words "TOPSECRET//SPECIAL ACCESS REQUIRED – FARRAGUT CENTER" at the center, just above the red band.

Daniel broke the seal on the corner and opened the file, examining the briefing note. "You're looking at Min Yong Jun," Ted stated, and Daniel lifted the color photograph up to the light, studying it intently. They had crossed paths once before. "Have you ever seen Rebel Without a Cause?" Min had

The Collateral Dividend

asked. What a prick, Daniel had thought, realizing that Min knew who he used to be. Ted's voice brought him back to the present. Min was a Chinese national, formerly working for Chinese intelligence in the eighties. He had strong ties with Gaillard, and tracking him had proved challenging for Langley. He would spend two months in Austria, only to disappear again for weeks. Ted's voice trailed off, and Paul continued the briefing, picking up the pace.

"He has similar patterns all over the world. Just as we start to pick up a trail, he vanishes," Paul explained.

"While you were in Hong Kong, he resurfaced on our radar. A case officer in Dubai spotted him at the Burj al Arab," Ted added.

"Nice place," Daniel interjected. "Big spender?"

Ted snorted. "Something like that," he replied.

Daniel frowned, looking up at his superior. "What does this have to do with what happened in Sudan?" he asked innocently. "What does any of this have to do with the money?"

"Everything," Ted replied, instructing Daniel to turn the page. They wouldn't be able to take down Gaillard until they secured this information. Paul didn't want to bring down the entire operation to eliminate one man. "The servers found at the Sudanese compound were receiving payments from banks based in Singapore, wired from subsidiaries owned by Min's company. Min is the next step in our pursuit of Gaillard. He likely knows both Gaillard's location and how the money is being funneled back to him. It appears that Min is working with Ralston to launder the money. The amount of laundering the funds underwent after leaving the market was extensive, making it difficult to trace. However, what's important is that we know Min has the data."

"Why?" Daniel asked.

"Because Min got caught using it," Paul interjected. "We reached out to our contacts in The Valley, and they are suing him for patent infringements on various products. Min's company is Asia's equivalent of a Valley tech giant, and it has strong ties to Imer Software. It's likely that the information went to Min first."

Daniel knew better than to ask unnecessary questions. He understood that if he was being briefed, someone needed to be eliminated. "Are we sending a message, or do you want to keep this quiet?" he asked, his eagerness evident, as he applied his logical approach to the tasks at hand.

"Neither," Ted paused, glancing over at Paul. "Did you enjoy Asia?" Paul asked, moving across the room.

"Not particularly," Daniel dryly replied, phrasing it politely.

211

Paul snorted. "Min has properties in Singapore, some of which are of particular interest to us. We'd like you to consider them."

"Such as?" Daniel inquired.

"The company's headquarters is there, and there's some dockside property that Canadian officers have identified as a temporary location for some of the money Gaillard stole," Paul explained. Both he and Daniel knew that most critical information would be kept as far away from the docks as possible. Paul believed that a private server would be necessary to store and process the extensive information they suspected Min had been using. Accessing such a server would be challenging, but an opportunity was arising that might grant them access.

"Well, it seems Min bit off more than he could chew. The lawsuit could bring him down, so it's best for us to go after him sooner rather than later," Ted stated.

"I assume this is relevant?" Daniel asked.

Paul's expression turned curt as he tried to dismiss Daniel's sarcasm. "We're going to insert you into one of the law firms handling the case. One of the senior partners defending Min is an old friend of mine. He used to work at the Department of Justice. Do you know him?" Paul handed Daniel a photograph of a man in his late thirties.

Daniel scrutinized the photo on the touchpad for a while before sliding it to the left, off the screen. He proceeded to read the accompanying synopsis. "Picking up where I left off, I see," he remarked with assumption.

"Hmm?" Paul asked, his mind already focused on tasks scheduled for the next month. While his phone's calendar was filled, he couldn't afford a personal secretary due to budget constraints.

They continued down the hall, with Paul leading the way. He entered a partially open door, and Daniel followed suit. With one hand in his pocket, Daniel used his other thumb to rub his fingers, glancing around the room. Paul turned on the lights and sat in the chair on the far side of the desk. Daniel repeated his previous question, and Paul looked at him over his reading glasses.

"Well, yes," Paul said matter-of-factly. "You're going to work for Tim Swinton. We've portrayed you as one of the senior associates transferred from one of the firm's satellite offices out east. The firm is headquartered in San Francisco, as you know, and nearly thirty partners will be involved in this case. You'll fit right in."

Paul sorted through a stack of papers, almost thirty pages thick. "The Valley was kind enough to provide us with most of their case," he said, handing Daniel

The Collateral Dividend

another file separate from the one he was currently perusing. "Their lawyers compiled it for you." Daniel would review the briefing during the flight. He was already familiar with the topic to some extent, as the legal battles between both parties had made headlines before. Allegedly, a Singapore-based firm had taken patents and designs, enticing several senior management members to join them. The company had been accused primarily of corporate espionage.

Daniel inquired about Min, who sat across from him with his leg crossed. Paul turned his computer screen toward Daniel, showing Min's photo next to his name. "He worked closely with the Russians toward the end of the war. After a stint in South America, he appeared in various locations around the world every month for five years. He bounced around Egypt and Singapore in 2008 for a few weeks before disappearing again. As far as we can tell, his company is legitimate and has no direct ties to Red China."

"But that doesn't mean they aren't involved," Daniel observed, knowing that masking affiliations was a classic Chinese tactic.

"Exactly. We're primarily concerned about the parent company's involvement," Paul confirmed. "Min has established quite an empire. Most of his operations revolve around distribution and manufacturing, but they span a wide range, from electronics manufacturing to corporate liquidation and property development. We found him after he entered the markets last September."

"And I'm sure Min's revenue stems from China," Daniel commented observantly, implying that China was skilled at hiding its affiliations.

Paul agreed. "Exactly. We're particularly interested in the direction of the parent company." He trailed off for a moment. "Min's operations are quite extensive. It would be challenging for him and his people to coordinate to the extent they have for Gaillard without logging and storing information on a server. Accessing that server won't be easy, but an opportunity is arising."

"When do I leave?" Daniel asked, realizing he wouldn't have time to change clothes before departing. He glanced at his watch, adjusted the alligator strap and gold clasp, and looked up at Paul, who made the same gesture.

"Private charter is scheduled to depart in an hour," Paul informed. Daniel promptly stood up, buttoned his suit, and retrieved the folder from the cluttered desk. "The car is waiting for you downstairs," Paul added, observing Daniel's brisk stride as he exited the room and closed the office door behind him.

Returning to Ted's office, Paul shut the door and locked it. With his hands jammed into his pockets, he approached the desk and patiently waited for Ted to begin his briefing. Having worked with Ted for a considerable time, Paul

213

knew that despite his wealth of experience, Ted often initiated briefings with lengthy lectures reminiscent of an old economics professor mumbling himself into irrelevancy. While occasionally relevant, Paul had dealt with a variety of challenging situations and felt he no longer required such lectures. If anyone should be lecturing, it should be him.

"How did the briefing go?" Ted abruptly inquired without looking up from his desk.

"Brief, sir," Paul replied.

"Has he left yet?" Ted asked, and Paul nodded, prompting a prolonged pause.

"Can't imagine the President was too pleased," Paul commented casually, once Ted had provided a long-winded explanation on how to avoid a repeat of last week's political fiasco. The Intelligence meeting at the White House had felt like a professional ransacking.

Ted shook his head and shrugged. "I was the President's personal punching bag," he confessed, settling into his seat at the office desk. He pulled out the top drawer and handed Paul a USB drive. "That's what Langley has on Min."

"I'll ensure it reaches the right people," Paul assured him. "I have a meeting today with some individuals from the Valley regarding the next generation of devices. There are rumors of programmable electronics jammers that can restrict certain aspects of devices."

"Could be useful," Ted acknowledged, though his attention seemed divided. He glanced up at Paul, pausing his writing. "Is that all, Mr. Irving?" he asked abruptly. When Paul confirmed it, the Chief-of-Staff understood that it was time for him to leave.

*   *   *

Daniel's flight to San Francisco had been tiresome. He arrived in the new time zone almost at the same time he had departed from the first, and the toll of hours spent flying seemed to catch up with him. Bags hung heavy underneath his eyes, and lines of exhaustion spread across his forehead.

During the flight, he reviewed the files. Despite not using his law degree for years, he found himself sharp and astute, quicker than he had expected. It turned out that Min had stolen information, and the Valley argued that senior-level managers had taken the information with them. That was certainly part of it. Paul had explained that they suspected Min had identified potential targets

The Collateral Dividend

through the hack on Farragut Center. Much of the data had resulted from the hack.

When the car pulled up to a curb on a street just off Fremont Street, Daniel climbed out and looked up at the towering square building. It was shadowed from the rising sun by the adjacent building and clad in tinted glass. The lobby had three-story ceilings, dimly illuminated by faded lighting above a false ceiling. A man stood near the side entrance of the building, next to a piece of abstract art in the plaza. There seemed to be a quick exchange of expressions between the man, the driver, and Daniel. The man took a final whiff of his cigarette and carelessly flicked it aside.

"Mister Faron, welcome to California," he said, and they shook hands. He introduced himself, and the door to the town car closed behind Daniel as the driver returned inside. The car pulled away. "Tim Swinton," he said, "it's a pleasure to finally meet you. Paul has only said great things." Daniel hoped so. It wouldn't be progressive if word got out about what he was doing there.

"Ralston will likely be there as well. I can imagine he'll be privately advising Min on these matters. He isn't the type to get too involved in litigation," Paul had mentioned back at the office in Washington. "He's a better banker than lawyer," Paul observed, and Daniel pondered the comment as he stood outside with Swinton in the morning heat.

"Long flight?" Swinton asked, gesturing towards the building entrance and leading the way. Daniel shrugged in response, thinking it best to gracefully elongate a pointless conversation. "Could be worse." By now, they had passed the front desk and entered one of the building's seventeen elevators. They reached the fortieth floor, and upon exiting, polished aluminum lettering displayed Criton Landon & Milburn on the interior lobby wall. Just outside the office, there was a bullpen of cubicles, and an old secretary entered Swinton's office, placing a stack of files onto his desk before closing the door on her way out.

"Take a seat," Swinton said, waving to the chair across from his cluttered desk. He laced his fingers and leaned forward. "We've been shorthanded lately due to some reshuffling by the head office. It has left us vulnerable in dealing with a few clients. There won't be much orientation around here. Since you've been with the firm for a while, I'll be straight with you. I have you working under me with a few other senior associates on the Min v. Valley case. Have you heard of it?" Daniel shrugged, "Only in the news." "Hell of a case," Swinton grunted, "a shit show if you ask me. You'll have to forgive me; it wasn't my first choice to utilize your resources this way." He handed Daniel a file that sat atop

215

his desk. Daniel assumed Min's lawyer was the one who liked to review their work, likely Ralston. "We're headed to Singapore next week to review the company files. Everything collected will be attorney's work product."

"Have we seen anything of theirs yet?" Daniel asked, shuffling through the papers, looking up at his boss.

'Not unless it's been filtered through this Ralston guy,' Swinton said. 'It should give us an idea of the type of damage we're dealing with.' There was a long and laborious process involved in preparing a case for litigation. They had been spending months just getting to where they were now. 'From what we've gathered, we will be able to swing two of the five patent breaches – technicalities in wording and process.' His voice trailed off. 'In terms of the non-compete contracts, it's all up in the air – and that needs to change.'

Swinton knew that this would not be a quick fix. The solution needed to be permanent, and that was where a great deal of billable hours were currently going. The Valley had a reputation for skewering companies in court, and if they failed in court, it wasn't uncommon to see them circle back once or twice for another go. Swinton had been tasked with trying to pull together the various potential arguments and try to undermine it. They needed to find a flaw in the armor before the battle had even begun.

Swinton had a cup of coffee on his desk, and by the time Daniel had arrived, it was lukewarm. He hadn't drunk any of it. He had started his day at the office around 6:30, much earlier than most of the partners, but there was a reason he had climbed to his perch so fast. He had been known as what they called a gunner – a Harvard grad who, in his first years, had logged more billing, more hours, and more work than any of his entering class. 'We meet normally around eight most mornings,' he said at forty-five to seven. 'Gives us the opportunity to get on the same page, a quick campfire with the teams working on the case.' Swinton stopped for a moment and looked past Daniel, through the glass wall of his office and into the hallway. He stood up, and Daniel reciprocated and followed Swinton to the door. There was a woman sitting near the desk of Swinton's secretary's cubicle. She stood up abruptly when Swinton came forward through the door. 'Daniel, I'd like you to meet Elizabeth Fisher, one of the senior associates here. You'll be working with her under me. She'll show you around the office – if you have any questions, I'm sure she would be happy to help.' Swinton stood there for a moment and waited until the two shook hands, and then he excused himself and said that he would see Daniel at eight.

Daniel found her quite attractive, but there felt as if there was a prudish undertone – an emotion that lacked conviction and feeling. It was not an emotional connection but rather purely professional and physical. The potential for chemistry seemed flat and unenthusiastic. She seemed boring to him; her smile just simply seemed less charming than Isabel's, and even when he wasn't thinking about her, he found a way to think about her again. He wondered what she was doing, where she was. Was she thinking about him as much as he was thinking about him?

'You from out east?' she asked when they were walking the hall along a long row of glass walls that looked into exterior-facing offices.

'Yes,' Daniel said, 'New York branch.' He followed her down the hall where she stopped abruptly at an office with its door open and the window facing north. The sun was casting through the window and onto the glass desk that was in the middle of the room.

"This is his office," she said, and she stood at the door while Daniel walked into the room and gave it a once-over. He was fiddling with the positioning of the desktop.

"This is his office," she said, standing at the door while Daniel entered the room and quickly surveyed it. He adjusted the position of the desktop computer screen and noticed a gift box on the table, accompanied by a cardstock paper with his name written in ink. In the corner, banker's boxes were stacked. Curious, Daniel approached the boxes and removed the lid of the top one. Inside, he found a note from Paul that read, "Just some things to make the room less bare." The box contained a few photographs, desk trinkets, pens, and other items to give his office a more permanent feel.

"How long have you been here?" Daniel asked the woman, realizing that he had been standing by the glass doorway.

"Seven years," she replied abruptly, effectively ending the conversation. It seemed she felt uneasy talking to him, her eyes darting around the room before settling on Daniel as he walked around the desk and dusted off the nearby chair. He adjusted his pants' height. "Rumor has it you worked at Langley for a while," she probed, but Daniel didn't take the bait, and she swiftly moved on. "The billing scheme is the same as New York, I'm told. You can find the company directory in the drawer." Daniel placed his briefcase on the table and opened its flaps. He then pulled out the directory from the drawer, glancing up at her. For a moment, it was evident that he felt comfortable settling in. "I'll leave you be," she said. "If you have any questions, I'll be next door until the meeting." With that, she closed the door upon leaving.

Paul sat back in his chair and glanced at the fax from New York one last time. It had been sent by their friends at Cable Schwartz. "We received this about two months ago, before the hack," the enclosed note explained. "It was listed for your man, so I made sure it was forwarded to you guys. Be sure that he sees to it." Paul took the package off his desk and opened it, finding a folded piece of paper with a lengthy text excerpt and a tie. He thought it was a shallow gift, and the apparent lack of sentiment made him more confident about sending it on to Daniel. He briefly considered not sending it, fearing it might unsettle him. However, he decided against it. If Rachel had sent something for Paul to Daniel, he would want to know. So Paul forwarded it along with the rest of Daniel's belongings, and it ended up on Daniel's desk early that morning, untouched and unopened.

Daniel pulled out his office chair and sank into it. The gift box on the table still caught his attention, and he lifted it, examining the checkered pattern before unfolding the cardstock. It read, "From your friend." Daniel removed the note with a strong frown and opened the box. "Thought of you and thought it was something that would make you smile. I hope you had a happy birthday, Daniel. I remembered you worrying about what the future held, and you told me about the old Latin phrase that said perhaps even the bad would be good to remember one day. I hope you enjoy what's inside." Daniel lifted the paper out of the box and stared at the end of the tie blade. It appeared to be a handmade cobalt blue silk tie, neither too wide nor too thin. Daniel looked at the gift and placed it on the counter. He wasn't quite sure how to react, other than to sit there and gaze out the window at the grandeur of the view. It was a nice gift, and he intended to make use of it, but how did it relate to the old Latin verse?

Perhaps he was overanalyzing, reading too much into it. It was the gesture of the gift that mattered. Daniel rubbed his face, then shifted his gaze back to his desk and the briefcase on the far side. The company laptop, which Paul and his team had heavily tampered with before Daniel's departure, sat on the desk. Daniel placed the briefcase beside his feet and positioned his smartphone next to the computer. Glancing at his watch, he realized he had half an hour before the meeting, which he used to settle in. It took him only about fifteen minutes to unpack the boxes that had been sent. He hung copies of his degrees on the far wall and adjusted the desk slightly to the left, creating a narrow seating area with a sofa, two chairs, and a coffee table.

Paul had included a few other useless trinkets that Daniel had no real use for but would be obliged to place on his desk — character-building, as Paul believed. It was now five minutes to eight, and Daniel waited briefly for the call from Paul. "Good morning," Paul greeted him. "Did you receive your belongings?"

The Collateral Dividend

"I did," Daniel replied.

"And what about the gift?"

"How did she find us?" Daniel asked. Paul explained that the executives at Cable Schwartz kindly forwarded it.

"I'm sorry if it bothered you," Paul said. "I know I've been insensitive about the situation in the past. Professionally, I'm still angry at you, but when I saw that she had sent it, I thought you would appreciate receiving it." Paul still believed that Daniel had ended things, viewing it as impractical. Paul thought Daniel didn't want to hurt her any more than he already had. "I hope that's all right. I thought it couldn't have been easy to end things because of your career, and I believe her sending this to you shows she still cares and has made peace with the choice." Paul rambled, trying to explain his decision. Daniel's breaths became shallow; Paul's words stung more than the gift itself. Paul had dissected the meaning of the words, assigning significance to them and creating a thought process behind the gift that made Daniel feel sick.

"It's fine," Daniel said, thanking Paul for forwarding it. "We have a meeting in five minutes. Do you suppose the sudden shortage of lawyers working on the case had anything to do with you?"

Paul laughed; he wasn't about to confirm what Daniel already knew. But yes, he had pulled strings at headquarters, reshuffling several lawyers to create shortages everywhere, leaving an opening for Daniel to step in. "Has he mentioned your trip to Singapore yet?"

"How did you find out about that?" Daniel asked, and Paul, eager to explain, interrupted him. Paul reasoned, "The wonders of physical incursion. I hijacked Swinton's schedule while you were in his office. There's a wireless jumper drive built into the latest variant of the phone we gave you. It wirelessly dumps collected data onto a cloud to send it back here, just like your old business cards." Paul paused. "What do you think?" he asked.

Daniel shrugged, leaning forward and staring intently out the window at the street below. He then leaned back in his chair and skimmed through the first pages of the briefing that Swinton had handed him. "No one here seems too optimistic about this," he remarked. And why should they be? They were fighting a losing battle, and everyone knew it. "Swinton seems friendly enough. How long have you known him?"

"A few years. Why? You don't trust him?"

"No," Daniel responded abruptly. "He works with Min. I certainly wouldn't trust him." There was a long silence, and then Daniel continued. "Do you?"

"I don't know," Paul admitted, shifting the topic away from Swinton. They would address Swinton later. "I've already arranged to have a field box shipped to Singapore for you. Once we find out where the stolen data went, I want you to terminate Min."

"For what happened in Sudan?" Daniel innocently asked.

"If that's what you wish to attribute it to, yes," Paul replied, exhaling deeply. "For once, something that doesn't attract attention would be preferable. I'd rather enjoy not having to clean up your mess once again," Paul scolded, while he sifted through the documents he had stolen from Swinton's computer. "How does the workload look?" Paul asked, but Daniel was already busy. Paul had considered telling Daniel about the offer extended to him, where the legal department in Langley would handle Daniel's work, but he suspected that Daniel would prefer doing it manually. Paul examined the most recent briefing from Sudan, which detailed the tracking of data from the hack to the downed drone. The drone had been taken to Sudan, where the information was extracted onto two computers and physically transferred to Singapore on discs in exchange for money. However, there were missing pieces. Where did the data go from there? Moreover, the data stolen from the hack was not enough to identify the client list they had discovered, nor was it sufficient to cover the other fragments of data they had recovered. Paul wondered where this additional information originated from.

Daniel checked his watch. "I'll have to call you back," he said and opened the door of his office, stepping out into the bustling hallway where Elizabeth awaited him. Daniel pondered whether she found the silence during their walk to Swinton's office awkward or not. Personally, he found it quite calming and had no discomfort in sharing silence with others. Holding the door, he allowed Elizabeth to enter first. When he entered the room, Swinton's eyes briefly met his, a flicker that was as close to a smile as Faron could expect.

"Good, you made it," Swinton greeted, his attention returning to the thick, bound document on the table. Daniel stood confidently, with his hands comfortably in his pockets and his shoulders set back, exuding an aura of confidence. It was a different demeanor from how he carried himself elsewhere, but there was still a sense of coolness and casual suavity about him. When he wore a suit, it just looked right.

"Take a seat," Swinton gestured to the empty chairs on the far side of the table. There were twelve seats in total, with more lawyers standing around the perimeter. Chairs from nearby offices had been brought in, and junior lawyers occupied them along the edge. They all stood with briefing packets and anxious

The Collateral Dividend

expressions. Daniel had quickly learned during his early days as an articling student to do good work, keep quiet, and remain invisible. It was a slow climb to the top, not achieved through flashy gestures. "This is Daniel Faron, everyone. He'll be joining the team," Swinton announced as Daniel took a seat.

A younger lawyer handed him a briefing packet. Daniel estimated him to be a fourth or maybe fifth-year associate. He wondered how many hours the junior lawyer was expected to work here. Swinton commanded the room, exuding a brusque and succinct demeanor. Anyone who wasn't quiet would have likely been fired. Daniel couldn't fathom how Swinton and Paul would have gotten along, but he tried not to speculate or judge the type of men they once were. People changed, Daniel thought. Or did they really? By Faron's calculations, Swinton would have already been an associate when he had met Paul, who was a young undergrad at Cornell. It wouldn't have surprised him if Swinton, an old boy from Harvard, had pulled strings to get the under-financed Paul into Harvard.

The meeting began with introductions, mostly from him, but there were also a few young associates who had been abruptly pulled into the fray when head office mysteriously transferred several lawyers to different parts of the country. By the time Daniel had said his piece, Swinton had already lost patience. At the start, Swinton informed the group that Min and his lawyers had sent over files – nearly 300 boxes of them. Swinton hoped that this would significantly impact the outcome of the case. Although unspoken, it was challenging to determine if Min's information had been obtained legally.

The discussion on how to approach the newly acquired information dragged on for nearly forty minutes, if one could even consider it a discussion with Swinton doing most of the talking and the room occasionally responding with one or two words. Daniel, who had never been a coffee drinker, suddenly contemplated pouring himself a cup just to stay awake. Eventually, they decided that one of the junior partners would lead a group of associates in categorizing and condensing the documents sent by Min for later use. Swinton moved on and announced that he, along with four other associates, including Daniel, would be traveling to Singapore to meet with Min, who refused to personally come to the States unless necessary. Word had gotten around that Daniel had expertise in contract law, and Swinton turned his charm on him.

"Daniel, I'd like you and a few others to examine the licensing agreements. Let's try to scrutinize them," Swinton said.

"Of course," Daniel responded when asked if he would lead the review. He reached for a jug of water, feeling his face heating up, but the shade of his skin masked any blushing.

"Good. Have something drafted up before we leave for Singapore," Swinton said before moving on to assert himself in another topic. By the end of the meeting, Swinton had forcibly recruited three lawyers to assist Daniel and agreed that they would all meet before departing for the airport on Friday. As the room dispersed, Daniel packed up his briefing packet, while Swinton pulled the three associates aside, waiting for Daniel outside the office.

"Daniel," the first of the three said aggressively, approaching Daniel the moment he left Swinton's office. "I'm Brian Chambers," the man said, extending his hand for a shake.

"Pleasure," Daniel replied briskly, eager to walk quickly. "Walk with me," he added, already moving down the hall. The men followed and positioned themselves at his side like eager pups. "And you are?" Daniel asked, as the other two introduced themselves. Daniel would be lying if he said he remembered their names. "Harvard?" he inquired about their education.

"No, sir. Stanford – most of us are. Rumor has it you went to Yale," Chambers replied, clearly the top achiever of his class.

"I did." Daniel was in his office. He took a seat at the far side of the desk. He gestured to the three chairs across from him. "Excuse the mess; I haven't quite settled in yet. Please, take a seat," he said, lacing his fingers together and resting them on his lap. "So," Daniel continued hesitantly, "I want all of you to review the information independently. Let's identify the pressure points in the contracts and see if we can argue that the two firms don't compete."

There was a shift in the room, and after a moment, Chambers cleared his throat and said, "There's a simple solution to this non-compete clause." He began to suspect Daniel's familiarity with practicing law in California. "California deems non-compete clauses unenforceable. It's just a matter of filing an injunction to move the proceedings to a California court."

"Great," Daniel replied with a hint of sarcasm. Having worked for the government, he knew better than to assume that such an injunction would solve the issue. Besides, this was a federal court case, not confined to California law. Leaning forward onto the desk, Daniel said, "Brian, let me tell you something." His statement oozed with sarcasm. "This is a multi-million-dollar case. Even if we could win the injunction, we could still suffer major losses right here on our own turf. Currently, we have a favorable judge, and while an injunction may buy us time, these contracts involve more than just non-compete clauses; they

The Collateral Dividend

include misrepresentation of trade secrets." Daniel then leaned back in his chair, looking at all three men. "Let's work on finding permanent solutions. If you have any questions, come find me." It was a snip of arrogance that Daniel had never seen in himself before. Almost instinctively, he had taken on the persona of the senior lawyers who used to berate the summer students in New York years ago. He remembered hating those assholes who would tell him and the other associates what to do, but somehow, it had made him a better lawyer, a harder worker.

Daniel waited for the men to leave, and then he locked himself up in the firm's main library, reminiscent of his undergraduate days. There was a table near the back of the library on the second floor, and he spread out his things across it. He had gathered casebooks that were nearly three inches thick, representing decades of legal cases.

He nearly dozed off once or twice, and after seven or eight hours of work, he was the only one still in the library. With the night approaching, he decided it was best to call it a night. His biological clock was so distorted that he no longer had an accurate sense of exhaustion. A company car awaited him just outside the courtyards, and Daniel stumbled out of the lobby with a briefcase filled with case files, ten minutes after calling for the car.

His hotel was several blocks northwest. Under better circumstances, he would have walked, but the exhaustion of being awake for over twenty consecutive hours had caught up with him. Daniel charged the town car to the client, checked into the hotel, and climbed the stairs to his room on the tenth floor. He fell headlong onto the queen bed's duvet, letting out a deep breath. After lying face-down for a few moments, he rolled onto his back, observing the long room with detachment. The closet door was pushed back, revealing his suit bag, which hung with all its contents dry-cleaned and turned around within a span of a 16-hour day. Daniel slipped off his brogue Oxford shoes, cracking his toes as if stretching his feet in his brightly colored socks. When he sat up and let out another sigh, he stowed away his brown shoes in the closet before undressing into an undershirt and a housecoat. He ordered room service and surfed through the television channels until the food arrived. He then attempted to familiarize himself further with misappropriation cases, but at this hour, it was of little use. By ten o'clock, Daniel felt lethargic and stifled long, crippling yawns every ten minutes. When Paul called to check in, Daniel had already brushed his teeth and was tucked beneath the covers of his bed.

"We'll keep this brief," Paul said, sounding almost as tired as Daniel. "I sent the files to some friends back at Langley's legal department to review.

223

Apparently, they found something." Paul paused for a moment. "They had some analysts at the NSA look into it further. The details should come through in the morning, but they helped us uncover how they got to us. Min used some of the trade secrets he picked up from Silicon Valley to intercept encrypted transmissions. It must have taken him months to decode the data packets." Paul's voice trailed off. "The encryption on all our communications should be re-secured and authenticated by the end of the week." They were resorting to wartime measures as Min focused on bringing down the operations that were tracking down Gaillard.

Paul didn't want to seem indecisive. So, he reassured Daniel that their actions were merely precautionary. The leaked information about Farragut Center employees, including their family members and medical records, was unforgivable. "We'll go old school for now - paper transfers and the whole deal. It doesn't make sense to communicate with Langley and MI6 in any other way. Min has hit us hard, and if he's not supplying the Chinese, he's definitely selling the information." The list of potential buyers among their enemies was extensive. Daniel couldn't even begin to fathom how they would approach terminating Min. A simple mugging would be too conspicuous, and suicide was out of the question. It required finesse, and determining the right approach would take time.

After clearing his throat, Paul spoke up. "Yes, so," he said, buying himself some time while he scanned through files. The unofficial word from Langley's legal department was grim. Rumor had it that the Senate Select Committee on Intelligence had requisitioned all resources related to the obsolete targeted killing department from the CIA. They hoped to catch any former key players involved in the Sudan mess. The last thing they needed was for the committee to start digging into former employees. While everyone at Farragut Center had an airtight cover, Senator Helpord was no pushover. The concentration of former Langley employees with specific skill sets working at the same place posed a risk of exposing the entire program. It wasn't just Paul's own well-being that concerned him; Daniel's profession made him even more vulnerable to the relentless legal system. At any moment, their legitimacy could be stripped away, leaving them destabilized. Their top priority was to keep Daniel out of the hearings and, above all, prevent politicians from obtaining the information.

Paul's mind was always racing, but now technicalities burdened his brilliant, macro-oriented thinking. He prided himself on staying one step ahead, but it seemed like he had lost that edge. Moreover, there was the lingering question of what Daniel had been doing for a month. After failing to locate Isabel and

The Collateral Dividend

encountering a complete blackout on Philippe Gaillard, Daniel had gone rogue and disappeared. Nobody, especially Paul, dared to ask the most pressing question. Office rumors circulated, fueled by reported sightings of Daniel around the world, but none of them yielded any useful information. Since his return, Daniel had kept his health and profession in the foreground, avoiding discussions about the past. This had greatly concerned Paul for some time.

"Anything else you need to tell me?" Daniel asked, holding the phone to his cheek while lying on the bed. Daniel's eyes were barely open, and he knew that Paul had been withholding his concerns.

"No, should there be?" Paul responded with a somber tone. When there was no reply, he waited a moment before adding, "That will be all for today, Daniel. Get some rest, and we'll keep you updated on the Senate hearings." Paul tried to assure him, but it was evident to Daniel, despite Paul's best efforts, that something was being concealed.

The political climate in Washington had shifted dramatically, and people were growing nervous about the Senate hearings, especially Paul. He didn't want to reveal all his cards to Daniel at once. After ending the call, Paul stood up from his office desk, turned off his computer terminal, and retrieved his coat from the hook near the door. He switched off the lights and, being the last person in the office, descended the back stairwell to the elevator and the underground parking facility.

Paul hung up the phone and placed it back on the receiver. He still drove the same car model he had during his time at Langley, but he had upgraded once in the five years since then, despite the salary increase and the passage of time. It was a Ford Fusion, and his girlfriend, who had accompanied him on the purchase, had convinced him to get the available eco-boost, something he didn't particularly care about. The car served its purpose, and he didn't give it much thought. During the events involving Philippe Gaillard in New York, Paul had been using the Metro as a cautious measure. The threat of Gaillard still loomed, and this fear had seeped into his daily life. At least the security in public places brought him some peace of mind, diverting his thoughts from his vulnerability during that time. When he arrived home and stumbled through the door, his girlfriend was sitting on the sofa watching the news.

Rachel stood up and observed him entering the room. As he collapsed onto the sofa beside her, resting his head on her shoulder and then readjusting so that his head rested against the edge of the sofa, she said with surprise, "You're home early." Her housecoat enveloped her as she sat back down, taking a sip of juice. "How was work?" She attempted to engage him in conversation, despite the limited topic. He had undone his tie, which now lay folded on the sofa beside him.

"Long, as always. Had back-to-back meetings since six thirty," he replied, grabbing the remote and switching through baseball highlights until he settled on a game between the Pittsburgh Pirates and the Baltimore Orioles. He had been a fan of his hometown team for as long as he could remember. Going to games at the old Three Rivers Stadium with his father was one of his earliest memories. "And what about your day?" he asked, resting his cheek on the crown of her head while surveying the living room in a casual, familiar manner. Like most nights, Rachel cooked dinner for two, and if Paul wasn't home by ten, she would refrigerate it for his lunch the next day, assuming he made it home at all. The kitchen lights were off, and the only illumination came from the television.

Something felt off in the room, and while Rachel recounted her day, Paul used the time to figure out what it was. "When did we get that?" he eventually asked, pointing to the new furniture in the dining room.

"Last week. I asked you about it three Mondays ago," Rachel replied, clearly displeased with his lack of attention. It was getting late, and she abruptly sat up, wrapping herself fully in her housecoat. "Okay, good night," she said, leaning forward to kiss him. "Don't stay up too late," she added as she made her way toward the kitchen. Paul remained seated, watching the remainder of the replayed game before finally joining her in bed. By then, his eyes were heavy, and as he lay in bed staring at the ceiling, he remained conscious for just over five minutes before succumbing to the embrace of sleep, the night's chill surrounding him.

THE CODE BREAKER

Washington was a ruthless city. The senators who had once worked hand in hand with Director Dunes were now more than willing to skewer him and leave him out in the sun to wither and die. The Capitol building was certainly no Westminster when it came to fake smiles, pats on the shoulder, and backstabbing. Still, it was the closest anyone not British would get. Things moved slowly there; it was uncommon for anything to progress in a manner that outpaced the private sector. The slow measure of legislation was tiresome.

The first preliminary hearings were scheduled for early Wednesday morning, preceding the investigation by a week. In the opinion of many informed bureaucrats, the investigation - backed by the Senate Select Committee on Intelligence - was a witch-hunt. The discussions regarding the investigations all occurred behind closed doors, and Ted Hawthorne, responsible for helping create the mess, attended all of them. He met with Gregory, the DNI, and one of the President's closest advisors, an hour before the hearing, and the four reviewed the exact wording Gregory would use to answer whatever the hearing tried to throw at him.

The press was already there by the time Director Dunes arrived, and they collapsed suddenly around him as the glob of reporters shuffled toward the hearing room door. The director emerged from the crowded doors as a solitary figure, leaving behind the drones of reporters not granted access to the hearing room. Of course, there were more press members seated at the back of the hearing room near the doors, and several in the space between the committee and the interviewee seating. Director Dunes was a holdover from the old days of the CIA, a breed nearly extinct. He and Ted were dinosaurs in an era of mammals. There existed a mantra that seemed to suggest there was no room for brutish and violent means to an end. However, many of these acts, in the conceived anarchic world, were the very things that kept the world intact. But no one would readily admit that the unmentionable acts were the very thing that let society continue unscathed, clean, pristine, and naive. Ted readily held the opinion that the primary purpose of his job was to maintain security, to sustain the state. The reality of that fact was quite clear. Unchecked freedom fundamentally required the admission and acceptance of insecurity. Restrictions had to be made if domestic freedoms were to exist. On the international level, constant insecurity existed, and it was that fundamental belief that allowed Ted to justify state-sponsored violence. He had spent years rehearsing these ideals, affirming them in his mind and actions.

The room was large, and across the far wall, fourteen seats were hidden behind a wooden desk that spanned nearly the entirety of the wall. Near the middle, the chairman of the committee, Senator Helpord, sat hunched over a thick stack of files, grumbling and mumbling into his own thoughts.

Dunes approached the foremost table and took a seat. He adjusted his tie and glanced back at the seating area where Ted Hawthorne was now sitting. Dunes poured himself a glass of water and took a long sip before greeting the legal aide to his right. He was nervous. He couldn't help but wonder if he would go to jail for this. He couldn't help but think about what would come of it all. Would anything? The aide sat there with her arms crossed and a plain expression on her face. What Dunes wouldn't give to be in her situation, divorced from the drama yet an active participant in the action.

Helpord turned toward the grand, oddly shaped room, cleared his throat, and leaned forward into the microphone. "I would say for this committee to come to order, but it seems we are already in order. Thank you for coming, Director Dunes, and all other witnesses whose testimony we will be hearing today. As you are all aware, this has become a public matter, and by that standard, we, as the United States Senate, hope that the public nature of these hearings will help determine accountability for past events and remedies for future ones." The chair of the committee was a pasty man with peppered grey hair combed over to one side, as if to hide his quickly receding hairline. He had been in the Senate for the better part of his life, and his appointment onto the Committee on Intelligence had been one he had participated in from the very beginning, notably because he was a residing senator from Virginia, the state where most of the intelligence community had clustered. "As many are aware, in events that occurred between May fifteenth and May twenty-sixth of this year, U.S. operatives were captured and eventually tortured and executed on a live online stream that was spread globally. The actions were no doubt acts of terrorism, displaying the deficiencies found in foreign protection of U.S. citizens and the failure of due diligence done to bring them home while operating missions abroad." The chair cleared his throat, reached forward on his desk, and took a sip of water. "Before this committee today, to help us understand the U.S. government's role in inserting these operatives into the field, we are joined by Gregory Joseph Dunes, the current Director of the Central Intelligence Agency. Mr. Dunes has had a long career within the CIA and U.S. intelligence community, and we would first like to thank him for his service to this country."

The Collateral Dividend

The chair caught his breath, looked at the paper on his desk, and waited a moment before continuing, "Mr. Dunes, without objections, you will have the opportunity to provide an opening statement that will be made part of the record, and all members will have five days to submit statements and questions, again for the record." He fiddled with something behind the high collar of the desk. "You may begin when you're ready, Director."

The old man gazed at the files on his desk, taking a deep breath. He peered over the brim of his square-framed glasses at the chairman of the committee before beginning. "Thank you, Mr. Chairman, ranking member, and members of the committee, for this opportunity. The events on May fifteen in North Sudan, which resulted in the execution of two brave Americans, Robert Kowalski and Mason Harper, were the outcome of operations conducted and coordinated by CIA operatives with high-priority national security objectives."

Dunes turned the page of his script, setting it aside, and briefly glanced up at the committee members before continuing. "Kowalski and Harper were employed by the Central Intelligence Agency at the time of their death. Therefore, I take full responsibility for their deaths. Both men possessed extensive experience with classified activities and were aware of the risks involved in operating on this specific classified and highly sensitive objective. As the director of the CIA, I authorized and oversaw the operation conducted in North Sudan. I accept all responsibility for our shortcomings. Allow me to first outline the circumstances that led to the execution of Mr. Kowalski and Harper, and then I will explain the critical nature of their roles in our current understanding."

"Not long before May fifteenth, ongoing investigations revealed a connection between rebel insurgencies in North Sudan and discrepancies in record losses by the New York Stock Exchange due to a market shutdown caused by ultranationalists from Greece. Our infrastructure and financial stability were compromised by electronic attacks. It became my office's responsibility to track down where the money had gone. Officials within the intelligence community successfully traced a connection between the ultranationalists and North Sudan."

Suddenly, there was a surge of camera flashes, and the hum of shutters filled the room, forcing Dunes to pause and collect his thoughts. What was he doing? This was a blatant lie, and if caught, there would be no going back. "We are constructing an explanation," Ted had told him, assuring that lying was the only way to avoid severe consequences. They needed to appeal to people's emotions. Dunes felt like a casualty of others' agendas.

E.R. Wychwood

"As is customary with high-priority intelligence, my office was notified, but I was personally informed only when the director of the National Clandestine Service presented me with a proposal for covert actions in Northern Sudan. It was at my suggestion that assets were deployed to determine the involvement of former Sudanese Army Colonel, terrorist, and extremist, Ali Omar Kutu, in the market crashes."

The cameras continued to flash even more rapidly now. Dunes felt dizzy. The occasional flash and loud shutter sounds created a disorienting situation. He tried to maintain his pace, using the break in his speech to glance around while taking a sip of water. He was hot, and the sweat trickling down the back of his neck reminded him of the pressure he was under. If he wasn't going to jail for this, he was surely heading for hell. It seemed as though the committee was hanging on to his every word, hoping for a slip-up, a foolish statement, a wrong word, or an incorrect disclosure. Had he already made one of those mistakes? Dunes placed the glass down, which had perspired, with water droplets collecting on the wooden tabletop.

"As the committee is aware, Colonel Kutu's removal is of utmost importance in restoring stability to the region. His collaboration with Al Qaeda and Somali pirates has put numerous American lives at risk. Kutu was also responsible for several attempted attacks on U.S. foreign properties, including the successful attacks on U.S. naval carriers in the Persian Gulf last spring. Robert and Mason were briefed and deployed with the objective of tagging the money and, if possible, capturing Kutu, before moving to a pre-disclosed extraction location. Many argue that the role of human assets in the field has become obsolete. While it is true that technology has made our jobs easier, individuals like Robert and Mason are indispensable. They directly contribute to sustaining American values and our way of life worldwide."

"As the director of the CIA for the past seven years, I have witnessed significant changes in the intelligence community. One thing remains true: Americans deployed on sensitive operations face risks and are aware of those risks. Many serve their country unrecognized, but it is their service that allows us to remain ignorant. Unfortunately, tough decisions sometimes need to be made, and I stand by mine. As this committee knows, the CIA plays a critical role in the intelligence community, crucial for national defense. I personally knew Robert and Mason. The decision not to send additional assets for rescue missions was not taken lightly. I hope that, with the partnership of this committee, changes will be made to strengthen the importance of human

The Collateral Dividend

intelligence operations and to prevent such events from recurring. Now, I'll be more than happy to answer your questions."

Dunes thought to himself, What a long-winded statement filled with nothing but lies and circular reasoning. He suspected that he would soon face the full fury of the entire committee, with undoubtedly harsh and numerous questions.

The chairman looked down toward the ends of the curved table that surrounded the witness in a semi-circular fashion. He exhaled deeply before leaning forward toward the microphone, grasping its base. "Well, Director, firstly, I would like to question something that you seemed to completely overlook. The primary concern of this operation is that the team in Sudan was captured and executed despite, and I quote, 'several unsuccessful extraction attempts.' Was this information provided to your office?"

"It... It was, sir," Dunes confirmed. Nobody, apart from those who had met with Dunes before, expected him to wholeheartedly take full responsibility for this investigation, and the decision caught the chairman off guard.

The committee chair reached for a follow-up paper, looking back at his aide, who handed him a folded paper with scribbled notes on it. Regaining his composure, he leaned forward again. "In that case, Director Dunes, what exactly prevented the attempts from being successful?"

"Well, Mr. Chairman, the current political environment in Africa and South Asia has fostered strong anti-American sentiment in the regions surrounding Sudan. The team's location made extraction impossible without facing heavy enemy fire while simultaneously maintaining operational security of the intelligence collected during the operation." Dunes drank more water.

Ted sat in the back corner, arms crossed, with a slightly strained expression on his face. The press was relentless, buying into the verbose and eloquent statements that came from the committee, many of whom asked the Director softball questions, allowing him to hit them out of the park. Ted was not surprised; many of the President's senatorial supporters on the committee would have preferred to avoid this hearing altogether.

The hearing lasted nearly two hours, with a large part of it consisting of the bipartisan committee lobbing partisan questions at Dunes. Ted left thirty minutes before the meeting was called to order and climbed into the back of the town car outside the building. He was glued to his smartphone for the duration of the drive. When he arrived at the tall building that housed Farragut Center, the back door of the car opened, and an umbrella appeared, protecting him from the rain. Ted followed the umbrella's path to the portico of the building and leaned against the frame after entering, knocking on Paul's door.

E.R. Wychwood

"How'd it go?" Paul asked immediately, looking away from his desk at Ted.

"Rough," Ted said, taking a seat across from Paul. "They grilled him, crucified him even," he sighed deeply, appearing exhausted. "If no new information comes to light, we should be fine." Ted slouched in the chair, rubbing his nose and gazing into the distance. "How is the security re-authentication going?" he asked, noticing Paul's reluctance to discuss it. Embarrassed by their unpreparedness, Paul preferred to forget about the incident. "So, what are we looking at across the globe currently?" Ted inquired, wanting to be updated.

A television screen, rarely used by Paul, was flush against the far wall of his office. He leaned back and turned on the screen, reflecting the image displayed on his computer—a global map with various colored circles. Some clusters overlapped, while others barely touched. Paul focused the screen on North America first. "Daniel is still in San Francisco, as you know. He's set to leave for Singapore at the end of the week," he informed Ted.

"What about the rest of the world?" Ted asked, and the screen shifted to Europe.

"I've been working with Langley to have twenty-four-hour drone surveillance of Kutu. The other two consist of Klaus and, of course, Alekos Tzavaras. Tzavaras hasn't shown up in nearly a month but has been displaying an unprecedented level of support, and the country has started to destabilize quickly. Riots are becoming weekly events," Paul explained. He enjoyed being in the role of the architect, instigating discussions and making decisions. "There is something more pressing that I think we should talk about, however," Paul said, adopting a confused tone. "I had some analysts review the information that Min was able to intercept from us, and, well, it doesn't add up. Some of this information couldn't be acquired unless Min knew someone within the community."

Ted, with a lifelong career at Langley, cringed at the idea of a leak. He had experienced counterintelligence manhunts conducted by Langley in the past and was not fond of the methods associated with spy hunting. "Within where exactly?" he asked.

Paul let out a deep breath, resting his chin on the palm of his hand. "Possibly within Farragut Center, within the two-specters," he referred to the colloquial term attached to Farragut Center and Heywood Lane. The latter was an offspring of the National Security Agency, a program comparable to Farragut Center.

Ted rubbed his forehead. "Have you contacted Mike and the others?" he asked in a murmur. Michael Winters was Paul's counterpart at Heywood, and they frequently met to discuss the current state of affairs.

'Not yet, I'm set to meet with him in thirty minutes,' Paul said as he glanced at his watch. The meeting had been on his mind all morning, and he already had an idea of what to expect.

He had devised a plan involving a mutual friend, someone whom Winters would approve of, to investigate their books. The task of spy hunting fell upon Harrison Wallace. Harrison, a former senior CIA CI who had transitioned into recruitment due to the tolls of business, had crossed paths with Paul in the past. When they first met, Paul was a young and impressionable undergraduate whom Wallace believed could be groomed into one of the agency's finest.

The Farragut Center, the closest and most discreet off-site location, was chosen for the meeting. Winters arrived and took a seat at the conference room desk, followed shortly by Harrison, who greeted Paul with a warm smile and a tight hug. The lines on Harrison's face moved upward, forming creases like cracks in dirt. He was a man from a bygone era, one who still held on to the principles of how the intelligence community should operate. In many ways, his vision resembled an old boys club. His weathered face reminded Paul of the harshness of wind and rain on sandstone, as years of service had worn away his once youthful appearance. Harrison entered the room and took a seat.

"So, what exactly do we hope to achieve with this?" Harrison eventually asked. Though it may have sounded like a simple question, the experienced man knew better than to embark on a search without a clear objective. Going in without a plan would only lead to aimless digging until something was discovered. "We need to be very cautious in our decision-making regarding matters like this. Having one's name associated with such investigations could quickly end careers," he added. Earlier in the day, he had been briefed on both programs, and the information was still swirling in his mind, forming a broth of thoughts.

Winters, the only one with counterintelligence experience, looked at Paul, seeking his approval before raising his hands and saying, "Ending someone's career is the least of my concerns. If these programs come anywhere near the ongoing Senate hearings, we could be facing serious charges."

Paul chimed in, tapping his pen against a pad of paper with a consistent rhythm. He had always enjoyed these types of meetings, where discussions had a gossip-like quality that exhilarated him. "Well, what do you suggest?" he asked.

E.R. Wychwood

Harrison sighed deeply, glancing at the papers for a moment. "No matter how you approach it, the investigation needs to be comprehensive. We should start with personnel files and finances. I have an old colleague from Yale who can assist in reviewing the financial records," he replied, adopting an old-school tone reminiscent of the time when he first joined the CIA in the sixties, a time when everyone knew everyone. The seasoned spymaster had returned solely for Paul's sake, though he couldn't express that openly with Winters present. Harrison held a great deal of respect for the young man, as Paul had never known his grandparents, or at least his impoverished parents had never introduced them to him. Harrison liked to think of himself as a figure resembling a grandparent to Paul. Clearing his throat, Harrison continued, "Once we identify any irregularities, I'll spend a few days in each of your operations centers and conduct interviews." Harrison was concise, astute, and above all, efficient. He had little patience for lies and even less for formalities. The excitement of returning to his former profession was causing Harrison to get ahead of himself. He had always loved puzzles, even as a boy, and the mental calculations required for a job like this surpassed any other. However, he couldn't help but be frank with himself; it had been years since he was active, and he couldn't fathom why the men sitting around him had agreed to employ him as their housekeeper.

The answer to that question was simple, always clear in Paul's mind. If Harrison had merely asked, Paul would have told him. Old habits die hard, and who better to review the books of an invisible entity than someone who had experienced the golden age of espionage? "Yes, well, perhaps you could start with Farragut Center," Paul suggested. He suspected that some local assets were taking orders from another department. It was unlikely to be foreign, but Paul believed someone within the American intelligence community was pulling strings beyond their jurisdiction. He had already lost an asset in Seoul due to operational security going awry. The increase in foreign assets had expanded operational reach but had come at the cost of reduced security.

Harrison made a perplexed expression. He couldn't understand why Paul would want to be the first under his scrutiny. "Of course, send me your books, and I'll start tomorrow," the early riser said. His silver-white hair had thinned, but he still attempted to part it to the left. He wore wire-framed glasses with thick bifocals at the bottom, resembling a hangover effect.

Satisfied, Paul finalized the details of subsequent meetings and, most importantly, how Harrison would contact them. Harrison's poor circulation made it a slow process for him to leave the building, and Paul assisted him.

The Collateral Dividend

Eventually, they found themselves standing outside the south entrance, beside Winters, who scowled at the torrential rain assaulting the city. "What do you think of all this?" Winters asked, his hands comfortably resting at his waist as he glanced down at his feet.

Paul shrugged. "Something's not right," he replied, but Winters already knew that. "It hasn't been right since Gaillard." Paul gazed across the street, just beyond the overhanging portico. Then he frowned, crossed his arms, and turned to face Michael. "How many assets do you have abroad?" he asked, speaking softly.

"What?" Michael responded with a smirk and a laugh. "Hell if I know."

"Oh, come on, humor me for God's sake. How many people do you have abroad?" Paul pressed. He estimated that Farragut Center had around twenty assets abroad, with only three possessing lethal capabilities comparable to Daniel's operational reach.

With his hands in his pockets, Winters exhaled, as if finishing a good workout. "I'd say seven. I've always had fewer Culper's than you. Wet work is your expertise, remember?" Winters said, laughing. He referred to the colloquial term for assets serving abroad, originating from one of the first spy rings under the direction of George Washington during the Revolutionary War. While Winters lacked foreign assets, his team compensated with signals and communication analysts. Paul, on the other hand, had around ten to fifteen analysts. Additionally, about ten others working for Grip were aware of Farragut Center.

"If this situation spirals out of control, I don't think I'm prepared to dismantle everything," Paul admitted in a hushed voice, below the hearing range of others. There was a weight to his words, as failing to take action would be disastrous and foolish. "I certainly don't want to destroy all we've built, hoping someone with an equally noble cause will eventually take up our mantle."

Winters retrieved a pack of gum, offering a piece to Paul who declined, before taking one for himself. "Look, you and I both know the leak didn't come from any of our senior staff, and the information we're dealing with is of senior management level. Who's to say someone at The Valley hasn't let something slip?" Both men understood that the suggestion was mere gossip, and Winters didn't want to indulge too much in his own speculative thoughts.

Paul kept his thoughts to himself. There was more to this situation than initially met the eye, and it made him uneasy. He had been keeping a close eye on Min since the first indications that he could become a problem, but it seemed like not all the cards had been played just yet.

E.R. Wychwood

*   *   *

Despite his age, Harrison exuded a youthful demeanor. His property just outside of Annapolis was large enough that in his younger years, he could go hunting in the unoccupied woods across the river. However, those days were now few and far between. His wife knew that espionage was an addiction for him, and his active involvement was the only way to subside the itch.

The personnel files had been delivered to his house in stacked boxes, confiscating a large portion of his home office. They reached from the floor to the ceiling in the small room with a long, narrow window. An old, heavy desk was pushed against the wall, while a green banker's light adorned the far corner. A massive computer screen was connected to a computer terminal that sat beside the desk.

He spent the first week reviewing the files, tackling several each night until he had nearly gone through all of them. During the day, he made trips to D.C. to observe the inner workings of the offices. Both Paul and Winters had established their own unique working cultures, and Harrison had been introduced to each group accordingly.

The initial days were spent at Farragut Center, where he was presented as a representative from one of the "neighbors," a term used for the center's sister agencies. The pace was fast, the tempo quicker and more energetic than what he remembered from Langley. Harrison observed everything meticulously, jotting down notes on peculiarities and unique factors. Operations ran around the clock with tight operational security. Checkpoints in every hallway monitored the comings and goings, while thermal and normal light cameras scrutinized movements outside the office spaces. Security logs and information requisitions were stored on three servers worldwide, recording the details of all personnel who requested any documents. Most terminals were highly modified, lacking USB or CD drives and running on independent networks.

Harrison found that similar arrangements existed at the other program, but Paul had taken it a step further. As part of the employment contract, many employees were required to surrender their location-based privacy rights. Harrison wasn't even sure if such an act was legal, but he assumed Paul had covered all bases after consulting with Daniel and other colleagues at Langley.

During his visits to Farragut Center, Harrison reviewed the operational protocols in the evenings. Their precision exceeded anything he had

The Collateral Dividend

encountered at Langley. The restrictions on employee freedoms were extensive, but they neither surprised nor offended the old Langley spymaster.

"...all employees surrender the right to privacy and authorize the tracking and review of all documents, rights, and information related to their citizenship. In exchange for this breach, the Government will provide ____ dollars per month. The Government reserves the right to revoke payment if the employee fails to maintain the operational security obligations outlined in S.35.b [in some cases, this includes surrendering the legal rights and obligations of U.S. citizens]."

At one point, Harrison read about Paul effectively creating an organization insulated from public scrutiny and pressures. It referenced the old days of espionage, the golden years of the sixties, and the protocols that had been resurrected to uphold operational security. While Harrison had not spent much time in the field, he understood the desire to return to the roots of old.

He submitted the financials of all employees to an old friend from Langley, who meticulously analyzed them for anomalies before returning them to Harrison. Being a numbers man, Harrison believed that numbers never lied. Although a well-trained asset could deceive an EEG machine, explaining financial irregularities almost always exposed the perfect honey trap.

Finally, the most challenging task lay ahead: analyzing the possibility that some of the most senior officers at the CIA had collaborated with the Soviets, or vice versa. Harrison had to consider the likelihood that it involved one of the heads of operation or, worse, one of the chiefs of staff. He began with Winters and worked his way backward until he reached Paul. Reviewing the files of those he was acquainted with always made him uneasy, and Paul's file was the most difficult to confront. Harrison only hoped that Paul wouldn't be suspected or, even worse, implicated.

THE PAPER TIGER

Mornings were becoming monotonous. And throughout the week, amidst the droning sounds of the city, Daniel repeated the same gestures with nearly precise clockwork. He no longer had to look over his shoulder. There was great comfort in knowing, or at least temporarily thinking, that he was safe and secure from lurking killers. Perhaps it was his fatigued appearance or the laziness that came from not actively scanning and surveying his surroundings, but Daniel had fallen into a heavy routine. He despised routines. He loathed the repetition and monotony, the prospect of endless months of the same thing without interruption. Although his work was far from repetitive or boring, the regimented consistency of his days wore him down.

Swinton had met him at the airport on the morning of their scheduled flight to Singapore. He had been quite frank that they would be charging Min for the flight and, furthermore, billing him for the hours they spent on the plane. The excuse was that they would be using the flight to prepare for things. Everyone knew better, including Min, Daniel suspected. Swinton, who could barely go an hour without a cigarette, had hastily smoked four before boarding and was now downing glasses of Irish whiskey in a last-ditched effort to get some sleep on the flight over.

Daniel, an experienced traveler by now, had already found a comfortable position in the spacious first-class seat and was slowly drifting in and out of consciousness. There was still a rustling of people boarding, and Swinton, who had never truly engaged in a one-on-one conversation lasting longer than an hour, looked at Daniel with almost envy at his tranquility. "Don't you drink?" he asked between sips, clearly judging. "Who doesn't drink?" he thought. Certainly not any lawyer Swinton knew.

With his eyes half-shut, Daniel let out a faint smirk from the corner of his mouth. "No," he said, and when asked why, he sat up, cleared his throat, and truthfully answered, "I ran into some trouble with not being able to control how often I was drinking. I eventually drank myself into sickness," he said. "I haven't gone back since." He crossed his arms now, looking down at the aisle floor, past Swinton's legs. It was as if he was recalling the vivid memory of his self-induced "drying-out."

Daniel felt as if he had been to hell and back, and the deep creases that furrowed his forehead made him appear much older than he was, especially

The Collateral Dividend

when he was tired. His eyes bore heavy, purple circles beneath them, further accentuating the emptiness of his gray gaze.

Daniel was weathered by his time away. He didn't look much older, but there was an aura about him that made him feel older. He looked down at his lap and stared at the end of his navy-blue tie. The narrow end peeked out to the side, revealing an embroidery in the same color as the rest of the tie along the bottom half of the narrow end. He wasn't sure how he hadn't noticed it until now. "Auspicium melioris aevi": a token of a better age. Daniel covered his mouth with his hand and pondered the Latin inscription. That must be what was meant by "inside." He held the end of the tie and examined it carefully. It was written in thick cursive text, taking up most of the width of the narrow end. "What a thoughtful thing to do," Daniel thought. He liked to believe that he had moved past the past, but in many ways, she still seemed to haunt him. He still longed for her, and in his mind, he wrestled with the idea that the gift was a gesture to reconnect, to extend a connection of some sort.

It had taken him months of contemplation to unravel the layers that had concealed exactly what had transpired. He had been vulnerable; he had always been, and letting down his guard had been reckless. In a way, he needed that pain – he needed to remember that in order to feel the highs, one must also feel the lows. But acknowledging that to himself only intensified his longing for her. He still yearned for her, for companionship both intellectual and physical. What had gone wrong, Daniel wondered. With thoughts of Isabel consuming him, he fell asleep, wondering if he would ever see her again.

The flight to Singapore was a grueling twenty-hour journey. By the time they arrived, it was clear why they had charged the client for first-class seats. Swinton, being slightly larger than most men, made it unimaginable for Daniel to endure a cramped, small, blue leather seat next to him for twenty hours. It would have been unbearable.

However, one can only sleep for so long. Daniel woke up when they were halfway over the Atlantic. He got up, paced the plane, and even took a shower before returning to his seat feeling refreshed.

"What are you watching?" Daniel asked as he leaned across the aisle. Swinton shrugged, took off his headphones, and looked at Daniel before turning off the screen. "Nothing," he lied. It had been a documentary on the prolific growth and history of Gaillard's firm. It was something that had always fascinated Swinton – how Gaillard's father had been so cunning. He had predicted many innovations, and it was his initial use of client "feedback" that had helped them grow. Or at least, that's what they were reporting. "What made

239

you make the leap from the Department of Justice?" Daniel asked as the video ended. He was having the in-flight lunch, opting for water instead of the offered wine.

Swinton took a breath and then glanced at Daniel with raised eyebrows. "Well, why did you leave?" he asked rhetorically before providing Daniel with a legitimate answer. "At the time, the changing administration was going in a direction that I disagreed with. I could make more money in private practice, and it was clear that I wouldn't be moving any further up the ladder in the public sector," he grunted. "I was in my late twenties and felt more comfortable with litigation on the corporate side of things." It was evident that he longed for the fast pace that came with the private sector, and Daniel couldn't blame him.

"Listen," Swinton said now, in a tone that implied he knew more than he was letting on. Moreover, it was said in such a way that Daniel swallowed hard and held his breath. For a moment, Daniel feared that Paul had disclosed the reason for his presence, and indeed he had. But Swinton didn't care.

"When we arrive there, we won't have the opportunity to meet Min until Monday, so you can lay low in the city until then. He's an odd character, likes respect, and isn't one for joking," Swinton quickly briefed Daniel, even though Daniel already knew most of the information.

"Do you like women?" Swinton asked suddenly. Daniel was certain Paul had mentioned that Swinton was married; he thought Swinton even had kids.

"I do," Daniel admitted, and Swinton suddenly went off on a roaring tangent. His face flushed with color, and his head tilted back, exposing the folds of his neck. Daniel looked at Swinton's short hair, crinkled and greying as if it had been singed. Swinton rambled on about a lovely little hole in the wall he had discovered during his first trip to visit Min nearly three years ago. There was a wonderful Asian woman, he told Daniel, from China, a small woman who couldn't have been much older than twenty-five. She had been working at the bar when Swinton first met her, paying off the crushing cost of college. Swinton implicitly referred to her as a tiger in bed, and suddenly the image of the large Swinton, hunched over this small, thin, tanned woman invaded Daniel's mind, and he wished it hadn't.

Daniel let him continue to talk. The more he knew about Swinton, the better. Swinton tried to describe her to Daniel, and by the end, Daniel had a vivid image of the woman in his mind. She had purple hair, a short bob cut, and a small square frame. Daniel wondered if Swinton's wife knew. Despite its plausibility, he dismissed the idea. Daniel didn't understand why they had flown in so early, but it quickly became apparent that Swinton had made the bookings,

The Collateral Dividend

and being the lecherous man he was, he wanted to arrive early to have leisure time. Swinton had reached the onset of a mid-life crisis nearly fifteen years too early. He enjoyed being dominated, which Daniel found peculiar, as lawyers usually avoided indulging in escorts, affairs, and violence. The potential troubles were not worth the benefit. Apparently, Swinton didn't care; he was either too careless or too bored with his life to worry about the legal issues.

The petite Asian girl satisfied Swinton in a way his wife couldn't. Or at least, that's what Swinton implied when he tried to describe her to Daniel. His wife was undoubtedly too busy between work and taking care of the kids to even fathom having a sex life.

Daniel had once seen a photo of Swinton's family on his office desk, and he juxtaposed the two very different personas that inhabited the same skin. There was a naivety in the way Daniel carried himself, or at least that's what he thought. Perhaps it could even be considered an old-fashioned persona. He hated the idea of infidelity and liked to believe that neither of his parents had ever been unfaithful. He never had the courage to ask Henry whether this image of his parents was a fallacy or not.

Daniel did not like the idea of being dominated, but he could understand why Swinton did. Swinton was a man of power; he thrived in it, and it was built into his very nature. This passion held an underlying desire to simply let go, to let someone else take control. Along with this powerful persona, Swinton had a short fuse; it was easy to imagine him tearing into opposing lawyers with obsessive ease. The two had made enough of a connection that Swinton felt comfortable making off-the-cuff comments to Daniel periodically until they reached the hotel. Three black Mercedes-Benz cars were waiting outside the arrivals area and took the team of lawyers to the downtown hotel.

Daniel enjoyed Singapore more than other cities. It was far from the neon-clad advertisements of Shanghai and nothing like the smoggy streets of Beijing or Seoul. Singapore was a city of glass and commerce, with a cool blue hue that enveloped the city and rolled in from the sea. The road into the city resembled a thick artery, pulsing along the river before cutting deep into the high rises of the core.

Ships moved slowly in the bay, indicating the port's immense daily transaction load. The amount of money that flowed through this port was staggering. Daniel marveled at the volume of commerce the city generated. It was impressive. However, there was something about the cleanliness and detachment the city seemed to inspire. There was an emptiness about the city— it felt artificial and shallow—encouraged by the dominance of glass, synthetic grass, and concrete. None of the hearty, soulful presence that came with stone, bricks, dirt, and grime, which could be found back in the capital. Perhaps that was a good thing, Daniel thought.

The hotel lobby perfectly embodied the building's luxury. It had been erected in record time and was made with dark, brooding slate and frosted glass. Daniel slung his suit bag over his shoulder and walked unassumingly into the hotel lobby. The building had a tall atrium with long draping chandeliers, and Daniel gave the expansive room a careful look. About thirty yards ahead, there was an Asian man with a closely shaved head. He approached them across the long pathway, following the wide red rug that led from the elevators to the front desk.

The man stared at Daniel and then Swinton, his gaze convincing, before coming forward and shaking Swinton's hand. He welcomed them all to Singapore and gestured to the porters, informing the group that their belongings would be sent up to their rooms.

It was mid-afternoon when they arrived. They were invited for an early dinner, and by the time everything settled down, Daniel felt bloated. He had eaten too much, and the weariness of the flight had begun to take hold. He wanted to stretch; the plane had stiffened his back, making him feel lethargic and immobile. The younger lawyers, along with Swinton, were planning to go out and explore the city's vibrant nightlife. For Swinton, this meant meeting up with his mistress and partying.

By late evening, Daniel had slipped away from the bustling festivities, finding solace amidst the chaos. He took a cold shower and sat in the rose-colored hotel room, lying in bed. There was something wonderful about a hotel bed. As strange as it may sound, a good hotel bed was comforting. The cold, soft sheets felt like an endless expanse waiting to be explored—a sea of white.

Since his time in Zurich, he had managed to find moments to read once again. Philosophy remained his enduring interest. He found great fascination in metaphysics, perhaps as an attempt to seek answers. His time at home had been one of the first instances where he truly appreciated Boston, taking advantage of the abundance of books and bringing back as many as he could find. He delved into the classics—Nietzsche, Mill, Hulme, Kant, Peirce, even Rawls—in search of an understanding of what it all meant. Was he doing the right thing? Did such a thing even exist? The fact that he couldn't explain how the world worked was beginning to gnaw at him, and he yearned to comprehend the connections. It wasn't that he wanted to believe in the theories; it was an endeavor to uncover why they were all here—the big questions, as he phrased it to Henry.

The Collateral Dividend

"You're going to drive yourself insane," Henry had told him. Daniel's love for exploring the metaphysical had stemmed from college when he took philosophy courses, despite not majoring in anything remotely similar.

In the late evenings and on weekends, Daniel would emerge from the library and sit with Henry, discussing how they perceived it all fitting together. Henry always encouraged learning without a predetermined goal—he had been a lover of philosophy for as long as Daniel could remember.

Now, standing up in the hotel room, Daniel found himself gazing out across the stark city lights that cast their glow on the hotel's glass. A busy artery ran adjacent to the building, dozens of floors below, and the tinged yellow lights of the streetlights pulsed as time passed. The reflection of the vast city stretched north and mirrored off the glass lining the balcony window. The city seemed to have grown organically in thick grids. The door to the terrace balcony was ajar, allowing the cool summer breeze to flow through, whirling about the hotel room. Daniel moved into the living room and noticed a figure standing on the balcony, overlooking the wide city avenue.

Daniel gripped his gun and aimed it forward, glancing quickly down the hallway that led to the bathroom. Deep breaths escaped his lips as he cautiously moved across the rug, his footsteps inaudible due to the severe angle. Pushing the door open, he stepped outside. The sky appeared ink black, scattered with faint shimmering stars that paled in comparison to the bright city lights. Continuing forward, as the figure became recognizable, he lowered his weapon. Setting the gun down, Daniel stood still for a moment, a sense of familiarity washing over him. He breathed heavily, his stomach dropping like he was descending a steep slope.

The woman wore a black dress, possibly made of jersey cotton, hugging her soft figure and reaching mid-thigh. Leaning against the balcony railing, her hair billowed in the warm coastal breeze, obscuring Daniel's view of her face. She was beautiful, standing with grace and proper posture, reminiscent of Isabel. Could it be her? How had she found him here? Lines etched on Daniel's face shifted downward as he peered intently. She felt familiar yet new, her image warming his heart. He found himself calling out her name, and as she turned and smiled at him from the far side of the balcony.

Daniel looked at her as if he were seeing a ghost, his long face drawn out. Walking toward her, he extended his hand, seemingly about to say something, but the words eluded him.

"I've been thinking about you a lot," she eventually said, expressing a desire to talk. Daniel approached her and held her close, enveloping her in a long embrace. Lost in his thoughts, time seemed to pass without notice. They had been talking, but Daniel couldn't recall the details. Eventually, as they stood inside, she reached for his hand, her touch gently conveying anguish. Slowly leaning forward, Daniel cupped her neck with his hand, hesitating at the edge of the bed. Then, he kissed her tenderly, pausing to gauge her response. After a moment, he kissed her again, this time more firmly, her arms draped around his neck. But then, she paused and studied him, her furrowed brows conveying concern. "Is everything alright?" she asked, sensing something amiss.

Daniel wasn't quite sure. Something felt wrong about this situation. He rose abruptly, a sense of someone's presence at the door. As he walked toward it, he glanced back at her from across the room. "I love you," he said with confidence, then turned and opened the door. To his horror, Mark Patel stood there, his clothes bloodied, and his hair disheveled.

Once again, Daniel brandished his gun and pointed it forward, firing two shots into Mark's chest. It should have been a clean kill, but Mark only staggered back, retaliating by pointing his own gun at Daniel. Despite Daniel's hazy attempts to subdue his attacker, a bullet pierced his chest. He felt as though he should have collapsed, but he remained standing. Looking back to where Isabel stood, he heard her emit a harsh scream. Mark shot Daniel again, causing him to sharply inhale before everything suddenly disappeared.

Daniel opened his eyes and stared blankly at the mundane ceiling above him for what felt like an eternity. His body was drenched in sweat, and despite his physical fitness, he struggled to catch his breath. Sitting up in bed, he gazed out at the balcony and then at the doorway. It had all been a dream. Daniel let out a laborious sigh and sank back onto the bed.

Nightmares occasionally jolted him awake in the dead of night, leaving him cold and shaken. The intense emotions stirred by these recurring horrors suggested they had deeply affected him. A lingering memory weighed heavily on his conscience. Daniel sat up for an hour, attempting to decipher their meaning. The consistency of these dreams held significance. Nightmares were not new to him; they had plagued him since his time at Farragut Center. But recently, Isabel had invaded his dreams, and he couldn't help but think there was a deeper meaning. He still felt emotionally attached to her, as if robbed of something precious that couldn't be replaced. Overwhelmed by a flood of emotions he couldn't comprehend, he knew exactly what it was: the sting of lost love, a lump in his throat.

Rolling onto his side, Daniel checked his watch. It was just past two in the morning in Singapore. Daniel brushed his hair back, away from his face. His eyes darted back and forth, revealing a discomfort with his own thoughts. Could she have affected him so strongly? "Pull yourself together," he thought. "It was only a dream, and a different outcome was never realistic." He inwardly chastised himself, feeling pathetic for wearing his heart on his sleeve as if the world were ending. But Isabel had once said, "Things have a way of working themselves out." He repeated those words aloud, hoping they held some truth. He wondered how true that phrase really was.

Daniel couldn't sleep for the rest of the morning. At six-thirty, he rose from bed, dressed in a suit, and took two pills from the refilled capsule provided by Paul. Eventually, he made his way downstairs for breakfast, where he encountered Swinton, nursing a tall glass of orange juice. Deep bags under Swinton's eyes suggested he had been rudely awakened. "Did you have a good night?" Daniel asked, though he knew Swinton's response would likely be indifferent. They still had another day of leisure before meeting Min, and the hungover lawyer hoped to make the most of it.

"Just slept," Daniel replied, expressing his concern about his disrupted sleep patterns and the impending sickness if he didn't recover. One of the younger lawyers chuckled, admitting they hadn't thought that far ahead.

Swinton appeared worn-out, looking like hell. "The guys are going to the Zoo later today. Are you going to join us?" It sounded terribly unbearable, even to Swinton who lacked enthusiasm. They indulged in a plated breakfast, enjoying a moment of silence. The grease seemed to be revitalizing Swinton. Earlier that morning, he doubted his ability to stand up straight. He asked the server for a tall cup of coffee, and by the time it arrived, he was salivating at the corners of his mouth.

Daniel shook his head, wiped the corners of his mouth, and finished his previous bite. "I still have some things to finalize before tomorrow," he said between bites. "If I finish early, I'll be sure to join you." Yesterday had been a write-off, and in order to settle everything before meeting Min, he needed the entire day to set things up.

Despite Swinton's piggishness, Daniel was growing fond of him. Swinton displayed a level of loyalty, at least as loyal as one could be while cheating on their spouse. Daniel considered it a good gauge of trustworthiness.

Daniel went for a walk, heading south down the long road that stretched through the city core. He walked along a wide, four-lane boulevard, neatly manicured and lined with tall buildings. After ten minutes of sitting in a courtyard shaded by a thick marble building, he ensured that no one was following him amidst the ebb and flow of the city streets. The city had a strange atmosphere, a mix of meticulous maintenance and neglect that reminded Daniel of neglected cities worldwide.

While Daniel appreciated cleanliness and despised neglect, he found Singapore's sterility overpowering. It lacked the vibrant charm that pulsated through cities like London, Paris, or New York. This feeling resonated deep within his soul. The city had a heart, but it felt feeble. It lacked presence. It looked like a city should, but sometimes, that wasn't enough. Daniel felt that the city lacked vitality. It offered a shallow experience where one could admire the architecture briefly, only to forget its existence mere hours later. Modernity had its merits, but the old world carried a sense of nostalgia and presence that couldn't be replicated.

At the corner of Philip and Church, Daniel hailed a blue and white taxi. He slouched in the back seat and instructed the driver to take him to the Port of Singapore. There was a warehouse near the harbor road where managers rented space for bulk corporate shipping. The building had a large, flat structure with a green corrugated steel roof and five tall garage doors leading to a loading bay. The highway snaked along the coast before reaching the southernmost tip of Singapore, where the driver stopped in front of the building. Daniel paid the driver to wait and carefully examined the facade. He wondered how Paul managed to find such businesses. The nearest garage door was open, revealing a dark, unlit space inside, casting a long shadow.

Daniel greeted the man inside and handed him a folded paper with a twelve-digit shipping number written neatly across the center. The man examined the number, gazing at the ceiling in thought. "This came from India, didn't it?" the man asked, and Daniel confirmed it. After leaving Washington, he had no idea where the package had gone. Nothing ever followed a direct route.

The man pulled out a cloth from the back of his pants and cleaned his hands before approaching a computer terminal mounted on the wall. He entered the shipping code, and a message appeared on the screen. The man glanced across the hall, toward the aisles of storage units.

Fetching the box would take a few minutes, so the man instructed Daniel to wait. He disappeared into the back room. Daniel glanced at the oily black soot on the ground and adjusted his trousers to rest higher on his waist, revealing a pair of bright green socks.

Daniel looked up at the overcast sky, hinting at rain. Occasionally, the sun pierced through the clouds, casting a sweaty, musky heat onto the city. Daniel Faron toyed with his sunglasses until the freight box emerged. He tucked the glasses into his breast pocket and took the case in both hands. It was dusty, with

The Collateral Dividend

a heavy, gray, scratched metal frame. He held the box close as he got back into the cab and rode in silence, lost in his thoughts.

With the box in hand, Daniel entered his hotel room, closed the door, and secured the deadbolt lock. He then approached the drawing table, where he placed the box with a heavy thump.

Removing his suit jacket, Daniel hung it over the back of a nearby chair and broke the seal on the crate, undoing the latches. The cover came off with a crack, and he leaned it against the leg of the desk. Inside, there was a tray lined with black felt, nearly two inches deep. It contained various documents, neither out of place nor too sensitive in nature. They seemed like forgotten belongings, which Daniel promptly discarded. He peeled back the felt lining with an obnoxious tear, revealing a keyhole along the side of the case's interior wall. Inserting a pin into the keyhole, he popped up the bottom of the case, releasing the latch on the false base. Daniel lifted the lead-lined cover and placed it on the floor.

The container's floor was filled with small plastic bags and fabric scraps, tightly packed compartments resembling drug smuggling. Daniel removed a thick stack of paper documents, which sat atop a hardcover book. He discarded the papers and placed the book on the table. The book, when opened, revealed a Smith and Wesson M&P 380 handgun painted in matte black. It was barely larger than his hand. Near the top half of the case, there was a fat, stalky suppressor. Daniel took out the handgun, placing it on the table, and then arranged the suppressor and three loaded magazines in an aesthetically pleasing manner.

On the other side of the case, a weathered, frayed holster made of gray fabric was folded in the top corner. When worn along the backside of his hip, inside his pants, it was almost impossible to notice. Wrapped in a bag, there were various devices with built-in tracking devices, along with a loaded pen gun stored on the far side.

Daniel marveled at the assortment of devices California had provided for him. He contemplated the countless ways he could use them to kill, which both fascinated and frightened him. He wondered if the developers sat in a room, concocting different methods of taking lives.

Out of habit, Daniel disassembled the weapon and cleaned it. He removed the slide, barrel, and spring mechanism before meticulously cleaning each part. He recalled hearing a story about Colt displaying the interchangeability of his revolvers by disassembling three and mixing the parts on a table before reassembling them. Daniel found the process soothing, providing a sense of calm. He took solace in the fact that he hadn't fired his gun in a long time but wondered about his marksmanship skills.

THE LONG STOP

Paul's morning had started early when he received a report from assets in Morocco who had been observing the rising rebel forces in the region. Since Daniel's tenure as a trainee, they had altered the criteria and methodology for recruiting and training individuals. Paul had managed to find a middle ground between freethinkers and regimental drones. Very few of the latter were still in active service, and none of the freethinkers, except for Daniel, had survived more than a year in the field.

In fact, only a handful of assets frequently returned to D.C. and were considered active participants in Farragut Center operations. Paul tried not to dwell on the careless waste that resulted from troubleshooting field operations actively. When the mental anomalies had begun with Daniel, Paul worried that he might have struck the wrong chord. He was concerned that the hallucinations would cripple the program. However, Ted had been convinced that they could find a way around them, and Paul eventually saw things his way. Several other assets reported visions and cognitive errors, but none as consistently as Daniel. The first recruit to follow Daniel had been a young man named Nathan Ramirez. They had tweaked both the search criteria and the training process, if one could call it that. The results were encouraging.

Paul had always known that the process resulted in reduced sensitivity to pain, and only once had he witnessed the horrible potential of that outcome. When someone completely lost feeling, they became prone to injury and accidental death. Paul wanted to find a happy medium, and that required time and a great deal of medical knowledge. After they modified Ramirez's responsiveness to pain, he displayed above-average sensation. The process was quite scientific. However, nobody seemed to have bothered to inform Daniel, and they had nearly botched his alterations. As a result, he became completely indifferent to the feeling of pain. His senses were still intact, but the threshold for pain tolerance had completely disappeared. Paul felt sorry for him and wondered if it was a contributing factor to his declining mental health.

Nathan, on the other hand, was the exception. He wasn't particularly large, but like most assets, he had become extremely adept at using his mass and muscles. Farragut Center had seen surprising results from its assets as the months passed, and Paul had a front-row seat to it all. They were no longer focused on state-sponsored espionage, and violent terrorism had largely become a thing of the past, a minor tool used to complement the truly effective methods of terror. Violence had become a distraction for the enemy, but it had also become the sword of the spy.

Violence no longer kept Paul awake at night. He was not a man afraid of a pointed gun, and he never shied away from a fight. What kept him up at night was the frequent use of electronic espionage with very real consequences. Computers were now more capable of inflicting damage than all the bombs of the world war. They had witnessed firsthand how billions could be stolen under the veil of legality, and technology was the warhorse that carried the new era along.

Nathan checked in at half-past three. It was morning in Europe, and he had eaten breakfast on the patio of a restaurant in Munich, confined to the narrow winding streets of the city's inner circle. Like most assets deployed abroad, he survived on limited sleep. He had been in the city for nearly three weeks, following a German businessman who had appeared on the center's radar a year ago when he bought nearly two hundred thousand shares of Philippe Gaillard's telecommunication giant. Nathan only knew him as Klaus, but Paul had dealt with the man before.

Paul adjusted the height of his office chair and rolled it further underneath the desk, examining his computer screen. "So how's he doing?" Paul asked to get the ball rolling. He was looking at a photo of Klaus Wilhelm Mauer, who, by all accounts, was not an unattractive man. He was young, much younger than the average age of the targets, but he looked about the same age. Paul had never considered Klaus a threat until late in the game when he began buying up shares of Gaillard's business and changed his estate plans to pay out Gaillard. It was then that Paul wanted to know everything there was to know about Klaus, which wasn't saying much.

They knew he was young but looked older than his age, and he possibly practiced Judaism on a handful of occasions. They also knew that he had been defiant to Gaillard for a time, but suddenly, nearly two months ago, he fell in line and never acted out again. Klaus's mobility, drive, and habits were drastically different after that moment, and no one could explain why.

Paul still had a few contacts in the German government, and despite hesitations, they were willing to cooperate with the Americans and hand over the files of one of their country's wealthiest citizens. It was then that Paul deployed a surveillance team to keep an eye on Klaus for nearly a month before Nathan moved in to make the final preparations. The young man had inherited his money from his father at eighteen. While attending school, he befriended

Gaillard and other executives of Europe's largest firms. His education evidently paid off as he successfully restructured the family bank before selling his shares for substantial profits.

Klaus's youth reflected in most of his actions, including his business endeavors. He dabbled in securities across the continent but never committed to a cause for more than six months. This behavior provided Paul with more information than it concealed – it revealed Klaus's impatience. When it was discovered that Klaus had acted as an intermediary for some of Gaillard's money, Paul had sent Nathan to eliminate him. However, things took an unexpected turn. Complications arose, especially due to the situation in Sudan, which put a halt on further terminations. Nathan had to maintain his distance and wait for authorization to proceed through proper channels. This shift in circumstances confused Paul, especially considering Klaus's newfound caution and professionalism in handling his affairs.

Although they were frequently called in to "finalize a deal," there were occasional scenarios where Paul would deploy assets for surveillance. Such actions stretched their resources thin, but Paul always made decisions based on what he believed was best for the mission.

Nathan informed Paul that Klaus had spent the night at a local hotel, which was unusual as Klaus was known for excessive partying. Nathan added, "It was a quiet night. The company car is waiting outside for him now."

Curious, Paul immediately asked, "Where's he headed?"

"He's headed to Zurich. He has a meeting with some business partners this evening," Nathan replied. He stood up, leaving money on the table, and crossed the narrow street. Nathan, appearing thuggish at times, tried to counter that image by wearing cream-colored jeans and a leather jacket resembling an old MA-1 flight jacket. With his head down and hands in his pockets, he approached a sedan parked several car lengths behind Klaus's black town car. Nathan climbed into the driver's seat, rubbed the top of his closely cut scalp, placed both hands on the wheel, and started the engine.

Curiosity piqued, Paul inquired, "What's the occasion?"

"Stocks, what else is new. He's considering another investment vehicle," Nathan responded. They hit the road again, with Nathan trailing the town car at a distance of at least a hundred yards. As they drove, Nathan noticed something was off. From the heart of the city, it made more sense for Klaus to head west until reaching the E54 highway, which they would take all the way to Switzerland. However, the car turned north and took the E45 until reaching the airport.

E.R. Wychwood

"I need a tail number traced," Nathan said once he connected with Paul on the phone. "Delta, Foxtrot, Sierra, Charlie, Foxtrot." The file appeared on Paul's screen, and he scrolled through the specifications before conducting a flight path inquiry. He sat forward in his chair, rested his chin on his hand, and examined the screen.

"The flight is headed to Singapore," Paul said, realizing his previous oversight.

Nathan remained seated in the car, holding his phone against his right ear with his shoulder. With his right hand, he took the phone away from his ear and accelerated away from the private entrance of the airport, heading towards general parking. "So, I'm assuming you want me to go after him?" Nathan asked. While the idea was noble, there was no need for two assets to be in the same city. Most of the assets were unaware of the exact breadth of Farragut Center's global reach, and Paul preferred to keep it that way.

"No," Paul abruptly responded, catching Nathan off guard. "Return back to the hotel and await further instructions." It was clear that the conversation had ended, leaving Nathan confused. He frowned, abruptly shifted lanes to avoid getting caught in long-term airport parking, and accelerated quickly, waiting for the call to end so he could toss the phone aside. Nathan was a man of vices and short temper. He wondered why they didn't want him to track down Klaus in Singapore. Was it a lack of trust? He contemplated how much free time he would have and acknowledged that the more he had, the more dangerous it became. Instead of avoiding his vices, he needed to regain control. Nathan drove fast, and upon returning to his hotel, he decided that nothing would happen that day. He then walked to one of the local clubs and consumed copious amounts of bottle service until the early morning.

Nathan was a troublemaker, and on several occasions, Paul had to maneuver through political and economic climates to get his asset out of trouble. Nathan had nearly killed a man in one of the bar fights he had gotten into. Paul believed it stemmed from boredom.

Early the next morning, Paul took the encrypted files stolen from Sudan to one of the SIGINT officers just down the hall. If he were honest with himself, he didn't think the recovered client list would provide much value. It was a starting point, but not much else. Paul needed something more substantial. Langley had briefly examined what they suspected to be a client list but deemed it lacking actionable information, so they returned it to Farragut Center. The physical packet arrived through a private courier that night, and the Center's

The Collateral Dividend

mailroom placed it in a sealed case for distribution to Paul's desk the next morning.

The cleaning staff woke him up, and after a grunted sigh, he sat up at the end of the cot. After a quick shower and morning tea, he took the file to Avery, suggesting, "Let's try to filter out the mess." It was up to Avery to decipher the encryption that had been corrupted during wireless data transfer. The coding and processes involved were too advanced to be hastily executed here. Avery had connections at the Department of Energy who owed her a favor or two, and they would repay those debts by running the encryption through one of the IBM supercomputers at a research facility near Knoxville, Tennessee. Although using one of the fastest computers in the country might seem like overkill, it would expedite the process. Decrypting the encryption would take a few hours, even with the help of multiple computers running calculations simultaneously.

A day later, Avery received the decrypted data and began examining the information. The nearly thirty-page document was only a fraction of the data they had intended to recover. Some parts were missing, pages ended abruptly, and information was incomplete. Despite these challenges, the file was readable. She took one of the conference rooms to lay out the information and gain a comprehensive understanding of its contents. It didn't take long for her to realize that it wasn't exactly a client list. Once she reached this conclusion, she transferred the file to a jump drive and hurried down the hallway, almost running, to Paul's closed office door. Ignoring any need for pleasantries, Avery walked in, and Paul, seated away from the door, turned around to observe her entrance, sensing her urgency.

"You need to look at this," she said, handing him the jumper drive and taking a seat across the desk. Paul plugged the USB stick into the desk and looked up at the young woman. He asked what he was supposed to be looking at, and she leaned forward with a frown. Her facial lines deepened, and her face turned pink.

"Well, we're missing parts, but it looks like a disposition matrix," she said, indicating that they were meant to see these files. Gaillard had intended for them to come across these files. They were corrupted, but still readable. At the top of the file, a familiar verse was written in Occitan: "They are refined better than gold in the burning fire, and however hears it more, understands it well." Paul asked her what she thought the significance of that was.

"He wants us to know he's going to sell this. Whoever possesses this will understand us," she replied.

253

E.R. Wychwood

Paul scrolled through the file, printed it off, and rolled back toward the printer, waiting for it to finish. "Like the disposition matrix?" The term had been coined by the Obama administration years before—a sort of who's-who of targets. It was a kill list, containing biographies, known locations, and even targeting practices of the enemies of the state.

"Not ours," she said, crossing her arms, her discomfort evident. "Someone else's. In this document, we're the targets," she added, and Paul looked up at her, making sure she wasn't joking.

"What do you mean we're the targets?" he sought clarification. He flipped through the document until he found Avery's name, and a few pages later, he came across something that resembled his own address.

"Here," she said, extending her hand and demanding the papers. Her movements were abrupt as she folded the stapled pages, then took a highlighter from the desk. She circled two listed names, and after a few more pages, she bracketed an entire paragraph. Finally, she handed the document and highlighter back to Paul.

"What am I looking at?" Paul asked before even reading the paper.

"Paul, we're on the list, and so is Daniel and Ted," she said. Paul looked up at Avery, who had her arms crossed and wore a long, stern frown. He then looked down at the page where his name, listed in full, was just two entries away from Ted's. Flipping through the pages, he found a detailed biography that covered everything from his social security number to information about Rachel's education, past loans, relationships, and daily practices.

He stood up and went to the door. He asked Avery to follow him and walked down the hall. By the time Ted realized, he had been briefed in full. Ted sat there, staring at the file. "Can I take this with me?" he asked. He considered what Brian Redding would say. Paul told him he could. They had a few other copies. Avery attempted to explain, but anxiety made it difficult to articulate.

"It's essentially a database, or at least a part of it, compiled not just as a kill list, but as a blueprint on how to capture, render, or kill those listed," Paul calmly stated. "We know it went from Sudan to two other computer terminals shortly before we obtained it. Based on the file type, it couldn't be saved on a computer; it had to be printed out."

"It doesn't stop with those on the list," Avery clarified. "It can be applied to future targets too."

Ted tossed the file onto his desk, and it slid to the edge. He took off his glasses and placed them on the desktop in one fluid motion. Comfortably seated in his office chair, he looked up at Paul with both hands on the armrests. "So

The Collateral Dividend

what you're saying is, what we thought was a manifest list is actually a playbook on how to take us down," he summarized.

Paul chimed in, "Avery suspects Gaillard gave him a teaser, possibly through Min."

"Explain," Ted requested.

"The encryption technique I described, where the file had to be printed, that's classic Min. We discovered that the data was compiled from a hack on our servers and involved someone within the intelligence community. My suspicion is that whoever compiled this information had contact with Min, who then forwarded it elsewhere. We don't know where. What we recovered was the initial distribution of information. The data passed through Kutu. He wasn't the compiler, but he acted as a conduit. The money transfers aligned with similar dates, suggesting that Kutu was responsible for collecting the data from the drone and sending it to Min. He served as an intermediary for the physical form of the document on its way somewhere else. Where it went, I don't know. That's what scares me. At least we know there are only a few physical copies that can be tracked."

"Christ, you couldn't make this shit up," Ted muttered, pressing the bridge of his nose to ward off a headache. "So what do I tell the DNI tomorrow?" Ted asked.

Paul let out a deep sigh. "Tell them the entire system is compromised. Everyone considered a high-value asset is potentially on these lists. We believe Min or someone connected to Min is selling specialized variants of a master list to the highest bidders."

Ted cursed under his breath, looking around the room as if familiarizing himself with its orientation. "Alright, keep me posted. I want this resolved quickly. Is that clear?"

Paul spent the rest of the night at the office. The next morning, he grabbed a fresh shirt and tie from the bottom drawer of his desk and met Ted in his office fifteen minutes past nine. "Late night?" Ted asked as Paul entered, and the operations manager nodded. Ted moved back behind his desk, checked his messages, and turned on his computer terminal. "The Senate hearing is in thirty minutes. I'm going to swing by there before a meeting on the hill. Want to tag along?" Ted invited. Paul mustered a weak smile and let out a faint laugh. There was no harm in observing the mess they had created. Besides, Daniel, who was twelve hours ahead, would soon report on the day's activities. Communications could be done from anywhere. The server hacking had made Paul skeptical of

255

Farragut Center's capabilities, but he reminded himself to suppress the paranoia if they were to accomplish anything.

They left the office at half-past, and a town car awaited them out front. Paul and Ted climbed into the back, patiently waiting until the city's traffic unraveled, and they arrived at the Hart Senate Office Building. Ted took the side entrance and followed one of the Senate staff down a long hall to a hearing room. There were seats near the back, and Ted took one, unbuttoning his jacket and exhaling deeply. Paul had his phone on his lap, legs crossed. "How's Dunes handling all of this?" Paul leaned over and asked.

"Not well," the older spymaster replied. "He's incredibly stressed. The press follows him constantly—it's his own special hell," Ted answered. Paul couldn't imagine. The thought of being under constant public scrutiny was disconcerting.

Eventually, Senator Helpord called the room to order, and Director Dunes took a deep breath, looking up at the senators before him. Seated in the middle of the room at a wooden table strewn with papers and empty water glasses, he waited for the chairman to reintroduce the members and then, once prompted and welcomed back, a senator near the far wall began preparing a statement. It seemed as if he were gathering the strength to speak once more. The senator delivered a lengthy and eloquent statement before questioning whether the funding cuts had contributed to the operational failures.

In Ted's opinion, Dunes knocked the question out of the park. But who in their right mind would have thought that budget cuts were the result of the catastrophe? Ted wondered how far gone some of these people were. Could an adequate budget truly have the effect of hurting operations, yet have nothing to do with whether or not the director of the CIA purposely chose to leave assets for dead?

"You'll have to forgive me, Director," Senator Helpord suddenly cut off Dunes. The ruthless interruption caught Dunes off guard, and he hadn't realized what had exactly happened. "I've just been informed that the media has new information - not previously available to this committee - and I find this information important." Senator Helpord was sifting through files that his chief of staff had handed him, and there was a long pause before he pressed his finger onto a line of text and read it aloud. "What has come to this committee's attention is, in my opinion, very disturbing." He glanced up at Dunes with a flicker in his eyes before returning his gaze to the desk. "Our understanding was that attempts were made for extraction. However, the evidence provided suggests otherwise, indicating that no attempts were made for extraction, and furthermore, to anyone's knowledge, authorization to break radio silence was

The Collateral Dividend

not given. I have also become aware that you authorized the extrajudicial removal of Kutu, which, need I remind you, is what got the CIA in so much trouble just a short time ago. Extrajudicial killings are gravely serious, and I question whether an investigation into CIA operations needs to be made to ensure they are not continuing in secret." The chair sat back in his seat, taking a deep breath. "So, I guess my question to you, sir, is: Was the authorization to deny extraction to the team deployed in North Sudan under your direction or that of your office?"

Dunes leaned forward, ensuring that the microphone could clearly pick up his voice. "Uh, yes, it was, Senator." In that moment, Ted knew that Dunes might as well have taken a bullet. The shot was fatal, and it was likely that Dunes' resignation would be requested once these hearings had ended. Ted had hoped not to throw his friend and confidant under the proverbial bus, but somehow he had just done that.

The cameras were now being turned off, and there seemed to be a reinvigorated interest in the hearings. Ted looked at Paul, who was already tapping away at his phone. Suddenly, Paul stood up amidst the disputes and pushed through the oak wood doors of the Senate hearing room, making his way to the hall. As he reached the vast building atrium, overlooked by offices up to eight stories above, he was already on the phone with Winters, waiting for one of the company vehicles to pull up outside. He stood by the towering aluminum mountains and the overhanging clouds of the sculpture, which shifted slowly above him.

"Yeah," Winters said when the private line clicked through. He was seated at his desk in the lower basement floors of the NSA headquarters in Fort Meade.

"It got leaked," Paul said in a hushed tone, glancing at his watch.

"When?" Winters asked, standing up, coming around his desk, and leaving his office hurriedly.

Paul looked up at the televisions playing the news. "Today," Paul replied. The information had been leaked to the media first. In fact, the television indicated that it was a Guardian news exclusive, with someone within the intelligence community willingly releasing vast terabytes of data. Farragut Center's secrets, Paul thought. "They sent it out to the press," Paul added. This made their job much harder. Finding information released onto the Internet was easy, but when it was acquired by a news channel or publication, hiding the existence of the information became extremely difficult. News agencies were skilled at hiding the sources of information, and it wasn't as easy as simply hacking the news servers. They couldn't just eliminate someone after they had gone public. Publicity was a shield that Paul sometimes couldn't stand to think about.

"Fuck," Winters cursed aloud, cutting down a narrow hall and entering the third door. It closed behind him, and he placed his mobile onto the table, tapping the screen. A momentary kickback occurred before the residual background noise of the Senate lobby played on the speaker. The phone was on speakerphone, and Winters searched the depths of the internet, trying to catch any hint of the information. He found the article online about the leaked information. Winters, an astute man, nodded in the direction of the young man who was at his keyboard. Winters approached the far side of the desk and rested his hand on the back of the young man's chair. They were already examining the company's servers, and the young man pulled up a search bar, typed in search criteria, and waited until the file returned. "We got it," Winters confirmed, and the young man highlighted the document and maximized it. "Sending it to your phone," he said. "Source known as Nowak."

"Who's the reporter?"

"It doesn't say. Could be a dead end," Winters reasoned. "Do you think it's our leak?"

"Possibly. But you'd think he'd be smart enough to cover his tracks." However, it occurred to Paul that perhaps the name was assigned to the mysterious source. The information that the company had surely encouraged the idea; there seemed to be an endless number of pages that any person with a half-wit of organization would no doubt attempt to label and categorize.

"I'll have my people pursue it as far as they can. Where are you now?" Winters asked, returning to the other side of the desk and taking a seat.

"Just leaving the hearing," Paul said, correctly assuming that Winters had no desire to hear about how Dunes had been betrayed. "I'll inform Harrison and relay anything I find to you," Paul assured as the town car pulled up. It wasn't raining, but it had earlier in the day, and there were still residual droplets clinging to the exterior of the town car. Paul descended the steps, climbed into the back of the car, and told the driver to take a smoke break. He held a large black binder, which he carried everywhere, and walked somewhat awkwardly along the narrow garden-flanked path to the front porch.

By the time he reached the door, he pulled the screen back and stepped inside to see Mrs. Wallace at the entrance to the mudroom. "You'll have to forgive him, Paul," she said in a tone that matched his grandmother's. "It's not a good day. He's out back," she said, offering him a cup of tea. Paul cupped his hands, took a seat in one of the chairs across from Harrison, and thanked Jean for the gesture. He looked at Harrison, already aware of his condition. There was a coffee table made of wicker between them, and Jean placed a tray of Marie biscuits on it.

"I wish it weren't," Paul said as he reached for the biscuits. Dipping them into tea had always been a chronic habit of his. He settled back into his chair, gazing out at the closely-cut lawn that sloped down toward a wharf. Many times in the past, they had spent hours fishing there. The river bank was adorned with low-hanging willow trees, their green fingers gently caressing the surface of the water.

Harrison cleared his throat and took a sip of wine. His cane rested between his legs, and he idly toyed with the handle using his thumbs. "It's definitely the same person," he said, pausing briefly before calling out to his wife, "Jeanie, can you grab those files Selwyn dropped off?" He then reached into the pocket of his deep maroon dress shirt. The shirt had a thick front pocket, where Harrison had folded a piece of paper. Unfolding it, he read the reminder note. Once he had the files in his hands, he carefully broke the seals on the far side, examining each one for a considerable time to differentiate between them. "Here," he said, handing one to Paul.

Paul examined the briefing attentively, his face growing solemn as he reached the last page. The document focused on a man who worked as an analyst within Farragut Center, responsible for Measurement and Signature Intelligence collection. "What's unusual about him?" Paul asked, taking a sip of his tea, crossing his legs, and leaning back.

Harrison cleared his throat. "He's developed a gambling problem. He found himself deeply in debt, but somehow managed to recover last month. It's completely unexplained how he came across nearly half a million," Harrison said, absentmindedly whittling his fingers. Such windfalls rarely happened in their families. There simply wasn't that much spare money.

Paul flipped through the file, reaching the back page, which consisted of a long sheet of financial numbers with several circled in red marker. He read through the entirety of the briefing, pausing at the sections marked in green. "What are these?" he inquired.

Harrison was unsure. They appeared to be additional payments of some kind. Perhaps the man was continuing to leak information. Suddenly, everything fell into place. An analyst with MASINT expertise would certainly possess the know-how and capacity to acquire such information. The money seemed to be sent shortly after the hack had occurred. Harrison wasn't the fastest with computers, but he had grown accustomed to using them. He used his access to

Farragut Center's files to examine the mole's computer logs. The analyst had accessed a significant amount of information, and they discovered that he had somehow transferred the data from the computer hard drives onto a USB stick, which was then sent through USPS. They were still waiting to determine the destination. The answers would come soon enough.

"Come into the office with me now," Harrison suggested, taking another sip of tea. "You can have a talk with this guy." Paul hesitated, then asked, "Did you find anything in the other departments?" He was overtly curious, burning with the desire to know that he wasn't the only one who had been deceived. He checked his watch to ensure they had enough time to return to the office before five.

Harrison nodded, providing Paul with a sense of relief. "A few; here." He handed Paul the remaining files, and the young man examined the names on each one. Only three others had suspicious transactions. Two of them had solid alibis, and apart from their finances, everything else seemed fine. The third person was a woman working for Winters's organization. She had gone AWOL shortly before the press release. Paul began to form an idea of what was happening, but he didn't want to jump to conclusions.

THE MOLE

When the car pulled up outside the building, the mood changed drastically. Paul had called ahead, and a support team met him outside the offices. There were four rather large men, and Paul instructed two of them to help Harrison inside. He then turned to the other two and asked them to come with him. Paul's mind raced. What nerve to sell secrets right under his nose. Was it possible that despite all the safeguards, they had failed to keep a secret? For Paul, it felt like a failure. The walk from the entrance of Farragut Center, down the hall, and toward an office on the far side of the building was long. It gave him a moment to reflect on how this could have happened. The hallway leading to the far side of the building was dark. They rarely lit the main hallways unless it was nighttime. Paul looked at the file folder again, holding out the information on Jeff Grossman as they walked. What a slimy bastard, Paul thought. In a moment, he folded the leather binder shut and stood at the door of Grossman's office with a blank expression. His face was flat, and he stood there as if reading Grossman's expression, hands folded over the binder.

Grossman stood up, his face turning all shades of red. Neither he nor Paul said anything, and Grossman glanced at the tall, burly men inside his office, then back at Paul. "Can I help you gentlemen?" he said. Paul thought at least Grossman was smart enough not to accidentally throw himself under a bus. Paul remained silent, his off-kilter stance telegraphed through his shoulders. He stood there with a blank, dreary expression, as if he were drunk. His eyes looked heavy, and his mouth remained small and motionless. He gazed in the direction of the nearest of the two men. The large man moved forward, taking Jeff by the arms, and reaching into his pocket. He produced an auto injector, which he swiftly stabbed into Jeff's neck. The second man stepped forward, slinging a black burlap bag over Jeff's head. Within moments, Jeff had fallen unconscious, and the men dragged him out of the office and down the hall.

Paul gave the office a strong look. The computer was still turned on, and he gravitated toward it, glancing at the screen and snooping around until he felt satisfied. He then proceeded down the hallway to the back of the building. A long, narrow corridor at the back of the Farragut Center, which employees had been told was unused office space, awaited him. First, there was a cushioning area, simply dead space filled with security features, trip alarms, and other surveillance methods. A corridor led through this web of security to another part of the office on the far side of the floor, which was unused. The support staff brought Jeff into a bland white room, seating him across from a steel table, while they stood back, blocking the door.

By the time Jeff woke up, Harrison was already in the room, sitting across from him, cleaning his glasses before putting them on and looking up with a stern and serious expression. "How was work today?" Harrison asked, clearing his throat. Jeff remained quiet, aware that he had been caught. The nature of his job meant he wouldn't get the chance to go to federal court. He had always wondered what they would do to him if they caught him. Part of him hoped he would never have to find out, but deep down, he suspected it was inevitable.

On the other side of the one-way glass, Paul hunched over a computer terminal, studying an fMRI of Jeff's skull. Harrison, once an expert interrogator, had a melodic way of initiating discussions. For now, he wanted to try the softer methods. If he failed, he knew Paul would have plenty of time to resort to harsher measures, such as waterboarding. That was something Harrison wasn't willing to be involved in.

They began discussing Jeff's personal life: memories of his childhood, the well-being of his parents, and whether they knew he was gay or that he worked for the government. After thirty minutes, Harrison had Jeff where he wanted him. "What about work here?" Harrison eventually asked, shifting the topic to Farragut Center. He showed Jeff some operational reports that had been increasingly inaccurate and tardy. He suggested that perhaps Jeff was distracted by other things, noting his sporadic and unreliable credit card payments.

"What exactly are you implying here?" Jeff asked, though he already knew. He chose to play coy rather than reveal all his cards. A puffy face surrounded his eyes, and Jeff appeared on the verge of tears. With short hair and a receding hairline, he resembled an old, nerdy programmer. He still wore thick glasses from the nineties, and his pale forehead sloped back toward his messy hair.

"To be frank," Harrison said blandly, lacing his hands in his lap, the rough rubbing of his palms audible in the quiet room, "I am not sure where you're getting the money to pay off your credit card. Now, Jeff," Harrison continued, clearing his throat with a heavy, raspy grunt, "you're a smart man. As you can imagine, this is disturbing to us. How about you explain to me what's going on?" Harrison waited for Jeff to respond, and when he eventually did, his answer was long-winded, supposedly definitive about his current position in life.

Jeff made it clear that he enjoyed working at Farragut Center. The pay was exceptional, and the environment was much more enjoyable than what he had experienced at the National Security Agency. He insisted that he was a patriot, a

The Collateral Dividend

lover of the United States. It became apparent to Harrison that Jeff wouldn't simply roll over and allow himself to be taken advantage of.

Jeff expressed his desire to speak with Paul, to have a lawyer present. He wanted to know where he was being held and requested the opportunity to contact his sister, brother, or someone they would allow into the building. Jeff's mind raced as he searched for something to say that would convince them to set him free. His arms moved vibrantly about as he explained his reasoning, while Harrison took notes on the pad of paper at the corner of the desk.

Suddenly, Jeff fell silent. The truth had dawned on him. The only thing that would set him free was the truth—it was just like that verse from the Bible in the Book of John. Jeff was familiar with it. Religion was one of the few things he would not betray for money. When he fell silent, he looked up at Harrison and realized they were going to kill him. But what scared him more was the painful death that awaited him if he failed to comply. He seemed to have momentarily forgotten his faith, despite actively thinking about it.

"I'm a patriot," he repeated. Falling behind on payments forced him to borrow money from an old friend from school, which he found embarrassing.

Harrison remained skeptical. He warned Jeff that if he wanted to survive, he needed to tell the truth. Having already investigated whether Jeff reached out to old college friends for money, Harrison found no evidence of any financial support. Flipping through the pages of his notepad, he interlocked his hands and let out a deep breath.

"All that would be quaint if we hadn't already checked," Harrison remarked, attempting to sound compassionate. "You owe nearly three hundred thousand to the banks. Did you get involved in gambling or face health issues?"

As it turned out, it was the latter. Jeff had recently developed a problem, and with a revelation that seemed long-lost, Harrison leaned back in his chair, exhaling heavily.

"I fell behind on payments, and the debt started piling up," Jeff frankly confessed. "I owed fifty thousand dollars to some dangerous people, and I have two kids in college with a mortgage that's barely a third paid off. I was on the verge of selling everything, even the house."

However, just as Jeff found himself sinking, a savior emerged from the shadows. They offered him a way out—provide them with information, and they would help alleviate his situation.

"Do you know how hard it is?" Jeff asked, knowing Harrison could never truly understand. "All I had to do was press a button and send that information. When you're faced with drowning in your own debt, you realize that pressing

263

that button gives you hope, a chance to survive. I didn't do it to betray my country. I'm a patriot. I did it to survive. You can never imagine how fear forces you to react until death is staring you in the face."

Harrison remained unimpressed. "What an asshole," he thought silently. "So, who approached you?" he asked calmly, realizing Jeff was spiraling out of control.

"I don't know, some man in a suit. We never spoke. It was a one-time deal," Jeff boldly stated. "He offered me $400,000 upfront and another fifty grand if I provided more information later."

With his hands resting on his lap, Jeff showed no signs of remorse, at least not visible to Paul. Harrison prodded him further, inquiring about everything he had shared with the man. Jeff's words flowed like a roaring engine, detailing every piece of information he had been granted access to. The security logs would provide specific evidence—field operatives, Farragut Center policies, program directors—everything needed to construct a framework of the center at any given time.

Still unsatisfied, Harrison pursed his lips, contemplating how to pose the next question. The well-worn lines on his face resembled a weathered road. Realizing it was unlikely Jeff would reveal more, it was Paul who took charge as they neared the end of their discussion. He stood in the corner of the room, gazing at a support staff member, silently conveying that Jeff needed to be eliminated. This action exceeded the support staff's typical duties, but Paul had little time and needed a swift solution. Jeff's death would be staged as an accident, somewhere between his current location and his home. To maintain appearances, flowers would be sent to his family.

Paul felt no remorse for Jeff. In fact, Paul didn't experience remorse for anyone. Resuming his seat in an office chair, he stared blankly at the conference room wall. A wide chart displaying everyone Jeff had encountered hung on the wall. Harrison informed Paul that there was another person collaborating with Jeff, likely the one responsible for leaking the information. Harrison suspected it was the woman. Both individuals shared the same handler, Harrison thought, and they were likely funneling information to the leaker.

Having personally examined the scanned data that had broken the story in the media earlier that morning, Paul believed he had deciphered part of the puzzle. The information paralleled the breach, traveling through the same data pipeline. Somewhere along the line, possibly through multiple intermediaries, the data reached Min and eventually Gaillard. If they wanted to apprehend

The Collateral Dividend

Gaillard, they would need to shut down this information pipeline. It was an arduous task, and stress turned Paul's face purple.

Pouring a glass of single malt scotch for Harrison from a decanter in one of his office drawers, Paul understood the importance of avoiding business discussions unless Harrison initiated them. The long day had undoubtedly taken a toll on Harrison, far more than it had on Paul. Time was not on Harrison's side due to his age.

"After all these years, are you still with that lovely girl of yours?" Harrison inquired after a while, refilling his own glass. Paul nodded quietly, reclining in his chair. "Marry the girl, Paul. Get her a nice ring, take some time off. It would be good for you." Harrison had heard all the excuses before. He rarely involved himself in others' personal lives, let alone expressed opinions about their spouses. However, he spoke with confidence, his eyes revealing a deep-seated belief. Harrison's list of regrets in life was short, and his ignorance of important matters, particularly his wife, ranked at the top. Despite enjoying his work at Langley, he often wondered if the memories he had lost to his job made it all worth it.

Paul saw himself mirrored in Harrison, and witnessing Paul follow the same path pained him. He feared Paul would lose Rachel if he failed to make an effort. "You won't find another one like her," Harrison added. Placing his glass on the table, his hands rested a few inches away from his chin. His farming accident had cost him part of his finger, and Harrison absentmindedly rubbed the stub, pondering how different life would have been with that extra inch on his right ring finger.

Once Harrison was on his way and Paul ensured his well-being, Paul drove himself home. For some reason, he couldn't bear listening to music during the ride, opting for silence and the hum of the engine. The sun barely grazed the horizon as Paul arrived home just after seven. Rachel was still cooking dinner. Paul had brought Chinese food—a seemingly simple, thoughtless gesture—but it held a memory from their first date.

Harrison's words resonated in Paul's mind as he contemplated them. He couldn't afford to let up now; they were on the verge of capturing Gaillard. Paul couldn't bear the thought of losing Rachel, but he was so consumed by his role at Farragut Center that he couldn't fathom taking time off.

Rachel knew Paul didn't want to lose her, yet she grew weary of the excuses, the long hours, and the lonely nights. Although he often reassured her of her importance, she couldn't help but feel a twinge of doubt. A nagging thought whispered in the back of her mind—if he truly cared, if he truly loved her, he would be willing to take time off. She acknowledged the absurdity of this notion but longed to believe it.

Late that night, they watched a movie together, both seated on the sofa. Paul woke up in the same position he had fallen asleep in hours earlier, a quarter past five. Rachel still nestled against his chest, and to avoid waking her, he carefully slipped out from underneath and covered her with a blanket, allowing her to remain curled up peacefully on the sofa. Paul prepared a bowl of cereal and watched her sleep from the opposite side of the living room. Scrolling through his phone, he continued until a company car arrived at a quarter to six, ready to transport him back to Farragut Center for another exhausting shift.

* * *

Daniel didn't accomplish as much as he had hoped. He found himself distracted, engrossed in reading obscure philosophers whose variations on Kantian ethics bridged the gaping void his profession had left sore and tender. When he finally looked up at the clock, he realized that the afternoon was marching towards darkness. The summer sun cast long orange shadows across the city, and he had only about an hour left before he needed to trek across town to meet up with the group. Daniel had taken a walk to a local park near the hotel and immersed himself in a book. Upon returning to the hotel, he ascended the stairs to his room and opened the door. The blinds were closed, and a whispering draft from the radiator made the room feel empty and cold. The chilly air rushed out into the hallway, contrasting the efforts of the air conditioning. The humid afternoon air seeped through the window seams, fogging up the corners and forcing the stale air to settle in the center of the room, evoking the feeling of a harsh winter's night.

Standing at the open doorway, Daniel cautiously entered the room, positioning his feet diagonally. He drew his gun, holding it pointed towards the ground, and slowly moved forward as the heavy steel door closed and locked behind him. Flicking the light switch, he directed the gun towards the retreating shadows of the room. Step by step, he advanced, turning on the light in the bathroom. The long draping housecoats near the showers hung pale-faced from the hooks, reaching down to the floor. Daniel exhaled deeply, releasing the tense breath that had been held in his chest, filling the room with a sense of relief.

The gun slipped out of his hand and landed with a clatter on the granite countertop. Daniel turned on the faucet, washing his face thoroughly to cleanse

The Collateral Dividend

himself of the sooty air that had clung to him in the humid afternoon. It was a temporary respite, but refreshing nonetheless. He turned off the faucet and gazed into the mirror, his own face reflecting back at him, marked by weariness and disinterest. The bags beneath his eyes tugged at wrinkles, evidence of a heavy blanket of experience. They were open eyelets that had witnessed too much. Sometimes, he couldn't help but recognize the toll it had taken. Drying his face with a towel near the door, he placed the briefing packet on the granite counter next to the gun.

Paul had always been capable of seeing the bigger picture. Though the information was outdated, it was the best Daniel could hope for in his current location. He correctly assumed that, with rumors of a leak floating around, the agencies would devour their own to uncover the responsible individuals. The agency had become a modern, distorted tale of Cronus, devouring its own young to maintain the status quo and unearth the moles within. Harshly horrific, Daniel thought, but somehow explainable. To Paul, the ends seemed to justify the means. Daniel wasn't sure how he felt about that, but one thing he knew was that he despised the archaic practice of paper transfers, finding them less reliable and prone to compromise due to the increased number of people handling the information.

The details of the mole-hunt had been tactfully omitted from the briefing note, and Paul had made the directives explicitly clear. Physically tracking Min was too dangerous. Countless man-hours had been invested in this operation, and it would not be in vain. Min was a high-priority asset, and specific protocols accompanied such a designation. Electronic tracking would be used to monitor Min's movements, but its effectiveness was limited.

Within the Farragut Center, it was no secret that Min had betrayed them. The identity of the individual Min had paid off within the center to obtain the information remained unclear. Under normal circumstances, Paul would handle this situation as he had dealt with previous leaks: with a quick termination. However, Min's control over the information obstructed their mission. They needed to reach Gaillard, and to do so, they had to secure and destroy the information.

Intelligence needed to be gathered with the sole objective of identifying the internal leak responsible. Subsequently, a swift and discreet takedown of Min, Gaillard, Ralston, and their conspirators would be executed. Paul believed that the initial link to the mole would be found on Min's company servers, likely something seemingly insignificant—a twenty-minute appointment, a phone call to Washington—details that had been added to the company calendar with little thought. Min would know who Jeff's handler was, and that was the information they sought. Obtaining this data wouldn't be easy, and Paul was candid about the difficulties they would face. Daniel continued reading. Paul had cleverly devised a plan that would authorize Daniel's access to the information. While Daniel's approach would largely be improvised, having a plan in place brought some sense of reassurance.

At first, Rachel was supportive of his new role. The early stages of his alluring profession had short hours and high pay, but that eventually changed, and soon he was working well into the nights. Paul had grown to discover that she thought he was having an affair – perhaps with his work – but certainly not with any other woman.

"I want to get out of the industry in five years," Paul said while explaining his plan to Harrison. Did he have that long, however? His relationship with Rachel seemed unable to last the year, let alone another five. Even with the time pressure, he wanted to be well off by the time he left. Paul had saved up a small fortune. He didn't care to tell Harrison how, but most of the money was made by exploiting the same market fluctuations that kept Farragut Center afloat. It was an act that was highly illegal. "I've also been thinking a lot about what you said," he had decided he was going to ask her to marry him, but he hadn't floated the idea out there yet, and he had hoped that today would have been that day. They had fought early in the morning, and it was clear that the mood of hurt had continued into the afternoon. Paul was no longer in the mood to ask such a question. He felt soured.

Paul had been carrying around the ring in his coat pocket for the past three weeks, a product of his sudden case of crippling anxiety. When he pulled it out to show Harrison, the old man sat back in his chair and looked at Paul through the bottom of his spectacles. It was a brash decision that he had made two or three weeks prior and had gone out right then and there to buy a ring. It was a large diamond, one that sparkled like the reflection of the morning sun off a watery beach.

"Are you sure about this?" Harrison asked with a hoarse voice. There existed a sort of paternal tone to his words, and Harrison fiddled with the silver bracket of his cane. He was looking at the ring from afar, through the spectacle of his glasses that rested along the bottom side of his nose.

Paul's eyes wavered in an extended expression across the pond, out to the field across the way. He was sure, he told Harrison, and it was said with such conviction and vigor that Harrison knew Paul was being serious.

The Collateral Dividend

"Then why wait any longer?" Harrison asked in a dry manner. It made one imagine he was cursing the young generation for their crippling inability to commit to things. "If you're sure of this, you can't simply hope that it will be the only thing to put you two on good terms. You need to clean up after yourself before you do anything," he looked at his old square watch with its metal band, and then his wrist shivered, and the sleeve of his shirt hid the watch face.

Paul had his thumb pressed against his lips and his hand clasped into a fist, as if he were thinking hard about telling Harrison no. By then, Rachel had arrived, and Paul came into the house and gave her a kiss. When they locked eyes, he smiled kindly at her. "Are you feeling alright?" Paul asked her; her face looked ill.

"I think I just need some air. I'm feeling awfully sick," she told him, and Paul took his coat from the hook.

"Harrison," he said to the old man from across the house, "we're just going to get some air. Rachel's feeling a little ill," and he threw on his boots and buttoned up a waxed Barbour that had full cut-out square pockets. With the collar put up, it made him look like he was hunting game.

There were trails throughout the forest that ran weaving patterns back and forth across the dense terrain, and the two set out across the gravel drive to an opening in the tree line about ten yards away. Rachel was still fiercely mad. Her face may as well have been an off-blue, and her arms were crossed high across her torso.

The trees narrowed, and there was a long muddy path that cut to the left, deeper into the forest. In the distance, one could hear the whine of birds and the soft rustle of leaves as the wind blew. "This isn't sustainable like this," Paul said eventually, and he asked her why she was acting so off. "I think it's something that we need to talk about."

Rachel was tired of all this drama. It felt as if Paul was never at fault, yet he clearly was. "Paul, I need you. I love you dearly, but I need to be shown I'm more than merely a convenient acquaintance to return home to," there was a sinking feeling that no matter how well she articulated, no matter how many times she repeated or stressed her pent-up emotion – her ability to communicate precisely what was needed had become lost. He was traversing across the broken bark, stacks of pine needles, and other things collected along the forest floor.

Paul quietly followed the path with his eyes, only for it to be interrupted by the methodical drip of old rain falling from leaves. She was still trying to express the same point but was doing it in a different manner. Paul was never around; it was as if he didn't care about her, and that hurt and bothered her. She knew, and had grown accustomed to the fact that Paul had never been a man who expressed emotion well, but since he took this job, things had gotten much worse. She asked him if he was having an affair. Paul seemed offended; he turned to look at her and stopped dead in his tracks. His hands were shoved deep into the square pockets of the coat, and he looked at her as if she were insane.

"I know that work's important, but it's not fair for me to always be making the effort to show I care and yet never hear anything in return." She had continued to walk along the path, and it was with a slow and drawn-out walk that made deliberate the measured pace. "Because you're right, Paul, it's not sustainable, and there's been very little that I haven't been willing to do to make it work. But I need you to be willing to put more effort in."

They had reached a clearing in the forest that was no more than twenty yards across. The high trees around the perimeter left the grey sky above feeling as if it were a high ceiling. Paul was standing only a few yards away from her, pushing down dirt with his boots. His hands were still in his pockets, and like a small child, he was staring down at the mud, playing in it with his feet.

Paul let out a grumble and then stared off in the distance toward the other side of the clearing, where the trail picked up again. He tried to muster one cohesive response to present to Rachel, but after several minutes, he was still empty-handed.

"The behavior has to change, Paul. I can't stand eating a dinner for two alone every week," Rachel still had her arms crossed, and every so often, Paul would look up at her, and he felt the urge to walk over to her and hug her and apologize and tell her that it would all change. But something held him back. "Am I not doing enough?" she asked, and then her tone shifted gears as if they were on another topic. "Paul, I need you to help me understand what is going on."

When they were together, things were good, but when work came into play and the chaos of the intelligence community grasped a hold of Paul and dragged him tooth and nail into the sooty, black abyss for weeks at a time, he would simply disappear. Paul would not exist, and it made Rachel feel as if she didn't either. Despite his constant assurances that everything was all right and that there was nothing she needed to worry about, Rachel could not shake the gnawing drone of worry. She had convinced herself that there was another woman, and nothing short of seeing one would satisfy her swirling worry.

The Collateral Dividend

It turned into a vicious cycle: Paul assured Rachel that everything was fine, and yet there was a seduction in character that simply didn't feel right. She had often attempted to lay out demands, plead with him that if it really was work, to simply spend less time there. Her demands were by no means unreasonable – she merely wanted to be noticed, to be cared about. There existed, however, a barrier that Paul erected in response to his demanding career. He became both emotionally and physically unavailable, and it was this presence, or lack thereof, which slowly ate away at the foundations of Rachel's self-esteem.

There was a mystique to Paul's profession that had rubbed off onto the man himself, and at the inception of the relationship, it had been exciting. As with all allures, it slowly eroded until there existed nothing but the barren silence of someone who was always on her mind but was never there.

Above all, this feeling of distance was the most frustrating. There was much she sacrificed for him; she did so happily and frequently. There was little that she wouldn't do if asked of her, and yet, despite all these efforts, there lacked a depth in the reciprocation. It felt shallow.

For if he was in this profession, she could never marry him. But she wouldn't dare tell him that decision. The intelligence industry was a black hole, consuming all things that surrounded it, and there came a point in time in which she had come to realize that possession – mere factual knowledge that someone was there – was not sufficient. They needed to be equally invested, equally drawn in. At what point did the bountiful acceptance of love reach its zenith? She couldn't help but wonder if there was one. It certainly sometimes felt as if there was. Consistently, she doubted whether someone was capable of changing course. At what point did loving someone become overwhelmed and crushed by the frustration, disappointment, and the pain of feeling abandoned? It was a thought that had embedded itself into her frame of mind and consumed a staggering amount of mental RAM.

She liked to think that there was no point, no end at all; that love was incapable of being crushed. But there was then the very valid point that love could not be controlled. Control, so it seemed, was the antecedent to love. It was incapable of being restrained or restricted to a narrowed avenue. Her attempts to do so only stifled it further. Her father had attempted to express this to her – but he was never one for words, and the attempt had been lost in the hours of catalogued conversations that laid the foundation for the library of her mind.

This was not a problem that had stayed internalized. Instead, it had proliferated out – exploding through the fabrics of her social circle to divulge an answer that suited her desires. She hadn't found many that did. There was, however, a clear divide between the two camps, and Rachel seemed inclined to have the second play out. It had been the rhetoric of many that there was a limit. One of her closest friends since university had told her that "there's only so much one can take."

Rachel stood still, breathing deeply in the clearing. She observed Paul as he continued to trudge through the dirt, staring off into the distance, as if he were looking for something that had long since disappeared. She contemplated the weight of her own words, wondering if they had finally begun to sink in, or if they would be disregarded like the countless other times.

Paul, oblivious to Rachel's contemplation, was deep in his own thoughts. He knew he had been neglectful, absent, and detached from their relationship. The weight of his guilt pressed heavily on his shoulders. He wanted to make things right, to salvage what remained of their love, but he also knew that words alone would not suffice. It required action, a fundamental change in his behavior.

Finally, Paul stopped his aimless wandering and turned to face Rachel. His eyes were filled with a mix of remorse and determination. "Rachel," he began, his voice shaky but sincere, "I can't express how sorry I am for neglecting you and our relationship. I've been consumed by work, and I've taken you for granted. But I want to change that. I want to be the partner you deserve, the one who supports you and cherishes you. Please give me a chance to make it right."

Rachel listened to his words, her heart heavy with conflicting emotions. She saw the genuine remorse in his eyes and sensed his sincerity. There was a part of her that longed to believe him, to hope that things could change. But there was also a fear, a fear of being hurt again, of falling into the same cycle of neglect and disappointment.

After a moment of silence, Rachel took a step closer to Paul. Her voice was soft but firm as she spoke, "Paul, I love you, but love alone cannot sustain a relationship. I need to see consistent effort and change from you. I need to feel valued and prioritized. If we are to continue, things must be different."

Paul nodded, his eyes filled with determination. "I understand, Rachel. I am committed to making things right. I don't want to lose you. Let's work on rebuilding our relationship, together."

As they stood there in the clearing, the weight of their words hung in the air. Both knew that the road ahead would be challenging, but they were willing to fight for their love. The future remained uncertain, but in that moment, there

The Collateral Dividend

was a glimmer of hope – hope for a renewed connection, hope for a brighter future together.

In the common room, there was a Zippo lighter. After Daniel finished reading the briefing packet, he tore off the cutaway bottom of the final page and placed it into the burn bag. Holding the bag above the sink, he lit the remainder ablaze in several places. He continued until he could no longer hold the paper, watching it disintegrate to char. Then, he turned on the tap and washed it down the drain.

Standing up, Daniel straightened his jacket and, with the tap still running, cleaned his hands. He smoothed down his hair, ensuring everything was in place. If Daniel did his job correctly, no one would notice. At least, that was Paul's perspective. However, Paul rarely ventured into the field, and unlike Daniel, he wasn't burdened by the taxes that clung to death and all those who touched it. Daniel had discovered that these feelings were particularly strong when one dealt out death. For a while, he had killed so frequently and in such succession that it might as well have been a playing card in a deck.

At ten-thirty that night, Daniel received an unscheduled call. The security features at Farragut Center were now back online, and Paul apologized for waking him. Paul had a good grasp of the briefing and informed Daniel that there might be as much action occurring in D.C. as there was in Singapore. "We have an asset in Germany who has tracked a target to Singapore," Paul stated matter-of-factly. "One of our airport contacts says he should be arriving in an hour. We'll send you his gate number and information when it arrives." Paul sent the photo of the German to Daniel's phone, and it vibrated. Daniel took the phone away from his ear, examined the photo dispassionately, and quickly put the phone back to his ear. Daniel asked Paul who the man was, and when Paul told him it was Klaus, Daniel fell silent. That was not Klaus. Daniel knew Klaus; he had seen him once before in Zurich, and the man in the photo was not him.

"Track him and wait for further instructions," Paul instructed.

"Is there anything else?" Daniel asked once he returned to his room. Seated at the edge of his bed, he stood up abruptly, pacing the room. He wondered if Paul was lying to him or if he was just misinformed.

"No, we'll send you further details tomorrow afternoon. We've checked our seals and found the leaks. Security is still at priority two for the time being," Paul explained. He had a busy morning and little time to delve into the intricacies of how they intended to solve the security breach.

E.R. Wychwood

Harrison had finally finished reviewing all he could, and while seated on the porch of his home, he shared the details of his search with Paul. He didn't think it necessary to reveal how much he disagreed with the actions of Farragut Center. Perhaps that discussion was for another time.

Paul checked his watch, waiting for Rachel to join them for dinner at the house. He wondered what was taking her so long. He and Harrison sat outside on the back porch, observing the cool rain cascading across the river bend.

Paul found himself thinking about Rachel once again. It was clear that their relationship was much more strained than anyone was comfortable admitting. It had reached a point where a lesser couple would seriously consider walking away. There was a tragedy in a failed relationship that made him very sad. His parents' marriage had failed miserably and imploded into a conflict that lasted three times longer than the marriage itself.

Paul felt it necessary to provide for them both adequately, and that meant he was always connected to his work through his phone. There was an irony in this fascination with financial success that many of Paul's generation missed entirely. It was a secret lost in childhood. The deathly grip of this fascination had the stark ability to silence the soft, supple wishes of a young man. One became convinced that a life shared with someone else was secondary and that money and work were all one needed to be satisfied. It was a fallacy that crushed a generation.

Harrison continued to nurse a scotch, fiddling with his cane as he looked at Paul. "So, what have you done about the leaks?" Any opportunity to discuss work was eagerly seized by Paul, as it wasn't often that Harrison wanted to engage in such conversation.

Paul smiled thinly. "Nothing yet. We're still waiting to hear back from the USPS," he replied with unshakeable courtesy. The cracks on Harrison's face telegraphed his expression before he even said a word. He nodded slowly, and his chin puckered upward, while the lines on his forehead descended as if a closing curtain had draped across his approval.

"You know there's more at stake here than just Dunes's dignity," Harrison eventually said. Paul acknowledged that he knew. The entire system was at risk of crumbling if the incident wasn't handled precisely and measuredly. There was a danger that the government might begin to question the legitimacy of intelligence operations. If that happened, it could raise doubts about the government's mandate—whether the current administration had the necessary legitimacy to claim it was operating in the name of the people.

The Collateral Dividend

"Why do I get the sense that you are not too fond of how things turned out?" Paul said after a long pause. The old spymaster gazed out at the lake, then looked back at Paul with a long face, his mouth slightly ajar. Harrison's greying hairs appeared long and tired, and he scrunched up his face, as if to accentuate his nose.

"What happened to that mole the other day? Where do you take them?" Harrison knew they couldn't deport them to the enemy—there was no physical place of the enemy anymore.

"Jeff?" Paul asked innocently, with the image of the man's dead body vivid in his mind. His face turned red, cheeks flushing. "Oh, we sent him home until we could transfer him to a prison somewhere."

Harrison seemed to have released some steam. He leaned back in his chair, forehead curling forward as he pondered those things. He had seen in the morning paper that Jeff had died in a car accident. He wondered if Paul had known and was lying to him or if he simply hadn't heard yet. He concluded that the first possibility was most likely. "You lads take security pretty seriously," he observed, and Paul affirmed that they did. "What happens when you find this other mole?"

Paul contemplated for a while, humming and hawing over the implications and available options. He detested the idea that a foreign operative had infiltrated Farragut Center, jeopardizing the entire program's existence. It now lurked on the surface like a malignant cancer, waiting to be expelled. But would they reach it in time before the cancer had the chance to spread?

Paul explained to Harrison that there were two scenarios that could unfold. It all depended on whether they could apprehend the mole before he revealed himself to the public eye. If they failed to reach him before the media did, the world would look very different. He would become a martyr—an untouchable among commoners. The mole must be aware of this and know that it was a race against time. If he could reach the media before Farragut Center got to him, the threat to his life would vanish. He claimed to be a white-hat hacker, how noble of him, Paul thought sarcastically, alleging that he was providing the people with what he believed they deserved to know.

"If we get to him after he goes public, touching him will be extremely difficult," Paul admitted, though not impossible—he considered adding that a moment later. Paul had always been a man of fair play, and he wasn't secretive about his desire to apprehend the mole before his identity became public. If the mole went on the run, Paul would order him to be killed. There was magic in watching Daniel carry out his work when done correctly. It was majestic,

275

measured, and brutal. Paul found a touch of romanticism in the bloody actions of espionage. They were dramatic and drawn out, yet so simple. He relished witnessing those events unfold.

Harrison contemplated this mysterious defector. "I suspect you only have another week or so before he goes public with his identity," Harrison estimated. "Without a public shield, he must know you'll get to him." Paul thought about correcting Harrison by informing him that they wouldn't just get to him—they would kill the mole. "Are you enjoying what you do?" Harrison asked, his tone uncharacteristically curious.

Paul assured him that he did. He found excitement in the fact that he controlled the cards, that he could alter an environment simply by sending someone to stand there. "You need to spend more time away from work," Harrison advised, expressing concern. Paul was married to his work in some ways, and that obsession with extrajudicial actions made Harrison feel uneasy, albeit a bit uncomfortable.

Paul's eyes once again drifted, indicating that his mind was elsewhere. Harrison cleared his throat and leaned forward. "How are things with you two?" he inquired with a curious tone.

Paul let out a deep breath, his cheeks puffing out before slowly subsiding as the air dissipated from his mouth. When he had initially joined Farragut Center, he had intended it to be temporary, merely helping Ted get operations off the ground. Did he truly want to be stuck in a role with no prospects for growth for the remainder of his career? At the time, he believed he knew the answer to that question. However, over time, his mood changed, and he became hooked on the highs of plotting thousands of operations a day. His role involved exhausting all information, and eventually, everything passed through Paul's desk among the forty or so people working at Farragut Center. Thousands and thousands of man-hours would be compressed into a single page and forwarded to Paul.

At first, Rachel was supportive of his new role. The early stages of his alluring profession had short hours and high pay, but that eventually changed, and soon he was working well into the nights. Paul had grown to discover that she thought he was having an affair – perhaps with his work – but certainly not with any other woman.

"I want to get out of the industry in five years," Paul said while explaining his plan to Harrison. However, did he have that long? His relationship with Rachel seemed unable to last the year, let alone another five. Even with the time pressure, he wanted to be well off by the time he left. Paul had saved up a small fortune. He didn't care to tell Harrison how, but most of the money was made by exploiting the same market fluctuations that kept Farragut Center afloat. It was an act that was highly illegal. "I've also been thinking a lot about what you said." He had decided he was going to ask her to marry him, but he hadn't floated the idea out there yet, and he had hoped that today would have been that day. They had fought early in the morning, and it was clear that the mood of hurt had continued into the afternoon. Paul was no longer in the mood to ask such a question. He felt soured.

For the past three weeks, Paul had been carrying the ring in his coat pocket, a product of his sudden case of crippling anxiety. When he pulled it out to show Harrison, the old man sat back in his chair and looked at Paul through the bottom of his spectacles. It was a brash decision that he had made two or three weeks prior, and he had gone out right then and there and bought a ring. It was a large diamond, one that sparkled like the reflection of the morning sun off a watery beach.

"Are you sure about this?" Harrison asked with a hoarse voice. There existed a sort of paternal tone to his words, and Harrison fiddled with the silver bracket of his cane. He was looking at the ring from afar, through the spectacle of his glasses that rested along the bottom side of his nose.

Paul's eyes wavered in an extended expression across the pond, out to the field across the way. He was sure, he told Harrison, and it was said with such conviction and vigor that Harrison knew Paul was being serious.

"Then why wait any longer?" Harrison asked in a dry manner. It made one imagine he was cursing the young generation for their crippling inability to commit to things. "If you're sure about this, you can't simply hope that it will be the only thing to put you two on good terms. You need to clean up after yourself before you do anything." He looked at his old square watch with its metal band, and then his wrist shivered, and the sleeve of his shirt hid the watch face.

Paul had his thumb pressed up against his lips, and his hand clasped into a fist as if he were thinking hard about telling Harrison no. By then, Rachel had arrived, and Paul came into the house and gave her a kiss. When they locked eyes, he smiled kindly at her. "Are you feeling alright?" Paul asked her; her face looked ill.

"I think I just need some air. I'm feeling awfully sick," she told him, and Paul took his coat from the hook.

"Harrison," he said to the old man from across the house, "we're just going to get some air. Rachel's feeling a little ill," and he threw on his boots and buttoned up a waxed Barbour that had fully cut-out square pockets. With the collar put up, it made him look like he was hunting game.

There were trails throughout the forest that ran weaving patterns back and forth across the dense terrain, and the two set out across the gravel drive to an opening in the tree line about ten yards away. Rachel was still fiercely mad. Her face may as well have been a pale blue, and her arms were crossed high across her torso.

The trees narrowed, and there was a long muddy path that cut to the left, deeper into the forest. In the distance, one could hear the whine of birds and the soft rustle of leaves as the wind blew. "This isn't sustainable like this," Paul said eventually, and he asked her why she was acting so off. "I think it's something that we need to talk about."

Rachel was exhausted from all the drama. It seemed like Paul was never at fault, even though he clearly was. "Paul, I need you. I love you deeply, but I need to feel more than just a convenient acquaintance to come home to," she expressed with a sinking feeling that her ability to communicate her pent-up emotions precisely had been lost, no matter how well she articulated or how often she repeated herself. Paul walked across the broken bark, navigating stacks of pine needles and debris scattered on the forest floor.

Silently, Paul followed the path with his eyes, only for it to be interrupted by the rhythmic drip of rainwater falling from leaves. Rachel continued trying to convey her point, albeit in a different manner. Paul's absence hurt and bothered her. She had grown accustomed to the fact that Paul struggled to express his emotions, but since he took this job, things had worsened. She even asked him if he was having an affair. Paul appeared offended, stopping dead in his tracks and turning to look at her, his hands deeply shoved into his coat pockets, his gaze suggesting she was insane.

"I know work is important, but it's unfair for me to always make the effort to show I care and never hear anything in return," Rachel expressed, walking along the path with deliberate, measured steps. "Because you're right, Paul. It's not sustainable, and I've been willing to do almost anything to make it work. But I need you to make more of an effort."

They reached a clearing in the forest, about twenty yards across. The tall trees surrounding them made the gray sky above feel like a high ceiling. Paul stood a few yards away, pushing dirt with his boots, his hands still in his pockets, absorbed in playing with the mud like a child.

The Collateral Dividend

Paul grumbled and then stared into the distance, where the trail picked up on the other side of the clearing. He tried to muster a cohesive response to present to Rachel, but after several minutes, he was still empty-handed.

"The behavior needs to change, Paul. I can't stand having dinner alone every week," Rachel said, her arms crossed. Occasionally, Paul would look up at her, feeling the urge to walk over, hug her, apologize, and promise that things would change. But something held him back. "Am I not doing enough?" Rachel asked, her tone shifting gears as if they were on another topic. "Paul, I need you to help me understand what's going on."

When they were together, things were good, but when work entered the picture and the chaos of the intelligence community consumed Paul, he would disappear for weeks at a time. It made Rachel feel as if she didn't exist either. Despite Paul's constant assurances that everything was fine and that she shouldn't worry, Rachel couldn't shake the gnawing worry. She convinced herself that there was another woman, and nothing short of seeing one would alleviate her swirling anxieties.

It became a vicious cycle: Paul assured Rachel that everything was fine, but there was a seductive aspect to his character that didn't feel right. She had often made demands, pleading with him to spend less time at work if it was truly the issue. Her demands were not unreasonable; she simply wanted to be noticed and cared about. However, Paul had built a barrier in response to his demanding career, making himself emotionally and physically unavailable. This absence slowly eroded Rachel's self-esteem.

There was a mystique surrounding Paul's profession that had initially intrigued Rachel when their relationship began. But like all allure, it gradually faded until there was nothing left but the desolate silence of someone who was always on her mind but never truly present.

Above all, the feeling of distance was the most frustrating. Rachel had sacrificed a great deal for Paul, willingly and frequently. There was little she wouldn't do if asked, yet the depth of reciprocation was lacking. It felt superficial.

If Paul remained in this profession, Rachel couldn't marry him, but she didn't dare reveal that decision to him. The intelligence industry was a black hole, consuming everything around it. Rachel had come to realize that mere knowledge of someone's presence wasn't enough. They needed to be equally invested, equally engaged. At what point did the abundant acceptance of love reach its peak? Rachel couldn't help but wonder if there was a limit, though it often felt like there was. She consistently doubted whether someone could change course. When did loving someone become overwhelmed by frustration, disappointment, and the pain of feeling abandoned? This thought consumed a significant amount of her mental capacity.

She liked to believe that love had no limits, that it couldn't be crushed. But there was a valid point that love couldn't be controlled. Control, it seemed, was the precursor to love. It couldn't be restrained or confined to a narrow path. Her attempts to do so only suffocated it further. Her father had tried to express this to her, but he wasn't one for words, and his attempt got lost amidst the countless conversations that filled her mind's library.

This problem had extended beyond Rachel's internal struggles. It had permeated her social circle as she sought answers that aligned with her desires. Unfortunately, she found few that did. There was a clear divide between two camps, and Rachel seemed inclined to side with the latter. Many argued that there was a limit. One of her closest friends since university had told her, "There are 7 billion people in this world, and not all of them have to love you. If Paul doesn't, someone else will." Rachel, known for her strong will, believed that enduring Paul for as long as she had was enough. Continuing to waste time would be fruitless if he was unwilling to change. This ongoing discussion had unfolded over the past four months, as the situation deteriorated.

Of course, Rachel still held onto the belief that there was potential for redemption in it all. She still believed that people were capable of change. She needed to believe it. However, the verdict on whether such a possibility was not only conceivable but also realistic remained uncertain.

Paul had been motionless for about three minutes, wandering aimlessly around the clearing. He released a deep breath. "I don't know if I'm capable of dedicating the time you need from me," he finally admitted.

Rachel sighed, the wind hitting her face and causing tears to stream down her cheeks. "What I'm asking for isn't unreasonable, Paul."

"No, absolutely," he responded, and suddenly, it all felt very cold. The damp air seemed to cling to everything, as if it wanted to escape.

"What exactly, then?" Rachel asked, her tone conveying that she wasn't open to negotiation.

"There are certain things that I can and can't do in my current role. Taking extended periods of time off is one of them," Paul explained, looking at her with heavy eyes set deep beneath his furrowed eyebrows. "Look, neither of us has had much sleep. Why don't we take it one step at a time?"

Rachel gazed across the clearing, murmuring words under her breath. The wind swayed the trees, creating a melodic sway of sound. "If that's the case, I need to know you're willing to put effort into making this work. There's no point in dragging this out if you're not willing to put in the work."

Rachel let out another sigh, her arms still crossed. She turned around, her boots sinking into the mud, and faced him. She stood there for a long moment before walking through the tall grass toward him. She extended her hand, holding onto his and hugged him, resting her head on top of his. After a moment, she let go and stood across from him, her face weary and drawn.

"What are you suggesting, then?" Paul asked, his tired voice conveying a sense of boredom that bothered Rachel. She looked at him with an almost harsh expression on her face, finding his tone careless. "I'm not suggesting anything, Paul," she said venomously. "I'm asking you to put in an effort. And if you're not willing to do that, maybe we should take a break." Her words came out bluntly and in an abruptly cold manner, slapping Paul across the face like a brisk morning wind. "Things weren't always like this, Paul, and I can't continue on without being an important part of your life." To her, he was careless, recklessly moving through his world, smashing the things he seemed to not care about and hoarding the things that he did. The uncertainty of which category she fell into slowly ate away at her conscience and sanity. She found herself in extended thoughts of self-doubt, even considering an affair on more than one occasion.

"Maybe we should take a break," Paul abruptly interjected, his tone off-color. He was so frustrated with Rachel that he had said it partially to sound dramatic, but largely to convey how seriously he took the situation. Surprising himself, he stared at her soft yet firm face, trying to understand his own logic.

"It may be a good idea," Rachel agreed, and suddenly it was decided. The whole situation had accelerated beyond comprehension. There was a part of her that feared if they took a break, Paul would never be able to refocus, never return. In some ways, that might be better for her sanity, but she selfishly didn't want that. She wasn't going to wait forever, and she cared enough for him not to want him to leave. A break would have been her last resort, but now that Paul had played the card himself, she wasn't about to disagree. She wanted to shake him, to wake him up and force him to realize how silly he was acting, how much he had to lose. "I think you need to take some time to think about what you want. Because if it's not me, then you need to leave." Arms crossed, her emotions still raw.

"Rachel, you're important to me. But I need you to understand the importance of my profession," he explained. "I can't simply take time off. My work is extremely crucial."

E.R. Wychwood

"I don't even know if you realize you're lying," she replied, shaking her head and turning to walk back to the house. Paul stepped forward and firmly grabbed her arm, but Rachel pulled away.

He was missing the point of the conversation, and it became clear that the discussion was quickly deteriorating. "I can't just conjure up my feelings. I need some time to think about all this," Paul finally said, his tone spiteful.

"If you need to seriously think about this, then I think you're wasting my time," she retorted cheekily. It was rather dramatic of her, but she had brought the discussion to this point, subtly wishing that Paul would vehemently disagree and express how important she was to him, how he intended to reduce his hours at work. The idea seemed like something out of a film, but it wasn't fictional. The world didn't work like that; people needed their own time, their own thoughts to comprehend what was happening. Sometimes people were indecisive. Paul understood that, but every time he tried to explain it to Rachel, she would retort with another statement.

It was all exhausting for him. He realized they were no longer listening to each other but rather hearing what they wanted to hear. It was a dangerous position to be in. Now that they had decided on this time apart, Paul couldn't think straight. What a mess he had gotten himself into. All he wanted was to leave things as they were. The status quo was calming, but clearly, he and Rachel had different ideas about what they wanted from the relationship. Paul missed work. Things were simpler there. Lines and relationships between people could be delineated, simplified, and used as examples to understand how information and money moved about. He was still thinking about work when Rachel sighed deeply, shaking her head. "Where did we go wrong, Paul?" she asked, and they found themselves standing in the middle of the forest again. Paul listened to the constant chirping of cardinals as they sang through the depths of the greenery. There was something about his name that made him hate hearing it from someone else's lips. He couldn't describe why, but the name seemed to cut through the air and conversation, perhaps stemming from a recessive childhood memory of constantly being called out by others, which had always carried forward in his mind.

"I don't know," he said, teetering on the brink of emotional stability. "If you'd like to go home, I'll cover for you here. I'll rent out some space to stay for a few weeks as well." Paul felt it was best not to discuss the future further. He felt sick. The idea of losing Rachel made him queasy, yet it was his own actions that had initiated the risk in the first place.

The Collateral Dividend

By the time they reached the house, Rachel stood on the porch, suddenly uncomfortable with going back inside. "I think I should go," she said after an awkward silence.

"Alright," Paul replied, his hurt feelings leaving him unsure of how to bid farewell. He gave her a long hug but felt a kiss would be out of place. As she started the car, Paul walked up the damp wooden steps of the porch and watched the car pull away from the door's edge. Wearing a baseball cap with the brim pulled down to cover his face, he didn't want to be seen as having cried, although it had happened.

Eventually, he regained his composure and went inside, telling the couple that Rachel wasn't feeling well and it would only be him for dinner.

"You've been off since you went for that walk," Harrison blurted out bluntly after dinner, as they sat in the backyard. He wore an old, harsh expression on his face, as if taking no prisoners.

"It's nothing," Paul assured him, but when Harrison persisted, Paul turned to the old man and admitted he wasn't sure things were going to work out between him and Rachel. They were skeet shooting, or rather, Paul was casually firing at clay pigeons launched by Harrison from a chair not far off the lawn. "We got into a fight," he said between shots.

"A fight?" Harrison replied bluntly, pulling the trigger again, but his shot missed as the clay pigeon flew uninterrupted into the river. "I don't know," Paul sighed. He fired at two more clay pigeons, hitting both with successive shots. Smoke rose from the barrel as two cartridges popped out of the weathered rifle with its old wood stock and nicked steel barrels. "What do you think?" Paul eventually asked.

Harrison grumbled deeply, shaking his head uncertainly, not sure what advice to give. "Paul, for as long as I've known you, you've had a thing for that girl. Sometimes we lose our way. It's hard to prosper in this industry with a significant other. Both of you need to be capable of dealing with its strains. I think you need to sit back and ponder what you want. Once you've figured that out, everything else will follow. Things have a way of sorting themselves out. It's about time you trusted that they will."

THE COVER OF FOG

Daniel had been waiting in the hotel lobby for an hour before the message finally arrived. The arrival of the messages felt cold and mechanical, almost intentionally so, Daniel mused. The sender had no phone number; the notification simply popped up, providing him with a flight number and the name of the airstrip where the flight would land. The message contained no further information and could only be extended by thirty seconds from the moment the screen was activated. After that time, the message vanished, and all attempts to trace its destination had been unsuccessful.

The evening air was cool, accompanied by fog rolling in from the sea, enveloping the damp city and clinging to the wide, empty boulevards and intersections. Daniel hailed a cab to the airport and waited at the reception for several minutes, making sure no one noticed his backtracking amidst the ebb and flow of pedestrian traffic. He had arranged with a housecleaner to have a nondescript vehicle waiting for him in the airport parking lot. Taking an enclosed catwalk to the third floor of the parking building, he found an old car that could blend in while still being identifiable once he knew what to look for. The private charter airstrip, located three or four miles outside the city core near the backwater plains of Singapore, was reserved for exclusive use. Daniel parked the car by the curb, just off to the side of the airport driveway, and sat inside for a brief moment.

Stepping out of the car, Daniel popped the trunk and changed into a set of soiled, old coveralls, zipping them up all the way to conceal his suit. He checked his reflection in the car glass to ensure everything looked right, donning a matching baseball cap and carrying a safety vest resembling those worn by ground crew members. Locking the car, he climbed the fence and broke the lock on the door leading to the nearest hangar. A black-clad sedan was parked nearby, idle, and when the charter plane arrived and slowed down past the hangar, the car shifted gears, pulled up parallel to the private aircraft, and stopped just off to the side.

With confident responses, Daniel managed to gain access to the airstrip's offices. By the time the aircraft landed, he had been instructed to assist with unloading the luggage. Daniel walked with the swagger of a worker, and as the loud screech of the landing aircraft pierced the air, he discreetly slipped a small plastic button, no larger than a quarter inch, containing a hollowed-out GPS transmitter, into Klaus's coat pocket. After completing his task of loading a large carry-on into the car, he gained insight into the impersonator of Klaus. Daniel caught a glimpse of a file folder with the words "Farragut Center" on the front, but when he attempted a second look, the folder had vanished.

Klaus descended the aircraft's stairs in a dramatic and unnecessary fashion, pausing at the foot of the stairwell to survey the surroundings—the foggy landscape, the city skyline illuminated by neon lights. Klaus inquired about their accommodations, receiving an itinerary packed with suggestions for exploring the nightlife. Although the impersonator had done thorough research, there were subtle traits he failed to mimic, which had alerted Daniel. Aside from the obvious age discrepancy, the original Klaus possessed a more impactful sense of style, a way of wearing his clothes that the impersonator couldn't grasp. Daniel desired to expose this imposter for his own purposes, to understand how he fit into Gaillard's scheme. Impatience began to gnaw at Daniel, but he managed to steady his breathing.

As Klaus approached the car door, Daniel maneuvered between the plane and the hangar, colliding with the German and discreetly dropping a tracking device shaped like a button into Klaus's pocket. Klaus stumbled back, revealing to Daniel that this impersonator was a professional, much like himself. The impersonator was well-versed in all the tricks of the trade. Facing Daniel, Klaus's narrowed eyes made it explicit that he wanted to lunge forward and snap Daniel's neck. Before one of the security detail members could intervene, the impersonator realized his mistake, swiftly turning back around. The security officer frisked him but found nothing suspicious, pushing him away forcefully. Daniel intentionally let himself fall to the ground, quickly getting up, wiping his hands and knees, and hurriedly making his way back toward the hangar, as if embarrassed. He observed the motorcade depart from the airstrip, heading towards the city center. Returning to his car, Daniel discarded the coveralls in the trunk and put on a chauffeur's hat before getting into the driver's seat.

Klaus's car moved slowly southward along the busy highway, and Daniel, in a rented black Mercedes C-Class with tinted windows, followed at a safe distance. The traffic provided enough cover for him to tail the town cars by approximately fifty meters without drawing attention. Eventually, the motorcade turned a wide corner, and beyond the thick forest foliage, the towering structures of downtown emerged. The cars descended into the underground, disappearing until they reached the heart of the city. Daniel continued to follow along the wide avenues until they approached the Wharf near the heritage promenade. In this section of the city, where glass buildings soared into the sky,

Min's latest achievement stood prominently, adorned with colorful lights. The building, situated on the inner side of the city harbor, seemed to float atop the water's edge.

Daniel glanced down the avenue, noticing green shrubbery separating the opposing lanes, while the cold night left the road empty, devoid of anything except dormant cars hugging the curbs and lush, green shrubbery reminiscent of the nearby forest. Min's buildings formed a tightly clustered group, some lacking any identification, while others displayed company logos near their roofs. One of the shorter buildings featured the infamous "G," widely recognized as Gaillard's company branding. Gaillard's building stood adjacent to the one where Klaus's car had parked beneath.

Klaus stepped out of the car, briefly glancing up at the towering structure before turning to his assistant and instructing them to bring several bottles and escorts to their room. Unbeknownst to Klaus, the tracking device hidden in his coat pocket captured the surrounding sounds. Daniel, leaning against the back door handle of the sedan, hands buried deep in his pockets and shoulders hunched forward against the damp wind, mimicked smoking a cigarette to avoid raising suspicion. Holding his phone to his ear, he waited for the automated dial tone before calling Paul's line. "Are you absolutely sure this is the person I'm supposed to be tracking?" he asked, sending Paul a photograph he had just taken.

Paul balanced the phone between his shoulder and ear, rising from his chair in the cafeteria room. He washed his hands in the sink, drying them on his trousers before responding, "Of course I'm sure. Is there something suggesting otherwise?"

Daniel hesitated. He preferred to pursue Klaus independently, allowing him to uncover the truth himself. He didn't want to rely on Paul's instructions to play it cool for a few days while they sorted out Daniel's claim. There had been a flurry of recent activity, with Klaus once again shuffling funds and transferring numerous properties to Gaillard's name. Halfway down the hall, Paul asked about Klaus's location, and Daniel provided the address, waiting for a moment before inquiring if Paul wanted him to apprehend Klaus. Daniel eagerly desired this opportunity, assuming there was more to the story than simply tailing Klaus. However, Paul shook his head, even though no one was present to witness his gesture. Paul had transferred the call to his office line, removed his suit jacket, hung it on a coat hook, and sat down. His gaze kept returning to a vial of pen ink on his desk, seemingly aiding his clarity of thought. After a pause, Paul finally responded to Daniel's query about what he should do next.

"Nothing more for tonight," Paul said in an almost apologetic tone. "It seems they have greater links than we had previously thought."

Daniel inquired further but was shut down. "That's all I need from you, Daniel," Paul sternly reiterated, suggesting it would be good for him to get some rest.

Paul sat in his chair, deep in thought about Klaus. These two men rarely met, and there was no record of recent business dealings between them. The last encounter Daniel witnessed was in Zurich, which seemed out of character or, at the very least, uncommon. This peculiarity caught Paul's attention, as it implied that one of the men possessed something Gaillard wanted the other to have. The question remained: what was that thing?

These facts piqued Paul's curiosity, compelling him to discover what that thing was. He took a deep breath while seated in his office chair, gently swaying back and forth. Resting most of his upper-body weight on his elbow, his fingers reached his mouth. Biting off his nails and spitting them onto the ground had become an unattractive habit, albeit one he had become adept at masking. He never indulged in this behavior in public or when he was relaxed.

Daniel disliked being kept out of the loop. He sensed that more was transpiring, and the lack of information made him uncomfortable. If he wanted to uncover these pieces of information himself, he would have to do so without the assistance or knowledge of Farragut Center. However, such an action was dangerous and potentially foolish. It would require careful planning and consideration. Daniel was hesitant to stumble into a trap or be caught snooping around by Min. Accusations of espionage from the government or any business would not bode well for him. He found himself contemplating the extent to which he was willing to pursue the truth.

Daniel's hotel was a block south, overlooking the harbor. He walked there from the marina, enjoying the beautifully illuminated scenery and the distant movement of seaborne vessels.

Upon entering his hotel room, Daniel found it enveloped in darkness. It remained undisturbed, and he wondered if anyone knew he was there. The thought of Min toying with him or Min's indifference to an American spy in their midst made him anxious. These worries added to his unease about the upcoming meeting with the assertive Min early the next morning. He pondered the consequences if his cover were blown. What would he do? To ease his mind, he thoroughly inspected the room once more, placed his gun in the nightstand, turned off the lamp, and sought a dreamless sleep.

E.R. Wychwood

The next morning, the meeting commenced early as usual. Daniel woke up earlier than the others, wandering around his room out of boredom before joining the group downstairs for breakfast.

Breakfast was served à la carte, and Daniel ordered a simple meal of over-easy eggs with toast, potatoes, and bacon. By eight-thirty, cars were waiting outside the hotel to drive them to Min's offices across town. This routine repeated for several days, and they still hadn't met Min himself. Daniel began to wonder if they ever would.

He still experienced errors in his vision. Shapes and images would play out late at night and early in the morning across the skyline, morphing through the shapes of flying bird flocks. He wondered if they would ever cease, but he had concluded that they probably wouldn't. Most of the time, he had learned to ignore them, but occasionally he would become so engrossed in the images that something had to snap him out of the trance.

Every morning, cars would pull up along one of the side roads that veined between two office towers, and the American lawyers would scurry across a courtyard approximately thirty feet in diameter to reach the door. On the first day of their travel, Min had come out to the front lobby and tried to meet each lawyer who had made the journey. When Min approached Daniel, he stopped and raised his finger, pointing it at Daniel as if he were about to reveal an important fact. "We've met before," Min said, recalling their encounter in Zurich.

Daniel attempted to act surprised. He looked confused, and his forehead wrinkled. Min crossed his arms and pondered for a moment. "Yes, we have met before," Min insisted. "Not long ago, we met in Zurich, at the Hotel Wein. We talked about James Dean and American films." He extended his hand and shook Daniel's hand firmly. "Don't you remember?" Min asked, but Daniel tried to dismiss the meeting as something he couldn't recall. Perhaps it was someone else, but Min vehemently persisted, "You were there with that wonderful girl. I'm terribly sorry to hear about the two of you. She told me what happened. I ran into her a few weeks ago." Daniel was now certain that he was being manipulated. He glanced at Min with a shallow smile. His face turned pink, and he could feel the mounting anger rising through his chest, gripping his heart like a strong fist.

"Wonderful to see you," Min said, adopting a cold and harsh tone as if passing judgment. He let out a soft smirk, indicating that Daniel's cover had been blown. "What a lovely surprise, such a coincidence meeting again," Min remarked.

The Collateral Dividend

"Here's to running into one another again, Chairman Min," Daniel said, using Min's position as a prefix, a common Chinese business practice.

"Oh, I have no doubt we will see each other again. My friends call me Min," Min replied, and Daniel wanted to retort but thought better of it. Daniel scrutinized Min's rugged face. He had short hair, an angular forehead, and a large head. His suit was well-tailored, but he wore it as if he had never been one to wear a suit.

Min knew who he was, Daniel thought. Oh, the danger that stemmed from that knowledge. He pondered whether it would be better to simply kill Min that evening and attempt to track down Gaillard before the information was exposed. It was an impulsive thought, and as he tried to calm down that afternoon, he realized it wasn't the best course of action. What if the information about Daniel outlined in the stolen files was released? Paul had mentioned that those files included operational reports Daniel had written about some of his first kills. If they reached the media, he would certainly be dead or, at the very least, imprisoned.

He began contemplating how to navigate the exposed position he found himself in. Gaillard and everyone he worked with, who had seen the files, knew who Daniel was. He had written a letter of resignation to the head offices in San Francisco and sent it by mail so that it would arrive by the time they finished their business in Singapore. It was another impulsive decision, but it had a calculated purpose. He did this in a small cubicle on the thirtieth floor, where temporary offices had been set up just a few feet away from the elevator doors.

The floor, two levels below Min's offices, had previously been a trading floor for a large Chinese bank. It had been gutted and cleaned out due to the harsh winds of the market. Apart from the cubicles designated for the team of lawyers, the floor stood empty. The old carpets had been removed, and concrete had been spread out until halted by the reflective glass windows. Describing it as barren would be an inadequate portrayal of its appearance.

It was within these cubicles that the lawyers were assigned to work, sifting through hours of files under the watchful eyes of security guards posted throughout the building. Many of the junior lawyers, who had been brought along to handle most of the tedious tasks, expressed discontent with the constant feeling of being observed, as if the foreign lawyers were suspects who needed to be treated with constant vigilance.

Daniel had been tasked with overseeing the document review based on specific criteria. Initially, he had hoped that this position would grant him access to Min's highly coveted servers. However, he was disappointed to discover that the computers provided to the lawyers were closed networks, connected to a "dump server." The dump server shared a one-way connection with Min's corporate server. Files could be shared with the lawyers at Min's discretion, but ultimately, access to what the lawyers saw was carefully curated. Undoubtedly, this was done to steer the case away from anything Min found unsavory. Although they had unrestricted access to the building at all hours, it also had its advantages. It was this vulnerability that Paul sought to exploit. Paul had left the planning to Daniel, who inquired if there was a way for them to gain access to the main servers by crashing the server the lawyers had access to. However, that approach seemed far-fetched, so Daniel took a different route.

There was frequent traffic between a conference room on the thirty-second floor and the temporary offices two floors below. The plan needed to be temporary; the secrecy of concealing their identity as the ones accessing the servers only had to last as long as Daniel was in Singapore. Consequently, Farragut Center bribed one of the building's staff to take a day off. Paul then forged documents to allow one of their operatives to gain access to the building.

By the time Daniel arrived the next morning for their final day in Singapore, there was a wireless router connected to a company computer upstairs. The router could only extend its signal within the building's wireless network to avoid arousing suspicion. Therefore, they would have to manually download all the files. That morning, Daniel placed a modified receiver, built into a briefcase, next to his desk and waited for it to detect the router's signal.

Paul received a message the moment the briefcase detected the network. He was in the middle of taking a gulp of coffee, which he quickly finished, and slid his office chair across the room to the computer terminal. A program file on his desktop was dropped into the open server connection as soon as the notification of the receiver being within range came through. They needed to bypass the Wi-Fi security before downloading anything onto the wireless hard drive built into the briefcase. Paul felt anxious and periodically checked his watch, appearing somewhat frantic. He had been tapping his fingers on the edge of the desk for nearly thirty seconds before the confirmation arrived. Paul then initiated the server download, consisting of a whopping two hundred terabytes of data.

By midday, Daniel made another trip up to the conference room, where he met Swinton. In a secluded area, he stowed the briefcase in a storage closet, ensuring it would continue collecting data. The briefcase could be retrieved later. The raw data was sent to Paul within the hour, and he promptly handed it over to two officers skilled in signals intelligence, entrusted with the arduous task of sifting through hours of metadata for careful examination at a later time. Unfortunately, the sheer volume of data they had received made it impossible to thoroughly examine all of it. In fact, they would likely never have the opportunity to review the majority of the files.

To address this issue, they relied on an incredibly powerful search algorithm that sifted through the files, attempting to identify flagged keywords. However, the system's intelligence was limited to its user, often lacking critical thinking in the choice of keywords. Ultimately, it came down to the cost-benefit analysis of sifting through data crucial to their objective, disregarding it for the sake of efficiency.

One thing was certain: Min no longer possessed the stolen files. This fact unsettled Paul and made him hesitate about pursuing Min for the crime. Clearly, someone had stolen critical information from the Valley, but the absence of a file made Paul wonder if Min was truly responsible. Beyond the uncertainties of responsibility, there was an underlying discussion about the file theft itself.

The distribution of the stolen file raised two significant issues that Paul couldn't ignore. First, everyone working for them was at risk as long as copies of the "who's who" file existed. Second, while all evidence pointed to Min as the original data thief, the absence of any file acknowledgement on Min's servers raised concerns. Initially, Paul thought it might be a security measure, but the lack of any record was simply poor recordkeeping.

Paul had once again utilized one of the conference rooms to carry out his work. One of these rooms had become a physical hub for all the information and resources related to his operation in Singapore. He aimed to map out the connections and interactions. How did they know that Min and Gaillard were involved? What were the links?

For a while, he spent almost his entire day in the room, jotting things down on whiteboards in an attempt to connect the dots. The files retrieved from Min's servers had been sifted through, and the ones flagged by the algorithm had been printed and stacked in banker's boxes, reaching a height of five feet. Paul started with a drawn web but eventually found it too complicated and switched to a three-dimensional diagram on the far wall. He supplemented the listed names with red strings connecting the printed photographs. As the data piled up, the web became increasingly intricate. More colors of string were added, with yellow representing mutual contacts Klaus had been flagged for networking with. Green and blue represented incoming and outgoing financial interactions. Gaillard stood at the center, with thick green and blue bundles of

291

string extending across the board and room. In some places, the bundles exceeded thirty strings, each representing an individual transaction over $10,000.

Stepping back, Paul looked at the web. Gaillard had close relationships with Klaus, Ralston, Tzavaras, and Min, and now he could see the method behind it all. The money had originated in New York, symbolized by a massively thick bundle of string. From there, the money had been transferred to various accounts worldwide before reaching Min. Some of that money would funnel back to Klaus and a charity in France. Ralston took his cut, and his fiscal involvement ended there.

Adding another colored string, this time to represent leaked information, Paul continued his analysis. The line started at Farragut Center and went on to Patel, who had been killed, marked by a line across his photo. They suspected that Philippe Gaillard was the recipient of the information, although the exact route was still disputed. The investigation was progressing rapidly, with two separate strands of information extending from Farragut Center. The first went from Farragut Center, through Patel, directly to Gaillard, possibly with a route through Ralston. They knew, however, that Ralston was not involved in the information leak. The second strand went to Jeff Grossman, and that was as far as they had discovered. There were no connections between Jeff and Min, and they were still waiting to hear back from the postal service to determine where Jeff had sent the information. Once the information reached Min, the trail heated up again.

Due to the hack that targeted Patel, Gaillard had used Kutu, the Sudanese rebel, to collect data from a crashed drone. Kutu served another purpose, as Paul had already established. The physical information sent by Jeff to an unknown party eventually reached Min in physical form. There was no digital copy of the data, which explained why there was no information on Min's servers. From Min, Paul knew the information went back to Kutu in a more concise form, but he didn't know the subsequent destination. He suspected Gaillard, but suspicions couldn't be recorded on the map just yet. By the end of the day, Paul had a narrowed understanding of how everything had unfolded, and he knew his next move.

There was a connection between Min and a man named Michael Brown, which initially came to light through Klaus. The leak of physical information from Farragut Center seemed to be a two-way street. They had recovered Klaus's American taxes to gain control over his finances, but it proved to be a challenging feat. Klaus had minimal physical assets in the United States, and what he had was negligible. Through a contact at Whitehall, one of Paul's analysts had found access to the European markets, managing to trace bulk trades to a private firm in Germany. Despite the firm's success, it appeared to be a family-exclusive wealth management firm. However, most of the wealth belonged to Klaus, with the remainder earned through trades made on Gaillard's behalf. Paul suspected a significant portion of the stolen money was involved.

The connection to the United States intrigued Paul. The firm owned a small number of shares in the Valley, enough to secure Klaus a seat on the board if he desired. While the board position didn't necessarily mean Klaus knew about the Valley's dealings with Farragut Center, it held more significance. If Klaus was already aware of those deals, having a seat on the board would expose the others who knew. Michael Brown fit perfectly into this scenario.

"Oh, Christ," Paul muttered as he delved deeper into his thoughts. Suddenly, everything made sense. "Damnit!" he exclaimed, louder this time, as if the first curse had not been sufficient. He then called Avery into the conference room. Paul stood on the far side of the room, hands on hips, and sleeves rolled up past his elbows.

"I found it," he immediately said, and Avery walked across the room to look down at the screen built into the table. "His name is Michael Brown," Paul continued, his dissatisfaction evident. "He used to work for the Valley under Marc Amon, our liaison and contact there. Brown would have had access to everything, our entire playbook," Paul said, displeased with how everything had unfolded. He stared at the engineer's photograph. "Did Brown have direct contact with any of our people?" he asked, and Avery leaned forward, tapping his profile. A set of clearance directives dropped down from a tab, and Paul tried to read through them all.

"Here," she said, pointing at Jeff Grossman's name. "He primarily dealt with Measurement and Signals or at least preferred to stick to that kind of analysis. That's what the Valley excels at." Brown had been cunning in his approach, instructed verbatim by the impersonator who pretended to be Klaus on how to engage Jeff. Avery then pointed at another highlighted name, the missing girl from Winters' outfit. "She's also important," Avery informed Paul. When he asked why, she gave him a cheeky remark and displayed something on her computer tablet. "The Postal Service informed us that the package was sent to Sarah Baker, staying at the Ritz-Carlton in Hong Kong."

"One of Winters' girls?" Paul asked, eyebrows furrowed.

Avery nodded. "She has a close relationship with Brown." Paul inquired about her recommendation, and finally, a connection between the leak at Farragut Center and Min emerged. Klaus had been the link, and the leaking of information from Farragut Center, which caused the current patent lawsuit the Valley was facing, was not solely Farragut Center's fault but also the responsibility of an executive from the Valley. Paul's face turned red as he contemplated how badly things had gone awry. They still needed to find the smoking gun, the golden ticket, but no such proof had been discovered in the files. Paul felt defeated.

"We need to go after both quickly. First Brown, then Sarah," Avery stated after collecting her thoughts on the matter. She would start working on retrieving Signals information on both of them.

Avery had access to nearly every database imaginable, which could make the task more tedious as she sifted through thousands of pages of data. She began with Brown, pulling his phone records and confidential data from past employers. This involved running his social security number and gaining access to tax, health, and credit card records. Brown had no living family, was a Canadian citizen, and spent most of his time in the United States working at various technology firms before landing a senior management position with the Valley. Avery had access to his school records and could retrieve confidential notes from banks, professors, and even some employers. She wondered if he had ever read these himself.

Next, she delved into his online presence. She obtained data from his smartphone until he left for Singapore, explored his Instagram and Facebook profiles, and traced all emails connected to a set of IP addresses. Brown seemed to watch copious amounts of porn, had few friends, and rarely visited websites other than Google, Facebook, and StumbleUpon. He spent hours surfing the internet but didn't engage in any significant activities. He loved to travel, or at least give the impression that he did. However, among all his interests and activities, one common theme emerged from his private photos online—Brown loved to drink and party. There was one particular bar in Singapore that had become his frequent watering hole, making it a reasonable bet that he would be there tonight.

Paul had decided to start with Brown. "He is low-profile enough – single, no living family, and a sporadic work schedule. His disappearance won't immediately raise eyebrows for a few days," Avery assured him once everything had been settled. She even cross-referenced Brown's information with the Valley patents to verify if Min had truly stolen the data. It was only a matter of time. There was no doubt now that the Valley wouldn't win its lawsuit. Patent laws often crossed boundaries and governments. If they couldn't get Min for the non-compete, they certainly would for patent infringement.

The Collateral Dividend

"We may have found him," Paul said smugly. Avery sat across from him in a chair, facing his office desk. Her face wore a soft, angled expression, and her pale skin flushed. The building was kept cold for most of the year, and Avery had a heavy cardigan drawn across her chest to keep warm.

"Who is he?" Daniel asked, still in a dreary slumber. His eyes were heavy, and he felt a discomfort along his lower jaw – a coiled tension that signaled fatigue.

"They leaked information from the Valley through one of the company's former executives. His name is Michael Brown. He had contact with a few of our people," Paul said, emphasizing the need to apprehend all those responsible quickly before they could leak more data to the media.

"So, what's going to be done about it?" Daniel inquired, eager to tie up loose ends. He sat up in a chair angled away from the drawing table pushed against the wall of the hotel room, gazing across at the closed blinds. He adjusted his suit on his shoulders and moved the phone higher up his ear.

"We need to move quickly," Paul said sternly. "Michael convinced two people to steal from us. We've taken care of the first one, but the second is in Hong Kong, undoubtedly trying to escape before releasing more data to the media. You'll receive information on both shortly." The policies that held the fabric of the intelligence community together had started to unravel, leaving Paul and the remaining individuals in the shadows to pick up the pieces.

"Then we go after Min?" Daniel asked, eager to take action.

Paul shook his head. "No," he replied, clearing his throat. "We leave Min for last, just like Gaillard. If we cut off their sources, they can't hurt us." Paul stared at Avery with an intense expression, as if consumed by his desire to bring Min to justice. The plan needed to be strategic; they would unravel it slowly and then strike all at once. They would start at the ends of the matrix drawn up in the conference room and work their way inward until they reached the epicenter. Only then, once they had reached the middle, could they take out Gaillard. For now, their focus was on Brown and then Sarah.

Paul had great trust in Daniel and conveyed that this was Daniel's show to run. He would be the one to see it through until the bitter end. The magnitude of Farragut Center's growth and the time demanded by this mission left Paul with no other choice. He made it sound as though Daniel was doing commendable work, so he trusted him. But the truth was that Paul didn't have any other choice. Micromanaging this, along with all the other operations happening around the world, would be overwhelming. Paul was a busy man, and his schedule was only getting busier.

E.R. Wychwood

House cleaners had been brought into Shanghai and would accompany Daniel. Brown was to be captured alive to ensure there were no others involved. Sarah, on the other hand, would not be as fortunate.

The wheels of creativity had been set in motion, and it was only a matter of time before the right people were in place for a snatch and grab operation.

"So, Brown brought secrets to Min from the Valley after being introduced through a contact, whom we suspect is Klaus," Daniel explained to himself. He rubbed his face and then ran his hand through his hair from front to back, trying to wake himself up. He continued speaking as he paced the room. "Min used the contacts through Brown to hijack our feeds and give Gaillard access to information that would damage Farragut Center and jeopardize American intelligence operations."

"Precisely," Paul replied matter-of-factly. He then told Daniel about what they had discovered the previous week – that the client list was, in reality, a disposition matrix capable of dismantling the entire intelligence community. It was a detailed list, identifying key players, their roles, connections, and whereabouts. It was a dangerous compilation.

Daniel's plan started with missing a flight. By then, the law firm's headquarters had confirmed his immediate release, so he didn't bother waking up early that day. It was the first time in a long while that he had managed to get any sleep, and Daniel took full advantage of it. As morning turned into midday, he found himself tossing and turning among shapeless dreams, unable to hold onto sleep any longer. Eventually, he gave up and sat at the end of the bed, trying to fully wake himself up.

"Well, this is certainly a surprise," Henry exclaimed when Daniel called him soon after getting out of bed. There was something calming and warming about Henry's voice. Daniel wished he could be back home in Boston.

"Henry, I'm struggling," Daniel confessed. He fastened his navy-blue tie with a Latin phrase on the narrow end, wondering why he put himself through this. Perhaps out of sheer curiosity or an effort not to forget, Daniel kept bringing these feelings upon himself. He told Henry that he was about to do something he wasn't proud of and was having a hard time with it. "Henry, no matter how pragmatic it all feels, I can't help but wonder if this is the right thing," he said, gazing out at the nearby park. He stood on the balcony, his hands tucked into the outer flaps of his suit jacket, causing the fabric to drape at awkward angles, but he didn't seem to care.

"Daniel," Henry said, as if he had uttered those words a thousand times before. How could such an intelligent man not understand this? "You question

The Collateral Dividend

whether this is right because you're a good man. You've known from the beginning that there is no traditional sense of justice in what you're doing," and it was the distorted notion of justice that troubled Daniel the most. "The measure of intelligence should never be your ability to function while understanding two opposing ideals. It's not just about functioning; it's about knowing what you'll do about those ideals once you figure them out."

"Is that Fitzgerald?" Daniel inquired.

Henry scoffed, "No," he said, as if it were he who had coined the phrase. "Although I imagine someone once said it." The line fell silent for a while, filled only with the strong sound from outside and the soft crackle of white noise through the phone. "Look, I have to run," Henry finally said. "Your sister asked about you again, and I'm never quite sure what to tell her other than that you're doing well." Henry let out a deep sigh. "I'm glad you called."

Daniel had always been unsure of what to say when someone complimented him. He found such situations awkward. He sat at the end of the bed for a while, trying to gather his thoughts for the day. He felt much better about everything, but if asked why, he wasn't sure he could explain.

By midday, Daniel had formulated a plan he was satisfied with. He had little more information than Brown's place of employment and his favorite bar downtown. Daniel knew not to make any moves on Min's turf, so the nightclub seemed like the best option. "We get him drunk, and then we bag him," he stated plainly, as if it were a simple task.

The nightclub was located in a short building, and bouncers with long sleeves and thick necks, each twice Daniel's size, guarded the entrance. A long line snaked along the old cinderblock wall of the converted warehouse, and the reverberations of music could be heard from inside, shaking the concrete sidewalk. The beat was heavy, pulsating with a pace that shook one's body to the core, giving off the illusion that the night was young, the liquor was cheap, and they were all invincible.

Paul had kept his promise and taken a back seat in the planning process. He found that Daniel was more creative and adhered to criteria when setting the rules himself. However, it didn't mean Paul left Daniel to fend for himself. On the contrary, he provided him with all the necessary tools to carefully craft a flawless operation. Daniel had called in a favor from an old contact in the region, who arranged for three young females from the Australian foreign affairs department to assist him. Daniel knew that a cold approach on his own would raise suspicion, so the female officers became invaluable. They were attractive and highly capable quick thinkers. He had contacted them a few hours before and outlined how the night was to unfold.

When Daniel arrived at the nightclub around midnight, he slipped two hundred-dollar bills to the bouncer to skip the line, stating his intention to buy a booth for the night. He claimed it was a celebration and had already pulled out his black American Express card. Daniel informed the manager that he wanted to show his friends, a group of Australian women there for the night, a good time. He emphasized their temporary presence and provided a few more details before being escorted past the dance floor to the back booths.

For someone as sober as Daniel, the initial shock of the pulsing neon lights was overwhelming. The grandeur of the room filled with young people swaying to the cocktail of drugs, alcohol, and music appeared so cool. But was it really? Daniel wondered. Most were too intoxicated to comprehend the events of the night, and they all wished to be treated as Daniel was.

"It had become a niche market in many places: the ability to sell the high-life experience in a pre-packaged night out. The ability to, at least for a few hours, feel as if one could recklessly spend money without a care in the world. They all wanted to party and pretend, if only for a moment, that they were important enough to have people want to take photos of them. It left this image, this falsified belief that they were celebrities. 'What a life one could live,' Daniel thought facetiously. 'They were all bloody idiots.'

The carelessness of unchecked spending on modern vices was what appealed to Daniel the most. He had seen many dabble in the party life during his time in college. He had even bought into the concept for a while before it began to bore him. Those nights, his early years of college, had been filled with excessive drinking and sex. He had witnessed far more experiential drugs than he had cared for. That wasn't the type of life he had wanted, and when it began to bore him and the lure of more intense things called, he knew it was time to leave.

Brown was only half a dozen years older than Daniel, but there was something clearly lacking in his level of maturity and mental composure. Brown worked hard and partied harder. Daniel wondered what drove the man. Perhaps it was the demand of his profession, but it certainly was not a lover or family. He wondered whether it was the deadness inside that pushed him further, seeking more money and expensive experiences to fill the gaping hole.

By the time he had gotten settled near the DJ booth, Daniel was still alone. Maybe he was overconfident, but he believed this to be easier than anyone thought. To attract Brown, he had bought a bottle of Belvedere and handed out drinks to anyone who would take them. There seemed to be a recent surge of fascination with espionage in Singapore, and Daniel found it rather quaint for such an oblivious group of people to find intrigue in what was truly a dirty world of shadows. He had come to this realization when he noticed that the club was 'espionage themed,' whatever the hell that meant. It wouldn't surprise him if there were people sauntering about, telling stories as grand and absurd as the ones he had personally experienced.

For a while, he contemplated telling someone he worked in 'murder and executions,' a line borrowed from a book he had once read. But the club culture was such that most people didn't truly listen. The comment would have been dismissed as dull wit. He reckoned he probably would have received a cheap laugh before being forced to come up with something else droningly interesting to talk about. The loud thumping of the club drowned out the space for intellectuals. The shallowness of the intellectual gene pool at the club was so low that very few were capable of comprehending, let alone reciprocating. So, Daniel adapted and tried to make himself appealing.

By the time the Australians arrived, they had made friends with a group of local girls, all of whom were happy to enjoy Daniel's free liquor and exclusive seats. It wasn't long after that Daniel spotted Brown from across the room. He immediately stood up and called out to Brown from the top of the steps that led down into the dance floor. Brown recognized Daniel from the many meetings over the past week, and the two exchanged hellos before Daniel invited him up to the booth. It was uncanny that they would run into each other at this bar in the city. It was simply fantastic. Daniel patted Brown on the back and then, in his best impression of a douche lawyer from Yale, introduced himself to the friends Brown had brought along. It was done with a subliminal tone, as if to tell them to go to hell. Brown's friends were both regulars here, and their tendency to get drunk beyond comprehension had become habitual and was on the verge of constituting an issue. Daniel used this to his advantage.

He couldn't help but think how pathetic it was that he actively sought to exploit the weaknesses of others, but he soon reassured himself of the shallowness of the group he was targeting, and the hesitation quickly subsided. He increased the pace at which the liquor arrived, and before long, they had lost count of the number of bottles the group had consumed. Yet, Daniel had still passed a glass of water as if it were vodka, and he would merely pretend to pour a shot and then fill it with a mixer. Daniel was habitual; he sipped the plastic cup slowly, looked around the club, and mentally mapped out the space. He did all this while pretending to be interested in what one of the Australians was telling him. People liked you more when you let them talk, so when he wasn't interested, he pretended he was and let them tell him their life story. His silence, at least for now, was interpreted as mystery rather than boredom.

Brown was on the far side of the booth, talking the ear off the other Australian girl, and there was an ebb and flow of people coming and going, attempting to take advantage of the free liquor. 'Is this your first time in the field?' Daniel eventually asked the woman when he was sure no one could hear him. He had been watching the room for prying eyes. The thumping of the speakers, not far off to the side, had canceled out any possibility of eavesdropping on the conversation.

'We don't get out much,' the Australian spook said sheepishly. Her hand grazed Daniel's knee as if she were making a pass. 'There isn't much work here,' she continued cryptically to Daniel. Singapore wasn't known for being a hotbed of intelligence activity, and it was clear why. There was little here. But that was changing. It had become a haven for trusts, with money flowing from China by the billions. Daniel suspected that it was the first time in the field for the two women from Australia. They seemed high-energy, eager to explore what it meant to collaborate with American intelligence collection.

Daniel let out a smirk and took another sip of water. 'It's not for everybody, you know. It's not as romantic as it's made out to be,' something in him urged him to explain more, to tell her all the things he knew. But what good would that do? Daniel would then be a spy with shallow standards of trust, trying to affirm those feelings by sharing secrets. The feeling of wanting to be desired and liked quickly subsided, and he again found himself comfortable with his own thoughts. There was security in that; they didn't try to exploit him.

He was reminded of a lesson taught to him by Mr. Pierce, his grade school teacher, who had been very clear about not divulging more than necessary. 'Your mind must be a vault, Daniel. I cannot continue to tell you these things just for you to tell others and seek their approval. A secret is a very rare thing in this world, and if you're told to keep one, guard it with every fiber of your being.'

It was one of those memories where Daniel could hear the speaker's voice, just as they would have said it. Trust undermines everything that you do, he thought to himself. What a funny coincidence that the very thing he struggled so greatly with was the very thing that supported his entire life. He wondered if there was anyone whom he truly, wholeheartedly trusted. Henry certainly. In all things, there was little that Daniel's guardian could do wrong, but that was a given. All proper guardians were trusted above all else. Daniel couldn't concern

The Collateral Dividend

his thoughts with those sorts of things. He wanted to know if there were others beyond the confines of family.

Daniel watched one of the Australians drop a dissolvable capsule into a drink and then hand it to Brown. How delicate love for another person was, Daniel thought. For a time, Isabel had been trusted, perhaps trusted more than anyone else, but something had changed. Daniel felt betrayed and pale. His mind forced thoughts as if to convince him that trusting Isabel was unsound. As the earth lurched forward, there were things he could no longer do without hesitating to think.

The capsule had dissolved, and Brown had drunk it. The final blow could be made. Daniel came around the far side of the booth and, in a brief moment of adjusting Brown's jacket collar, he attached a tracking device to the underside of the collar near the seam. By then, Brown was barely able to form a cohesive sentence.

The capsule had contained Rohypnol, a date-rape drug that had become notorious for its effects. The dosage was concentrated enough that Brown would soon lose consciousness. It had been embarrassingly straightforward. Brown trusted these women, apparently with his life, and that had been his first mistake.

Brown was a brashly impatient man, and things began to get complicated when one of Brown's friends emerged from the woodwork and took Brown by the arm, intending to bring him home. For a moment, Daniel thought of reacting, of standing up and knocking the man back, telling him that he would take Brown home. But Daniel realized the value in this change. There would be no link, Brown's disappearance would be shifted onto his friend, and Daniel could remain invisible. So he remained motionless and watched the group prepare to leave. The longer he waited, the better. He was now completely absolved of all suspicion. He waited for thirty minutes, and from the chair at the back of the bar, he followed the movement of the tracking device through his phone. Then he made a quick exit and ensured he wasn't being followed.

Daniel stumbled out of the entrance, where the deafening sound of electronic music dissipated into mere thumping murmurs that extended down the street. There was a line snaking out from the steel door, and he looked around to orient himself. There was a taxicab parked out front, and he climbed into the back, slouching down so that the back of the seat masked his head.

He felt guilty for abandoning the Australians, but he realized that they would only slow down the process rather than expedite it. Slouched down in the back seat, his face was illuminated by the dull glow of his phone. Every so often, he would look up to check the fare.

Upon returning to the hotel, Daniel headed upstairs to change, leaving his suit hanging on a hanger against the closet door. He switched into running gear and made his way downstairs to the lobby, purposefully catching the attention of local security cameras. Carrying a GPS system programmed to record movements once he returned to the hotel, he had pre-recorded the entire route to mask his true travel. The date and time stamps had been falsified along a long path north.

In an effort to maintain legitimacy, he initially headed north in the opposite direction of Brown's condominium. He continued along this route for nearly two-thirds of a kilometer before crossing several blocks west and doubling back south.

The night was cold and the weather miserable. The gloom of an encroaching rainstorm had appeared a few hours earlier, and harsh winds swept across the city from the bay, hinting at what was to come. The rain started at quarter past eleven, nearly three hours ago, and showed no signs of stopping. Thick droplets fell hard, as if poured from a deep goblet. Thankfully, his waterproof running gear kept him dry, except for the reflective fluorescent-orange windbreaker he wore. The rest of his attire was all black.

The tracking device led him to a condominium building along the coast, not far from Min's offices, a block east. The front entrance was impassable, not due to physical barricades but because of heightened security with doormen and security cameras. It would be difficult to enter unnoticed. However, there was a side door along the road connected to the emergency stairwell system. It was undoubtedly armed to set off an alarm if opened. Daniel placed his digital runner's watch against the edge of the door near the hinge and waited thirty seconds. Beneath the resonance of clapping thunder, a quiet click ensued. He then used a metal device resembling a credit card to cut three wires along the serenaded edge of the door. Moving to the lock, he pressed his watch against the lock fob, and with a swift turn, the internal components of the watch deactivated the alarm system and unlocked the door. He cautiously pulled the door open ajar and peered into the dark, foreboding entrance.

A long hallway with several doors on each side led to the center of the building. Another large fire door restricted access to the cavernous stairwell, which felt like a narrow wind tunnel ascending to the upper floors. With the door behind him closed, silencing the patter of the evening rain, Daniel found

The Collateral Dividend

himself standing at the end of a dark hall. His hair was slicked back and parted, drenched, heavy with the rain.

Daniel removed his coat and placed it on the floor. There was a waterproof pouch in the back, allowing the jacket to be folded and stored. Underneath the coat, he wore a full-zip black sweater, lacking any sheen and with a sporty texture. From the pocket in the back of the raincoat, he retrieved his handgun, a smartphone, and several other devices he would need later. He folded the coat and secured it around his waist with the pouch hanging low. He blended into the hallway with a tactical aura, dressed entirely in black. It was a shrewd, eerily menacing presence. His shoes had rubber booties to keep them dry, and he removed them, clipping them to the coat pouch.

Brown resided several floors above, but the building's design prevented Daniel from simply climbing the stairwell unnoticed. His first destination was a room that stored the security features on a floor above. Overriding the system required a file downloaded from a USB drive, a quick and painless process.

It took Daniel more than five minutes to acquire what he needed. Paul now had access to the building's security feeds. Daniel swiftly moved through the floor, reaching Brown's floor. Paul and the others at Farragut Center had successfully disabled the building's security features. Daniel reached for the handle and pushed it down. The door leading to Brown's apartment was unlocked. He hesitated for a moment, then entered the room with conviction. His gun pointed forward as he made his way into the kitchen, scanning the living room. The far wall was lined from floor to ceiling with windows, offering a view of the bay and the faint glow of sea-bound lights piercing through the fog. The skyline was painted with a haze of green and red.

Daniel crossed the hardwood floor, heading toward a home office located through the doorway leading to the bedroom down the hall. The city's long shadows seeped into the condominium, casting tall figures on the walls in shades of black. His heart raced in his chest—an uncomfortable feeling as his mind outpaced his body.

Based on their findings, Brown was skilled at covering his tracks, which explained his appointment as vice president in charge of software. The office was small, with a glass desk pushed against the sidewall. Opposite it stood a cluttered bookshelf filled with old books and magazines. A computer terminal sat neatly against the legs of the glass table, its cables concealed within a custom port built into the wall.

The room was silent, save for the soothing hum of the computer's background programs. Occasionally, it would spring to life, as if taking a deep breath. Daniel positioned himself on hands and knees. Softly closing the door, leaving it slightly ajar to maintain a view down the hall, he pulled the terminal out from under the desk and placed it on the adjacent chair. Although the terminal was sealed, Daniel could remove the side cover, revealing the computer's internal components. With his phone, he connected an adapter to the bottom port, while a metallic clamp covered the base of a cluster of white cables stemming from the hard drive. This rerouted the data, and the phone's screen displayed a login screen resembling the terminal's desktop. An automated algorithm ran, allowing Daniel to place the phone down and momentarily gaze out across the city.

The city was vast, engulfed in darkness by the storm front, making it nearly impossible to see the other side of the bay. Rain and wind relentlessly battled each other at this height, with little to obstruct their fierce interaction.

Files began to pour in, initially a few dozen at a time, until the computer had been completely cloned. The data was stored on a digital cloud with near-impossible encryption. The process took no more than ten minutes. As it concluded, Daniel stood up, returned the computer drive to its original position, and examined the remaining contents of the room in greater detail. Unfortunately, there was nothing of interest, just the occasional childhood photograph and an improperly disposed work file. Nothing significant enough to warrant photographing or taking with them.

After scanning through the bookshelf, Daniel covertly contacted local housecleaners, and they parked an unregistered delivery van behind the building near the loading docks. Exiting the van, they left the doors unlocked and used the supply elevator to reach Daniel's location. A few moments later, Daniel answered the door, allowing the two men dressed in blue coveralls to enter. Moving down the hallway with his gun pointed at the closed door leading to the bedroom, Daniel found Brown collapsed onto the bed in a disheveled state. Daniel checked his pulse and opened the bathroom door, turning on the light.

The others entered the bedroom, administering another shot to Brown before placing him in a fabric bag to facilitate transportation downstairs. They laid him flat on his back on the sofa in the living room, his mouth agape in apparent awe. Standing in the hallway, Daniel inquired whether the housecleaners had encountered difficulties gaining entry to the building. The more experienced of the two shook his head and proceeded to clean the rest of the condominium, creating the illusion that Brown had abruptly left town. It wasn't their first time making someone disappear under such circumstances. This strategy required meticulous planning and execution. Paul had used

The Collateral Dividend

Brown's credit card information to purchase a ticket to an Asian destination, while the housecleaners packed Brown's bags—items that would accompany him on his journey, not to Asia but to one of Farragut Center's undisclosed and unlisted "black sites," used as illegal prisons.

Accompanied by the housecleaners, Daniel rode the supply elevator down to the delivery van. He put on his coat and began a quick run back to his hotel, intending to return immediately. However, despite his initial intentions, he found himself several miles east of the hotel after a twenty-minute burst of running, his thoughts consumed by the downpour. In the midst of such heavy rain, he felt an irresistible urge to keep running until he could run no more. And so, he found himself sprinting at a near-full speed.

There was a certain serenity that accompanied the rain, something Daniel wholeheartedly embraced as the aftermath of a quiet yet stormy night. He found solace in the idea that enduring a storm required endurance and, perhaps, a touch of wit rather than brute strength, hoping it would never recur.

The rain had fallen in such a manner that by the time Daniel returned to his hotel, he was almost entirely drenched. It was nearly three-thirty in the morning, and the doorman looked at him as if he had seen a ghost. After taking a long, hot shower, Daniel packed his belongings into two black suitcases, placing them at the foot of the bed. Despite the early hour, he woke up just before five for his flight out of Singapore, scheduled to depart at eight-thirty. Daniel waited in the morning sun for about twenty minutes, and when the charter arrived, one of the co-pilots emerged to assist him with his bags. "It may be a bit of a rough ride," the co-pilot said as Daniel settled into the back. "I'm Jack, by the way. Is there anything I can get you?" he asked, and Daniel shook his head apologetically.

Since Jack had transitioned to the commercial industry several years ago, he could barely recall the number of times clients had requested to deactivate the tracking system and fly below radar detectors. Surprisingly, it was a frequent occurrence, often for mundane reasons. However, in this particular scenario, they had been provided with false tracking numbers, and the plane had removable tail numbers. This allowed them to drop below radar for several hours and emerge hundreds of miles away as an entirely different aircraft. It was peculiar but acceptable. It was only in the airspace between Indonesia and Australia that the flight would reduce its altitude to avoid radar detection before immediately deviating northeast toward Japan. There, Daniel would lay low and await further instructions.

E.R. Wychwood

The flight from Japan to Hong Kong was swift, and upon arriving at the airport, Daniel used his phone to access a briefing packet on Sarah and her business in Hong Kong. Daniel's suspicions were confirmed when he learned that Sarah was to meet with a reporter from the UK Guardian. She had come to Hong Kong to escape the looming shadows of the intelligence community, seeking refuge in a world under Farragut Center's grip. Or at least, that's what she believed.

Surrounded by the sea on all sides, the city's airport left Daniel with an unsettling feeling as the small aircraft descended for landing, almost as if they were crashing. The thick brilliance of thousands of blinding lights illuminated the harbor upon his arrival. By the time he reached his destination, new intelligence on Sarah had altered the nature of his mission. Initially, Sarah had been staying in a hotel beyond the central district, in a low-traffic area where any advances would be easily detected, and any death, even if disguised as an accident, would be scrutinized.

Paul, however, knew the best way to draw her out into the open. First, they gained access to the Guardian reporter's accounts, starting with his cell phone, and then hacked into his computer to gain access to his other accounts. Through one of the reporter's emails, they reached out to Sarah, requesting a meeting at a hotel across town the following afternoon.

And so, they waited.

Paul wasn't entirely convinced they would receive a response, but he believed that the reasoning he provided in the email seemed legitimate enough for Sarah to believe it. To his surprise, she responded an hour later, and suddenly the operation was in motion. Paul finalized the location and time. They knew she wouldn't travel by road, as targeted killings disguised as car accidents had become a calling card for intelligence agencies. No one in the community would be foolish enough to think such methods were still effective. Paul hoped that subtlety was not dead. For a paranoid analyst on the run, understanding the world in shades of gray was crucial. The stark contrast between black and white no longer existed. Once on the run, all previous instances of logic and reason collapsed in favor of self-preservation. It was this intensity that Paul aimed to exploit.

If all went according to plan, they would be in and out of Hong Kong by nightfall the next day. Paul's tone conveyed austerity as he briefed Daniel on the day's operational requirements. Clear "Kill-no-capture" directives had been given. A delicate balance sustained the critical operations of Farragut Center and its sister organizations, and recent events had disrupted this balance, necessitating harsh remedies to restore it. In this case, it meant eliminating the anomalies that had caused the issues in the first place.

Initially, Paul had wanted to capture Sarah and afford her the same rights as any other common criminal, but Ted Hawthorne vetoed the proposition and classified the killing under national security protocols. It was a decision driven entirely by Farragut Center's self-preservation. Paul couldn't help but wonder if this decision mirrored the irrationality they sought to exploit in Sarah. Removing old liabilities to minimize risk exposure had its merits.

Daniel knew his stay in Hong Kong would be brief. He had rented a hotel room in the central district and spent the night showering and attempting to clear his mind for the emotional turmoil he would face the following day. He had only taken the life of a woman once before, and it had been a brutal and violent encounter. The conditions of that encounter were likely influenced by Daniel's own hesitations, and he couldn't forget the woman's superior hand-to-hand skills. Had he not been highly trained, he would have surely perished. Taking someone's life was an intimate and harrowing experience. Daniel acknowledged that thinking in such a way might be sexist, reinforcing pre-existing gender roles that had long enveloped society. But in his defense, he believed there was something particularly disturbing about it all. He felt embarrassed by his hesitations and the act itself, and he tried not to dwell on it. However, today, the idea persisted and couldn't be shaken.

Early the next morning, Daniel dressed and made his way to the subway station across the street from Sarah's hotel. He waited in a plain-colored sedan parked across the wide avenue. The windows were tinted, and he gazed out across the boulevard, observing Sarah emerging from the hotel's side entrance. She wore beige flats, blue jeans, a gray down coat, and a baseball cap pulled down to conceal most of her face with a tightly curved brim.

Sarah appeared entirely unremarkable, failing to fit any media narrative portraying the intelligence community as a masculine industry. She exuded femininity and thoughtfulness. Unlike the military, espionage required a femininity that shattered expectations of machismo.

Sarah stood outside the hotel for several moments, smoking a cigarette to calm her rising nerves. She found herself in the most dangerous phase—the delicate balance between the rule of law and anarchy. It was no secret that Farragut Center's capacity involved killing. Sarah refused to become a victim and carried a gun, remaining vigilant for others who might do the same.

However, carrying a gun in the city proved too cumbersome. It was loud, inaccurate, and too conspicuous. Daniel wanted to remain invisible, sending no messages. He followed Sarah down the street for about five minutes before stopping to watch her pick up the morning paper from a small kiosk beside the subway entrance.

It was at that moment he caught a glimpse of himself in the reflection of the window across the street. A tall, blue-suited man with a cobalt tie, stark white shirt, and pocket square adorned with a hint of silver from the tie bar stared back at him. He glanced toward the subway station, where a housecleaner had disguised himself as a homeless man.

As part of the operation, Daniel was tasked with establishing the operation's boundaries. He had personally briefed the housecleaners and assessed as many factors as possible within that zone. There was a park bench nearby, and Daniel took a seat, pulled out a cigarette, and went through the motions of smoking it. According to his watch, Sarah had waited under the sun for about five minutes before descending into the depths of the Hong Kong underground. Daniel quickly took the parallel entrance stairs and scanned the lobby for any signs of his target before confidently bypassing the turnstiles with an overridden card. He seamlessly blended into the morning rush of passengers, feeling the crush against the wall as they waited for the northbound Red line.

CCTV feeds hung above, looping in fifteen-minute cycles, masking the feeling that the trains were not running on time. Utilizing facial tracking software, Daniel pinpointed Sarah on the boarding platform across from him. By then, an inbound train had begun slowing its approach, and the screeching sound echoed through the cavernous tunnel.

The automated syringe built into Daniel's phone activated, and the needle protruded from the audio jack at the bottom. He positioned himself behind Sarah, pressing his head low against his chest, and swiftly jabbed her in the lower back with the syringe. The device fired, and Sarah felt an injection-like shiver traveling down her back. Daniel quickly moved to the far end of the subway car, looking down the narrow pathway without turning back.

Sarah managed to secure a seat near the middle of the car, clutching her bag tightly against her chest. However, as she sat down and caught her breath, she began feeling violently ill. A woozy sensation washed over her, and her body temperature seemed to rise, resembling a fever. A shiver down her spine forced her back into the seat, as if utterly exhausted. She looked around, but her movements started to slur, and the relaxation of sinking back into the seat became overwhelming.

Paralysis had set in. She stared at the subway car, and in that moment, the realization dawned upon her. She was being killed, and there was nothing she

The Collateral Dividend

could do. No one looked at her. She was dying alone in a train full of people, and nothing could change that fact. Sarah felt a wave of fear strike her like searing heat. It felt as if her life was flashing before her, but it was merely the actions she regretted. These images played out before her like a nightmare, worsening until she tried everything to wake up from the bad dream. In the peak of her regret, her eyes fell shut, and she slumped back into the seat, as if suddenly falling asleep. The emotion drained from her cheeks and forehead, leaving her with a taciturn expression.

Daniel found it difficult to look in her direction. There was something unsettling about knowing she wasn't sleeping. He rode the train to the next stop, climbed back up to street level, and glanced across the street at a gray van parked temporarily along the curb. As he climbed into the back, he closed the sliding door and faced the passenger. "Has Paul been notified?" he asked, and the man nodded.

The van dropped him off at the hotel room, and he took the stairs to his floor, entering the room with a soured and desolate expression. The night was still young, but he felt no motivation beyond lying inert in bed. Somehow, he couldn't help but feel that this was a consequence of his ruthless actions. There was something shallow about the way his superiors approached death. It was a solution, horribly filthy, used to maintain cleanliness. What great irony, Daniel thought. It was a contradiction ingrained in the very fabric of the intelligence community. They claimed that sacrificing security for increased security was justified, but was it? Daniel was no longer sure. He found himself caught on the fence between the belief that if one had nothing to hide, then unreasonable searches weren't an issue, and the realization that those searches encouraged people in power to make unjust decisions. Daniel disliked self-righteous TSA officers or highway patrolmen. It bothered him how they exploited rights through the ignorance of others. At least when Daniel violated people's rights, he did so within a legitimate legal framework—or so he told himself.

Two housecleaners had been sent to meticulously search through Sarah's life. One had broken into her hotel room in the central district, while the other did the same at her house in Alexandria, Virginia. Paul sat at his office desk, watching the live feed of the operation streaming onto his computer screen. Sarah's hotel room was a mess, disheveled, with scribbled notes on white printer paper, documenting her communications with Jeff.

The paper was laid out on the floor in a grid pattern. It solidified the fact that she had been involved in distributing stolen information. The matrix on the floor contained photographs of several key actors in Farragut Center. Paul was one of them, and when he brought this to Ted, the head of Farragut Center, Ted informed Paul that all those listed were to be pulled from the field or provided private security until the conflict was resolved. They found a copy of the Farragut Center matrix in a file folder hidden beneath the hotel's mattress, giving them the first glimpse of what they had lost in its complete form.

A chemical process had been applied to the papers - a vial of blue liquid spilled onto the paper. If the paper had been photocopied or duplicated, it would turn red. Fortunately, that wasn't the case. Paul felt relieved, knowing that one less copy was in circulation. However, determining how many more copies were floating about became his next concern.

They had retrieved her personal effects from the city morgue, adding them to Paul's wall of strings. This process helped him connect Sarah to Jeff and Brown. It became clear that Ezra Cohen, posing as Klaus, was the link between Brown and Min. Min had been happy to refer a few candidates.

Paul's discovery of Cohen complicated things. It didn't make sense how Cohen was connected to all the information. Cohen seemed to operate above the string matrix, linking to Min and a few others, but the details eluded Paul. From his perspective, he had been at the helm, the central actor in stealing funds from the markets.

Min had been responsible for most of the heavy lifting, orchestrating the logistics of the attacks and their aftermath. Along with Klaus, he now represented Gaillard's public face in their secluded life. Then, a breakthrough came around mid-day. Farragut Center stumbled upon a golden ticket by pure coincidence. A homeless man in lower Manhattan discovered a secure-looking flash drive among the banking district's trash. The company Min worked for had manufactured the drive. When the homeless man brought it to an Internet café, it caused the company's entire network to crash. The digital signature was identified by Heywood and forwarded to Farragut Center, prompting swift action to secure the drive. Before long, Paul found himself staring at a schematic of trade directives and bank accounts worth hundreds of thousands. The money had been moved in tiny increments across numerous accounts, managing to evade taxes. This brought Gaillard tantalizingly close to their grasp, and Paul felt a rush of excitement as the information closed in.

For nearly a week straight, Paul had been working to keep a constant stream of information flowing to Nathan Ramirez. It was around that time they learned about Klaus's death. Ezra had been lurking around Europe, finalizing the last of the trades as per Gaillard's demands. Paul wanted to ensure Ezra, or Klaus, or whoever this person claimed to be, was eliminated swiftly. Klaus was next in

The Collateral Dividend

line to receive the information Sarah had sent. Paul wanted the data isolated. He wanted Min and Gaillard cornered, so they would be the last ones standing and could eventually be targeted without risking the exposure of the information. There was still an unsettling risk that Congress could discover Farragut Center, which would bring everyone involved crashing down.

Eventually, Nathan tracked Klaus down, thanks to Daniel's work, in a bar in the South of France. He entered through the back entrance and made his way through the kitchen. There was an air of arrogance and cruel efficiency in the way he moved. In the kitchen, a group of gangsters lounged around, with two sitting on stainless-steel counters, and a group of prostitutes present. As Ramirez entered, a tall and bulky French gangster stood up, looking at him with a stern expression. Ramirez received a cleaned handgun, checked the discharge port, coiled the weapon, and tucked it into his waistband. He continued his seamless journey, walking out of the kitchen and into the nightclub. The loud music and strobe lights obscured any sense of coherence.

Ezra sat on the far side of the nightclub, accompanied by a group of girls and an old associate from Israel. They had considered hiring a group of gangsters to handle Farragut Center's dirty work. However, with increased attention from the Senate hearings, it seemed best to keep things in-house. In retrospect, Paul realized it was foolish not to make things appear accidental. At the time, though, the goal was to send a clear message, and Paul had confidence in Nathan Ramirez's ability to disappear. Nathan approached Ezra's table, reached behind into his waistband, pulled out the handgun, and aimed it at Ezra, opening fire. He calmly lowered the gun and stared at the lifeless body. Before he could regain his bearings, he was tackled to the ground and restrained.

An hour before the Senate hearing, Paul received a blocked phone call. As soon as he answered, he sensed something was amiss. Ramirez was now imprisoned, awaiting trial for murder. However, that wasn't the main issue. Somehow, he had been connected back to the intelligence community. It was revealed that he was one of Dune's own. Paul felt his face flush with embarrassment.

"Nathan Ramirez hasn't said a word," Director Dunes stated. But that wasn't the reason for his call. "The Senate received a delivery this morning through CNN. It listed Nathan Ramirez as an Agency asset and claimed his murder of Klaus was an attempt to cover up more evidence from being released. Is this true?"

311

E.R. Wychwood

Ted cursed under his breath. It was evident that Gaillard was retaliating. "It is," Ted eventually confirmed.

"I'm told they're working with French authorities to bring him back to the U.S. for trial. The Attorney General is considering whether they can subpoena him for the hearings."

Ted crossed his arms. "Director, Ramirez is one of our best. He's been trained not to talk," Ted assured. With the news spreading and gaining popularity, coordinating Ramirez's extraction had become impossible. Ramirez might as well have been killed; there was no way to retrieve him now.

"I think we need to tackle this head-on," Paul suggested abruptly. Ted asked for clarification, and Paul continued, "Everyone will come up with their own theories about Ramirez. If we don't provide our own narrative, we might as well surrender. Why don't we have Dunes start with some circular arguments, frustrating the committee, and then lay out a clear, concise story: Ramirez was an agency asset pursuing leads on explicit threats to American lives."

"They'll accuse me of violating the constitution, authorizing an extrajudicial killing," Dunes interjected.

"Yes, but that's a charge we can defend," Paul argued. "If we don't address this now, the committee will keep subpoenaing people until someone talks. That's a risk we can't afford."

"You know that would force me to resign as soon as the hearing begins. What if the new Director decides to comply with the Senate, and it's revealed that we were bluffing all along?" Dunes, sitting hunched over his office desk, eating a tangerine piece by piece, raised valid concerns.

"Paul is right, Gregory," Ted interjected. "Finding a suitable replacement will be easier than facing a full-blown investigation."

"For Christ's sake, Ted! Taking the fall for some shoddy work in Sudan by my own boys is one thing. But sacrificing myself so that some Harvard prick can play leviathan is bullshit," Dunes expressed his frustration, glancing at Paul.

Paul slammed his hand on the table. "It's about sending a bloody message!" he shouted. "Sometimes, you need to make a splash to catch the fish. I'm not surprised you're angry; the CIA has never been good at gracefully handling blowback. You were already doomed. We took the hit deliberately, knowing you would have to shoulder the blame. We sent the message we wanted, and now we have a lead to trace back and find Gaillard. If Gaillard had the information we've been tracking, he would have released it after we killed Klaus. So don't tell me I made a mistake when you're clearly—"

"That's enough, Paul," Ted intervened firmly, rising from his seat. "Gregory, this is non-negotiable now. It will be much easier to defend your order for an assassination based on national security than to defend your involvement in creating an entirely isolated targeted killing center. We all have our roles to play, and you have made your choice. This is about protecting the government and its policies, not saving one person's career."

Late to the hearing, Paul sat at the back of the room. The media was captivated by the revelation that the CIA had authorized a modern-day assassination attempt, bringing immense attention to Director Dunes. The opposition had the strongest objections, questioning how such an event could occur under the government's watch.

Senator Helpord took a moment and tried to reiterate what he had initially intended to convey. According to Winters, who Paul was seated beside, Dunes consistently misinterpreted the questions asked. In some cases, it made him appear callous, taking poorly constructed sentences too literally. Eventually, the senators' staffers caught on and began asking tightly worded questions that couldn't be misconstrued. Dunes seemed increasingly disconnected, as if mentally absent. "Mr. Dunes, I believe you're missing the point of the question," Senator Helpord said while Paul entered the hearing room. "I wanted you to explain the recent information released through the media, linking a murder in France to an American accused of working for the CIA."

"What specifically would you like me to explain?" Dunes asked, determined to make them work for it. If he was going to take the blame for one of Paul's mistakes, he was going to do it in style.

"Could you please elaborate on your knowledge of the events described and when they occurred?"

"I don't recall the date of the situation you're referring to, Senator," Dunes replied, beginning to stonewall. It became apparent that the President would likely force him into retirement, and ultimately, Dunes would be held accountable for orders that neither he nor his office had ever made.

"Director Dunes, to your knowledge, did the CIA or any member of the intelligence community train or authorize operations carried out by the American Nathan Ramirez?"

"I don't recall," Dunes repeated. It quickly became clear that Dunes conveniently couldn't recall any specifics beyond what he had previously briefed the Senate on. The committee grew desperate and began considering subpoenaing deputy directors and other agency officials, both current and former, to determine the level of authorization within the CIA and whether these events were exceptional.

"Was Nathan Ramirez following orders from your office or any other office within the intelligence community when he shot Klaus with the intention of killing him?" Gregory Dunes took a long sip of water, scanning the crowd for a familiar face. The room fell into a hushed silence, as if any sound could trigger chaos. "I ask again, Mr. Dunes, can you please answer the question?" the senator pressed after a moment, and Dunes locked eyes with him.

"May we take a ten-minute recess?"

"Let's reconvene here at half past," the speaker agreed, taking a sip of water and settling into his chair until the designated time arrived. During the break, he observed Dunes, who made notes on his desk and absentmindedly doodled in the top corner of the briefing packet his aide had handed him. When they returned, the senator restated the question and inquired if Dunes was ready to answer. It seemed criminal charges were looming over him.

Dunes let out an exasperated sigh, as if defeated and beaten at his own game. "I have hesitated to state this for a few days because I have been unprepared for duties beyond my role as the Director of Central Intelligence. These commitments extend into the personal realm. It is my understanding that Nathan Ramirez targeted Ezra Cohen under orders personally sent from my office. Mr. Cohen was targeted due to suspected involvement in recent terrorist activities. He was financially connected to events that unfolded in Sudan," Dunes took a deep breath, fixing his gaze on the glass of water directly ahead. "It was at the direction and discretion of my office, and my office alone, that the judgment for extraction of American assets in Sudan was made. Furthermore, it was my discretion to authorize Nathan Ramirez to go beyond his standard call of duty and carry out extrajudicial targeting of Ezra Cohen. I attempted to delay the discovery of this from the Senate and the American public to protect agency personnel who were following my explicit directions. I would like to apologize to the Senate and the American people for my actions."

The room exploded, and a surge of camera flashes followed. Dunes looked up at the committee, as if left in awe. He stared up at the chairperson, and Senator Helpord hesitated for a moment. They had found exactly what they were looking for, but if he were being honest, he had never been convinced they would ever find it. Helpord let out a deep breath and glanced back at his senior staffer, who handed him a folded note. Helpord opened it and placed it on the table. "Director Dunes, I would like to thank you for your testimony today. Your forthcoming attitude will, I am sure, be invaluable to our further investigations," he didn't feel the need to inform Dunes that they expected his resignation. That went unsaid. Many experts on national news agencies had already assured the public that Dunes would resign within the day, and by eight-thirty the next morning, Dunes had submitted his resignation to the President and quietly retreated to the remote backwaters of Kentucky or Kansas, somewhere with fewer people and more farms.

Ted had made sure to visit the old boy the night before he left the district and told him he was sorry. In some ways, Ted felt like he had betrayed Dunes. The reality was that there was little anyone could do beyond offering condolences; after all, Dunes had volunteered for the role. It was a clean way to sever ties with the community. There would be no temptations to be pulled back in, and certainly, no one would be foolish enough to ask for his help. Dunes saw it as bittersweet. He wondered how long he would continue to feel that way. With the community in the spotlight, Farragut Center couldn't rely on many more men like him to take the fall for shoddy work. For at least a few months, Farragut Center had to operate flawlessly. Dunes didn't think it was a question of how, but rather if they could do it at all.

THE UNRAVELING WEB

Sergei's return home was less than spectacular. He found himself doing paperwork as a skewed form of punishment for months, until eventually, in some sort of miracle, he was let back out into the field. His father had told him that he was proud, but Sergei sensed a hint of disappointment. Vladimir was no longer interested in sticking it to the Americans, and he secretly thought that anyone who was interested in doing so was wasting their time. Sergei hated that he needed his father's reassurance to stay sane, to believe that what he had done was the right thing. It hadn't been.

The old Russian wasn't certain it had been the right thing. He had long since handed over his authority to a much more politically connected deputy director. The political pressures had bogged him down, and now he only kept the role symbolically. It was out of respect rather than utility. Even though they clearly owed Philippe Gaillard a great deal, Vladimir wanted his son to have nothing to do with the Frenchman. That's why Sergei found himself thrown into a dizzying array of archival work. It took months before he saw the light of day again, months since he had held a gun or checked his shoulder for the threat of a follower. By the time he emerged from the archives, he barely had the patience to do either of those things anymore.

It wasn't until he was sent to a field office in Austria that any hint of the name Philippe Gaillard reentered his mind. The aftermath of his work in New York had been unlike any other operation he had ever undertaken. A bank account made under his name in Ukraine had received a deposit of several million dollars, and he was comfortable enough to live a life of leisure if he wished. He felt uncomfortable about using the money, but eventually, he found a use for it.

Four months later, the account balance hovered dangerously low. He had become addicted to the high of cocaine. There were few days when he hadn't sniffed. His summoning to Austria had been at the request of a local asset there. The asset had specifically asked for him and had told the Russian Embassy that there was intel the Russian government would be interested in. The asset showed the first page of the stolen files from Farragut Center. It wasn't until Sergei arrived in Austria and found himself seated at a park bench across from Philippe Gaillard that he realized the intel had merely been a honey pot to lure the Russian Kroysgin into Austria and back within Gaillard's reach.

The Collateral Dividend

"It's been too long," Gaillard said at once, crossing his leg and leaning back into the park bench. They were along the Danube River. It was late spring, and the weather seemed to think that summer had already arrived. "What's it been, five months?" Gaillard asked, and Sergei shrugged. Gaillard had spent a great deal of time thinking about what needed to be done. He tried to hide his hands; their constant shaking made him even more anxious.

"Not long enough," Sergei said. "I am no longer at the whim of your orders. Are you actually selling something to us, or are you only here to ask me to help with something else?"

"Of course, I wish to sell. But I also came to discuss some questions I had." Gaillard pulled out a file folder from a briefcase, and with unsteady hands, he held it up for Sergei to see. "The current rate is a hundred million. You can't see it until you at least pay half." Gaillard knew Sergei couldn't say yes without consulting his handlers back home. Sergei had contacted them and outlined the contents, and when he was given authorization, an immediate wire had been sent to a dummy account in China, routing the money around the world and eventually into Gaillard's hands. Several days later, when they met up, Gaillard cleared his throat and whimsically asked, "Say, my dear friend, what ever happened to that flash drive containing the trade order? What did you end up doing with it after your work was all said and done?"

Sergei's heart fell, and he felt a strong lump in his throat. "I disposed of it behind the building," he said truthfully.

Gaillard thought it might have been found. In fact, he knew it had been found. That would have been the only way to uncover a connection between Min and himself. Gaillard had fumed over this idea for days, pacing his room and thinking about how the events would play out. There was a methodical pace to the way Gaillard had structured his life. He thought about what he would say to Sergei and when, how he would say it. It was a micromanagement of communication and thought so pristine that any unexpected action by Sergei would cause Gaillard to lose his sanity. Gaillard's web, so tightly and intricately woven, had collapsed.

"You failed us all, Sergei. Your drugs and your arrogance doomed you from the start. It was a mistake to involve you. Now, I fear you and your father must pay for all this," Gaillard said, letting out a deep sigh. "It was a pleasure as always, Sergei."

Sergei had destroyed his family's reputation with Gaillard. It was enough of a disruption that his father would have disowned him upon his return to Russia. He seemed content with accepting his fate. He couldn't bear to face the wrath of his unrelenting father. What upset him even more was the brutal reality that he would never see the motherland again, but he would die a martyr.

"My condolences for your failure, Sergei. I'm sure you are just as aware as I am that the consequences will be far greater than what you can afford. And thank you for your support in Zurich," Gaillard said, and Sergei laughed.

As Sergei leaned against the backrest of the park bench, he suddenly felt himself pulled over it and wrestled to the ground. A wire was wrapped around his neck, suffocating him with an iron grip. The attacker kept Sergei subdued and reacted against his violent jitters as the Russian tried to get in one last breath. Sergei clamored for air and attempted to reach his attacker's face until the coning of black left him dead in an unspectacular heap.

When his body fell limp, Gaillard stood up from the park bench in a matter-of-fact tone. He looked around and watched as his men pushed the corpse into the riverbanks, using a cement block to drag it to the bottom. Gaillard then took a car back up into the secluded Austrian countryside. Here, he found the lifestyle enjoyable, but often longed for the ambiance of France. Things were no longer as simple as they once were. He felt it unsafe to return home until Farragut Center had been 'handled'. However, what he failed to see was that he was in a losing battle. The upper hand had long since waned. This was no longer the invisible war he perceived it to be. At the Center's request, the French had begun to investigate Gaillard's involvement in funding terrorism. Firms owned by Philippe Gaillard had been explicitly connected to money stolen from the stock market. Although only a few people suspected that the owner himself had been involved in such a heist, the effects had already begun. Those companies were on their last legs, but Gaillard himself was still, in many ways, untouchable. Pierre had timidly attempted to inform Gaillard of the losing ground, and as a result, the head of security found himself murdered.

Gaillard's social leprosy and political demise were now nearing their zenith. He stayed in Vienna for two reasons. The first was that it provided close access to the company that coordinated most of the stolen assets. The second was that it kept him out of the media's eye and within reach of some of the world's premier doctors for his type of dementia. Here in Austria, he could hide comfortably while attempting to prolong his own life, a luxury not possible in France.

All this finesse meant that Daniel needed to be extremely astute in his execution. Gaillard, above all others, needed to die by accident. Gaillard could not meet a sloppy or suspicious death. It had to be an accident. Only through that method could Paul work with the necessary people to return most of the

The Collateral Dividend

money into an internal account and excuse the discrepancy as a computer error. Paul wanted to solve this, track the money, and return it as if nothing had happened. In truth, he wanted to bury the evidence as quickly as possible. Whether such a thing was possible was another matter that needed to be examined once everything had been ironed out for good.

They didn't find the body until the following week. The new teams eventually discovered that he was Russian and had, at least for a brief period, been involved in the government. His face had been deformed, and the dental records were inconsistent with any on record. They wondered how Gaillard had successfully changed Sergei's appearance.

Gaillard's money made lips tight, but in the world of money and wealth, there was always the offer of more, the allure of power. Stroking egos could be enough to convince a person to do nearly anything.

Paul called early the next morning. The recent weeks had been a marathon, and the wear began to hold an audible resonance in Paul's tone and mannerisms. He had begun to sound like an old man.

Avery had tracked funds to Sudan, where they were to wait before heading to China. It had taken them a good deal of time, but they traced the money to one central account. All of it stemmed from Switzerland and ended in Austria. It turned out that the account was opened during Sergei and Gaillard's time in Switzerland. They were registered to a corporation based in Austria that paid its taxes and did little else. The firm was a holding company for several dozen cash operations, masking the shadowy nature of the business. In conjunction with Sergei's death, things seemed as if they were narrowing. The world felt very narrow, and Daniel did not like the fact that it made him feel awfully alone.

Where he was going in Austria, the communities were mostly backwater, with many housing massive estates that offered rural privacy unmatched anywhere else in the world. It was that privacy that Daniel hoped to exploit. There was a sense of privacy that was impervious to electronic eavesdropping, as if a relic of the old world. The Austrian company manually filed taxes, and the paper trail must have been mountainous, Daniel thought. How they intended to sift through all the data was a question that had yet to be answered. Daniel felt best traveling to visually see the files. He had never been comfortable with the idea of freshly scanned documents and wished to see them himself.

The flight to Austria arrived in Vienna at quarter to seven, and the sunny morning welcomed Daniel with a warm breeze from the Danube River. When he arrived at the hotel nearly an hour later, a special parcel had been shipped and was waiting for him at the airport. Upon entering the hotel room, he closed the door and the blinds, and in the dark, he placed the package onto the bed. Using the blade of a key, he opened the cardboard folds. Inside was a locked case, and Daniel used the key to open it.

Inside the case was a matte black handgun with a threaded suppressor. Subtle scratches along the edges indicated wear and tear that had eroded the paint. He disassembled and cleaned the weapon before reassembling it with a loaded magazine. He put the suppressor into the outside pocket of his suit jacket, and the handgun went snugly into the holster inside his waistband.

There were two smaller cardboard boxes inside the larger box, and Daniel took the first one out, cut it open, and pulled out a small device resembling an LED flashlight. He put it into his pocket.

The second box was larger and securely packed. Inside was a pair of thick-framed glasses with false lenses. On the inside of the right arm of the frames, there was a button. When pressed, the frames could be placed onto a document, and the device would scan the ink, printing the page while piecing together minute images for analysis. The scan could also identify fingerprints, printing errors, and photocopy errors, which would help speculate where the original documents had been produced. It was a wireless means of scanning the documents without having to take them back to Washington. The technology was brilliant, although Daniel had no idea how it worked and, like many things, he didn't particularly care.

At the bottom of the package, there was a briefing packet—a fifty-page document bound with a thick staple in the top right corner. Paul had begun orchestrating the most efficient and brutal operations to date. The process was highly regimented. They had already eliminated Klaus, and with the death of Sergei, only Tzavaras, Min, and, of course, Gaillard remained. Through a contact at Whitehall, Paul had sent out a general call, but it felt as if the intelligence communities had suffered from lethargy. Daniel's work in the Far East had provided them with valuable information on Min, and they now had the capacity to track him almost anywhere. Paul's directives were clear: there were three targets, and they all had to be eliminated before the end of the month, which was less than a week away. Daniel was to be at the helm of the operation, and Paul had communicated that there was zero margin for error. Paul was growing tired of the Senate and its special hearings; he did not want his operations to fall under the scrutiny of the public eye.

Min had been a thorn in many sides, and his attempts to undermine The Valley were the icing on the cake. Their chase was no longer driven by legitimate reasons but rather by the desire to find Farragut Center's slippery foes. Paul had abandoned the idea of internal legitimacy long ago. There was a time when he desired to find definitive proof so that when Farragut Center reflected on their actions, they could rest assured knowing they did what was reasonably justifiable. However, Paul had become immensely focused on tracking down Gaillard and the others, to the point where he had a wanton disregard for justice. He had told Avery many times that he simply wanted the end result—he wanted to find Gaillard and kill him.

Paul was determined to create a narrative that would shape the perception of who was the villain and who was the hero. Daniel, on the other hand, had a different approach. He valued due diligence and legitimate due process, and his primary goal was to find Isabel and understand her carelessness and ignorance in the relationship. His suppressed emotions made it difficult for him to assess his work objectively.

Daniel also struggled with recurring nightmares, which were becoming more frequent. In these dreams, he would find himself in an old elevator, with the doors closing and the flickering light creating a dark and eerie atmosphere. The elevator would descend, leading him to a cold and dark corridor with billowing lights and long shadows through fog. These nightmares played with his mind, challenging his perception of reality. To cope with the anxiety, Daniel would regulate his breathing and try to confront his fears, hoping to find solace in facing the truth.

Min had traveled extensively through China and ended up in Venice, which was close to Vienna, the place Daniel intended to visit first if given the chance. Heywood Lane had uncovered a series of financial transactions matching Min's travel patterns, ultimately leading them to him.

The briefing packet Daniel received was dense but lacked substantial evidence. Apart from what he already knew, the packet only contained a transmission stating that additional sources had confirmed suspicions, instructing Daniel to pursue Min and Gaillard relentlessly. Daniel never suspected that Paul had ulterior motives. There seemed to be no reason to suspect such a thing, as Paul's aggression couldn't solely stem from the desire to destroy Gaillard. Or could it?

Paul had omitted the evidence against Min or Gaillard from Farragut Center, but Daniel trusted that Paul wouldn't initiate an attack based solely on speculation. However, Daniel sensed that Paul's focus was no longer on airtight evidence. Paul wanted to bring the operation to a close and clean up the mess, perhaps out of exhaustion.

E.R. Wychwood

It wasn't until the following day that Daniel went to the archives. Dressed in a dark blue suit, he exuded a sense of confidence and elegance, with fake reading glasses tucked into his breast pocket. As Daniel entered the room, the shadowy morning cast a gloomy shade through the windows, creating an atmosphere of foggy uncertainty. Daniel's well-fitted suit accentuated his posture, standing with his hips forward and shoulders pulled back, his hair neatly combed and eyebrows slightly furrowed.

Although Daniel wasn't entirely sure what he was searching for, he believed someone back at Farragut Center would discover something valuable. The stack of files was extensive, and he quickly skimmed through most of them until he stumbled upon a file dated three months ago. It marked the first significant sum of money entering the account, followed by subsequent transactions to an account in Luxembourg. Daniel made a note of the frequent interaction with this account, suspecting that Paul would link it to Gaillard. The meticulous consistency of the payments, always in cash and two days before the due date, hinted at Gaillard's involvement. Daniel questioned whether their search was biased, whether they were merely finding evidence to support their views or genuinely seeking the truth.

The most recent tax payment had been made just a day ago, but the account was registered under a pseudonym that led to a dead-end address. Initially, Daniel considered it a convenient coincidence, but he realized it was only a matter of time before the payment period resumed. He asked the archival clerk if the bank also stored surveillance footage, hoping it would aid in his search. Convinced it was relevant, they led him to a back room, where Daniel carefully reviewed nearly fifteen hours of film.

Suddenly, a significant portion of the financial transactions became clear and understandable. Most of the money Klaus was moving around was linked to Gaillard.

From the hallway of the archives, Daniel asked, "So what would you like me to do about it?" The long granite hallway with high ceilings and tall windows cast a dark and eerie shadow, as if the outside fog had seeped into the building and accumulated on the roof.

"We're going after them," Paul recalled saying. He assured Daniel that the data obtained from the archives provided sufficient evidence of Gaillard's involvement. However, Daniel's doubts began to grow. He wanted to believe Paul and uncover the truth behind this conspiracy, but he questioned whether Gaillard's death by their hand was the right course of action.

The Collateral Dividend

Paul believed that both Min and Gaillard were nearby and would soon instruct Daniel to apprehend them. He had manipulated documents and concealed his zealous actions to avoid detection by internal regulators. By the time Daniel received authorization, assets related to Whitehall confirmed Min's presence in Venice and informed Paul that Min had been meeting with representatives of organizations interested in illegal activities. Paul suspected that Min was attempting to sell the stolen data from the Valley, disguised as legitimate business transactions. The private closed bidding only heightened Paul's suspicion, with rumors suggesting that someone was willing to pay hundreds of millions for Min's secrets. Pressure from Washington to conclude the operation and let Farragut Center lie low added to Paul's urgency. He wanted to rectify his mistakes and ensure the sacrifices made were justified, but he knew it couldn't be accomplished overnight. Paul's attempts to fix previous events only worsened Farragut Center's financial and political position, and he could sense his waning popularity. Paul needed a substantial achievement to reverse the sentiments, even if public recognition was unattainable. He aimed to gain political recognition for Farragut Center as an essential element of the intelligence community.

Finding Min required luring him into a sale to narrow down his location. Min was cautious and wouldn't agree to meet without having some control over the situation and environment. This paranoia presented a considerable challenge for Paul. However, it also had advantages since they could eventually trace Min's whereabouts. Paul referred to this tracking method as "bread crumbing," which involved following a surrogate long enough to lead Farragut Center to Min. It required patience and significant financial resources to conduct surveillance for days or even weeks. Paul had to involve their financial backers, though he worried that accountants increasingly influenced the center's operations. Such was the reality of their operation.

*   *   *

Min and Gaillard needed to be on the same page; that much was imperative. They kept in constant contact throughout the week, with a phone call every two days. Owning a telecom giant had its advantages. Several prospective buyers were interested in the information, and the stakes had risen to nearly half a billion dollars. Initially, when things were new, they considered giving the information away to news agencies at a fraction of the market cost. In the hands of the media, it would have been devastating. However, Gaillard eventually conjured up a plan that Min wholeheartedly agreed to. They would sell the list to two buyers and then again, at a much cheaper cost, months later to a few of the larger news agencies. The two men had long known that they would be hunted for their actions. Gaillard no longer cared; he simply wanted his money back so that his pride could remain intact. Min was more cautious than Gaillard. He believed that Gaillard's lack of constant motion, vigilance in hiding, and always being suspect and on the run was due to arrogance. This tactic was a double-edged sword. Disappearing forever was rare. If one stayed still, they ran the risk that eventually someone would look in the right place. On the contrary, if they kept moving, they would no doubt eventually attract attention. Ports of travel, common routes, movement—these naturally attracted visual attention. Either way, it had always been a matter of time. That was why they had plans. There were alternatives, backups, and pre-laid scenarios in case the inevitable ever came.

*   *   *

Venice was sunny, with a warm breeze across the vastness of the harbor wafting above the narrow canals. Daniel arrived by boat and reached the heart of the city by noon. The meeting Paul had arranged had already occurred in the early morning, and an unmanned drone had trailed the seller through the city until they identified where Min was staying. It was a small three-story building with red bricks, overlooking a rather wide canal with a sidewalk on the near side, which extended for about three hundred yards.

Daniel didn't even bother to check into a hotel. It wasn't that he didn't particularly enjoy Venice; Daniel merely wanted nothing more than to get everything done and return home as soon as reasonably possible. He had been thinking a great deal about his role in all of this, and the recent news out of France was that Ramirez was not going to be given an extraction. They had left him out to dry. That was the reality of this business. Daniel had increasingly become uncomfortable with the fact that Farragut Center had not even lifted a finger when word spread that Ramirez had been arrested.

He couldn't help but wonder whether the same would be said for him. These thoughts were dangerous. Did he trust the certainty of Farragut Center's word? Worse still, Farragut Center could be vengeful toward his failures to keep his promises. Was the Center capable of letting him disappear? Or would they claw him back into the world of espionage and force him to remain? It had all started rather romantically—the notion that he had been seduced into a way of life that

The Collateral Dividend

held great promise at the expense of many things. But now, the chickens were coming home to roost, and he had been wondering for a long time whether they were doing the right thing. He wondered whether his consent even mattered.

There was a part of Daniel that had wanted to storm into the room and shoot Min dead. However, he realized that such thinking was shallow, lacking creativity and reason. Daniel contemplated the stupidity of killing Min without subjecting him to questioning. If Min was going to meet his demise, it had to be executed flawlessly. Tact was of utmost importance. Paul had informed Daniel that he knew some people who could assist, guaranteeing that everything would fall into place. Daniel began to wonder how many people actually owed Paul a favor.

Daniel had expressed his intent and deep desire to kill Min, but Paul deterred him with alternative plans. Documents were prepared and sent to the Valley. Eventually, these doctored files found their way to the D.A.'s office in San Francisco. The legal wolves would eventually seize the opportunity to bring Min down. Paul aimed to present Min on a silver platter, ensuring that everything was perfect and in its rightful place.

"What exactly did you do?" Daniel inquired upon witnessing Paul's anger-driven intention.

"Sometimes, Daniel, the best use of force is no force at all," Paul quipped cryptically. Daniel questioned whether Paul's sanity had completely deserted him. The state of mind at Farragut Center seemed unstable. Daniel had been concealing his traumas for far too long, haunted by scarring and horrifying hallucinations that occasionally resurfaced, triggering fears of his deteriorating sanity.

Revenge was best served cold, and Paul had just revealed his main course. Almost a year since it all began, Paul had delivered a deadly blow. However, there was something unsatisfying about this achievement. Pinning Min down with an impossibly complex legal case and a life sentence was less gratifying than knowing Min was dead and gone.

When Daniel arrived at the apartment, he ascended the stairs and paused outside the door for a moment. Perhaps it was arrogance or stupidity, but Min had minimal security. He detested feeling cluttered, despising the presence of burly men attempting to control his actions and thoughts. Though aware of the danger, Min craved solitude. There was a possibility that Min sensed the end drawing near, but Daniel preferred to maintain the illusion that they had taken him by surprise. Daniel knocked on the door and awaited one of Min's men to answer. As the door swung open, Daniel stood unarmed and silent. After assessing the room and identifying all the individuals present, he swiftly seized the nearest attacker, slamming him hard into the nearby wall. Daniel then drew his handgun and, in broad daylight, stormed into the room, shooting two more of Min's men dead.

The room exuded intimacy. Daniel glanced across the lengthy space and settled onto a sofa near the far wall. Min had been knocked to the floor, looking up at Daniel as he sat up and leaned against the wall. "Daniel Faron, how your legal morals have faltered," Min remarked, furrowing his brows into a scowl. A beam of light streaked through the window, casting a harsh line across Min's face. "You don't have to hide the fact that you don't trust them from me. Every man questions his convictions to his country at some point. Eventually, you won't be able to provide them with what they want, and you'll be left for dead, just like your friend Ramirez."

Daniel peered through the blinds of the far-side window, his gaze fixed on the narrow street below. After a quick glance back at Min, he knew better than to engage in a debate. Min was infamous for his persuasive speeches, and Daniel had no desire to endure an argument whose conclusions he already knew. Engaging would undoubtedly expose him to unwelcome truths, causing him great distress.

A knock interrupted his thoughts, prompting Daniel to approach the door with a gun in hand. Opening it, he found a man with a briefcase and a fedora. Neither of them uttered a word. Daniel's gaze shifted across the room to where Min leaned against the wall. "He's all yours. I'll report it in," Daniel said before stepping into the hallway. "We need to go after him now," he asserted as soon as the line connected with Paul. However, Paul hesitated, preferring a measured response rather than rushing into an operation without thorough planning. He was wary of the consequences rebounding on him. Paul's paranoia grew, fearing exposure for his involvement in forging documents and gathering sensitive information. Although it had been a necessary means to an end, he wasn't particularly proud of his actions, yet he acknowledged they were not his most egregious offenses.

"Hold on, Daniel," Paul interjected. "What do you know that I don't?"

"Nothing," Daniel replied. "But it would be foolish to assume they lack digital copies. My guess is that it's stored online. If news of Min's demise spreads, Gaillard can release the information at any moment through a wireless link. The same would have happened if we had targeted Gaillard first. It's a fail-safe. If someone threatens them, they can release the information, making themselves politically untouchable."

The Collateral Dividend

Paul sighed deeply, running his hands through his hair, and checked his watch. If they were to act swiftly, they needed to move immediately. "Well, we still don't have a precise location for Gaillard," he pointed out, highlighting the obvious obstacle. They had a general idea but lacked certainty.

"But Min does," Daniel stated, glancing back at the doorway he had just exited.

"That depends on whether you think he'll talk. Do you believe he will?" Paul pondered the question before responding.

Daniel wasn't certain, but it wouldn't hurt to try. It was then that Daniel asked if he could return to Vienna, citing exhaustion as the reason. He assured Paul it wasn't personal, but the day's events had taken their toll, and he needed rest. Paul saw through the feeble attempt to conceal his discomfort with witnessing another interrogation. The last one had been horrifying, haunting his thoughts.

"I don't think you would be of much use elsewhere," Paul remarked, reluctantly acknowledging Daniel's request. "However, there is some paperwork that should be dealt with soon. If you prefer, you can handle that." Paul understood Daniel's inability to openly express his anxieties, so he approached the situation with caution. He treated his field operatives as delicate machines, requiring maintenance and care, not to be pushed beyond their limits.

Min proved to be elusive and resistant to torture. However, over time, exhaustion eroded his sense of right and wrong. Min had been trained to withstand torture and interrogation, but there came a point when self-preservation overshadowed his stubborn silence. He realized they would never release him unless he cooperated, and Gaillard's cause was faltering. It became clear that the only way for Min to see freedom again was to betray Gaillard. The path of least resistance was the most viable. Nearly ten hours later, in the dead of night, Daniel returned to Vienna, and Min's voice finally cracked. He looked up pathetically at the interrogator. "Wilkes Hall," he managed to utter. "He's at Wilkes Hall." Exhausted, Min's head slumped onto his chest. The interrogator smiled, gently supporting Min's head and patting him on the back, then promptly called Paul.

The following day, Paul met with Harrison to review their findings. The remnants of the spy ring had been subdued, and Harrison sat in Paul's office, cane in hand, contemplating his role. "So we've apprehended them all," Harrison remarked, to which Paul nodded, offering a smile.

"It seems so. Harrison, I genuinely appreciate your assistance," Paul expressed his gratitude, while Harrison brushed it off, enjoying the opportunity to become involved once again. "If there's anything else you think I might find interesting, feel free to share it with me. I'll be happy to take a look."

Paul nodded. "For now, we're just tying up loose ends," he replied, and both men understood the implications. The custodians had done their job, and now it was time to deal with those responsible without hesitation.

"That's my boy," Harrison said with a smile. "And what about the senate hearings?"

Paul shook his head. The proceedings had turned into a mess, raising legislative questions that threatened to undermine the current government. "We've been closely monitoring them," Paul admitted. He contemplated eliminating Nathan Ramirez to simplify matters. He had grown less hesitant, making deliberate moves. Removing Ramirez wasn't an attempt to silence opposition, but rather a step to eliminate potential complications. No one was fooling anyone. The hearings meant Dunes would have to resign. No government, especially a minority one, could withstand the relentless scrutiny of the judiciary. The official opposition demanded retribution, and the President would be forced to comply. Without the option to prorogue, the government had to provide answers. The committee overseeing the controversy would undoubtedly continue digging into Nathan Ramirez's background and any potential associates.

At least he was shielded from the witch-hunt, Paul thought. His boldness exemplified his confidence. Throughout his education, Paul had delved deep into the world of politics. It was a peculiar realm, understood by only a few. Paul glanced at Harrison, shaking his head. Listening to politics often made his blood boil, as most people failed to grasp how things truly worked, their meanings. What Farragut Center was doing was legally justified. "The problem is that politics is too frequently muddled by those who misunderstand the realities of espionage and the law," Paul expressed his frustration.

Harrison groaned discontentedly. "Then they need to be educated, but political activism serves as an assurance," he argued.

Paul snorted, realizing that these individuals would never comprehend. "The Greeks recognized the flaws of democracy early in their experiments," Harrison pointed out, explaining how the Greeks believed that majority rule was a closer approximation to the greater good. Paul wasn't entirely convinced; perhaps those who understood politics best were better suited to lead. He couldn't help but think of Socrates' concept of philosopher kings, an idea centered on fulfilling the common good administered by a select few. But was that truly

The Collateral Dividend

democracy? Such governance certainly didn't allow for free will, and what purpose did all this serve if not to protect the right to free will?

"Have you spoken to Rachel?" Harrison abruptly shifted the conversation's tone, diverting from their previous discussion. Paul shook his head, indicating he hadn't. Harrison grunted, leaning forward in his chair to rest his arms on the cane's handle. "Paul, there's a secret about life that I discovered too late for my own good. I regret it every day since I found out," he began, capturing Paul's undivided attention. Paul took a sip of coffee and turned off the computer screen, visually demonstrating his complete focus on Harrison's words.

"It's exceptionally rare to find someone you love wholeheartedly, someone you can't go a day without thinking about. There's comfort in that, but often, that comfort betrays you. The biggest mistake I ever made was forgetting how much I valued her. You only bring pain to yourself and others when you subject yourself to loneliness just to test whether you can live without someone," Harrison confessed, clearing his throat. "Now, Paul, I've known you for many years, and maybe I'm completely wrong about this, but I have never seen you happier, even when you're angry, than when you're with Rachel. Everyone's journey has its bumps, but don't let a few obstacles on the road prevent you from reaching your desired destination."

Struggling to stand up, Harrison finally managed to rise from his chair. He approached the office door and swung it open. "How about you arrange for one of the company cars to take me home?" he requested, grunting slightly. Moving on from their conversation, Harrison left Paul deep in thought, staring at the wall.

"Absolutely," Paul said, leading him downstairs and helping him into the back of the car. Afterwards, Paul went upstairs, trying to process what Harrison had said. A strong wave of doubt washed over him, making him uncomfortably warm. Had he made the right decision? Or was Harrison correct? What troubled him even more than his own self-doubt was the lack of opportunity to sit back and contemplate the consequences and effects of his choice. Almost two years had been dedicated relentlessly to the program. Paul had spent nearly all his time in the office, and in the past two weeks alone, he had only gone home once, if one could even call a hotel room home. Since the breakup, he hadn't even had a chance to search for a place to rent. In that realization, he finally identified the gnawing thoughts in his mind as a peculiar form of boredom. He hadn't engaged in anything outside of work for months, and apart from interacting with assets Ted and Harrison, Rachel had been his sole connection to the outside world. Lost in his own thoughts, sanity felt like it was slipping away.

Paul had left everything behind in the house. During their discussion on the drive, he had agreed not to return. The things he would need to retrieve were merely material possessions and temporary. There were no valuables he desired, though Rachel might have argued otherwise, but at the time, she wasn't in the mood for another argument. The house felt empty, almost darker, but perhaps that was just a reflection of her mood. In the first month, she clung to the hope that Paul would wake up one day and realize his mistake. She wished he would storm in and confess that he couldn't live without her. But that day never came.

Gradually, Rachel began to branch out and spend more time with her friends, some of whom she hadn't seen since college. She attempted dating, but it always left her feeling uninspired and uninterested. When things were good between her and Paul, they were amazing. That feeling became her litmus test, but she failed to find a chemistry that matched. However, a more diligent approach would have been to compare the lows, for they were the catalyst that led to her decision to end the relationship.

She was determined not to regress under any circumstances. Rachel knew she deserved better treatment and wasn't willing to allow it to happen again. Yet, there were moments when thoughts of Paul invaded her mind. When dining at a new restaurant or passing by the national mall, she would find herself thinking about him and wondering. On one occasion, she had called Harrison, asking if it would be alright to talk. "You did the right thing, dear," he had replied. "Be prepared to accept that he may never be ready or may never return. But there's value in hearing him out if he's willing to change. You wouldn't be foolish for considering it, just like you wouldn't refuse to return to a restaurant simply because they once refused to seat you. If he can prove he's changed, it's not foolish to give it a thought." Harrison's advice seemed invaluable to her, or at least that's how she interpreted it. It was clear they loved each other, but Harrison cautioned that Paul's words may never align with his actions, presenting a real danger. Still, Harrison believed it would be unwise for Rachel to dismiss the idea of listening to Paul. If she wasn't interested, it would be more beneficial to focus on moving on rather than wondering if Paul's actions could ever change. After some time, it became evident that Harrison's advice was sound. Rachel pondered the situation extensively and concluded that she desired a relationship but refused to accept the same mistreatment. Paul needed to understand the consequences of his actions.

The Collateral Dividend

Ironically, less than a month later, a knock on the door disrupted Rachel's thoughts. Opening it, she found Paul standing there, a mist in his eyes as he stared at her for a long while. Neither of them said a word. Earlier, Paul had stood in his office, fixated on a bottle of cologne. Would using it help regain Rachel's trust? "I was wrong," he finally said when she answered the door. Tension lingered between them. It was the first time they had seen each other since their fight, and Paul would have been lying if he claimed he hadn't thought about her every day.

Rachel tried to remain closed off, reluctant to welcome Paul with open arms after his prolonged silence. "Paul, it doesn't work like that," she said candidly. "I don't trust you."

"You certainly don't have any reason to," Paul conceded. "Can we start again?" he asked, hoping for a fresh start to prove he had changed. Stepping forward into the doorway, he reached out and held her hand, his other hand gently resting on the nape of her neck as he kissed her. "I've missed you," he said softly.

Rachel let out a deep breath, feeling conflicted about going against her own words. However, she would be lying if she said this wasn't the outcome she had hoped for during their break. The prospect of moving on seemed messy and lethargic. Uncertainty plagued her mind, wondering what Paul had been up to during the long periods of no contact. This lingering doubt threatened their future.

"I've missed you too, Paul," she replied, emphasizing that for her to feel more comfortable, he needed to start trying and showing that he was willing to put in the work required for the relationship. Rachel took a moment to look into his eyes. "I think it's best that you're aware I don't entirely trust you," she said. "I'd like to take it slow." Rachel's vulnerability and lack of trust presented a significant obstacle that needed to be overcome if they were to move forward. It would be a slow process, and she still wasn't sure if she could fully overcome it.

THE CONFRONTING SHADOW

The house was grand and old, shrouded in the summer mist that crept up from the cool lake after heavy rain, enveloping the evening mountains. It surrounded the country house, choking it for the better part of the day until the sun cast long shadows near twilight. Situated nearly a mile east of Vienna, the castle stood on the outskirts of the sleepy town of Enzersdorf, gazing wearily at the distant city like a tired aristocrat.

Daniel had rented a car and made the journey from Vienna to the tranquil town of Enzersdorf, just outside the federal district. He had yet to sleep, still clad in yesterday's clothes, which hung untidily from his shoulders. His unkempt hair was pulled back, perhaps disguising the fact that he hadn't rested, save for leaning his head against the train window during the trip into Vienna.

With an obsessive mind, Daniel embarked on his day. In the late afternoon, he arrived at the imposing house, driving up the winding road for nearly a hundred yards to the front gates. He parked in the gravel car park nestled at the foot of the cresting hill, where the estate stood. The surrounding Vienna woods suffocated any hint of the outside world, and silence delicately hung on the rustling leaves.

Sitting in the car, Daniel took a moment to steady his breathing. This was something he had yearned for a long time. The peril of carelessness had reached its peak. He closed his eyes and attempted to still his trembling hands. Taking a deep breath, he finally emerged from the car and made his way towards the path leading to the front of the estate. The arched front entrance seemed diminutive compared to the tall wings that flanked it on either side. The central building, with its subtle off-white coloring and black clay-shingled roof, was reminiscent of a bygone era.

Daniel stepped into the building, acknowledging the front desk manager with a polite yet uncomfortable gesture. Passing through the intimate atrium, he proceeded to the left, beyond the private dining hall. The walls of the hall were painted in a muted green, and a sign on the door identified it as the green room.

The layout of the old castle proved challenging to navigate. The main house, relatively newer than the surrounding structures, was constructed with battleship grey bricks, dating back to the 18th century. Adjacent to the old main house, a red brick mansion in old French styling stood revitalized. To the right of the main house's conservatory, there was an entrance leading to a large and imposing castle that extended over the cliff, descending two or three stories. Guests would stay in this castle, traversing the colonnades lining the narrow castle walls.

Daniel studied a map on the wall for several moments before crossing the large common rooms. Each of the three hearths crackled with fire, casting a shadowy ambience that exuded intimacy.

For a brief moment, Daniel stood still, sensing that lingering any longer would make him seem indecisive. He needed to walk with purpose, displaying a consistent and confident demeanor, asserting his right to be there. The back half of the ground floor was dominated by the dining hall, blocked by a black grand piano adorned with thick candles. The old hardwood floors, weathered and neglected, exuded a charm befitting their age. Antique rugs adorned high-traffic areas, and small clusters of chairs were arranged throughout the seating areas. Daniel imagined the room would be enchanting in winter, though the absence of central heating meant heavy blankets, sweaters, and a warm fire would be essential.

Daniel continued past the largest of the private rooms until he reached a small hallway with two closed doors, leading to a vintage elevator. The door directly in front of him was slightly ajar, and sounds of the bustling kitchen staff seeped through the cracks. Daniel opted for the second door, descending the stairwell into the narrow basement hallways. Alone in this hollowed path, he was reminded of a faded memory he had all but forgotten—a recollection of an underground facility with medical connotations. The gleaming pot lighting along the narrow plaster walls startled him, and suddenly he found himself standing near a curved stairwell at the end of the hall. The hallway led to curving stairwells, following the contours of the castle tower, ascending to enclosed colonnades providing access to guest rooms. Glass windows offered views of the main house, while guarded doorways led to suites perched on the cliff, overlooking the countryside.

In one corner, there was a maid's closet. Daniel entered it and placed one of the wooden room service trays on his shoulder, creating the appearance of being prepared. He closed the maid's closet, walked down the hall to the far corner, checked his watch, and at quarter past the hour, he knocked on the door twice. He positioned himself in a way that the room service tray obstructed his face from the peephole. The sound of the deadbolt retracting reached Daniel's ears as the door opened slightly. Seizing the opportunity, Daniel threw his shoulder into the door, causing it to swing open and knock the man at the door off balance. The man stumbled down the stairwell and into the living room.

E.R. Wychwood

With his weapon drawn, Daniel swiftly closed the door, firing a shot that ended the man's life. The sound of the handgun was faint, drowned out by the ensuing silence and the clatter of broken dinnerware. The wooden tray fell to the floor, cracking, and porcelain plates shattered, creating a messy blend of old wine and food juices.

Daniel cautiously advanced into the room, his gun held out, his breathing steady but rapid. Taking cover behind a corner, he observed as another man appeared, walking past the corner and approaching the fallen comrade on the floor. Capitalizing on his advantageous position, Daniel shot the man in the back of the neck, causing him to collapse. A third man emerged, prompting Daniel to swing around the corner and fire two more shots. The recoil of the gun unsettled him, and a bullet grazed the far wall. His heart pounded in his ears. The return fire shattered a nearby lamp, but the third man had already been hit, convulsing and falling backward onto the ground near the kitchenette.

Emerging from his hiding spot, Daniel pointed the gun forward, assuming a wide stance. With his right hand, he retrieved a device from his trouser pocket that resembled a flashlight. Activating it, the room's lights flickered, and the nearby television displayed a blank blue screen. The computer emitted a final whimper before falling silent.

Gaillard, having finished washing his hands in the washroom, had witnessed the events unfolding at the main room's entrance. By the time Daniel reached the room, Gaillard stood at the washroom doorframe, holding a towel. Positioned on the far side of the room, Daniel could see the entire length of the room from over the curvature of the bed. Lifeless bodies lay scattered across the floor, blood forming a slippery pool. Another guard lay face down near the writing desk. Gaillard walked over to the man, checking his pulse, only to confirm that he had been shot in the chest. Gaillard looked over at Daniel, who stood on the far side of the room, gun still drawn, pointing directly at the Frenchman.

Daniel gestured towards the sofa positioned in the middle of the living room, calmly instructing Gaillard to sit down. Gaillard, raising his hands, cautiously walked towards the sofa and complied with Daniel's command. He glanced awkwardly at Daniel, then surveyed the room, which included a bowl of snacks on the coffee table. Daniel maintained his aim at Gaillard, saying nothing as he picked at the nuts, specifically searching for cashews. Throughout this process, he tapped his foot with methodical precision, matching the rhythm of the wood clock on the mantle. After cleaning his mouth and placing the napkin on the table, Daniel stood up and surveyed the room once again.

The Collateral Dividend

Daniel crossed the room and picked up a wooden chair by its back, carrying it over to where Gaillard was seated. He placed it down and took a seat. "What a coincidence to have you here tonight, Mister Gaillard," Daniel said, picking up a homemade French fry from the nearest plate and eating it. He scratched the back of his head and ran his hand through his hair, as if to pull it away from his forehead. "It has been a long year, hasn't it?" He smiled. "You know, I can't begin to express how deeply I have wanted this moment to come." Daniel's kind smile offset his harsh, cynical tone.

Gaillard replied softly, "Business is business," looking at Daniel with a sheepish grin. Daniel found it eerie how Gaillard looked directly at him, as if he could see through Daniel's soul and read his mind with piercing clarity.

Daniel was hoping the juxtaposition of the dead bodies would create a more explicit effect. Staging dramatic illusions was one of his favorite aspects of this job. He enjoyed setting up implied conclusions so that his intellectual adversaries could carry the thought forward. He found this method of mental sparring much more effective at conveying his message.

The Frenchman shrugged and said in a cold, matter-of-fact tone, "It was never personal. With the Yates family, there was a hint of revenge, yes, but stealing from the markets was merely an opportunity. I couldn't let all those banks come after me and not retaliate." Gaillard had clearly lost his sense of timing. No one in the financial industry had even been concerned with Gaillard's actions.

"What was her involvement in all this?" Daniel asked, sitting back now with his hands laced between his thighs, examining the wounds on his knuckles. He couldn't help but think of her, with her soft skin and brilliant blue eyes, so different from his own cold, ironical gaze. "Who?" Gaillard asked, realizing that Daniel was referring to Isabel. He smirked. "She played you better than anyone could." Daniel couldn't tell if Gaillard was lying. His emotions couldn't discern the difference.

"I'm sure she did," Daniel said. He didn't want to believe Gaillard, but he had to accept the possibility. For now, he needed to try and out-bluff Gaillard. "Where is she?"

"I don't know," Gaillard replied, and Daniel gave him a look that conveyed, "Please, we aren't fooling anyone here. The game is done; just tell me what I want to know." "You see, this is what you don't understand, old boy. You can't arrest me. To everyone other than your precious little Farragut Center, I've done nothing wrong. The world believes in due diligence, justice, and conscience, and through those lenses, you can do nothing to me."

E.R. Wychwood

Daniel looked back at the dead body on the other side of the room. "I don't think we're going to be involving the legal system any time soon."

"You're bluffing," Gaillard said. "If you wanted me dead, I would be dead already. You need something from me, and yet the risk of keeping me alive is immeasurable. I am a walking liability for your leash-holders, but they are unwilling to admit that my wealth makes me untouchable for people like you."

"Try me," Daniel paused, and Gaillard said nothing. "What exactly happened with her?"

"Ask her yourself."

Daniel smiled. "You and I know that's not possible."

Gaillard smiled and snickered, assuming that she had been targeted and eventually removed like Min, a casualty of the underground war he had waged. He quite liked his own ideas about his role in all of this. He saw himself as the kingpin, the measured and reasoned voice that would not be silenced. They craved men like him, men who would fuel their agencies and special access programs with illegal information for a special price and an ignorance compliance committee. He wouldn't end up dead; he would end up employed by them.

"At first, we thought you had picked her up and whisked her away to some place. But it eventually became clear that she had merely run away from you," he said, letting out a long breath and intentionally creating an uncomfortable pause. "When I eventually found her, I knew her death would bring her actions under suspicion. It was better that she remained invisible. It left the illusion that she had stolen the money herself."

"How did she end up where she was?" Daniel asked.

"She retained her own free will until it became clear she was considering returning to society. We picked her up in Malaysia less than a month ago. Tzavaras was kind enough to keep her under house arrest in Greece while he worked on his little project of toppling the government. Eventually, I would have liked to see her fall ill and die. It would have been a nice capstone to the whole affair. What ever happened to Tzavaras? Is he also dead?" Gaillard sat back in his chair, appearing sheepishly caught in a white lie. Daniel couldn't ignore Gaillard's casual demeanor throughout their discussion.

"Not yet," Daniel replied, trying to convey the same calmness as Gaillard. He looked up at Gaillard with a withering grin, and the Frenchman suddenly realized he had been played into divulging information. Daniel had bluffed.

"So somehow you thought you'd get away with this? How did you expect to pin this plot onto someone else without people like us finding out?" Daniel asked.

Gaillard laughed, his head drawing back exaggeratedly. "You and I both know, dear boy, that the only reason you stumbled upon all this was dumb luck. If you think it was because of your sharp wits or clever mind, you truly are a goddamn idiot. It was never about 'getting away' with anything, Daniel Faron. It's about changing the world. That, I'm sure, you know a little something about. I have no doubt your reliance on necessary means to reach necessary ends will soon make you no different than I."

Daniel let out a deep breath, resembling a grunted sigh. "Philippe, you and I are nothing alike."

"We are everything alike, Daniel," Gaillard said, leaning forward. "Revenge, at least, is an emotion that runs in a harsh cyclical motion, a flat circle of time."

At that moment, there was a knock on the door. Daniel got up, opened it, and allowed the housecleaners to come in and begin their work. He returned to the room, sitting across from Gaillard. His arm rested along the side of the chair, and he crossed his leg over the other. Daniel looked at Gaillard for a long while, as if expecting him to say more.

"If you hadn't gotten involved and caused her to run away, no one would have gotten hurt. We wouldn't have had to involve her at all, you know. Daniel, you are just like me because you manipulate people and hurt them carelessly and brutally. What is the phrase you Americans love? We are two sides of the same coin," Gaillard said, laughing. "After all this time, that's what gets you, doesn't it?" he added. Daniel tried to ignore the belligerent Frenchman, but his rhetoric had begun to gnaw at Daniel's conscience.

"I disagree. I know the difference between right and wrong. There is a line that I won't cross," Daniel asserted.

"Everyone has a line they won't cross, Daniel. But when you continually push that line further, eventually there may as well be no line at all. We both do the same things; it's just a matter of whose will is stronger and whose cause is more convincing. My efforts are no more just than yours—the difference is that my pragmatic values have the tolerance to flex underneath the weight of my actions. You Americans and your rigid values and weighty actions will always be faced with the crushing belief that what you do must be right and must be the only way."

Daniel tried not to dwell on what Gaillard was saying. "Are you almost done?" he eventually asked with a hint of sarcasm.

E.R. Wychwood

"I'm better off dead now than alive," Gaillard said, and he was right. The government would be lucky if they could touch him. Most evidence was classified, and that which wasn't was circumstantial at best. He either needed to be locked away for good or killed. "But you and I both know that if you were to kill me, you'd only confirm that you are no better than me," Gaillard said with a smile.

Daniel agreed. "There are those who don't deserve to live and those who deserve to die. If I'm incapable of granting both, then why should I deprive one of either?" Daniel had thought long and hard about this day and what he would do when it came. Finally, once he realized that Gaillard would not respond, he continued, "Your men were in self-defense, but you're right. My judgment on your life would make me no better."

"Are you not going to kill me, Mister Faron? After all the pain I put you through, surely you must feel some desire to fulfill business as usual," Gaillard asked bluntly, his blond hair fallen forward along his right temple. His mustache was much thicker than Daniel had vividly remembered. "Min's people will come for us, you know."

"Then I do hope you can defend yourself," Daniel said as he rose up and tossed the crust of the bread slice onto the coffee table.

"If you're not here to kill me, then why are you here?" Gaillard inquired.

Daniel walked over to Philippe Gaillard and pulled out his reading glasses from his breast pocket, handing them to the Frenchman. "There is a cyanide capsule inside the left arm if you feel the need to take your own life before the remainder of my people arrive. Otherwise, you can wait to enjoy the remainder of your life somewhere between here and Diego Garcia," he said, threading the suppressor so it came off the handgun and returning it to his coat pocket. "Oh, and don't worry. We'll be sure to parade you through Paris in your sorrows before we lock you away. Your legacy charity will only wither and die, bankrupt and pathetically remembered."

Gaillard sat there and stared up at Daniel, remaining silent in the empty room. He was no longer interested in escape. There was a warm, searing feeling that cascaded over his face, warming his skin to a hot boil. He knew it was over. Gaillard sat there for a few moments, fiddling with the frames before he cracked the seal on the backside of the left arm and let a capsule fall into his hand. He stared at it and then up at the other men in the room, who completely ignored his presence. It was as if Gaillard were not even there. He put the capsule into his mouth and bit down onto the aluminum casing. The cyanide spilled out and, on contact, began to eat away at bone and melt the fragility of his skull. Gaillard looked down at his hands and then closed his eyes.

Paul had told Daniel that he had done good work. The house cleaners had staged the house with a 22 caliber Makarov and put it into Gaillard's hand, making it appear as if he had murdered his own security and then himself. They left no suicide note; notes were too cliché and there was no need to explain the actions of an unstable man. "You were right," Paul had said to Daniel when the young man called from the train the next afternoon. Isabel had never been involved. "Gaillard took the easy route. Though I'm surprised you didn't act on the opportunity yourself," Paul said.

"Why?" Daniel asked, almost offended. He was wearing a button-down shirt and cashmere sweater, a subtle reference to his need for comfort. Today he felt vulnerable.

"Daniel, you've been waiting for this for a long time. I'm surprised you didn't capitalize on the opportunity for closure."

He had been thinking about his actions over the last few years for most of the ride. "I'm not proud of what we had to do to get to that point. I think when this is all said and done, we need to talk about where we both go from here," Daniel suggested.

"Just remember what's at stake here," Paul cautioned.

Daniel looked out the window of the train as they crossed through Macedonia. The sloping arid hills reached far into the sky before stopping abruptly at a snow-capped peak. He was due to arrive in Thessaloniki later that same day. Daniel tried to keep himself occupied with thoughts other than the sense of regret he associated with Isabel. However, he found it difficult. There hadn't been a day since that he hadn't wondered what had triggered her to leave. In some ways, what Gaillard had said resonated with him much stronger than he had wished. If Daniel hadn't been involved, she might not have been involved at all. But there was still the possibility of salvaging this. He had to believe that right up until the last moments of his life, he could rectify his mistake. It was a rather pessimistic thought, blaming oneself for events beyond direct control, but that was often what defined Daniel's beliefs.

There was a disconnect between his feelings for Farragut Center and his feelings toward his profession. He believed that he was being manipulated, having witnessed the center's ruthlessness and how quickly they discarded field assets. He had also observed their treatment of others and himself, which made him uncertain about trusting them. The fear of being made a fool and the possibility of a cold sweat overwhelmed him. He took a deep breath, attempting to dismiss these thoughts and focus on the task at hand. However, distractions persisted. Despite the pressures, he knew that staying present was crucial for his sanity.

"Suddenly," Daniel asked Paul, "have you ever considered that we might not be doing the right thing? We achieved our goals and did what was necessary, but at what moral cost?"

Paul had never been a firm believer in morals; he was more pragmatic, prioritizing convenience as truth. They had saved lives and protected American sovereignty, which he believed was the ultimate goal. The concept of moral culpability seemed absurd to him. As long as they didn't unjustly infringe on written rights, Paul could sleep at night. He couldn't understand how someone like Rachel could fall for someone as straightforward as him. Her work focused on establishing the idea that all humans had rights beyond institutional constructs, but Paul didn't share that belief. It aligned with his Lockean perspective, although he acknowledged that many disagreed.

"Dangerous thinking, Daniel," Paul eventually responded. "We have a purpose here, and we did the right thing. I've forwarded the details to your phone. The President publicly condemned Alekos Tzavaras' actions and assured the international community that we would do everything in our power to prevent his attempts to topple a democratically elected government."

The region of Arcadia wasn't as vast as its history suggested. However, there was a small village named Karytaina nestled in the foothills of the River Alpheios. Its lineage could be traced back to a crusader conquest in 1205 CE. Outsiders often considered it a backwater area of Greece. Karytaina had a population of barely two hundred, and the village exuded a sense of tranquility that appealed to Tzavaras.

Tzavaras' family originated from Karytaina. They had sought refuge here while fleeing the Ottoman Empire. Tzavaras found symbolism in his family's escape from the empire, believing that it was for the purpose of growing strong and returning.

During the civil war that engulfed Greece, Tzavaras became a prominent figure. His family owned a sprawling villa located in the hills above Karytaina's city center. The seclusion provided an ideal command post for Tzavaras, as he led his rebels in their march toward Athens. Thanks to meticulous military planning and significant financial support from Philippe Gaillard, Tzavaras gained popularity and became untouchable by the government.

When Daniel arrived in Corinth by train, he realized he needed to rent a car to travel further into the heart of the Peloponnese peninsula. The narrow and

The Collateral Dividend

winding road led him through the city of Karytaina before heading north. Daniel parked his car in a public lot that overlooked the river valley to the south. The road was paved with white cobblestone, similar to the rock used to construct the quaint houses with colorful wooden shutters and faded red shingles. Green shrubs adorned parts of the road. Stepping out of the car, Daniel gazed up at the steep hill, noticing a stairwell between two houses that ascended to the road's level. He climbed to the top, reaching the edge of the city, and looked down into the valley before turning his attention to the villa perched on the hillside's peak.

The house stood as a stronghold, fortified by Tzavaras' newfound publicity, which attracted fanatics willing to die for the ultranationalist cause. If Daniel had attempted to take on the building alone, certain death awaited him. Unfortunately, the urgency of the operation prevented them from exploiting any security weaknesses. Given more time, they could have patiently waited for Tzavaras to leave or travel elsewhere, taking advantage of potential accidents or unforeseen events.

Farragut Center found itself coordinating a military operation rather than a civilian one, a deliberate decision. While the Greeks refrained from targeting Tzavaras, the Americans had no qualms about doing so. Daniel would lead the charge, advancing as far forward as possible on his own. His path would likely take him through the western half of the villa, toward the south wing. Paul had arranged for Delta Force operators to create a diversion on the east side of the building, drawing attention away from their true objective.

Daniel ascended the stairwell and knocked on the door, waiting for an eye-level letterbox to open, revealing a pair of eyes on the other side. "Who are you?" a voice inquired in Greek.

"I'm a friend of Tzavaras. I have something from Gaillard," Daniel responded, prompting the man to ask for the item to be handed through the opening. However, Daniel stated that it wasn't something physical; he was meant to deliver it directly to Tzavaras himself. He also mentioned the security word from the previous week, "Tartarus."

"That was last week's," the man replied. Using his silver tongue, Daniel managed to momentarily convince the Greek that he was mistaken, making him believe that Daniel had knowledge but had simply gotten the details mixed up. It was an old spy trick that often proved useful in extracting information willingly from adversaries.

Upon entering the main courtyard, Daniel was informed that he would be taken upstairs. A man in a suit, suspicious of Daniel, asked, "Are you one of

Gaillard's?" He intended to determine whether Daniel needed to be searched for weapons. Tzavaras had explicitly instructed that Gaillard and his people should not be subjected to searches, as a gesture of trust and gratitude for Gaillard's support. Daniel nodded in response, and the man pondered the matter briefly. "Where's Gaillard?" he inquired, already aware of the answer, though few others were.

"Vienna," Daniel replied. "If you'd like, I can give him a call, but I'd be sure to inform him that you were giving me a hard time."

The man fiddled with his thumb, standing about ten yards ahead of Daniel. It was clear that his jaw had set into place. "That won't be necessary," Tzavaras was informed and was to meet Daniel upstairs. Several cars were parked on the far side of the courtyard, near a grand entrance and a fountain. One of the more casually dressed Greeks, a man who appeared to be of higher rank than the one at the door, signaled for Daniel to follow him down the far side of the courtyard through a side door and down a narrow hallway.

Daniel could think on his feet, but when the Greek asked him whether he knew what had happened to Piere, it quickly became clear that his cover had been blown. Daniel hadn't even thought the question through. He wasn't even aware of who Piere was. It would have been foolish for anyone from Gaillard's camp to not know who Piere was or what had happened to him. The realization struck Daniel almost instantaneously. He was the first to react, swiftly knocking down the suited Greek and the other two men standing behind him. Drawing his gun, he pointed it down the hallway.

The first shots came from his gun. As he turned the corner and ascended the first flight of stairs, he shot and killed the three men standing there, though one of them managed to get a few shots off before falling. That was when the shooting began on the far side of the building. Hopefully, it would divert attention and support to the opposite side. Daniel hoped it would provide an opportunity for him to slip past undetected, though he knew it was likely wishful thinking.

It wasn't until he reached the kitchen that he encountered another firefight. The group had planned to flank the attackers from the east, but once Daniel's position was exposed, any element of surprise was lost. He found himself pinned down against an alcove in the hallway, periodically firing shots to keep the attackers at bay. Across the hall, about four yards behind him, there was a doorway leading to a library with a window. Daniel timed his run so that when he flung himself across the hallway, he hoped to avoid getting shot.

The Collateral Dividend

Returning fire, he tumbled back into the library and slammed the door shut, falling hard to the ground. He pointed his gun at the door and waited, but nothing happened. Daniel got up and surveyed the room. On the far side, just beyond the rolling wall ladder, there was a window. He walked over to it.

Daniel Faron opened the window and looked in both directions. The ledge of the villa window hung over a steep cliff, and the hill dropped down into a valley a few hundred yards away. He was terrified of heights, and the sight of the seven-story drop below made him dizzy. Checking his pocket, he found one more magazine and two bullets in his gun. He knew he couldn't fight his way through the hallway, so he would be forced to scale the exterior wall.

He turned back around and considered his options. Climbing up the ladder, he released the bolts holding the book frame to the wall, causing it to nudge out of place. Daniel jumped off the ladder, kicked the wheels out, and the entire bookshelf collapsed, resting precariously on the ladder. He pushed the ladder across the room and positioned it so that when the door swung in, it would knock the ladder over, bringing down the bookshelf. As an added measure, a grenade, primed with its pin connected by a string to the door handle, was there for good measure.

Daniel pressed himself against the alcove of the window, trying to catch his breath. Glancing down at the cliff below, he kicked a rock off the ledge to gauge the height. As he reached up and grabbed the ledge of the floor above, he noticed natural grips in the stone used to build the exterior wall. Daniel scaled the wall until he was beside the window. His feet dangled from the ground, and he reached out, attempting to catch the lip of the windowsill with his extended foot. But as he lunged forward to take refuge on the windowsill, he lost his footing and fell hard.

He had nearly fallen entirely off the building but managed to hold onto the ledge and pull himself up. Trying to map out the floor, he realized there was a winding hallway that stretched from one side of the house to the other. They had bribed a local maid to help them reconstruct the building's layout from memory. Paul had made sure to link the schematics to Daniel's phone, and now Daniel sat near the door in a bedroom, scrolling through the layout, attempting to commit it to memory.

According to the maid's account, there was a locked wooden door in a part of the house she was only allowed to enter occasionally. She described a quiet and sad British woman usually present there. The maid recalled it being in the south wing, on the far side of the house. That was where Daniel wanted to go first. He took the hallway until he reached a small courtyard, and across from it stood a large wooden door, guarded by a man. Daniel shot him dead as soon as he stood up, and he crumpled to the ground.

The padlocked door resisted Daniel's search for a key, and finding none on the dead Greek's body, he used the remaining bullets in his magazine to weaken the wood around the clasp. With a few forceful kicks, the door swung open, revealing a dark room filled with swirling dust illuminated by sunlight. Daniel pointed his handgun forward and surveyed the room.

Suddenly, Tzavaras emerged from the right and hit him hard, reaching for his own gun to shoot Daniel point-blank. However, the gun was pointed at the ceiling, and Daniel wrestled with Tzavaras until it discharged the remaining bullets into the roof. Daniel tried to gain the upper hand, knocking Tzavaras' legs out from under him, causing Alekos to stumble forward. The gun fell to the side.

Tzavaras punched back, and before Daniel could subdue him, Tzavaras landed a hard blow across Daniel's face, tackling him into the wooden door, which broke off its hinges and crashed onto the concrete patio. Tzavaras positioned himself so that Daniel was beneath him, rolling to get a firm grip around Daniel's neck. Tzavaras was a skilled fighter, far better than Daniel. Daniel struck Tzavaras repeatedly in the gut until his grip weakened, allowing Daniel to scramble up. Daniel swung, but Alekos ducked and delivered a powerful punch that stunned Daniel, followed by a series of punches to his face until Daniel fell back and collapsed against the patio wall. Blood dripped from his mouth as he sat there in a daze, while Tzavaras crossed the room and picked up a handgun from the ground. He returned to where Daniel was seated and spat on him.

"You, my friend, are going to die," Tzavaras said, standing up and clenching his teeth. He smirked before stomping on Daniel's right knee repeatedly, causing Daniel to cry out in pain. After a while, it seemed that Daniel could no longer endure the agony of his torn ligaments.

After a while, it became apparent that Daniel was alone. He mustered the strength to crawl towards the handgun lying near the corner of the patio, with patio furniture and a nearby pool in sight. Daniel speculated that the ledge across the way offered a splendid view. He managed to cover three-quarters of the distance when a gunshot echoed, and Alekos Tzavaras reappeared on the patio, accompanied by Isabel. Earlier, Isabel had been staying in one of Gaillard's guarded rooms, where she was treated with some respect. Tzavaras had been kind enough to offer her accommodations in one wing of his home, occasionally visiting her and insisting they go for a swim. However, he dared not

The Collateral Dividend

challenge Gaillard or his men when it came to Isabel's well-being. Tzavaras led Isabel to a patio lawn chair, running his hand through his hair and wiping the sweat off his forehead.

'If you're here, then I assume Gaillard is dead. What a shame, he was a remarkable man, the only reason our friend here is still breathing,' he said, petting Isabel's head and pulling her close to his torso. Daniel wondered what Isabel thought, seeing him in this situation. 'I must admit, you have impeccable taste in women,' Alekos commented, glancing at Daniel. 'Gaillard told me all about you. Quite an intriguing case you are,' he continued, mimicking the filed reports. 'Apparently, you're difficult to control and may be suffering from severe mental trauma. They think you're unfit for active service.' He chuckled. 'It seems even your friends don't trust you.'

Caressing Isabel's cheek, Tzavaras kept the gun's muzzle near her head. Then, he grabbed her by the nape of her neck, pulling her forward and pointing the gun at her back. Daniel could hear her hysterical weeping.

'I've been waiting for this moment. I couldn't just kill her outright, could I?' Tzavaras glanced at Daniel, gauging his reaction. 'You love her, don't you? There's nothing that would torment you more than seeing her suffer.' Tzavaras laughed, fully intending to assault her. Uncomfortable with the situation, Daniel made feeble attempts to subdue Isabel, but Tzavaras interrupted him each time, ruthlessly beating him until Daniel could no longer muster the strength to stand. It played into Alekos's plan, albeit with some delay. The handgun remained just out of Daniel's reach, but he persisted, lunging forward to grab it.

In a bloodied heap, Daniel lunged once more, rolling onto his back and pulling the trigger. Tzavaras reached for the gun, quickly turning it towards Daniel. The trigger released, and three rounds burst out across the garden. Daniel panted heavily. A shiver ran down Tzavaras's spine, causing his head to snap back before he crumpled to the ground and splashed into the pool dramatically. Daniel crawled against the wall, trying to stand upright. Disregarding the handgun, he stumbled towards Isabel's fallen form. She lay curled over, facing away, and upon reaching her, Daniel realized that the blood pooling near her was not Tzavaras's. Her abdomen, just below her ribcage, was stained red. A searing pain surged through her consciousness, intensifying a few moments after the initial shock had subsided, making her breathing deeper."

Daniel gently laid her on her side, using his jacket to stem the bleeding from a clean gunshot wound. Isabel's breathing became shallow and labored, as if she were congested and struggling for air. She felt as if she were drowning. "I shouldn't have left," she said, her words faint. Daniel brushed off her concerns,

345

but her eyes were already rolling back into her head. He urged her to conserve her strength, knowing deep down that this might be their last chance. "I got scared, and I didn't know what to do. It was never personal," she reassured him. But Daniel's focus was on slowing the bleeding, realizing he had only bought them an additional ten minutes.

"Isabel, you're dying," Daniel abruptly stated, interrupting her. He attempted to keep his voice calm, but a quiver betrayed his emotions. "I know," she responded, her blood pooling on his lap, staining his shirt sleeves a deep claret red. "I do love you, you know," she added with a hint of awkwardness. She tried to lift his hand towards her ear, a gesture that painfully reminded him of Switzerland. Fatigue began to weigh heavily on her. "Things have a way of sorting themselves out, don't they?" Isabel spoke with assurance, but Daniel wasn't so sure.

A lingering sense of resentment for being abandoned still nagged at him, but he knew this was their only chance for reconciliation. Daniel stood up, gazing out at the hesitant gathering of townspeople on the street below. If they could reach a hospital, there might be a chance for Isabel to survive, he thought, as he tried to carry her towards the street, his voice now filled with desperation. A local resident came forward to assist, helping Daniel carry Isabel across the street. Urgency fueled Daniel's actions as he placed her gently on the top of a café table just outside the compound. Clearing the table and dragging another one beside it, he arranged all three tables in a row before carefully straightening Isabel and enlisting the help of the local and café owner to stem the bleeding. Blood oozed through the table's slats, forming a thick pool that dripped onto the cobblestone streets. Isabel's body hung limply, intensifying the sense of urgency. "Stay with me," Daniel pleaded, his hands trembling as he tried to secure her neck. But it was futile. She had slipped into the final embrace of sleep, her face a pale mask. Daniel kissed her, desperately attempting to keep her heart beating, but a pulse never came.

An overwhelming emotional shock engulfed him, radiating through his entire being. He felt frozen in place. More locals gathered, their eyes fixed on the scene. Daniel knew the police would arrive soon. As he stared at Isabel's lifeless body, he stepped back, slowly retreating into the midst of the crowd. Part of him longed to stay with her, to cling to some semblance of emotional stability. Angst and desperation were clearly etched on his face. What had he done? She deserved better than this. Daniel questioned whether he was to blame.

The Collateral Dividend

By the time the house cleaners arrived at the villa, Daniel had already fled. The police quickly followed, questioning the foreigner who had discovered the body. It was then that the search began, but it would be in vain. Faron had found a secluded spot on a rooftop a few miles uphill. He held the gold necklace she had been wearing, wrapping it around his palm and touching it to his lips. It was there that he first uttered aloud that she had died. Saying the words out loud caused him to cry. The words felt like a cancerous plague, consuming anyone who dared utter them. The weight of the calamity descended upon him. He felt even worse for leaving her lifeless body on the street. Taking several shallow breaths, his vision started to blur. Overwhelmed by grief, he held his head in his own arms and wept. He pondered the emotional insecurity that led to his collapse, considering it as the defining aspect of his weakness.

For the second time in his life, he felt utterly helpless. Suddenly, he found himself standing in the forest of his old school, with the field stretching out to the road before him. He remembered why he had buried his feelings so deep. He despised this feeling—the sudden and permanent absence of an integral part of his life.

However, his experiences in the past year had changed him. He had grown significantly. There was a reason why it hurt so much. He had tried relentlessly to remove all emotional attachments from his life, suppressing his natural human instincts. Yet, this path had led him astray. In eradicating the pain, he had also eradicated happiness.

Driving proved to be soothing. He found solace in feeling the gears shift and the gentle vibrations of the suspension on a narrow road. After collecting his thoughts, Daniel rented a car and embarked on a aimless journey. He drove for days, without a specific destination or route. Driving helped him think. There was a melodic drone to a fast-moving car, and for the first time in a long while, he found himself able to process and understand his own emotions.

He had reached Denmark, driving along a road that ran alongside a picturesque lake. He pulled over and watched as the sky shifted above him. The clouds seemed to compete for dominance. Sometimes, he spoke aloud to himself, allowing his distress to surface. He admitted that it was okay to be as devastated as he was. He acknowledged his love for her and his own confusion about his actions. Daniel felt like he was navigating through life blindly, relying on instinct alone.

The pain he felt went beyond the loss of a single love. Throughout his years, Daniel had somehow managed to avoid confronting the trauma of his parents' death. "They're gone, Daniel," he had told himself while driving along a highway in Belgium. "Eventually, you must accept that there's nothing you can do to bring them back. Although you miss them terribly, their memory is more powerful than the feeling of loss." As he uttered these words, it took a moment for the profound wisdom within them to sink in. Eventually, he realized that, twisted as it was, happiness still emerged from his loss. When he thought of Isabel, his heart felt weightless. He felt warmth, and although tears welled up in his eyes, a smile also graced his face. Daniel was not a religious man, but perhaps there was some truth to the idea that he remained connected to loved ones long gone.

By the time he returned to the United States, four days after the events had unfolded in Greece, Daniel felt uncertain about this theory. It seemed too absurdly coincidental, too mystical. The sun had long since set in Washington when he arrived, and a company car met him at the airport, driving him to his apartment. Restlessness overcame him as he paced the living room for an hour or two. By a quarter past eleven, he was so restless that he put on a raincoat, took an umbrella from the hook, and went for a walk.

A sedan stopped just ahead of the building entrance, and Ted, the familiar figure, opened the back door, collecting his umbrella, briefcase, and fedora from the seat beside him. He stepped out onto the city street, under the overhanging portico and into the condominium complex. He hooked the umbrella's wooden handle around his forearm, allowing its tip to tap against his thigh as he walked. With his free hand, he reached into the trench coat pocket for his keys. The mackintosh he wore held a warming sense of familiarity, having been in his possession since before the fall of the Soviet regime. Ted fondled the keys until he reached the apartment door. Placing the briefcase on the ground beside him, he jiggled the key until it slid into place, and the door sneered open. He entered the unassuming foyer, turning on the hall light to harshly illuminate the narrow hallway's dark crevices. Ted placed the umbrella in the stand and hung his coat on the adjacent hook.

He proceeded down the hall and into the kitchen. On the counter, there was a coffee machine, and above it, Ted reached for a mug from the cupboard. However, he suddenly halted when he noticed that the coffee machine had been used. He pressed his rough palm against the still scorching glass pot beneath the dispenser. It was freshly made.

Ted cursed as he reached for his pocket, realizing he had carelessly left his handgun in his briefcase down the hall. He contemplated calling out, but acknowledging the presence of an intruder would diminish his advantage. Ted focused on remaining calm. Walking down the narrow hallway, he arrived near the entrance of the living room, where his briefcase lay at his feet. The heavy, worn-in saddleback leather case had served him faithfully over the years.

The rain continued unabated, its rhythmic drumming against the living room windows. Kneeling, Ted faced the dark hallway, allowing his hand to reach into the bag. He gestured around the vintage Indian rug that stretched the length of the hall, pulling back the sturdy leather flap, and revealing the open bag. The Glock handgun was nestled in a sealed compartment near the seam. Ted drew the weapon with his right hand and cautiously moved toward the living room, where the dark windows stood ominously behind tall, looming curtains. Ted pointed the gun forward and briefly surveyed the bathroom before stepping back into the kitchen.

"Oh, for God's sake, you certainly aren't scaring me," a familiar figure emerged from the shadows, their presence shrouded by the darkness beyond the window. Ted turned to face the emerging shadow and glanced at the handgun before placing it on the granite countertop. He rubbed his hand against his face, as if brushing away crumbs from the corners of his mouth. "I believe some congratulations are in order. Many happy returns," Daniel said, removing his brown leather gloves and stacking them atop one another on the arm of the sofa. He took a seat, as though he had been there before, still limping. Ted wondered how Daniel had gained entry and how he knew it was Ted's birthday.

"Normally, guests bring something," Ted remarked.

"I made coffee," the young man responded sheepishly, with a touch of cheekiness, gesturing toward the kitchen behind Ted. The comment didn't sit well with Ted, and he took a deep breath to clear his mind. "What happened?" Ted questioned.

"Nothing."

"The reports certainly don't imply nothing. If you're hurt, there's no shame in admitting it."

"There's a difference between being hurt and trying to ignore that you're hurt."

"Absolutely," Ted agreed, glancing at his watch. It was just past eleven. "So what did you want to talk about?" Ted's stern look conveyed that Daniel wouldn't have come there if he didn't want to talk. He gestured toward the liquor cabinet.

Daniel declined and said, "Haven't had a drop-in in months. I wanted to talk about what exactly we did, whether you thought it was the right thing. As I sit here, after all this is done, and I look back at what happened, I can't say for certain that we did the right thing."

E.R. Wychwood
"We did."

"How can you be so certain?" Daniel's fragile tone betrayed his uncertainty.

"There are people like Gaillard who enjoy seeing others suffer. Make no mistake, Daniel, the people we've targeted, even if through extrajudicial means, have all been dangerous individuals. We're not concerned with small fish here," Ted explained.

"And what about Sarah or Jeff? Were they small fish?"

Ted let out a deep sigh. "We are not the same as them, Daniel. You are not the same as them. We worked hard to implement behavioral modification, so you would barely react to violence. It may have been a mistake. Those emotions are what set you apart."

Daniel's head cocked to the side, seemingly intrigued by the theory. Ted continued, "Years of political philosophy revolve around the central concept that the role of the state is to provide some form of security to its citizens. When we executed our operations with drones, there was no human cost that limited our discretion. If someone was a target, we knew everything about them, but other than the drone pilot, no one felt anything when they were killed. Now, we all feel it, and I assure you, Daniel, we all feel it."

"But how can you sit there and assure me that this lack of moral character or checks and balances is not a risk for future abuse? Just because the reins are in safe hands now does not mean that thirty years from now they still will be," she argued.

"I don't. Or rather, I can't assure you of that. But the same could be said for many types of work. Sometimes we get lost in things. But I think eventually things always straighten out," Ted replied. Under his breath, Daniel muttered, "They have a way of doing that, don't they?" Ted then looked up at Daniel and asked, "Did you find what you were looking for?"

"In a way, yes. What about you?" Daniel inquired.

"No," Ted immediately responded, his deliberate tone hinting at a hidden undertone that suggested Ted's attempt to convince himself that he had found closure, despite his actual experience proving otherwise. It had been a textbook case of what vengeance could do. "I assume I wasn't supposed to," Ted continued. "Much like you, I tried to subdue the pain."

Daniel Faron let out a deep sigh. "I've learned that the pain should never have been a testament to how much the bad hurt. It was and always will be a reminder of how great the good was."

"That's a well-thought-out perspective, very philosophical," Ted remarked, his tone leaving Daniel uncertain whether he was joking or not.

"You know mockery won't get you anywhere," Daniel quibbled back.

"I do know that," Ted said with a grin. "You should also know that we never betrayed you. Not if Paul is where he is."

"That doesn't make the thought cross my mind any less," Daniel confessed.

"Hm," Ted responded with a heavy tone. "No, I don't imagine so. But do know that he values you more than the others, whether you realize it or not. Sometimes we all need to be reminded of that."

Daniel nodded, acknowledging the statement superficially. "Well, rest well, sir," he said, making his way to the door.

"Daniel, it wasn't your fault, you know," Ted suddenly interjected. Daniel looked back at him, smiled, and nodded. That was something even harder to believe. When he thought about Tzavaras, worse still Isabel, anger washed over him like a hot, white bath. It was almost as if he couldn't conceive the reality that what he remembered was indeed fact. He wished it was just his imagination. There was a hint of embarrassment in how it had all played out. He suspected that while Paul hadn't left Daniel out to dry, it wouldn't have surprised him if Paul believed that using Isabel as bait had been the reason they had been able to get Gaillard so quickly. That was the center of Daniel's discomfort, something he would have to deal with. It was over now, and despite his desires, there was no going back. The future lay before him, and he faced the difficult decision of whether to return to Farragut Center.

It was perfectly reasonable to forgive but not to forget, Daniel thought. That would be best. Despite all his uncertainties, he wanted to believe they were doing the right thing here. Above all, it was his life, and no disapproval from Henry or anyone else would change that. What he feared, however, was the possibility that it would happen again. He was afraid of being made a fool of, a pushover. Above all else, he feared that the rhetoric he was being told was merely there out of convenience, that he was being told what he wanted to hear to align his own ideals with Farragut Center's.

"This turmoil was not something that could be resolved within a day, or even something Daniel believed could be resolved at all. It was a question he wasn't meant to know the answer to. He chose not to fret over it, or at least that was his opinion. By destroying Gaillard, Daniel somehow destroyed a part of himself, freeing himself from the bounds that made him the homo sacer. In a stairwell, for the first time in a long while, he pondered the words spoken long ago. He had somehow found his place amidst the mess.

Things changed swiftly. It marked the first major victory for Farragut Center, and as expected, the President wanted an accurate and truthful account.

Paul had prepared the briefing packet for Ted to take to the White House, comprehensively outlining the progress made. However, some within the President's inner circle remained unconvinced. They shared Daniel's view that perhaps the authority to carry out targeted killings should not reside with any department. They questioned whether drones or humans could grapple with the existential issues surrounding extrajudicial force. Despite this, it was unlikely their opinion would sway many, and little was expected to change.

Paul was eager to temporarily halt operations to conduct internal assessments. Farragut Center endured another round of evaluations, starting with security checks and progressing to psychological assessments.

Daniel wasn't enthusiastic about undergoing the tests, but deep down, he found some enjoyment in them. There was a sense of routine and comfort in conversing with the agency's psychiatrist. She was one of the few who understood the mental demands of their profession.

He met with Acres for the first time since before all this began. Paul had arranged the meeting, emphasizing that Daniel needed clearance from Acres if he wished to return to the field. Acres made it clear that she wouldn't participate unless Paul took her recommendations seriously. It had been months since Daniel had last spoken to Acres, and now she entered a conference room in Washington, holding a thick file folder.

"How have you been?" she asked to break the ice. "I was wondering if you could tell me about Isabel Yates."

"What about her?" Daniel responded with a hint of hostility.

"You had a strong emotional connection to her. She was important to you. Last time we spoke, you struggled with the lack of closure. Is that still the case?"

"She's no less important to me now than she was then. I cared a great deal for her."

"It's quite a change from the last time we spoke, Daniel—your honesty about your emotions."

"I've thought a lot about closure and what it means to embrace one's feelings."

"As humans, we aren't designed to ignore our feelings, Daniel."

"It forced me to think about the loss of my parents," he said frankly. "Eventually, you're faced with a choice: let the event consume or define you. Well..." Daniel paused, looking at Acres, who sat with her legs crossed. She scribbled on a pad of paper in her lap and then looked up, waiting for him to finish his thought. "You move on," he said. His experiences had shaped him, and he didn't regret them for a moment. Simultaneously, he didn't hesitate to express that they had also led him to believe the world was random. The events of his life lacked consistency, and he made sure Doctor Acres understood this. While there seemed to be a recurring trend of the things he cherished being abruptly torn away, Acres dismissed it as coincidence. There was no such thing as fate or luck. Or was there?

Daniel's tone conveyed a sense of contentment with the choices he had made in his life. He was acutely aware of the gravity attached to his actions. He vividly remembered the harshness of his deeds and looked up at the psychiatrist.

"I can't help but feel that what we were doing was morally wrong."

"Why do you say that?" Acres inquired. Daniel struggled to find a better description, and when he relayed his thoughts to Acres, she made a note and pondered the question for a while. It seemed to her that Daniel had started to comprehend the emotional trauma stemming from his childhood.

"Daniel, what you do for a living was fueled by your ignorance and the pain from your childhood. Now, I'm going to share my observations, and I need you to listen until the end. I believe you fell in love with Isabel, and it showed you that you were capable of feeling something other than the horror of your first kill." Daniel had undergone extensive behavioral modification, which Acres suspected had loosened a few repressed emotions. "Do you still want to continue working in the field?"

"Yes," Daniel replied.

"Why?" she asked. Daniel hadn't given it much thought, but the answer was remarkably simple. Somehow, he felt at ease. There was warmth in being invisible. The thrill of danger and the immediacy of results fascinated him. Acres made more notes. Eventually, she informed Daniel that she had gathered all the necessary information and recommended meeting again in a few weeks.

Acres encountered Paul in the hallway, exchanged greetings, and got down to business as soon as the door closed. "As I mentioned before, he's sorted himself out. I see no reason why he shouldn't be deployed to the field if he chooses to. The question, Mr. Irving, is whether he wants to."

Paul reviewed the client notes Acres had compiled and stood on the far side of the desk. He set down the file folder, looked up at the psychiatrist, and placed his hand on his hip. "Overall, we seem to have a relatively healthy department."

"Generally," Acres acknowledged. "But there are some concerns. Paul, I've known you for a long time, and I've never seen you as stressed as you were a few weeks ago. Whatever has changed, you need to realize it hasn't been for the better. Daniel learned the hard way that this profession can't be everything in life. If you're running a department of human assets, attempting to humanize targeted killing, you mustn't overlook the human aspects. Do you understand?" Paul did.

"I believe all of you have forgotten the importance of relationships, in any form," Acres continued. Her comment made Paul feel foolish. After a brief pause, she stood up. "I'll be back later in the week to discuss other matters," she said, referring to her increased involvement in overseas operations. Paul saw her out, then returned to his seat, crossed his arms, and contemplated Rachel. He considered himself fortunate to have such an understanding partner. However, he still grappled with the hesitation he felt toward everything. It seemed like pessimism, irrational thoughts creeping into his mind due to circumstances. Only time would tell. As for Acres, she found herself deeply embedded within Farragut Center. Her experience in dealing with Paul and the team proved invaluable. In a way, she worried about all of them. Trust was a vulnerability in their line of work. There were legitimate reasons for concern, yet she believed they would all be fine. Despite Daniel's misconceptions, Acres hoped they understood that vulnerability didn't equate to the need for complete shutdown. It was a sign of feeling, of trust, but never weakness or stupidity. To be vulnerable was to truly experience. Too often, people misinterpreted vulnerability as weakness rather than strength.

Paul had spent too much time watching television, feeling like he was overloading his brain. The Federal Reserve had announced that, after several months of investigation, a dormant security account had recovered the missing money from the stock market, leading to a sudden rebound in the markets. The amount was so significant that it needed to be reintroduced gradually to avoid hyperinflation. The effects of the missing money had dealt a serious blow to domestic markets, but the fact that it had been recovered brought relief, although not all of it. To maintain consistency, Paul had briefed the executive on how the CIA and their fiasco in Sudan tied into the situation. The stolen money had been traced to family accounts owned by Klaus. Both Klaus' actions and the events in Sudan were inexcusable and impossible to hide. However, the rest of Daniel's actions remained invisible to the public.

For the first time in nearly two years, Paul found himself sitting in his office, doing nothing. It was an extremely foreign feeling to him, and he wasn't sure if he liked it. Nevertheless, he looked forward to sleeping in a bed rather than the cot stowed behind the office door.

Although the battles still raged on, the death of Aleko Tzavaras had dealt a critical blow to the ultranationalists. The notion of American involvement had

The Collateral Dividend

been dismissed as preposterous, even though those in the know were aware of its truth. As often happened, the chaos of politics soon shifted the interest away from uncovering secret intelligence departments, favoring other senatorial showboating. Unfortunately, this came at the expense of Director Dunes' career.

The next day, Daniel entered Paul's office to discuss their next steps. Faron accompanied him, limping along with the aid of a cane. A fall in Greece had torn ligaments in his knee, and his recovery was slow. He wore a well-fitted suit, handmade with a grey tie and a white button-down shirt. The dark mahogany cane had belonged to his great-grandfather, with the letters "AF" engraved just above the gold band separating the handle from the shaft. When Faron gripped the handle, the letters flashed in gold. "Good morning," Daniel said as he entered, and Paul welcomed him in.

"How are you feeling?" Paul asked, genuinely concerned, as he came around his office desk and took a seat, looking across at Daniel.

"The leg could be better," Daniel replied in a cheeky tone. "So, where do we go from here?" He asked, settling into his seat and resting his laced fingers on top of the cane.

Paul adjusted his posture. "There isn't much work at the moment, just some minor things that need tidying up. I assume you've moved on from Gaillard?"

Daniel grunted. "They say you're done with something when it no longer affects you. I don't think I'm fully done with this one yet," he said, thinking about getting over the emotional impact of it all. He wanted some time to himself. "If it's all the same to you, I'd like to take some time."

"Absolutely," Paul responded, reaching into his desk and pulling out a file, which he handed to Daniel. "I thought you might be interested in this." Daniel opened the file and then looked up at Paul. Paul had taken it upon himself to sort things out with the Yates family and the S.E.C., clearing all the discrepancies surrounding Isabel's name. "She's buried in a family plot up in Kensal Green if you're interested in visiting. And Daniel, I am truly sorry. We all are. When you're ready to return, let me know. There's a place for you here," Paul said, his face filled with angst.

Daniel gave a warm smile, somehow knowing that things would turn out all right. "You don't have to worry about me," he said. "Things have a way of sorting themselves out, don't they?" Before Paul could look up from his desk, Daniel took the elevator alone and disappeared into the cold and wet November morning, for the first time in a long while.

Printed in Great Britain
by Amazon